ORR: THE TELLTALE Y

By Lynn Marron

A Grace Farrington DNA Mystery

Book and Cover Design By Lynn Marron and Leonard J. Bloom, Jr.

Published by Kear Press
Stratford, CT

LIBRARY OF CONGRESS: 2017956884

ISBN: 978-1-942888-17-8

e-book ISBN 978-1-942888-18-5

This book is dedicated to:

Dick and Betty Booth

Who drew People into

Their Warm Circles of Friendship,

And Never Stopped Preserving History,

While With Their Examples

They Encouraged Everyone

to Be Prepared and Be Better!

1918 the town of Yekaterinburg in the Urals

Long after they were sleeping, a guard hammered on the bedroom door, yelling that the girls must get dressed. As her three sisters started dressing, seventeen-year-old Anastasia pulled on the heavy bodice lumpy with the hidden diamonds, rubies, emeralds and sapphires sewed in. It uncomfortably pushed against her chest. Their spaniel Jemmy jumped on her leg to be petted. Why had they still let him stay? The soldiers had taken everything else.

With bayoneted guns the soldiers herded them down steep wooden stairs in the old house, saying they must wait for a truck to move them to another, safer house. Finally, the sisters stepped down into a windowless cellar with a dirt floor and saw their three servants, who still stayed, with them also standing. She saw Alexi's spaniel, Joy, nervously wagging his tail. Anastasia's dog Jemmy growled at another guard and frightened of the man her mother's maid, Anna, quickly picked up the spaniel to hush him. Now Anastasia saw Poppa coming in, looking around the bare cellar he asked for two chairs. Momma soon sat in the room beside little Alexi with Dr. Botkin hovering nearby.

These soldiers were not the regular guards, they were roughly dressed, and shoved everybody about meanly, but they had brought the two chairs for Momma and Alexi. Anastasia looked on, frightened for her brother, Alexi's leg was swelling again, would these cruel-faced men let the doctor help him?

Each time they had been moved they were hurried to assemble and then stood waiting for hours. Would the rest of their clothing be packed to go with them? The servants were down here. Poppa stood nearer Momma, resting his hand on her shoulder to comfort her. Momma looked up at him and tried to smile bravely, not looking to the glowering guards.

Anastasia's sister Tatiana looked about, then quietly asked the soldier near her, "There are medicines in the bedroom that we need, can I go get them?"

The soldier ignored her.

Another soldier roughly ordered, "Stand in two lines for a photograph to prove you have not escaped." Anastasia moved to stand beside Tatiana, and behind Momma, with the wall at their back. There were frightening sounds coming down, heavy boots hurrying as big men rushed into the cellar. Now there were at least ten armed men in the room. The first man read loudly from a paper, "Nikolai Alexandrovich, in view of the fact that your relatives are continuing their attack on Soviet Russia, the Ural Executive Committee has decided to execute you."

Poppa said, "What, what..."

The room flashed with light, gunshots, and smoke.

Screaming Anastasia felt hard painful hits to her chest knocking her to the wall, but the bullets were bouncing off the concealed jewels. In shock and pain, she fell to the floor. Jemmy, the dog, barked, then squealed.

Silence. Then her sisters started to cry–their corsets of jewels had protected them too. Olga was rising up. Not understanding how they survived their bullets the panicky soldiers cursed and yelled prayers as they mercilessly shot Olga in the head and stabbed Titania and Marie through with bayonets. Anastasia stayed still, too terrified to speak as a warm wetness ran down her leg and blackness covered her eyes.

Someone moaned. Then a cold wind hit Anastasia as the door was opened to let out the smoke.

Soon a big man tossed her body over his shoulder, carrying her like a rag doll, out into the bitter cold. Terrified Anastasia found herself being thrown on top of a pile of rags. Warm rags-- the bodies of her parents and sisters. Did they kill little Alexi? And Jemmy, her dog? Even the maids and the doctor? She heard the soldiers' boots scraping on the gravel as they moved away, as stiff and cold, a terrified Anastasia lay listening...

1994 Announcement in Moscow, Russia

In the boggy Ural woods, following written testimony of the Bolsheviks' death squad a group of history-loving geologists uncovered the smashed bones of nine individuals believed to be the remains of those slaughtered in The House of Special Purpose in 1918.

Extracting DNA from all nine skeletons, investigators determined five of these individuals were related as a family. Further comparing DNA with that donated by Prince Philip, the Duke of Edinburgh, and the exhumed brother of Nicholas, five of the nine bodies have been identified as Tsar Nicholas II's murdered family. It was also determined that two of his children, the male heir Alexi, and one of his sisters--either Marie or Anastasia–were still missing.

Chapter 1

The waters near São Tomé Island off of West Africa

The rented science ship for the Nature channel had seen better days, but the equipment mounted in the tight cabin was nearly adequate and air-conditioned, opposed to the broiling sunlit deck. Grace slapped on that silly, huge brimmed, pink straw hat that covered her face, shoulders, and everything almost. Her friend Freya had conspired with Kurt to substitute a bag of *'resort clothing'* for her usual suitcase with its business like pants suits and stacks of submitted research papers to be reviewed for various DNA journals.

Seeing them off at the airport Freya pronounced, "You're finally getting a real, non-working vacation!"

Traveling with Kurt MacKay, they made a well-matched pair, both with black hair, blue eyes and about five foot eight in height. They were fortyish, having just a touch of silver in their hair; being on the thin side, Kurt was surprisingly strong for a man of his slight build. Grace wore her hair short with natural curls at the top; Kurt's was short with a van dyke beard. From his constant exposure to the sun with his marine studies, Kurt's skin had tanned a bit more, and while socially Grace preferred to be ignored by people, Kurt constantly went for shock or confrontation for the pure fun of it.

On this trip, Kurt pushed for her to take time off, so in front of the crew, photographers, and students he referred to her as 'Gorgeous' and kept pushing her to go ashore while *'the real scientists worked.'* The first day dumped on the island country of São Tomé and Principe, Grace got sunburnt. With no lab to go to she felt lost, with no DNA to study, no e-mails to reply to...it just left her walking aimlessly about the São Tomé tourist shops and tents, looking at carved elephant necklaces and cargo cloth dresses. It seemed horrible to be without work--without what made her tick; she had to kill endless wasted hours until she could take the tender boat back to the ship for dinner. But by the second day, Grace had a gallon of suntan lotion, swimsuit, bottles of water, a sandwich lunch, and a borrowed Juliet Blackwell mystery to read. This time laying on a towel in the warm sand kind of appealed to her.

The third day there, she walked about the island and saw Great Dog Peak, a misty rock sticking up high like some Easter Island idol. Grace passed tin covered shacks alongside fruit and fish markets open to all sides with just jerry-rigged sunshades above them. She watched dark-faced little kids filling buckets at the public water station and giggling as they ran away home. Grace walked farther, seeing gray parrots eating fruit and endlessly chattering to their feathered friends in the green drenched jungle. A buzzing hum of insects and Grace found herself swatting mosquitoes that were eating at her, as she took a closer look at those splashes of color in among the green. Reaching out she felt delicate, velvety orange, pale green, and white orchids, so many different varieties growing wild here. She heard the São Tomé and Principe islands were trying to increase tourist traffic, a shame because they had such an unspoiled paradise here.

Heading back to the white sand beach, Grace realized back home in Connecticut the snow should still be melting, but now she stretched out in a baking sun. When warmed enough, she cooled off swimming in the bright turquoise water that felt like being in a warm bathtub. Swimming in the sea again, Grace rolled over for a backstroke, then just stopped and floated with her eyes closed, as gentle waves bobbed her up and down. Letting her legs sink she narrowed her eyes from the tropical sun's white reflection as she looked about, seeing the palm treed shore, paddling around more she could see the white painted research ship riding at anchor.

Grace smelled bananas and could hear the students from the science ship excitedly calling out what their traps were bringing up, but she just treads water at peace with the world. This being lazy actually felt like fun–if she married David Gardiner she could be doing this the rest of her life, on his private island in Greece or where ever in the world his money could take them.

No, Grace didn't want idleness for the rest of her life, but it was nice for now, and she could manipulate elusive Denisovan DNA sequences in her mind. Grace swam out farther, and as wind rippled the waves, again she lowered her feet down into a bottomless sea and treaded water a bit. On board the ship they were filming Kurt today, he'd be standing on the platform lowered to sea level. The script called for footage of him frowning in concentration as he dipped collection jars into the sea. Then he'd be back up on deck talking to the interviewer about overseeing the setting up of a series of satellite-monitored buoys to map ocean currents for his studies in sea mammal migrations.

Kurt would also discuss his theories of oceanic effects on the climate and on hurricane genesis, and the counter-predicted cycle of mild storms and hurricanes. The interviewer would casually bring up Kurt's dramatic underwater rescue back home in Oyster River Harbor, and Kurt would look appropriately modest --hard for him--as he told the story. They had discussed her coming over on camera at that moment, but Grace's reputation as a pioneer in the DNA field would totally overshadow Kurt's marine achievements. No, this trip she would remain the non-working 'Gorgeous,' beach bunny extraordinaire.

Chapter 2

An hour before dinner Grace climbed aboard the beached tender boat taking her back to the ship. The curly, black-bearded cameraman running it gave her a thumbs up saying "Kurt did great. One take, we got all his stuff, and it's going to look good."

"Did he talk about the rescue?" Grace asked settling onto the hard wood-board seat. The guy pushed the prow off the sand and then jumped in, climbing over board seats to the outboard motor in the stern.

"Jesus, that must have been terrifying for you," the guy said, pulling the cord to turn over the motor.

Tears warmed in Grace's eyes. "I thought he was going to die, that cold black water...the underwater wreck was being washed out in the undertow, but Kurt still kept diving..."

The cameraman stared at her, saying quietly, "If I could get that on tape?"

No, this show was only Kurt's, she shook her head. "I'm just a bring-a-long on this trip."

Seeing he had lost, the guy was gracious enough to just nod in acceptance and not argue further, but then he said, "I'm Jason Lindell. Besides doing the camera work, I'm co-producer on this project." Grace smiled wryly--this guy probably knew Grace's legendary inability to recognize people unless she had known them for years, but he was continuing, "The Science Channel is interested in a documentary on the Oyster River Research facility-its long history as a Noble prize incubator in cellular research..." The small boat plowed through bright sapphire water that darkened to black in the greater depths, as the cameraman studied her closely, seeming to be evaluating her image.

Grace just watched the water change color as she said,

"Eric Larsen passed away suddenly at fifty-eight; he was our last working Nobel."

"My sources say you nearly had it last year."

Yet a man with the third of her discoveries got it instead. "But I didn't get it–and perhaps I never will."

"You received the MacAlpin Guru award. That's pretty prestigious."

That first year's thousands all went into her laboratory for another specialized, double glass-doored specimen freezer that didn't defrost, but the yearly income would help going forward. "Every bit that I can put into my research counts."

He only smiled at that. "Like you, Barbara McClintock revolutionized the field of genetic studies, and she didn't get her Nobel until fifty-six years after she entered the field."

That fact had bothered Grace for years. "The only reason to want the Nobel is for the money that can buy equipment to further your work, or perhaps the prestige that gives you entry into an optimal research situation..."

Speaking loudly over the motor's roar he yelled, "You have that at Oyster River don't you?"

She stopped to think about it. When she was an unknown, unfairly disgraced researcher, Eric Larsen had thrown his weight as a Nobel winner and had gotten her a job there. "Yes, Oyster River allows me to work in my own laboratory, on projects I chose, with a free condo right down the road. And researching at Oyster River has offered me a chance to meet and work with extraordinary minds, like Dr. Kurt Mackay's. Yes, ORR has been good to me."

"But if such a documentary was filmed, would you talk on camera? Let us watch you at work in your laboratory?"

She owed Adam and Oyster River a lot, but said, "I'll give an interview in the large front room I use for my office, but as for filming in my clean room," Grace shook her head,

"I can not have intrusive DNA where I'm processing a single toe bone from ninety thousand years ago."

Holding up a hand, he backed off a bit to make her more comfortable. "You'll set the rules, of course, we'll do your office if you wish, but if we could go in the clean room, we'll go in wrapped like mummies in protective gear, with the cameras in sterilized underwater filming boxes," he promised.

Grace didn't really want to commit to anything. "You'll have to make arrangements through Adam Greenfield's office, he's president of ORR." They had reached that floating platform and ladder beside the ship. Jason reached out a hand to steady Grace as she climbed out.

She asked, "Do you know where Kurt is?"

"When I left he was glued to his computer screen below decks in lab 2."

Up on deck, Grace took the steps–no 'ladder'-- down as other scientists and students were heading up to the mess hall for dinner. It'd be another goat stew with freshly baked bread that Grace admitted smelled delicious. She found Kurt in the science cabin downstairs, so deeply engrossed in the computer screens before him that he wasn't even aware she was there. Again, Grace gave in to the temptation to glance through the stacks of DNA readouts the students had produced. After about twenty pages she looked up to see Kurt still intently studying the computer screen, stroking his short van dyke beard.

Another man she couldn't marry, but Grace immensely enjoyed spending time with Kurt and his so un-politically correct altitude. While his pugnacious nature appalled her at times, his endless curiosity about everything oriented to sea life resonated with her. Yes, as President of Oyster River, Adam pushed this trip to promote Kurt as one of ORR'S scientists, but Kurt really seemed to like being a 'senior' scientist to these graduate students. Yet, even here he came determined to do some serious marine studies. Yeah, like her, he'd work through dinner again if she didn't interrupt him. Still, the stew would last, or they could get cold cuts for sandwiches, and Grace wanted to spend more time scanning sheets of the students' DNA readouts.

"Damn it." He straightened in the fold-up chair and rubbed his back as he looked at her. "I thought we'd be together more here. Want to go with me to the beach and do some sunbathing?

Grace looked at the clock on the wall. "Only if you want to sunbathe in the moonlight."

He looked over surprised and then stiffly stood up. "That late already?" Also glancing at the clock, he shook his head as if coming out of sleep, then looked back to the screen. "I wish we were going to be here in July instead of March."

"What happens in July?"

"The big'uns come out," he said wishfully.

"Miss Universe contest is held here?"

He laughed. "Nope, Humpback whales swim and breach in these warmer waters, when the females come looking for places to mate and calf."

"I've seen some dolphins," she said absentmindedly, still scanning the student DNA printouts.

Walking over he bent down and kissed the back of her neck. "You too bored on the beach?"

Looking up at him she could honestly say, "No, I'm having fun."

He stared at her with those intense dark eyes. "My part of filming is done at the end of the week. If we change those airplane tickets to add another week, one of the students tells me there's a real nice cabin his aunt's got, and we could share it for a pittance?"

"Share the price?"

"Well, it's one room, and we'll be sharing the bed..." he said shrugging.

That was Kurt Mackay alright--get a love nest to

seduce a woman, and send her half the bill, but for years Grace's best friend, Freya, had been on her back to just '*enjoy life a little,*' and Grace couldn't think of a better place than here. "It's a deal."

He looked at the printouts in her hands. "Those kids got anything?"

Not looking at him, she stared back at the rows of base pairs. "Where did they get these samples?"

"Pickups on the beach, dipping nets off the ship, buying bones and fossilized sharks teeth from the open air fish markets. Check their log."

Grace reached for the specimen extraction log, a bunch of bent-edged, poorly mimeographed sheets with handwritten notations in colored pencil, pen and ink, and one which looked like it was scribbled in a blunt, brown eyebrow pencil. "You ever show these guys about those new marvels, computers?"

He smiled. "Actually, I think some of them are inputting the data into their cell phones."

Making a face of disapproval, Grace glanced back at the readouts and pointed to the line that corresponded to catalog number on the printouts. "It's an obviously incomplete genome, but they may have something here..." She studied the repeating sequencing of chemical base pairs of adenine and thymine, coupled with cytosine and guanine, the only four chemical bases that carry the complete instructions for building and maintaining all organisms. Just like the twenty-six letters of the alphabet, those two base pairs could be read in millions of different ways.

Seeing she was on to something he asked, "What do you think it is?"

"From this ship could you connect me to an overseas database?"

"We got satellite. Which one you want?"

"That scientist friend of yours at Woods Hole. The

one who publishes genomes of special significance on the Internet?"

"Dr. Dowan Dai. Might be able to get him from here." He moved to another computer while she copied the sheet's date and page number into her pocket notebook added a quick notation, then started on the stack again.

But Kurt rolled his eyes toward the white metal ceiling. "Oh, no, Gorgeous! No more DNA sleuthing today, you're just a bring-a-long assistant this trip! Now we're getting something to eat–then we are going to my cabin to make like the happy humpbacks."

Chapter 3

The next day it looked like rain, but Grace still decided to take the tender boat to shore and hang around town anyways. She spent most of the day drinking hot chocolate and reading in a bar near the surf. When she got back, Kurt wanted to know only one thing asking, "You got pantyhose with ya?"

"I did, in that suitcase you and Freya deep-sixed. I don't have any now. Maybe I could buy some in town. Why?"

"I want to teach these kids how to make an impromptu dragnet for specimens–and pantyhose works real fine."

She cocked her head to one side. "The Kurt MacKay I know would be sidling up to all the large racked girls, asking what they're wearing under their jeans?"

He flushed deeply. "Since I'm coming across as an elder statesman this trip, I don't want to rock the boat."

* * *

Their last day onboard, Grace packed her suitcase to be taken by boat to the cabin they'd rented. Now she switched out her orange resort wear for a blue shirt and shorts that she'd bought in São Tomé and headed down to the main lab. Seeing her, the bearded co-producer automatically reached for his camera, but Grace shook her head 'no,' and he put it down. She looked around: some general scientists, eight earnest graduate students, even a couple of local high school kids. From their looks, she knew a few of them recognized her from the beginning, but all were careful to respect her wish of anonymity. This she blew now. "Gentlemen, ladies, gather around. As some of you probably know, when I not being called 'Gorgeous,' my name is Dr. Grace Farrington." From the students who hadn't guessed that there was an intake of breaths. "Now, you've really been working hard, and I assume learning something. Dr. MacKay and I are leaving today, so after this talk, I will answer any questions until we leave, but first, there are some things I want to point out."

She picked up that disgrace of a specimen log. "This is ridiculous, guys. Your whole extractions and DNA profiles must tie back to your original sample, and where it came from. Look at this list: some samples have names attached, some don't; none have origins; some only have initials that are unreadable. There are samples here that do not even have their processing number! If you find something really worth studying further, how are you going to trace it back?"

They looked like little kids being scolded for stealing cooling cookies, but Grace didn't care, they had to learn. She picked up their DNA printouts and quickly paged through to a place she'd seen before. Studying it again briefly she then turned back to the specimen log. "Now in this log, I see two initials 'CJA's' in different handwritings?"

The bearded producer looked pained at keeping his documentary camera off, but he did explain, "That would be Carl Jorge Abramson or Calvin Joe Abano."

She nodded. "Okay. We're looking at CJA's sample 6876?" Grace looked from one blank face to the other. "You also must have some idea of the work you are doing!"

A gangly, cinnamon-skinned male moved to her and looked where she was pointing in the log, saying hesitantly with a faint British accent, "That's mine. I'm Calvin." He stood about six two, with short cut fuzzy red hair and he looked nervous.

She turned on him demanding, "Do you remember this sample?"

He hurried over to a cubby filled with loose-leaf books and brought one back. In front of Grace, he paged through what looked to be neatly hand-printed pages.

But she still commented tartly, "If you input into a computer, you can print out something readable."

He gave a big toothy grin. "Where I collect samples, there is no electricity." Calvin hunted down further on his list, then glanced up a bit nervously. "Is there is something wrong with it?"

"No," she said. "In fact, it looks like something good."

Calvin relaxed a bit. "Well, then..." he pointed to a young woman and another guy anxiously hovering behind a table. "Beverly and Thomas picked this up with me at the market near the brick water station."

Grace didn't care much about attribution. "Do you have more of this sample on ice?"

Regretfully he shook his head. "No, mam, no room to keep it."

Biting her lip, Grace looked at the printout. "You certainly don't have a complete genome, you know that, but you do have an interesting configuration. It's not totally something that I recognize, but I think it is within the same species..."

Calvin looked at his loose-leaf log. "It's a 'tank fish'- called that 'cause it's big with thick scales. Some fisherman must have caught it in his net."

Electricity shot through Grace. "The specimen was alive? You didn't extract this sample from a fossil bone?"

"Been alive that morning," said Calvin who looked to his friends for confirmation. "It was alive before it was netted. It's a rare fish, but I've seen some before."

"Can you get another?" asked an excited Grace.

He didn't look hopeful. "I've only seen maybe two or three on the market tables in my lifetime."

The woman in collection group stepped forward. "I've got pictures of all we collected on my cell-phone." She was busily thumbing through hundreds of pictures. Finally, she shoved the screen at Grace. It showed a light blue, almost lavender fish, with pale white and gray spots and multiple fins. Grace studied it and passed the cell-phone to Kurt.

He looked at it. "Definitely a three-lobed caudal fin. Cosmoid scales and paired fins, but smaller head than pictures

I've seen–but I ain't seen many. Maybe a variation, or might be a new subspecies?"

Grace looked down at the print out again, "Chris Amemiya's group published the coelacanth fish genome. I've compared the partial results you have with the Coelacanthiformes on a database Kurt managed to contact for me. What I think you have here is not a coelacanth, but a close relative."

Puzzled, one of the other students asked, "With just the DNA readouts how can you look a line of repeating bases and then match that to a strange fish?"

Kurt smiled ironically. "Gracie can't remember your name or the name of this ship, but she has memorized hundreds of thousands of DNA patterns and can recall them all."

"Not all of them," Grace protested. "But I recognized a pattern that reads as fish, primitive fish, and then one as close--but not the same--as the coelacanth. But I had to verify that with a database."

"The coelacanth's extinct isn't it?" a red-headed post-doctorate asked.

Again Kurt took point explaining, "Scientists figured the coelacanth went extinct after the late Cretaceous, about sixty-six million years ago, but then in 1938 some fisherman hauled in a live one off of South Africa. Looks like you guys found its mate."

"Or its son, or its great-grandfather," started Grace meditatively, "or more likely a distant cousin. We now know coelacanths exist in the Indian ocean, and the current belief is that their line diverged from Lungfish about three hundred ninety million years ago. Lungfish are thought to have been the ancestors of all land animals, but if we learned more about the coelacanth and its cousins, that theory could change. By being able to read DNA and its variations, we're finding previous mapping and dating of organisms' family trees have to be drastically revised."

A meditative Kurt added, "Coelacanths are still evolving, but slowly. The present fishes have been observed by submersibles, some over six foot long that weigh in around two hundred pounds. Those were actually larger than the previously found fossil samples."

Looking at the readout again, Grace said, "I just wish we had a complete sample to work with."

Calvin shrugged, not holding out too much hope. "I can ask around. This fish's meat is oily and smelly, not usually sold for food, mostly thrown away."

The young girl still held out her phone. "We can print out posters with its picture and maybe offer a reward?"

Grace gave them a beaming smile. "Yes. Do that! And what would help other scientists--and maybe yourselves--is publishing the find. Dr. Dowan Dai, a friend of Kurt's at Woods Hole, publishes significant genomes online that are open for anyone to study. That's where I picked up the coelacanth I compared with this."

"You're going to publish it?" asked Calvin excitedly.

"No," said Grace. "You guys discovered it. That's your decision, but putting it online will help other scientists, and if this is a new subspecies, publishing may establish that you found it first." She studied the readout once again. "It's a little premature right now--especially on incomplete data-- but if this proves out, you three might start thinking of a scientific name for your discovery."

"We'll name it after you!" proclaimed Thomas.

Shaking her head, Grace glanced at Kurt and then smiled. "Actually I already have been given that honor. No, give it some thought, pick something that has meaning for the three of you. But today, let Kurt know if you will agree to upload your gene profile so he can do it before we leave."

A glowing Beverly had a smile on her sunburned face. "Yes. Yes." Delightedly she looked to Thomas and Calvin, who just stood basking in the excitement and envy of the rest of group.

Turning to the whole group, Grace finished, "Now, as I said before we leave today I'll answer any questions you have." Most had questions--some actually had a few of Grace's books to be signed. It was over another two hours before Kurt finally called a halt, announcing to the whole group, "We have to be going."

Grace looked at the eager, determined faces of scientists just beginning their careers, and she said, "You're starting on a grand scientific hunt–there is nothing more intoxicating! I envy you all."

Jason the co-producer had put down his movie camera and now had a Nikon in his hands. "Since our resident expert, Kurt, is leaving the ship today, I thought we might get a photo of everybody on deck?" They all marched upstairs and lined up on either side of Kurt. Grace had moved into the shade, but Kurt called out, "C'mon, Gorgeous, I want you in this picture with the kids."

A murmur of excitement as Grace moved to slip within Kurt's arm. The camera clicked, and Grace patiently stood posing for smaller groups. Finally, Kurt pointed to Jason, "Give that camera to somebody else, and you get over here with me and Gracie."

Even behind the wild, curly beard Grace could see the guy's happy smile as he joined them; it was close to sunset when Kurt and Grace finally climbed into the bobbing tender boat and headed for their vacation destination together.

Chapter 4

Yeah, their destination on São Tomé was only a rough cabin built from storm-grayed boards on a white sand beach. The entrance faced the sea, with a wide open porch set with a long red painted bench and a small pink table. Inside everything looked neat and clean, with the primitive wood walls painted a soft Naples yellow. The one big room had a double bed with a large lemon yellow flowered coverlet, aimed so that when you woke up in the morning, you were seeing the ocean through the large glassless window that could be shuttered in driving rain or at night. A small butter yellow dining table was also set before the window, with two sap green painted chairs. The back of the cabin had a tiny primitive open kitchen with no refrigerator, and next to it was a small bathroom with only a high, pull-chain tank toilet, sink, and shower. Very basic, but Grace loved it. Kurt stowed his suitcase on the other side of the bed. "Okay, Calvin said there were some places to eat, even some bars with a little nightlife around here."

Grace pulled a pink and purple flowered sarong from her suitcase and examined Freya's pick critically. She was going to look like an upholstered sofa in this, but only said, "Okay, let's go party."

As they walked into town, he picked a wild, white orchid for her hair. Dinner was meat pastries they purchased from an outdoor vendor. The bar proved to be even more basic than their cabin, and after something strong with rum Grace found herself walking barefoot with Kurt on the beach, finally kissing in the moonlight as the gray surf crashed on the shore.

* * *

The next morning, to Grace's surprise, Kurt had made a deal with some woman who sold meals on the beach, so they were to have a breakfast tray delivered each morning. The first day,

Grace found a platter of cut bananas, cheeses, cornbread, shrimp, glasses of coconut milk, and a pot of very strong coffee. Together they ate out on the porch sitting on that long bench facing the rolling waves that now sent foam lace up on the smooth sands, as raucous seagulls swooped in for scuttling crabs.

That was the second delight of the morning.

Then as Grace leaned back on the bench, Kurt put his arm around her saying, "This shacking up is going pretty good."

"Aaup," she mimicked him, contentedly sliding into his shoulder.

"Remember, we're supposed to be deciding if you're going to move down to my boat or I'm going to move into your condo?"

Yes, the night they both nearly drowned, Grace had fervently promised herself that given another chance she'd make some big changes in her life...yet, things were going so well. "Can't we just keep going like this? Making more of an effort to spend time together, but still living and working independently?"

"That usually doesn't work for most people..." he stopped and then leaned back to look out at the in rolling foamy crests before he continued, "but you and I aren't most people. Yeah, let's keep it going as it is."

White clouds drifted across the sky, as clear, translucent green waves lapped on the damp sand. Grace could hear parrots chattering from the jungle behind, and seagulls squabbling over some half-ate crab that washed up. Yes, nothing could be more peaceful than this, but as she watched Kurt's face, she saw him frowning, and Grace knew the drill. "Okay, what don't you want to tell me?"

He didn't seem surprised she could read him. "At the end of this week, we were planning to embark on the trip to go home to Oyster River."

"You planning something different now?"

"This science ship is taking off, following the currents. Seems like I film kind of good," he puffed up his chest saying, "so they've offered me money to go with the ship and be the resident Humpback expert for the next month and a half..."

"That's a lot more time to take off from your studies back in Oyster River?"

"Yeah," he didn't sound happy. "That'll be sticking Bobby for another month or two with all my ocean sampling..."

But Grace knew Kurt really wanted to go, so she said, "With three kids in diapers Bobby'll love all the overtime money and a chance to get out of the house. Almost as much as you'll love the chance to see your breeching whales."

"They told me I could bring you along?" he offered. "They kind of like having Gorgeous aboard?"

"No." She looked over that long beach, the misty hills in the background and the sharp leaved palm trees. "This has been fun, but the end of the week I've got to get back to my lab."

"Yeah," he looked to the white ship out at anchor, saying in a dreamlike voice, "a chance to see the Cape of Good Hope... Antarctic waters...me showing on TV as a marine expert..."

"You've never even seen a humpback whale," she reminded him.

"Whal, they want my ocean current know how. And my rugged seaman looking face..."

"Trim your nose hairs," Grace advised tartly.

He laughed, kissing her, brushing her with stiff chin whiskers. "I haven't decided yet..."

She looked deeply into his dark eyes. "Yes, you have."

Kurt flushed a bit. "Aaup, but you and I still have got the rest of the week."

But they didn't. The next morning's breakfast tray contained the teapot Grace asked for as a substitute for the coffee and fresh pineapple, grilled fish and a rasined beskuit-- a crispy, African sweet bread. As the two of them sat on the porch bench devouring each delicious bit, Grace looked up to see a familiar cinnamon colored face, whose name she couldn't remember. "We've got a visitor."

Kurt looked up. "Calvin from the ship."

The young guy trudging up the beach did not look like he was bringing good news.

"Calvin," Kurt called out, "am I needed onboard?"

"No, sir, the radio guy got a message for Dr. Farrington."

Noting Calvin used her proper name, Grace took a folded paper from him, frowning as she read the brief handwritten message.

Kurt asked, "What is it?"

In shock, Grace looked up at him. "Freya's accused of murdering a man..."

Chapter 5

In Bradley International Airport, Grace pulled her luggage off the carousel and headed out into pale, cold sunlight. March in Connecticut. She'd sent an e-mail asking Freya to pick her up, but she didn't get an answer. Grace should probably have asked one of her assistants to pick her up, but Freya usually did, then Grace would treat her to a lunch a fancy restaurant. Well, Grace would just have to get a cab. A tall figure waving to her. Not six foot one Freya, but her six foot five son, Mac. Sandy-haired like his mother, with her bright blue eyes, big bones, and an easy going way, he walked to Grace.

"Aren't you on duty?" she asked.

Mac looked down at her suitcase, "Umm...I'm kind off duty at the moment."

"They suspended you?"

"Well, my Captain strongly suggested I take my vacation time. Hell, it looks like my mother is chief suspect in a murder." Mac picked up Grace's suitcase and laptop and sounded worried as he said, "Ma planned to pick you up, but the police are questioning her again."

"Again? Just because she found the body?"

Mac looked away from her and started walking out to the parking lot. "It's a bit more complicated than that."

"The Internet said Freya discovered a body on someone's private estate. Why was she there?"

He was stowing her suitcase in the back of his blue RAM 1500 truck. When he joined her inside, Grace looked at him, waiting. Finally, as he was pulling out, Mac answered, "She won't tell me why she was there, or even how she knew this guy."

"Is that why the detectives keep questioning her," asked Grace. "When she just found a body, that shouldn't instantly make her a murder suspect?"

He turned his truck out of the parking lot on to The

main road. "The guy's skull got crushed from behind by a tenth-century Norwegian trimming axe."

Oh, shit. "A trimming axe–like the one Freya specially ordered from Ireland for the two of you to work on that Viking faering boat?"

"Aaup. The same one. Probably the only ten century, reproduction Norwegian trimming axe in Connecticut, maybe even the United States."

Oh, God, Grace had first seen that axe when Freya ordered it: three foot of wooden handle topped by an iron head. It took a strong person to lift it, much less swing it at the back of grown man's head. "Who was this guy?"

"He was a caretaker of the Kincaid family compound. They're a big, politically-connected family that have had an estate on the Long Island Sound for generations. They show up here once in awhile, especially now that Aldon Kincaid is the local Congressman. This is supposed to be his residence of record, but he spends more time in Washington or at his New York City apartment."

"Why was Freya there? The Kincaids don't sound like her kind of people."

Turning on to I-91 East Mac said, "Ma would surprise you--a lot of the people that attend those seances of hers have big, big money. Not that Freya really cares."

"Has your mother got a lawyer?"

Mac looked angry. "Freya says she doesn't need one and won't talk to one. You know Ma, there is no one more stubborn." He changed lanes easily, doing the same speed as most of the traffic, way over the fifty-five mile an hour speed limit. At least as a cop he had a badge if they were stopped. Grace studied Mac's strong profile for a moment, remembering that awkward, long-legged boy who gathered horseshoe crabs and seaweed for her. Then it seemed like only a short time, and she and Freya were raising money for his junior college. Mac Dell was the closest thing Grace had to a son, and a very, very fine one he'd grown up to be.

As they turned on to I-95 West, Grace put a call into her lab and got her undergraduate student assistant, Inger. "Mac will be dropping me off in half an hour, did the delivery come in?"

Of course, there were a lot of deliveries since she'd been gone, but the one that counted was a tiny toe bone from a believed to be human, that may have walked the earth eighty million years ago. A simple package expressed from a lab in the Atai mountains of Siberia. If they got lucky, and if she and her team could extract DNA, they might have another look at rare Denisovan genes, or perhaps that of an as a yet unidentified human lineage Professor Abrantes and she were looking for.

"It's here waiting for you," Inger happily reassured her.

Past Stamford, Mac turned off I-95 to older roads leading East toward the small towns that ran along the Long Island Sound as he headed for Oyster River Harbor; a harbor town that once sent its whalers out to sea for years at a time. Before the town itself, Mac turned off on a road that led toward the fish hatchery on the left, and on the right, the entrance to ORR-Oyster River Research-facility, her home for so many years of work.

As Mac turned his truck right, he asked, "Where do you want to go—condo or lab?"

"Lab."

Feeling very happy to be coming home, Grace looked to 'The Roost,' a mustard yellow Italianesque Victorian mansion with its central tower that faced the road. Built by a sea captain in 1840s, it now housed a large meeting hall and conference rooms above. The Roost formed the first building in a research institute started by wealthy summer residents in the 1800s, with the goal of eradicating cancer. Work continued in the quiet place with woods and harbor, where an amazing assortment of questing minds were drawn, but finally, Dr. Stewart Brewster put it all together and created an institute known worldwide for research into cellular development.

Parking his truck in front of a two-story, whiteboard building, he asked, "Want me to take your suitcases up to your apartment?"

Well, that suitcase and the resort wear inside it really belonged to Freya, not that she could fit in any of it, but Grace only nodded. "You've still got my key, right?"

"Yeah. And I had time to fix that kitchen faucet while you were gone."

"Thanks." She slipped out of his truck, focused totally on the place that--for her--was really home. Grace headed into the smell of citrus disinfectant in the black and white tiled foyer, where three labs and a lecture amphitheater filled the building. Grace headed to the door of lab 5, and, as usual, that stupid security system acted up. It refused to recognize her thumbprint or the number she tried to key in. Finally, Grace hit the buzzer–with no answer. Either Inger had left, or she was suited up in the clean room. The buzzer should work in there, but Grace wound up hammering on the front door. David and his stupid ideas of '*protection*'!

Finally, the door was answered by tall, blonde Inger explaining, "I can see you on the screen, but the buzz-in isn't working again."

"Leave it unlocked when we're in here," sighed Grace.

"Have fun on the trip?"

Inside a wide, white painted room opened up with long wooden tables and chairs in the center. Longer computer desks lined the end of the room near the door to the airlock suiting up room, before the clean room with its banks of specialty freezers and the latest equipment for DNA extraction.

In this entry room, two walls of fish tanks bubbled

away, some dry, some with rubber-banded clawed lobsters crawling about. Subjects for a current skin cream study Grace shared with Kurt, and more samples for an inquiry into the twisted shell disease infecting the harbor lobsters, with some normal ones for controls. In the front, windows overlooking the harbor and that handsome maple burl, a multi-drawered cabinet that once belonged to the generations of anal dentists, that left her with a treasure of DNA. The room looked bare, sterile and everything Grace found comforting; to her, it seemed she'd returned from 'work' to start her permanent 'vacation' here. "The bone tip?"

"Is logged in, and deposited in the main freezer. Are you going to start the extraction today? Nick hoped you'd let him do it tomorrow?"

"Yes, but under my supervision. And I want you to watch that one too--we might be making history." What about Bobby? He'd be too busy teaching her classes, and while really skilled with his extractions, Nick needed the high profile experience that bone could give. That settled, Grace wanted to settle in and find out what was going on with her best friend. Grace dialed The Haunts of Wôdan, got no answer, then tried Freya's home number. Mac had gotten his mother a cell phone, what number was that? She should have gotten it, but didn't--still, Inger might have. Grace checked her phone list on the computer, yes, Inger had inputted the cell number. Grace called it, no answer, but she once again blessed Inger's organizational ability as Grace turned back to her work.

Minutes passed. Hours? Hearing a voice, Grace looked up.

"Dr. Farrington, I've been wanting to meet you," a voice came from above her desk. A stunning beautiful blonde held out a hand, and Grace realized she should rise and shake it. She did. Then what?

Inger came out from restocking the airlock with boxes

of paper booties. "Oh," she said walking over, "This is Nicole Duval, Dr. Huang's new assistant."

"Associate," Nicole corrected, then turned to Grace. "I don't know if you've heard of my work, I developed Erratum, it's..."

She started, but Grace finished, "Software that attempts to winnow out errors from merged gene segments." Grace thought a bit, then added, "It's an interesting concept. I've bought a copy for my lab, but we haven't installed it yet."

Nicole looked gratified. "If you have any questions, call me–and when I'm ready to get the next version out, I'll get you a working copy to test."

"Thank you." Grace had the sneaking suspicion she would now be listed as Nicole's latest 'associate', as she turned to get back to her computer.

Taking the hint, Nicole glanced about the lab and then walked out. Seeing Grace settled in, Inger headed over to the corner counter with its sink, mini-fridge, and coffee maker that was only used for hot water to make tea. She came back over with a steaming cup that smelled of lemon tea and set it beside a grateful Grace.

"I needed that, thank you." Stirring the cup to cool it with the wooden stick Inger provided, Grace asked, "What do you think of Huang's new associate?"

"She's got everyone entranced, especially the men," Inger supplied, sounding a bit envious. "Looks like a model and as an undergraduate wrote a program that everybody wants..."

"Actually..." Grace gave it some thought before saying, "I think Erratum has a very limited market, probably won't even justify the cost of selling it."

Finally drinking her lemon tea, Grace studied her computer screen as her mind worked. If she managed to extract workable DNA from a bone Professor Abrantes felt might be eighty thousand years old, she would be privileged to work on it. And if they both were correct and tremendously lucky, they might have another Denisovan gene line from a pool of extinct humans to work on or even a rarer find of a proposed, but as yet unfound human lineage. So far the world had only a few Denisovan molars and bones, starting with the tip of one female child's finger bone from forty thousand years ago. If she could culture this find, it would be a true treasure! The next step would be to determine if this bone also carried genes that are still found in small segments of the human genome. With a genetic readout she would have to pull out Denisovan genes, but there must be some way to filter them out?

"Grace? Grace, do you hear me?"

Chapter 6

Again, another annoying voice brought her back to her laboratory world. The tea was cold, Inger was gone, it was one o'clock, so her assistant's part-time hours were finished for today. Knowing she should be alone, Grace looked up at the tall man standing there--tanned skin, blue shirt, construction work clothes. It was Adam, President of Oyster River Research, a voluntary position, but not just an honorary title. Not really her boss, but Adam ran ORR and offered Grace her contracts, a laboratory to work in, and a free condo. Although she really just wished he'd go away now, Grace forced a smile, "Adam."

"How did the filming go?" he asked, sounding a bit anxious. "After all MacKay's representing ORR and some of the things he spouts off..."

"The cameraman said Kurt showed marvelously, in fact as their senior scientist he's going with the Science ship to Antarctica waters to get more on film."

Always annoyed to be taking time off from the construction company he owned, Adam really wasn't paying much attention to Kurt's trip as he sat down in the chair opposite her desk. Grace had to suppress a groan; whatever he wanted to talk about, she didn't have the time to waste. He started out saying, "Inger hasn't gotten back to me on your attendance at our Spring buffet fundraiser at the Roost? Congressman Aldon Kincaid will be speaking. He's taking time out from his run for the Senate, well, actually he'll be kicking off his run for the Senate here, trying to tie his campaign in with Oyster River's cutting-edge research."

"That should sell some tickets," she said noncommittally, wondering when this talk would be over.

"We need you there."

Shit. "I really don't have the time..." *She hated being*

led out in the dog and pony show. 'Here are our scientists, one of them is due to get a Nobel, sometime...maybe...'

"Grace, I would personally appreciate you attending."

And she owed ORR a lot. "Yes, I will be there. I'll eat something, and you can introduce me, and then I'll leave.."

"That's very good. I understand you consider it a time waste–still we have projects that need funding," he stopped and then started again, sounding embarrassed, "but today, I'm here for something else..."

Grace waited.

"You know Aldon Kincaid is married?"

"No," said Grace, not really caring if this politician had one wife or twenty.

"His wife is Maura Kincaid. She's very interested in you and your work."

If Grace offered this woman a tour of her lab would Adam leave? "You want me to talk to her?"

"Actually, she wants a favor. She'd like to see how you work."

"Is she a geneticist? Or at least a scientist? Adam, you know I don't allow random tours through my clean room, it's in my contract."

Adam held up two open hands in a stop gesture. "I didn't phrase that quite right. Maura doesn't want to see your work, she wants you to work for her. Maura wants you to compare some DNA for her."

Grace certainly did that occasionally for other scientists, friends, and locals, more to study the results herself, but this was not going to become a regular ORR fundraising promo. "How much DNA?"

He shrugged. "She didn't tell me. In fact, she seemed not to want to talk about that at all. She asked if your work was confidential."

"It is." And Grace wanted to get back to it. "If it's two or three samples, I can have Nick and Inger culture them."

"She wants you to work on it," he pointed out.

"I will supervise them. What result is she trying for?" He shrugged. More wasted time."So, it sounds like I'll have to talk with her directly. Have her make an appointment with Inger."

"Actually Mrs. Kincaid is waiting outside." Relieved that his part was over, Adam started to stand up, then obviously felt he should add, "Grace, you are aware that for generations the Kincaids have donated to this facility and numerous other charities. They are a socially responsible, wealthy, very politically-connected family."

She knew the drill. Getting up, Grace moved to pull on a white laboratory coat as Adam left. He shortly returned with an attractive dark chestnut haired woman in her thirties, wearing a cream-colored, mink-trimmed car coat. Mrs. Kincaid looked doubtfully about the white painted wood lab that was originally built in the 1920's.

"Maura Kincaid, this is the renowned Dr. Grace Farrington."

She smiled tightly at Grace, who tightly smiled back. Nobody spoke, so finally Grace asked her, "I understand you want me to culture some DNA for you?"

The woman looked at Adam, with embarrassment staining her cheeks. The first to figure that out, Adam also looked embarrassed as he said, "You know I'm late for...I'll just leave you two to talk."

Saying that, Adam hurried out, but Maura waited until the door closed behind him, then she turned to Grace asking, "Adam said you've done work with DNA identification before?"

Well, that established Mrs. Kincaid knew nothing about the *'great Dr. Farrington's reputation,'* so Grace indicated two chairs at one of the lab tables. "Let's sit down. You want two or more DNA samples tested confidentially, is that correct?"

The woman seemed relieved Grace was getting to the point. "Yes, two samples." She started pulling a checkbook out of her handbag. "How much will that cost?"

Grace had the wild desire to say '*fifty thousand*' and see the look on her face. Instead she said, "First I need to know why you want this done, Mrs. Kincaid?"

"Just Maura, please."

"Then it's Grace."

"You know that in 1918 the Bolsheviks executed the last Russian Tsar and his family?"

"Yes."

"Their youngest daughter, Anastasia, survived the massacre."

Oh, lord, not this stupid business again!

Maura continued earnestly, "In 1918, the seven Romanovs and their four servants disappeared..."

Grace picked it up, "Leaving rumors that the whole family escaped and were sailing in the Arctic sea on their yacht the Standart, or that Alexi escaped to Eurasia, or that Anastasia had escaped to Paris, London, Beijing, the city of Baltimore..."

"Yes, there were wild rumors and imposters," Maura reluctantly admitted.

But Grace continued relentlessly, "At one point there were about ten Anastasia Romanovs, each claiming to be Nicholas and Alexandra's lost daughter. Of course, they didn't have DNA in the early twentieth century to disprove their fraudulent claims. It was only after her death that saved medical samples disproved Anna Anderson, as DNA would have disproved all the others."

"My great-great-grandmother Dagmar isn't like that."

"Is she still alive?" Grace thought about it. "One of Tsar Nicholas's daughters would be over a hundred years old?"

"Oh, she was dead before I was born. I only know of

her because of the impression she made on my grandmother, who talked of her grandmother Dagmar constantly."

"So your great-what ever-grandmother claimed to be the real Grand Duchess Anastasia?"

"Not publicly. She wasn't like an Anna Anderson, a Nadezhda Vasilyeva, or even a Eugenia Smith living on the reputation of being the Tsar's lost daughter. My grandmother and her husband came to the United States as refugees after World War II. As Dagmar Pancoff, she settled at Brighton Beach in New York City. When widowed, she began working as a seamstress--remember Empress Alexandra had trained all her daughters to embroider and sew?

"Dagmar worked in my great-great-grandfather's garment factory, where he met and later married her. She was very shy, but everyone who ever saw my great-great-grandmother spoke of her dignity-- and as a short woman, she still walked and sat with an imperial stature."

As Grace tried to patiently listen, she saw no happy outcome from this exercise. Chances are Grace couldn't prove the relationship--more likely she would disprove it-- but Maura continued excitedly, "Her name, Dagmar, of course, you know Anastasia's grandmother, Maria Feodorovna, the Dowager Empress of Russia, was born into the Danish royal family as Princess Dagmar?"

"But your Dagmar claimed to be the missing Grand Duchess Anastasia?"

"No, not at the beginning. It was obvious she had suffered terribly in World War I, then the Russian revolution. After her marriage, she rarely left the family estate and insisted they keep guards with trained german shepherds patrolling the property constantly. She told her husband the truth and years later--just before her death--she told the rest of her family about her Imperial parents; and her sisters and brother Alexi; their life in the Winter Palace; and then the horror of her families' execution at Yekaterinburg."

"How did Dagmar escape?"

"Armored in a jewel-sewn corset, Anastasia survived the initial shooting of her family and fainted. While the soldiers went out front to wait for a truck, servants coming out to view the bodies heard her crying; they hid Anastasia. When the White army reached Yekaterinburg, she managed to attract a young soldier, Nicholas Pancoff, who married her, and eventually smuggled her into the United States, where he was killed by a runaway carriage horse."

"An interesting story..." Grace started, shifting uncomfortably, wanting to end this interview.

Maura ignored that. "I have pictures of Dagmar at thirty, that looks just like a thinner, older Anastasia."

Yes, she probably had dark hair, two eyes, a nose, and mouth-instant resemblance to the Grand Duchess. This was going nowhere. "Yes, the original bodies were concealed for over ninety years, but I believe the Russians did find and test nine bodies and were satisfied that five of those were Nicholas II and his family."

"Yes," she said excitedly. "So they can test bones for a family relationship?"

"Depending on the condition of the bones, yes they can." Grace wished she didn't have to do this, but she added, "Articles I've read in *Nature Genetics* and in *PloS ONE* discuss a second grave, found nearby years later with the bones of two other individuals."

"Yes," said Maura without hesitation. "In 2007."

Now, Grace had to crush her hopes. "I understand they found the two smallest victims were burned by acid, fire, and lime as per the murder squad's testimony. These tested as Alexi and one of the daughters of Nicholas and Alexandra. They thought it was Marie, but that has been disputed, and it's claimed the bones were Anastasia's."

With the look of a true believer, Maura pushed back. "And you're saying they couldn't have made a mistake with ninety-year-old DNA? They were looking for a Marie or Anastasia–so they found her. Don't you know scientists, that whatever the results of an experiment, they still always decide their original theories were proven correct?"

Actually, Grace did, but she said, "But the number of bodies is correct..."

"Couldn't there have been a young housemaid also killed? Or that the murderers finding they were short a body, hadn't gone out and killed another young girl so that they could show their superiors the proper number of victims? Do you personally know these bones to be the seven Romanovs?"

"I didn't work on the DNA matching, and, yes, there are some discordant voices citing the DNA from Nicholas's blood in the Japanese incident doesn't match, and others arguing the attributions were wrong on various grounds."

"What do you believe, Dr. Farrington?"

"The only interest I had in the Romanov affair was in the procedures used in preparing the damaged bones for DNA extraction."

"So you will admit there could have been a mistake?"

This woman would not be stopped by reasoning. "If you could prove your great-great-grandmother was Anastasia what do you plan to do? Write a book, sell a movie script? Claim any Romanov money still left in British bank accounts?"

She seemed surprised at the question. "No, I hadn't even thought of that. I don't want publicity, and I certainly don't need money since I'm married to Aldon Kincaid..." Maura frowned, then finally said, "I just want to know who I am descended from."

"Then hire a genealogist and trace your family tree."

"Looking at just written records, they aren't going to find any more information than I already have."

Why couldn't Maura see reason? "Right now you're

sure you're descended from your great-great-grandmother Dagmar, who you believe was a lost Romanov Grand Duchess. I think you should be satisfied with that, because-- if I do testing--odds are I am going to prove that Dagmar Pancoff was not Tsar Nicholas' surviving daughter."

Still frowning, Maura had apparently given this a lot of thought. "Yes, I do understand. I understand that could happen, and I accept the risk."

Well, maybe Grace could end this on the grounds of practicality. "I can't do DNA comparisons without samples."

Seeing she might get her way, Maura brightened up again. "The family preserved some of Dagmar's tissues in formaldehyde..."

Sadly Grace shook her head, saying, "That will probably have degraded the DNA. A big problem with the sea monster samples people keep sending me."

The woman looked deflated. "Oh, maybe we could have her body exhumed?"

"That's extremely difficult to do, especially if her husband and her immediate family have also passed away."

Maura stood there, obviously wanting this so very badly."My grandmother left me a locket with Dagmar's hair inside–could you get her DNA from hair?"

That was a definite possibility–a tenuous one, but a possibility. "A hair shaft doesn't have a nucleus or normal cell structure, but there is a chance that there might be a root follicle on the hair or perhaps skin cells attached. The hair root contains keratinocytes, cells which are ideal for the extraction of nuclear DNA. Do not open up the locket, just bring here, and I'll look at your samples under the brightfield microscope. Are you a direct female line descendant of Dagmar?"

"Yes."

"Then we can test you too."

"Can you do that?"

"Of course," Grace pointed out, "but you understand in order to prove or disprove relationship with the Romanov Royal family I would need samples of their DNA. I believe Anna Anderson's claim to be Anastasia was proven false by a sample from the British Royal family."

"Yes," agreed Maura. "Prince Philip, the Duke of Edinburgh, he is related to Alexandra on his maternal line and to the Romanov males on his paternal side."

This was impossible. "I can't just call up Windsor Castle and ask the Queen to swab her husband's cheek..."

"You can't and I can't, but my husband is a Kincaid. I'll just tell him you need it for your research, he won't ask why; the Kincaids have always been supportive of Oyster River Research. My mother-in-law Charlotte was just talking to the Prime minister of England the other evening. The Prime minister's husband is on a board of one of the Kincaid holdings. And if Prince Philip's already been tested, perhaps they could just send those results to you?"

"That might have what we'd need." Grace studied this obviously deeply driven woman trying to understand. "Why is this so important to you?"

Maura raised her head proudly. "I'm married to a man who expects to be President of the United States someday; his mother is on the boards of multiple corporations; his uncle-- the late senator--there is talk of canonizing him in the Catholic church. Aldon's cousins are governors, surgeons, archeologists, the Kincaids are American royalty."

"And now you're part of that," said Grace.

"Yes," she hesitated, then started more carefully, "Branches of my family have been successful merchants and manufacturers in America since the eighteen hundreds. They came from Portsmouth, England, but before that, we can't trace anything..."

"DNA autosomal testing that maps ethnicity could tell your ancestors' geographical movements over the centuries..."

"Autosomal?" Maura asked.

"A term for the non-sex linked DNA."

"I'm not interested in tracing my family tree to some fisherman in Grimsby, but if Dagmar Petrov Pancoff Clark can be proven to be Anastasia, daughter of Tsar Nicholas II, that would mean I am descended from the ruling houses of Europe. I'd be part of European nobility, on par with my husband's American aristocracy."

To Grace, a person was what work they did, or even how they treated other people in this life, not who sent down their genes. "If you're a Romanov, you'd be a descendant of Ivan the Terrible, who in a fit of temper struck his son with an iron-tipped staff, killing him, or Peter the Great, who one day ordered the torture and murder of over a thousand men just because they dared question his commands."

Maura just stared at her levelly saying, "The Romanovs were strong men, that was the type of leader needed in violent times."

Grace thought there was one more thing she might try. "By DNA testing, it is estimated that all modern humans today are descended from an 'Eve' who lived roughly two hundred thousand years ago, and an 'Adam' who may have lived one hundred thousand years ago. If you believe that, just by being born homo sapiens, you are related to the Romanovs, and the Japanese Imperial family, even the last Inca."

Maura did a mock smile. "Yes, I know, these days everyone is 'special'..., but you study DNA, you must know families like the Kincaids or the Romanovs who produce generation after generation of leaders, creative geniuses, physically superior people. There must be something in their genetic makeup..." Embarrassed Maura looked down at her hands saying, "You think I'm crazy."

"No. What you're saying is not exactly 'politically correct,' but yes, some families do seem to produce surprisingly high percentages of persons with superior intelligence, physical endurance, or creativity. But how to separate out what of that is the result of nature or nurture, or the interaction of both, is a whole inquiry that is way beyond the scope of my current research."

"But you understand why I need to know the truth about Dagmar's origins?"

"Yes, but I think you're making a mistake, risking losing a cherished, sustaining belief for the more likely cold, dampening shower of reality."

"I'll speak to Charlotte about Prince Philip's DNA, and I'll bring it over when I get it."

Grace noted that Maura said 'when' not 'if' she got it, so Grace reached into her desk drawer and pulled out her business card which she handed to Maura. "It would be better if they e-mailed my lab directly."

"I know you think I'm foolish..." She took the card, then sat looking at Grace, finally saying, "I know Dagmar was Anastasia, but even if your tests were to prove she wasn't, I still have to know."

Yes, Grace had figured that out some time ago. "If you can provide the samples, I'll do the extractions and comparisons."

Maura's face lit up. "When can you test me?"

"Now." Grace opened her desk drawer for a sterile testing vial with a five-centimeter stick inside.

"Will it hurt?" Maura asked a bit nervously.

Grace smiled reassuringly. "It's painless. You'll just swab the inside of your cheek at least three times with the cotton end of the stick, then return it to the vial, and recap it."

Maura eagerly reached for the vial. "Please, don't tell my family—or leave a phone message. That sounds weird I know, it's just that I'd like Dagmar's truth to be a surprise...if I told anyone, and I just might not." Saying that, Maura finished her test, then after smiling brightly to Grace, she headed out.

Chapter 7

Knowing hunting yet another fake Anastasia was an incredible waste of time, and angry with herself because she hadn't turned Maura Kincaid down, Grace decided to take a break. It was past lunchtime and her work was already interrupted, so Grace felt she had to talk with Freya. She called Haunts of Wôdan, letting it ring long and not getting an answer; Grace tried getting Freya at home; also no answer. The police couldn't still be questioning her?

A sound by the entrance made Grace look up; she thought she had set the remote lock on the door. Did she forget or was that security system acting up again? Now a solid, middle-aged man walked in, wearing a jacket that was open over a business shirt. He looked all about her lab, then walked to her desk. Grace did not encourage sightseers. "May I help you?"

Again he looked at the white room, "What is this place?"

"Laboratory 5," Grace answered in a cool, dismissing voice.

The man's face spread wide with an ingratiating smile. "I'm Harry Corman, Aldon Kincaid's campaign manager." She just silently waited for him to state his business, so still smiling he asked, "You are?"

"Grace."

"Grace. Do you have a last name, Grace?"

"This is a private laboratory that it is not open to the public, so unless you have business here, you'll have to leave."

He looked about, "You have a boss I can talk with? Is he in the back there?"

"No."

Stopping, he mentally drew back a little. "The boss is a lady, right? You?" Again, the lopsided insider smile that said '*you and I are going to be friends.*' "You modern gals run everything, and do it better than us guys, I'll admit it! But as I explained, I work for the Kincaids, and I saw Maura coming out of here? Again Grace stayed silent, forcing him to try again. "What do *you* do here?"

"Work."

"Yeah, this is a lab. You, people, do In-Vitro? I mean, I know Maura's having difficulty getting pregnant--she lost those three babies--is that why she was here?"

"If you are so close to the Kincaids, why don't you ask her?"

His voice got a little rougher. "You, know, mam, I do a lot for the Kincaids. In fact, as campaign and business manager, I write all their checks for them, so if Oyster River is expecting a donation, it may be Kincaid Foundation money, but that check is going to have my name signed at the bottom." He shrugged. "And, you know, sometimes I kind of lose the checkbook."

This was too much! Grace reached for the landline still on her desk. "If you don't leave now, I will have to call security." Actually, Grace knew because of budget cuts ORR only had security patrols at night, but fortunately, this gentlemen didn't seem to know that. Harry raised his hand's palms out in a '*no harm meant*' gesture. "No, problem, Grace. It is Grace? Got to remember that name, but I'm leaving."

Again, with a sweeping look at the computer screens, microscopes and data printouts covering tables her visitor walked out, leaving Grace with questions. The man obviously had no idea of what her lab did--maybe even what Oyster River Research did--so how did he happen to be here? Did he follow Maura here? He claimed to know her, be employed by her husband. If he was truly only a friend, why hadn't he walked in while she was still here? Should Grace tell Maura this guy was asking about her? Grace didn't like this at all–yes, she was going to have to start using that security lock-buzz system David had ORR install for her.

Again she tried calling Freya--no answer. Feeling down and hungry, getting on her jacket, she locked up the lab and headed outside. Ahead, the gray harbor water ruffed with lacy whitecaps. Soon the trees should start budding, but now Grace found herself shivering from the chill wind whipping skeleton branches framed against low gray clouds.

Built over the years, ORR could only be called a hodgepodge of architectural styles, from eighteen-century firehouse floated across the harbor, to the nineteen fifties' brick and wood labs, to the guest lecturer's apartment atop the boathouse once belonging to the mansion on the point. Now she headed inside the brown and beige brick contemporary Administration building. To her right, the glassed-in ORR research library, to the left the glassed-in Café and ahead was Gail's desk in front of the short hall to the President's office. That desk was empty now.

Grace turned into the next glass cube, with the ORR Café. Really a glorified cafeteria, but since they out-sourced food service to The Gourmet Cheese Shop catering, the food quality had really gone up. Inside, several people sat at tables, and Grace immediately spied Gail Travinski in the corner. The blue-eyed, full figured, but curvy self-proclaimed 'polish doll' was reading from a book as Grace walked over. "What's good today?"

Looking up surprised, Gail slipped her book into her handbag, as if she didn't want Grace to see it, but she only said, "I thought you'd be late. I've got the tuna salad, but I bet you'd like the barbecue beef hero and New England clam chowder. And could you please pick me up a package of potato chips?"

Nodding, Grace walked over, picked up the tray and headed into the walled-off food area. A refrigerated section of plated salads and desserts, then racks of wrapped sandwiches, a small grill, and on the other side: plates, napkins, plastic ware, and condiments and two heated urns of soup--today clam chowder--and a chili. Grace picked up a slice of cherry pie swathed in plastic wrap, then she ordered a barbecue beef on a kaiser roll, ladled herself some thick, creamy clam chowder in a cardboard cup, and picked up a bottle of iced tea. She made these Café lunches the main meals of her day. At the end, she grabbed up a packet of oyster crackers, and the baked potato chips Gail preferred. After Grace got her sandwich, she used her employee card to put it on her tab, then walked out to the dining room.

"Grace." The well-coiffed blonde who had been ahead of her in line smiled back at her. "Would you like to join us? Adam and Huang are with me, we're eating over there."

She should know who this woman was--Grace was sure she'd just met her--but, as usual, she stumbled over the name, "Ah...actually I'm at the table over there, with Gail."

The woman glanced over at Gail eating her tuna salad and said coolly, "You're eating with a secretary?"

"A temporary secretary," Grace amiably confirmed.

"You're turning down the President of ORR? Is that politic?" From her tone, the lady obviously didn't think it was.

"Adam will understand." Not waiting for an answer, Grace carried her tray over to Gail's table. And as she sat down, she noticed Gail slipped her book into her handbag a second time. She usually just left her books on the table, and Grace had stuffed a journal in her jacket pocket so they both would read as they ate. Grace passed the chip bag to Gail, who reached for her handbag to pay. "Never mind–with the Guru award I can afford some chips."

"Do you have pictures of São Tomé?" Gail asked eagerly.

"Loads." Grace fished for her cell phone, handing it to

Gail. "You would have loved it. The white sand beaches were out of a vacation brochure..."

"Adam's really excited that they are filming more of Kurt and that ORR is getting more coverage."

"They're very impressed with him. Kurt did a marvelous job acting as a senior scientist."

Happily murmuring Gail thumbed through the vacation photos as Grace bit into her sandwich. The vinegary coleslaw that came with it tasted marvelous.

Gail lowered her voice a bit. "I see Nicole is trying to recruit you for her team."

Nicole, Huang's new assistant, that was her name? "She's got a team?"

"Huang hired a Barbie doll to teach his classes and clean up his lab. Instead, he's got a student of Machiavelli's tactics who probably plans to be top dog around here someday," reported Gail.

"She doing any work of interest?"

"Outside her undergraduate software break-through? No. Her curriculum vitae lists her field as 'interpreting the secrets of life'..."

Grace choked with laughter at that. "You're kidding?"

"Nope. But madam's been making the acquaintance of all the Board Members, and makes Adam start flushing the moment she walks in and turns that thousand-watt smile on him."

"Oh, boy. Wait till Kurt sees her."

Gail titled her head, giving that some thought. "I don't know what she will make of him with his red neck front and motorcycle gang. I would have said she wouldn't bother with him at all, but if he comes back as a superstar of the Science Channel..." Gail shrugged her shoulders. "We'll have to see..."

"Has Adam spoken any more about making you a permanent employee?"

"No," Gail said, lowering her head and obviously not wanting to elaborate.

"Have you pointed out he'll pay you less if he's not paying the agency's fee?" Grace took another fork full of the coleslaw.

Gail still looked down, and said slowly, "But, if I were a permanent employee, he'd have to pay social security, vacations, retirement, and he'd have to put me on the medical plan." She looked so sad. "I could really use that medical plan."

Grace stopped eating. "You're sick?"

"No." The secretary shook her head, but wouldn't meet Grace's eyes. "No,... it's just that a medical plan would be nice, that's all."

"If there's something wrong...I'll lend you money for a doctor's visit, to get you checked out. In fact, I'll pay for it!"

"Not needed. I was just looking at doctor's prices without insurance. It's expensive."

"Why do you want to see a doctor?"

Looking away, Gail only said, "No reason. Just thinking of a checkup. I-I'll speak to Adam again, but I don't think he'll want to change things at this time."

"You're certainly worth it to ORR," pointed out Grace.

Gail looked unhappily at her salad. "I don't know if Adam will think so."

"He will. We're going to work on it," stated Grace firmly.

There was silence, then as Grace started on her cherry pie, Gail asked her, "Didn't you ever want children?"

Where did that come from? Grace would have considered that her own personal business, but she had a long friendship with Gail, so answered honestly, "My work is my family, my projects my babies..."

"Not really." Gail stared at her plate. "Didn't you ever

want to form a family so you won't be alone? Or have your genes keep on living after you are gone?"

The question seemed very important to Gail, so Grace took a little more time before answering, "There have been moments, when I turned thirty especially, yes, I had a strong, biological urge to procreate, but I wasn't married, or even in a steady relationship. And whatever my desires were, a child demands a level of commitment that I knew I couldn't give."

Gail looked back up at her. "They take donor eggs from women. They even pay for it. Quite a lot."

Grace chuckled. "Not for eggs from a woman over forty."

"In your case, it would be different! The eggs of a genius, any woman would want that–like getting a donation from the Noble Prize Winners Sperm bank."

"I don't think that's in business anymore. A shame, since Stewart Brewster still feels that it had some really worth-while ideas. But no, if my eggs produced a child, I'd feel obligated to raise her."

"You don't think making an infertile couple happy would be worth it?"

"Not for me–I'd always wonder how the child made out if it was treated kindly. I'd feel responsible for bringing a baby into the world that I didn't know..."

Gail looked back down to her plate, and Grace gently asked, "Are you thinking of donating to get money? In that case, I do think helping an infertile couple would be right. And maybe you could arrange some sort of an open adoption deal, where you were allowed to keep in touch with the family as the baby grows up?"

"No. No, I don't want to donate," Gail said picked up her tray. "I've got to get back to my desk."

Usually, they finished eating, and they talked a bit. Gail was a very practical, bright person, and Grace valued her opinion, but today, she just watched the secretary hurry away.

Back in her lab, Grace tried first Freya's New Age store, then the home phone again. She finally got an answer on that.

"Hello?"

"Freya, it's Grace."

"Where are you?" asked her excited friend.

"Back in my lab."

The voice saddened immediately. "Did you cut your vacation short because of me?"

"No," Grace lied. "The ship moved out early, headed to Antarctica and Kurt went with it."

"Tell me everything–no, I'm making spaghetti sauce, come for dinner after work. Mac's bringing home someone...it would probably be better if you're here. I might not kill her."

Chapter 8

Grace got off the phone thinking that with Freya being questioned in a murder, her friend better watch the macabre jokes; although Freya hadn't sounded like she was kidding. Logging in Maura Kincaid's sample without a name attached to the number, and only a notation in her small private notebook to identify that number, Grace headed to the clean room. At the door outside the airlock, Grace shut off the ultraviolet lamps that sterilized the suiting up room and laboratory when no one was inside to kill any funguses, molds or stray DNA in the air. The negative air pressure filtration units kept going all the time. Inside the airlock, she began pulling on her white Tyvek jumpsuit, hair net cap, gloves, disposable booties, then finally the surgical mask and face shield helmet for her work in the clean room. Deciding to take a chance they would get a royal sample to test against, Grace started the extraction of Maura's DNA herself.

Her assistant, Inger, came in after her classes and reminded Grace of her dinner engagement with Freya (knowing Grace's ability to get lost in work, Freya called Inger to remind her). So Grace found herself driving out of ORR, past the Roost, and turning left along the end of the Harbor. A majestic white heron rose from the wintered yellowed marshlands, as she continued on the road left toward the town of Oyster River on the other side of a deep water harbor sheltered by ORR's peninsula. In the 1800s whaling ships had docked in Oyster River, then the town went into a long depression. The poverty of their owners ironically saved the beautiful old New England houses from destruction and 'improvement.'

In time, Oyster River became a summering spot for rich families escaping from New York City's unbearable heat and the stink of the cart horse droppings. Along Main Street, most of the town's clapboard houses became elegant shops for clothing, gourmet food, fine art, and jewelry. Freya's family house perched on the harbor two very old, narrow streets over from Main Street. Driving on a road once laid out for horse and buggies was hard enough, without trying to park, so Grace turned into the small municipal parking lot opposite a row of stores.

For a house gift, Grace picked up a bottle of wine and then dropped in the gourmet cheese shop for Freya's favorite rice crackers, a round of Brie, and beer-cheese dip for herself. She then walked past the expensive dress shops and the seamen's church, finally reaching a side street, turned left, then left again. Frey's white-painted clapboard house had been old before the Revolutionary War. Her son Mac had a Bilco door entrance--on the side--to his basement apartment, and another renter usually lived on the second floor with an outside porch entrance. Freya had the whole first floor, with a back staircase that went from the cellar to the attic. Grace knocked lightly on the front door painted a bright red, and then just walked in.

The foyer held a rising staircase, now blocked off at the top for the renter's privacy. To the left stood a parlor usually closed off by the pocket doors where Freya kept her endless craft projects: pinecone based candle holders and painted rocks; stained glass sun catchers being constructed; a frame for weaving, a spindle for spinning. It was here Grace had first seen that tenth-century trimming axe, the one they now claimed Freya murdered a man with.

Pushing that thought from her mind, Grace turned to the left parlor. Its pocket doors were open to show heavy Victorian Empire furniture, and purple velvet hangings darkened the windows. A large crystal ball set in an ornate brass dragon stand took pride of place on the carved mahogany coffee table. Here Freya did her tarot readings, crystal gazing, and psychic interpretations for her private clients. Grace stopped by an end table and looked to a triple deck of worn cards on top of a thick, green-bound astrological ephemeris. Freya worked hard for every dollar she got.

And Freya sincerely believed that her cards--or whatever--channeled some intelligence beyond herself. Over the years, Grace's best friend had read her cards or polished stones representing the planets cast on black velvet, or brass Chinese coins–all methods of divination that Grace found almost impossible to believe in, but...she had to admit, at times Freya had given her warnings of things that later came true. Facts and future events that Grace knew Freya had no way of pulling out of either her conscious or unconscious mind. But if out-of-worldly voices really did whisper to Freya, why hadn't they warned her to stay away from that boathouse and the dead man it held?

Calling out a loud, "Hello," Grace pulled aside the rainbow-beaded curtain and headed into the dining room. Here the blond table and chairs were Swedish modern, and the tall windows were hung with Freya's stained glass sun catchers in glowing colors. Smelling baking bread and a rich sausage, meatball spaghetti sauce, Grace headed through a door to an oversized country kitchen, with its gray wooden cabinets and big work table in the center. On the wall to the right, a door led to a hall with a bathroom and small bedroom, that ran behind to the other front parlor. To the left, there was a large ancient brick fireplace in one wall, once the main cooking area of a pre-Revolutionary War fisherman's house. On the East wall, a backdoor led out to a small wooden porch that over-looked the harbor. Alongside that door stood counters, a sink, an old refrigerator and a fancy, commercial-grade stove Freya bought second hand from a bankrupt bed and breakfast. To the right was the door to a full pantry of food and craft project supplies.

As Grace walked in, Freya saw her and rushed over to envelop her in a big bear hug. "You're okay? And tanned? Did you really do some resting on the beach?"

"Days of it. But what about you and this caretaker that was killed?"

Freya drew back. "They questioned me for eight hours today, each new detective asking the same stupid questions."

"Have you gotten a lawyer?"

"Don't need one. I'm not guilty of anything!"

"Freya..." Grace started to lecture.

But her friend cut her off with a raised hand. "I do not want to talk about this tonight!" She turned back to the wooden counter top where she was chopping a purple onion on a plastic board. "Good, you've brought red wine. I just poured the last of the Brotherhood Holiday spice wine into the spaghetti sauce–smell it."

Grace inhaled, and it was marvelous. "You're making my mouth water."

"Pour your wine and tell me about São Tomé," Freya instructed.

Getting a bottle opener from a counter drawer, Grace scraped at the foil bottle cover. "São Tomé is beautiful. Rainy jungles with lots of wild orchids, and those beaches, endless white sand with water that looked like an aquamarine jewel."

Freya nodded eagerly. "I read up about São Tomé. They have colonial architecture, one hundred unique kinds of orchids, and waterfalls, including a seawater fountain..."

No, Grace hadn't seen all that. "I spent a lot of time reading on the beaches, and it was warm enough to swim."

Her face glowing, Freya imagined it all as if she was there herself. "That sounds wonderful." Then she frowned, "You are sure because of me you didn't cut your stay short?"

"No," Grace lied again. "Do you want me to set the kitchen table?"

Freya didn't look happy. "No, the dining room, with my green embroidered tablecloth, and the good china for Mac's '*guest*.'"

Formal tonight. "Who is your son bringing?" Grace

usually would have opted out if she knew others were coming.

"Mac is bringing over that little bitch, Samantha Carson."

So that relationship was still on. "I thought we were working on being not judgmental?"

"My son is an idiot! His choice in women has been consistently bad! He's always bringing home the weak, the wounded, or just outright predators!"

To herself, Grace thought that sounded a lot like his mother's choice of boyfriends, but she only murmured, "Maybe it will be different this time."

"You know why she's coming," Freya demanded, dumping the onions in the sauce and then starting to chop up fried sausage. "She coming because I'm accused of murder, and the girl reporter wants the inside scoop."

"Or maybe she's coming because your son is an unmarried hunk and she lusts after his muscular body?"

Freya glared at her. "You know what she did to you–that hatchet job about Dr. Grace Farrington being a hermit, who didn't want to help other women get ahead!"

"Sam apologized for that. And it was partly my fault when I refused to take time off to give her an interview. She had to write something, then her editor wrote a lot of that 'anti-other-women's success' stuff,'"

"Do you know she writes for the tabloids under a fake name, 'Kit Samuel'?"

"A lot of writers use pseudonyms. Mark Twain was really Samuel Clemens."

"She did a story about this murder at the boathouse–about me!"

"Murder is news, Freya, she had to write about it. Did she mention your name?"

"No. Just that the body in the boathouse at the *'Kincaids' palatial harbor side estate'* was found by '*a local woman.*' Made it sound like I was the cleaning lady," Freya grumbled as she turned up the flame under her sauce pot.

"That's bending over backward not to use your name." Grace started taking out flatware from the drawer, and tried to sound neutral as she asked, "Why were you at the Kincaid boathouse?"

Crushing garlic with a broad knife, Freya wouldn't meet her eyes as she recited, "I'm planning on doing a new book in my Oyster River series. This time it will be *The Boats of Oyster River Harbor.*"

"You're switching from ghosts and hauntings to fancy boats?"

"Why not? The caretaker had been tooling around the harbor in a magnificent varnished wood motorboat from the nineteen-fifties. I needed his permission to use photographs of that boat in my book." Freya sounded like she had rehearsed this well, maybe a little too often.

"But wasn't this man just a caretaker there?" Grace pulled out the good paper napkins in antique gold. "Doesn't the boat belong to the Kincaids?"

Freya hesitated, then went back to stirring her spaghetti sauce. "I didn't know. It could have been his. Yes, I think he told me it was."

Her longtime friend thought cynically that Freya was a lousy liar, but Grace only said, "Then why are the police still questioning you?"

Checking on the twin loaves of Italian bread baking in the oven below, Freya carelessly shrugged as she said. "I don't know. The killer was probably that slutty girlfriend he was living with."

Grace wasn't going to let that pass. "Why did she use your trimming axe to kill him?"

"How did you know that–my big mouthed son told you?" Freya turned, putting her hands on her hips, and still holding the stirring spoon, she dripped blood-red tomato sauce on the worn linoleum floor as she said most firmly, "I am sick of being questioned on this matter. If you want to have dinner here tonight, you will change the topic!" She turned around and drained her wine glass.

Silence, then Grace cautiously asked, "Do you want some more wine?"

Freya nodded and turned back to her sauce. After a little time, she asked softly, "Tell me more about São Tomé. Did you really have any vacation at all?"

"Oh, yes. Kurt introduced me as 'Gorgeous,' a science groupie, and he ordered me off the boat and on to the island every day. I wore the two-piece bathing suit you sent and laid on a white sand beach..." What else did she do? "I read mysteries and swam and studied wild parrots and orchids in the jungle."

Her blue eyes brightened as Freya asked, "You did explore the island?" For as long as Grace had known her, Freya planned elaborate vacations to far off islands, sending for color brochures, picking distant destinations, and working out budgets, then she spent all her money on her son, helping her friends, or saving homeless animals...

Grace wanted to make São Tomé sound like a paradise Freya could vicariously visit. "I explored the open air markets and the jungle. I've brought home wooden carvings as presents for all of you–I should have brought them tonight." She paused, what else would Freya dream about? "At night Kurt and I went bar hopping–well there aren't too many bars on São Tomé, but we drank pineapple rum concoctions, and walked the beaches in the moonlight." After refilling Freya's goblet, Grace carried the wine over to the counter by the stove. "Then we hired a cabin..."

"We?"

"I chipped in half."

"That cheap..." Freya threw down her hotpot mitt in disgust.

But Grace felt she had to be fair. "I make more money than he does."

"Kurt MacKay is an obnoxious red neck who tells everybody he's in the KKK, he runs with a biker gang...I never understand why you have anything to do with him!"

"He's also in Mensa and the Masons. Kurt likes to shock people, but he's a very good scientist, and a gentlemen in his own way." Freya pulled out a leaf-shaped wood platter for the appetizers and Grace automatically got out the cheese knives as she continued, "When Kurt finished his filming on the ship and his studies, we shared that small, one room cabin on the beach. Freya, you would have loved it! From the porch you could walk right onto the sand, and see warm, sudsy waves coming at you. Kurt hired some woman to bring us breakfast trays: bananas and shrimp and corn bread, and things I don't even know the names of--marvelous meals. I wish you could have tasted them." As she talked Grace unpacked her paper bag from the cheese store, then pulled some more cheeses out of Freya's fridge. Soon she sliced up blocks of cheddar and Swiss, as the microwave heated the crusty brie for the burl wood platter Freya had set out. Grace finished off by adding her beer cheese spread crock, saltines, and the rice crackers. Needing something more, she dug back into the fridge and found seedless green grapes, which she rinsed out to complete the appetizer platter.

"You do look rested," Freya said, sounding happy, as if it were her vacation too, as she hauled out two golden-topped french breads from the oven. Hearing voices in the dining room, Freya's face slid from happy to ready for battle.

Grace stepped closer and put a hand on her friend's arm softly saying, "Try to give her a chance, for Mac's sake."

Chapter 9

When they walked into the dining room, Grace carried the appetizers and Freya followed with the wine. Totally oblivious to them, six foot five Mac leaned down to kiss five foot nine, red-haired Samantha. As a reporter, she worked in pants suits and jeans, but every time Grace had seen them as a couple, Sam wore a filmy chiffon skirt outfit, now in soft mauve. Both fair-skinned, they flushed when they realized they had an audience.

Freya just puts down the wine bottle and headed back into the kitchen. Sam quickly looked to Mac, but Grace only said, "She's bringing in more wine glasses for us. Let's sit and talk a bit. Should we sit in here? Or in the front parlor?"

Mac frowned as he suggested, "That parlor looks like Halloween, maybe the porch off the kitchen?"

The porch would be cold, and Grace knew the right front parlor would be cluttered with Freya's ongoing projects of seashell flowers, carved candles, and fishbone jewelry, all to eventually be sold in her new age store. Awkwardly they waited until the lady of the house returned with a tray of wine glasses, pronouncing, "We'll do the front parlor, it is for guests. It's too cold for an open porch."

"A shame, the view of the harbor is spectacular," added Grace.

In the psychic's parlor Freya settled herself on a tall chair, a one-of-a-kind piece that spread out behind her like a peacock's tail; hand-carved and brightly painted with writhing birds, fishes, snakes, and stalking cats--it was a marvel, carved by one of the artists who sold consignment pieces in Freya's store, and who gave it to her as a birthday present.

Seeming a bit uptight, Samantha just stood awkwardly waiting, as Mac started to pour ruby wine in the goblets Freya had put down on the coffee table. Leaving the stiff horse hair-cushioned Empire couch for Sam and Mac, Grace set down the cheese tray, and settled on a purple velvet chair, hoping the wine will loosen things up. Maybe instead she should have brought the fixings for apricot old fashions?

Mac tried first saying, "Sam got an exclusive interview with Congressman Aldon Kincaid."

That put a glow on Samantha's face. "Yes, it won't be printed until after he announces his run for the Senate at Oyster River Research's Spring fundraiser..."

Freya looked to Grace. "So he's using ORR as a front?"

"A front?" asked Sam as she flashed a questioning look to Mac.

He closed his eyes in pain. "Ma has kind of prickly relationship with the Kincaid family..."

His mother glared at him. "It's not just me! The Kincaid Compound took over a town's bird sanctuary."

"The Town sold it to them, in when was that, 1940?" Her son asked, looking weary of the subject.

"1942. Your grandfather was on the Council and voted against it."

Inclining her head, Grace said, "Sounds like the statue of limitations has run out on that one."

Freya looked primed for a fight. "Well, then let's talk about what they're currently doing. Who is funding the Kincaid campaign? There are rumors that the Kincaid International Helping Fund is pushing money back his way."

Immediately Samantha took up the defense. "That Foundation is for worldwide work, helping women and children gain their freedom, seeing that the African populations are vaccinated..."

That only made Freya raise a questioning eyebrow. "I hear Saudi Arabia has just given the Kincaid foundation a hefty donation, are they interested in 'helping women gain their freedom' too? For all that money, what are they expecting from an American politician?"

"Some people in Saudi Arabia may be more enlightened than others," said Sam defensively, not wanting to fight this.

But Freya was on the attack. "And I hear press people who write favorable articles get jobs with that Foundation? Or at least get to go on junkets to Egypt or some tourist paradise to '*check*' on the Foundation's '*good works.*'"

Sam's cheeks flamed. "I support Aldon Kincaid, and no one has offered me any trips."

"But you'd take one if they did?" Freya shot back.

Grace wanted to change the conversation, get them all talking about the aroma of Freya's baked bread, or the warming weather, or anything. She looked desperately to Mac, who just sat there with tight lips, watching his mother and girlfriend go at each other.

"Yes, I would," said Sam stiffly. "And that wouldn't change my reporting one bit! The Kincaid men have always had their flaws, but they are progressives who are trying to change the world. To make it better for everybody..."

Freya raised an eyebrow again. "They talk a lot about their good intentions, but what have any of them accomplished? What has Aldon accomplished that makes him worthy of being a United States Senator?"

Unconsciously sliding closer to Mac, Sam sounded on the defensive. "He's a junior congressman from a small, liberal state, there isn't much he could have done, but he's co-sponsored a lot of bills...to protect children from guns..."

"Yes, going along with George Soros to disarm the citizenry worldwide, and then you can legislate whatever you want, and nobody can stop you! That's why our Founding Fathers gave us the Bill of Rights and particularly the Second Amendment because they knew there would be people trying to enrich themselves by using taxpayer money to buy voters, and citizens should be armed to resist a tyrannical government."

Grace wondered when Freya suddenly started sounding like a conservative? "Freya," she interrupted, "if Aldon's a progressive, aren't you a progressive too?"

Obviously angry, her friend turned on her. "Grace, what do you know about politics? You're totally disinterested in anything that's not being dissected in your clean room!"

"That's not completely true," protested Grace weakly.

Freya ignored her. "Being a progressive is more than talking about it to a fundraising crowd. The Kincaids have long been known for selling out any cause to the highest bidder."

Audibly catching a calming breath, Sam said, "You're talking about the late Senator Al Kincaid ..."

"Not only him! The whole family: Aldon voting on subsidies for projects turned over to his mother's companies; his cousins are setting up '*heating for poor*' charities, then paying themselves hundreds of thousands of dollars in salaries..."

"Executive expertise is worth fair compensation," defended Sam.

"What is the extent of their expertise?" Freya demanded. "Being born wealthy? Going to papa's Ivy League college? Getting fat government grants pushed through by their cousin?"

Taking another sip of wine, Grace realized Freya couldn't be shut up, and it didn't look like the flushed faced reporter could either.

Again Sam tried, "Aldon's his own man..."

"Oh, yes. Quite a ladies man, too, I've heard. You know that girl who died--where was the press on that? A brief mention of her working for his campaign in the first story, then nothing else. No inquiry as to why she died? No investigative series to get at the truth?"

In a disciplined fashion, Sam turned her eyes to the appetizers, reaching for a cheese and cracker as she replied,

"The woman had a troubled history, she apparently was depressed..."

"Suiciding without leaving a note?" Freya asked.

"Only thirty percent of suicides leave a note," returned Sam wearily, seemed to remember this woman she verbally dueled with was Mac's mother, but she continued, "Aldon isn't perfect, but he's charismatic, he has name recognition, he wants a better world, and as Senator Kincaid he might just accomplish that."

"Or he might make everything worse–look at his record! Look at who is paying for his campaign," Freya said hotly. "Why can't your paper get behind a true progressive, someone honest like Astrid Ahlgren, President of C.U.R.S.?"

Those initials meant something to Grace, but before she could remember, Sam nodded her head and said, "Creatures' Universal Rights Save, yes, they are a dedicated organization, but journalists can't take sides, we just report..."

"Oh," said Freya raising that eyebrow again. "You–a journalist–do not take sides? You report equally on Astrid as you do on Aldon Kincaid?"

"I've written articles on her demonstrations..." Sam shifted uncomfortably.

"I've read them," Freya said her voice filled with anger. "For Aldon you use words like 'progressive,' 'caring' and 'born to leadership,' but with Astrid, you write stories that refer to her as 'a reactionary,' 'her Don Quixote missions', and 'her unrealistic worldview.'"

Eyes lowering, Sam didn't deny Freya's facts. Instead, she pointed out, "Astrid is honest, committed, steadfast, and unwavering I'll agree, but no one is going to vote for her except a few fringe nutcases."

"So you think I'm a 'fringe nutcase'?" Freya started, but a pager went off.

Mac reached for his belt, but the buzzing pager belonged to Samantha. Sam glanced down, then started dialing her phone, soon saying, "Carson." After listening briefly, she rose up. "There's a fire on I-95 in Stamford, tractor-trailer pile up. I've got to go do a story and pictures."

Freya also rose, saying anxiously, "But you haven't eaten yet? I'll put it on the table right now."

"Fires don't wait for photographers," said Sam heading for the foyer looking a bit relieved.

"You need an escort by a vehicle with a police siren?" Mac asked following her.

"No." Stopping she put her hand on his chest gently saying, "Your mother's gone through all that work for a lovely dinner, it smells great." She looked Freya, murmuring in a neutral tone, "Some other time." Saying that, Sam hurried to unhook her jacket hanging in the hallway, but she stopped at the door when Mac followed her. Sam looked up, and he reached down and kissed her.

It actually hurt Grace to see the pain on Freya's face. Yes, to a woman who dedicated nearly her whole life to raising her son, seeing that son walking away to another woman must cut so deeply. But Freya said nothing more as she went back to the kitchen to boil spaghetti for a family dinner that had already clearly failed.

But--as ever--the spaghetti sauce bubbled richly and smelled of sausage and garlic. The newly baked bread had been broiled with butter and mozzarella. Freya smothered the crisp salad with one of her homemade dressings–this one a creamy peppercorn ranch. And for dessert, she served a raspberry ice cream roll–Mac's favorite. Whatever she felt about her son's new girlfriend, Freya had put a lot of work into that meal.

Mac and Grace stayed to help with the dishes, but Freya said she had a headache, and retired to her bedroom, ending the evening. Finished cleaning up, Grace got her jacket as Mac asked, "Why don't you let me drive you to your car?"

"Thank you."

As they reached his truck, Mac commented, "Well, that went better than I'd expected."

Looking hard at him, Grace realized he wasn't joking.

* * *

Driving back to ORR Grace parked in front of her two-story condo building. She thought of dropping in on her assistant Bobby and his wife, but she didn't hear a baby crying, which probably meant Sara had managed to get the twins and Ginjer to sleep so she wouldn't appreciate someone ringing the doorbell. Instead, Grace unlocked her mail-slot and picked up the usual load of bills, advertisements, and the textbooks, authors sent her in hopes she would comment on them. The speaking requests and medical questions usually went to her lab, so she didn't have to lug that all up to the second floor. She was so glad to be back in her neat little condo, with its pale blue walls and a long room leading to the sliding glass doors that closed off her small patio overlooking the harbor. The moon hadn't risen, but Grace always liked to see the shining lights across the harbor reflected in the black water.

She dumped the mail on the table just before the kitchen. The small open kitchen looked neat and empty. Usually, Freya would have packed some extra bread and a jar of sauce to take home for her. Not tonight. What with being suspect in a murder, and seeing her son in a relationship she disapproved of, Freya had enough on her mind for a dozen headaches. Grace went to the second bedroom she used as an office and junk room. In the rest of the apartment, she made a half-hearted effort to keep it looking neat, only for herself, it was so rare she had visitors; actually, it was usually just Kurt or David, and them not too often. What happened to her resolve to be more social?

In the guest room office, Grace made little effort to straighten out the mess. This extra bedroom had shelves of her own books, that overlooked stacks of other DNA tomes printouts and journals covered two chairs and the daybed.

Grace had a very comfortable black leather executive chair, before her desk that was made of cheap prefab board from Ikea. Figuring to get through some e-mails, Grace took her thumb drive on her keychain and plugged it into the laptop on that desk, but she couldn't really get her mind into anything. Most of all she worried about her friend Freya facing a murder charge.

To work out her theories and then set up experiments to either prove or disprove them, Grace used spreadsheets to focus her mind. Clicking on her keyboard, she opened one up and started to labeled it the 'Murder of' ...of who? Freya hadn't given her the caretaker's name, and Mac's reporter had carefully not mentioned the murder. Okay, it will be 'Murder of the Caretaker.' Then she set up column headings, 'Suspect,' 'Motive,' 'Means,' 'Pro,' and 'Con,' then 'Total,' followed by a 'To Do' column.

By giving subjective percentages, Grace could plot out the direction her studies would go in. But normally she had more than one suspect. She studied Freya's row, with 'Motive ?,' 'Means 25 %' on site and with her own trimming axe as the murder weapon, 50 %. With no other suspect beside 'Unknown Killer,' Freya led the list. Most murders are committed by someone with some kind of relationship with the victim. This caretaker lived on the Kincaid estate, and Grace knew nothing of the Kincaids. She put a note on the 'To do' list: Find out more about the Kincaids--maybe through Maura?

But Freya had mentioned the Caretaker had a 'slutty' girlfriend that he lived with. Her friend was obviously very upset over Sam dating her son, so lately she said some uncharacteristically unkind things. Normally Freya lived the Wiccan creed, 'Let it harm none, do as ye will.' Freya accepted people for what they were, and normally didn't make judgments on their lifestyles, yet she referred to the victim's girlfriend as a 'slut.' Usually, a woman did that when she had feelings for the man involved.

Grace opened up another row for...had Freya given this significant other a name? No, Grace didn't think so. She just labeled the row 'Slutty girlfriend'. Motive, that was a problem, 'money'? 'jealousy?' Who could Ms. Slut have been jealous of? Freya? Would she have gone to the Boat Building barn and stolen Freya's trimming ax, using it as the murder weapon to implicate Freya? More research needed, and, again, Maura might be able to get her into the Kincaid compound where Grace could meet Ms. Slut.

Chapter 10

The next morning, Maura Kincaid actually showed at Grace's lab. Now Maura wore a business looking navy pants suit, and she carried a black briefcase. This she opened on Grace's desk, lifting out a small object wrapped in white tissue paper, which she unwrapped to show a gold trimmed locket, that she placed before Grace on the desk asking, "Will you have to destroy the entire hair lock?"

"Probably not."

"Can you do it now while I watch?"

Maura just stood there, waiting eagerly, so Grace had to explain. "No, it will be processed in the clean room to minimize contamination with our DNA. The extraction of DNA takes time. For a fresh, uncomplicated sample, you should allow two or three days before it can be read, but for something like a hair lock –that's what, seventy years old-- there might not be any DNA left. At the least, we can assume the hair was contaminated when it was cut and touched and breathed on over many years so it will take much longer to process, even longer to separate out any contamination, if I can get anything at all. The extraction of King Tut's chromosomes took over six months..."

"Six months?" Maura sounded dismayed.

"And they were only successful because of a combination of the dry climate of Egypt, elaborate body-embalming procedures, and centuries of a pretty consistent temperature in his tomb. Even then it took months of work before they got lucky and figured out how to filter out a darkening chemical embedded during the mummification process."

Grace studied the golden chain and flat, oval locket on her desk. It had a rim of tiny pearls, some missing, some yellowed, that surrounded a cream and caramel cameo. Picking it up, Grace studied the carving of a beautiful young girl, with a miniature chain and tiny diamond chip pendant around her neck.

Maura sounded eager, urging, "Can't you just open it?"

"Not out here. I'll look at it in the clean room later." Grace put the locket down.

Not looking too happy, Maura said, "Please call me when you have something."

"Yes." Now, could Grace get on to Maura's property to see the murder site? She started awkwardly, "Maybe I could deliver it to your house? I've heard the Kincaid estate is something to see."

"No, not on the estate. We'll do Dagmar's information in private here at your lab." But thinking about it, Maura nodded, and said slowly, "but Adam says you're famous?" Then the woman got a speculative look like Maura couldn't quite believe it. "Adam said David Gardiner has been seeing you? He is 'marriage platinum,' is he really interested in you?"

"As a friend, yes, but David's living in the Mediterranean right now," said Grace devoutly wishing Adam could keep his big mouth shut.

Dating a Gardiner apparently pushed Grace up to a higher status in Maura's eyes as she proposed, "My mother-in-law is organizing a series of weekly 'power teas' for influential women. Yes, I could certainly invite you. Are you free this Thursday at two?"

"I could be, yes, I'd like that." Grace forced a smile, another time waster, and although she doubted the boathouse murder scene would be on the tour, attending the power tea would get her on to the property. And there was another, even more, awkward topic. "Uh, Maura," Grace didn't know how to say this, didn't even know if she should say it. "After you left the other day, a man came in and asked about you."

"What?" She looked surprised.

"His name was...Barry Orman or Lorman or something..."

"What did he look like?"

"Uh...older...balding," Grace stumbled.

"Harry Corman. He is my husband's campaign manager. Formerly he was our business manager--well he still does that." Her face suddenly looked frightened. "Did you have to tell him about Dagmar?"

"No!" Grace could be firm on that. "Certainly not. What we talk about in my lab is none of his business. He didn't even seem to know who I was or what I do...he seemed to think I was a fertility lab doing In-Vitro?"

Although she still looked a bit upset, Maura only said, "Harry's overprotective, but he's harmless."

"How did he find Oyster River Research–do you think he could have followed you?"

Maura stopped to think about it. "Only if he thought I was doing something that could reflect badly on Aldon's Senate campaign. That's what we're all focused on now." She closed up her briefcase, getting ready to leave. "Please call me when you get something on Dagmar–but don't leave a text or a phone message. Talk to me directly. Don't even say what it's about, just ask me to come to your office."

"But we still need the profile from Prince Philip..."

"My mother-in-law spoke to the British Prime Minister's husband last evening, and it's being arranged. It will be sent to your lab at the address on the card you gave me."

When Maura left Grace looked distastefully at the locket and found herself feeling she was now part of some International-class spy ring conspiracy.

Later that afternoon, a suited-up Grace and two of her assistants opened that locket in the clean room. Inside lay a coiled lock of silver hair between the photographs of a stern looking older man and a young woman with dark hair and sad eyes. Using tweezers, Grace herself pulled out several strands of the dry hair, putting it between glass in a slide that she slipped under a high powered microscope. Grace studied the scaled hairs that looked like logs in a primeval forest. Slowly she moved the slide around, finally zeroing in on two hair roots and what looked like several dried skin cells. Grace suspected the skin cells might be contamination from the hair lock being cut and handled, but she still said, "Nick, come over here, please. Later I want you to try an extraction on these, the two roots and all the skin cells. But first, you will attempt a gene extraction from that eighty-thousand-year-old bone that might be Denisovan."

Nick did it with a nervous Grace and Inger staring over his shoulder, holding their breaths. To her supreme frustration, Grace wouldn't know for days if they had a successful extraction from the bone chip, but it looked good.

Finishing her tasks in the clean room, Grace unsuited and then headed out to the main lab. She needed to answer her e-mails that had accumulated in the weeks she was gone. Inger winnowed the thousands into something more manageable, then Grace took the paying consultations first. Mostly stuff she could answer without having to think hard, so she found her mind drifting to Freya's problems. Finally, unable to stop running various scenarios in her mind, Grace decided to do something positive.

First, she looked up Mark Silverstein's name and number and tried calling the lawyer. The receptionist said he was out, and Grace didn't want to leave a message. She wanted to make her appeal directly, so she said she'd call later. Grace planned to get back to work, but it was near lunchtime, so continuing her break with her routine, she opened up her laptop and pulled up the murder spreadsheet. She still didn't have a name for the victim–she should have asked Maura-- no, Sam. Yes, the newspaper reporter could and would tell her.

Grace glanced over the spreadsheet. Right now with 50 % Freya lead Unknown Killer. Supposedly Freya went to interview the Caretaker concerning a new book on motor boats. Yes, Freya's books usually concerned ghosts and hauntings, but there was no reason she wouldn't be trying to find a new market. Still, from being so close to Freya for some many years, Grace could tell when her friend was deviating from the truth. She might not be totally lying, but there was a lot Freya wasn't telling about going to that boathouse.

Yet, Grace couldn't see the earth mother she had known for years as a killer.

So Grace added a row for the Kincaid family; they were onsite, and must have had a relationship with the Caretaker that could have soured. She'd give the whole family a 25 %. 'To Do' learn more about Kincaids; attend Power Tea; talk to Sam? There was another possibility Grace'd been unconsciously ignoring. Hating it, she added a row for Mac Dell. He would have access to his mother's trimming axe, so Means 25 %, but no reason to be on site, and no motive to kill the Caretaker. Leave it a 25 %, and 'To do' learn more about the Caretaker.

She studied the spreadsheet critically, then she added another row for that annoying campaign manager, Barry Corman, no Henry, no Harry Corman. Harry probably was on site 25 %; probably had a relationship with the Caretaker so another 25 %, and in the 'Pro' column has shown himself to be a manipulator 25 %; but in the 'Con' how did he get Freya's Trimming Axe for the murder weapon? So minus -25 %. Giving him a total of 50 %, a match with Freya, but Grace still needed a motive for Harry.

And she had years of a built-in warning alarm that went off when she tried to twist the data into a predetermined pattern. Yes, Freya was her best friend, and yes, Grace knew she couldn't be guilty of murder, but Grace vividly remembering seeing Freya swing that heavy medieval axe high as she worked on the Viking fishing boat she and Mac were building. Grace knew her friend had the physical strength to kill, but the mental strength to murder?

Sadly, Grace realized Freya raised her son as a single mother through some really tough times-- she would have both the mental and physical strength to do whatever was required. But why would Freya need to kill the Caretaker?

* * *

At lunchtime Grace headed out with an envelope of printouts to be picked by Fed Express at Admin, but as she looked out over the lawns to the docks, Grace saw a hunched figure sitting on the yellow grass of the cold hillside, facing the water. A figure that looked familiar.

Changing direction, Grace walked over and around to look at the woman sitting there–Gail. But now the cheerful secretary's eyes were red with crying. "Gail?" Grace asked in a concerned voice. "What's the matter?"

"Nothing." The girl stared out to the green-gray sea. "I'm fine."

"You look it," said Grace sarcastically, sitting down beside her, feeling the chill earth under her bottom even through her wool pants. "Please tell me what's wrong?"

Gail bobbed her head down. "I've got my period. I've got bad cramps..."

"So you come outside, in the damp wind, to sit on a freezing hillside, to make things worse...?"

That brought an ironic smile to Gail's face. "Yeah. Polish logic." She looked back to the Admin building. "I've got to go inside, back to my desk. Get some aspirin...or something..." She used the back of her hand to wipe her cheek and running red nose.

"I can get you two Tylenol from my fanny pack, or I could get cherry brandy from my condo–no--Kurt's boat is closer, and he'll have at least a couple of bottles of Scotch?"

There was silence, with just the sounds of the waves coming in and seagulls calling as they swooped, before Gail said brokenly, "I didn't want to get my period."

"It usually comes at a bad time..." Grace agreed.

"No." Gail shook her head, holding back tears. "You don't understand, I was overdue...I thought I...was pregnant."

Unmarried Gail rented half a basement for an apartment, drove a twelve-year-old car, and worked at a temporary job--with no benefits-- that could end tomorrow. "What about the father, does he want this baby?"

With her bright blue eyes, Gail looked to Grace in surprise. "I wasn't going to tell him. If Steve knew he might get angry and beat me up."

Oh, great. Grace needed lunch needed to finish some extractions, and now she would be giving advice on a section of life that she hadn't navigated too well herself. "In that case, I wouldn't tell him."

"Steve's not a bad guy," said Gail in pleading mode. "You don't understand. I was using him to make a baby... he doesn't like wearing a condom, but he thinks I'm on the pill...it's me that is not being fair to him."

"Well, if he won't protect you, he deserves what he gets." Grace sighed, then said, "But I'm more worried about you. Babies need someone twenty-four hours a day. You don't even have a medical plan to pay for the pregnancy check-ups or the delivery. If there are complications, that can run to hundreds of thousands of dollars..."

Not meeting her eyes Gail looked out over the water as she said softly, "Fourteen-year-old girls have babies and live on welfare. I could do that until the child is old enough to go to school...then I can go back to work."

This really wasn't Grace's business, but she liked Gail and didn't want her to be making a big mistake. "Those pregnant fourteen-year-olds probably have mothers and grandmothers and sisters and maybe aunts who are willing to pitch in. You've never mentioned family–do have anyone who would help? A mother, a cousin?"

"I have a mother and cousins, but no, they wouldn't help." Gail smiled a bit bitterly at the thought.

And Grace knew Gail worked through Christmas and all the holidays if she could, every extra hour she could get, for what–not much above minimum wage? "I know there are strong biological urges, but giving in to them may not be in your best long-term interest."

ORR's secretary spoke in a dead voice. "Grace, I don't want to be alone the rest of my life."

Yes, that bothered Grace herself at times. "It's a frightening thought for anyone. But you're not that old, there is still time to find someone to marry, and have a parcel of kids..."

"I'm thirty, and I've been trying to have a baby for over a year now."

That didn't sound good. "Have you seen a fertility specialist?"

"I called one. Without insurance it will cost me two hundred and thirty just to talk to him with no tests," said a dispirited Gail.

This was sounding worse and worse. "This boyfriend, if you'll get pregnant...will he marry you?"

Her arms tightly across her chest, Gail shook her head. "Steve's already living with another woman, and he will never marry me or her, or any of the others he's with." Gail covered her face with her hands as she started to sob again. Awkwardly, Grace just put a comforting arm around her shoulders. Finally, the sobs stopped as Gail struggled to regain control. "How do you handle it... the emptiness, seeing other women with babies..."

That called for an honest answer. "I have doubts. Sometimes I wonder if there is still a chance. David talked about us having children–but I know I wouldn't make a good mother to anybody--I'm too selfish with my time."

They sat there in silence, the cold biting deep through Grace's jacket; she had to get Gail inside, off of this chilling ground. Grace started again, "But I was also lucky, at my worse '*I want to have a baby stage*' I met Freya, and she was willing to share Mac with me." Shivering a bit, Grace remembered that time. "Freya made me a sort of an honorary aunt and kind of let me co-parent. Not that I was any good at it. My 'genius' does not extend to throwing baseballs real hard or disciplining fourteen-year-olds that are taller than me..."

Gail forced a smile. "Since I'm not pregnant, I could use some of that Scotch? It would help kill the cramps."

Rising Grace reached down to help her up. "You go back to your office. I'll get you Kurt's booze, but only if you promise not to drive your desk over twenty miles an hour."

After getting some of Kurt's Scotch into a less pale Gail, Grace returned to her own office, to get a frantic call from Brazil, from Señor Cardozo. "The leaf rust has spread downwind to other valleys of our coffee crops', the copper sprays are not holding it!"

"Señor, we've talked about this before, the sprays are only a temporary solution, damaging your soil with copper build up."

"You want us to breed stronger plants," he said in a tired voice.

"In your situation, yes, I think that is your best long-term hope. The Columbian lab I've been working with has turned out some interesting crosses that I think might help you. I'll have Inger e-mail you their address."

"Yes, yes. But in the meantime can you look at the rust fungus and see if it has a weakness we can exploit?"

Could her lab take on more work now–especially with Bobby doing extra sampling duty for Kurt? But the coffee planters needed her now. "Yes. Airmail me twenty-five samples of the affected leaves, and also send me the leaves of any plants in that area that are not showing signs of infestation. Like the last time, look on my website for my standard contract, I'll need that signed, and returned with the samples, and a deposit in U.S. dollars before I begin."

"We get the mass discount again?" asked Señor Cardozo.

"Yes. Keep me updated on the progress of the infestation, and I tell you if I need more samples."

"Thank you, Senorita."

* * *

The eighty-thousand-year-old bone DNA extraction failed. There was some more material, a tiny bit, that would be sacrificed if she tried again and failed. Discouraged, Grace left the clean room, with its white walls and bright lights, and in the airlock she took off her plastic face shield helmet, surgical mask, disposable booties, and wiped her sweat away. Then she started out of the white Tyvek jumpsuit, finally stripping off the latex gloves and dumping them in the trash can.

Grace knew Nick had done everything right--she had been standing alongside watching. But the next time she would try the extraction herself if Professor Abrantes would allow the sacrifice of the last bit of the precious sample. She'd call him for permission, but not tonight, when she was so disappointed and exhausted. Yes, if her lab did another extraction attempt, she would do it. If they were going to destroy an irreplaceable trace of human ancestry, let it be on her head.

Time to go for supper, but first Grace sat down at her desk and typed in the latest, disheartening results. Soon she started on her endless e-mails. The next time she looked up a man stood there. He was only five foot nine but stood with a commanding stature that projected wealth and influence, even if his navy blue Savile Row suit didn't. Try as she might to suppress it, this man always made her body tingle a bit. His sandy hair was brushed to the side, and his fair skin was freckled from riding steeplechase, but that face did not have his characteristic ironic smile. Today he looked annoyed. "You're here all alone, and your door is not locked?"

"David? Oh, that buzz-in you had installed–I do use it...sometimes. It's been having problems lately."

"Using it 'sometimes' isn't going to protect you," he said sternly.

She wanted to change the topic. "I thought you were on your private island in Greece?"

"I had some matters to take care of, and I still have the house here. And since I'm around, I thought I'd drop by and ask you out for dinner."

"Why?" Grace asked, her mind really still preoccupied with that finger bone.

"Why eat dinner? Aren't you hungry?" he countered.

She was, desperately. Grace looked around. "Yes, I am. Let me close up."

He watched her until she put on her jacket, then asked, "Aren't you shutting down the computers?"

"No. Inger will be coming in to make up her hours. She's been busy during the day working with her class team on their term project due this week."

He nodded, waited until she checked on the lobster tank temperatures, then as she locked the door from the lobby he asked, "Are you still considering my marriage proposal?"

Grace closed eyes. "How about just dinner tonight and no pressure?"

"Let's make it half and half, dinner and you tell me about the latest murder you are involved in?"

That came as a surprise. "Who called you? Adam? Gail?"

"Actually, I got a call from that friend of yours, Mr. MacKay." David always said Kurt's name with a touch of distaste.

"He called you?" With Kurt's disdainful attitude toward 'Mr. Big bucks', Grace couldn't imagine him calling a man he considered a rival.

But David further explained, "Apparently MacKay's too involved in marine research to keep you out of trouble, so he let me know you might need rescuing."

That rankled a bit. "I don't need rescuing, but I would love to have dinner with you again."

It was dark, with ORR's lamplights reflecting off the harbor water in long yellow greenish streams as he said, "Still cool out here for March. On my island, it's almost warm enough to swim."

"How is the shopping mall you're building coming?"

"Frustrating, as most major projects are." He stopped to look deeply into her eyes. "But it just requires cash and tenacity, and I have a lot of both...for any project, I feel worth pursuing."

Grace did a mental eye roll, but it did feel good to see him and smell that rich aftershave lotion of his. Someone was joining them--a woman in jeans, who started speaking, "Grace, I saw your car outside, so I knew you'd be here. The black Escalade?"

Actually, Grace's car was a beat up old Subaru Forester station wagon, but the woman was continuing talking to David, and holding out her hand to shake, "I'm Dr. Nicole Duval, Dr. Huang's associate."

"David Gardiner, a friend of Grace's," he said politely.

"The David Gardiner, the philanthropist?"

"It's just David."

An awkward silence, then Nicole started again looking at Grace. "I've been meaning to get over and talk with you about Erratum. Maybe we could get together someday? For lunch? Dinner?" She looked hopefully from Grace to David.

Even in a leather motorcycle jacket and slim fit jeans

Nicole looked good, and Grace had the feeling the woman was more interested in sharing a meal with David then herself, but David only took Grace's elbow to steer her away as he smiled saying politely, "Perhaps some other time." Grace felt a little embarrassed just leaving Nicole standing there, but David propelled her forward to his car still parked in front of her lab. While he opened the passenger door for her, Grace saw Inger, who waved as she headed for the laboratory to finish her hours.

As he started the car, David asked, "ORR will be having your Spring fundraiser soon."

"Yes."

"I've bought a table, and my daughter and sons will be there. I was hoping you could join us?"

Another problem she didn't want to deal with. "Let's settle dinner tonight?"

"What would you like to eat?" he asked, heading out of ORR.

Grace thought about it. "Steak would be nice."

"Then there's the Captain's Mansion, or how about that place up toward Greenwich? The Japanese place, with that hibachi you liked?"

That surprised Grace. "The last time we went there you said you'd never eaten hibachi before?"

He turned left and headed toward the Post road. "Since then, I've eaten quite a bit of it. I especially like those salmon rolls, all that sushi is pretty good. Only, instead of us sitting around the hibachi grill table with a lot of strangers, let's get a private table, and have the food carried to us."

"They don't usually do it that way..." Grace started.

He turned a little way to her, raising an eyebrow slightly, "If they want my money, they will do as we wish."

And they did. Grace and David were escorted to a private booth, they gave their orders: David wanted the hibachi steak rare and shrimp; while Grace ordered medium steak and scallops. Then he ordered the 'sushi boat,' that came in a wooden bowl shaped like a Viking craft, with an appetizing variety of rice rolled raw salmon, avocado, crabmeat--all with its spicy green wasabi paste, and shredded, sweet, pink pickled-ginger. Digging in, Grace's chewed on a bit of shrimp and rice as David's cell phone rang. He listened a bit, then said laconically, "Grace, is your phone turned off again?"

She dug into her handbag and pulled out a black, blank screen. "Needs to be recharged."

"It's Inger." He said to Grace, then turned to the phone asking, "Did you want to talk to her?" David listened, then he hung up, explaining, "Your assistant said you wanted to know when Prince Philip's DNA had arrived?"

"Good," said Grace, looking down to dip another artfully designed piece of sushi in soy sauce flavored with pickled ginger.

David sat staring at her in amazement, finally asking, "Dear, is that Prince Philip, Duke of Edinburgh's DNA? Husband of Queen Elizabeth II of Britain?"

"Yes."

David raised an eyebrow. "Checking to see if one of his grandsons might be the result of Princess Diana's dalliance with the riding master?"

Grace found herself coloring, "No. Since Philip was related to Tsar Nicholas and Tsarina Alexandra on both the paternal and maternal lines, his genetic profile was used to authenticate the bones found in Russia that were claimed to be Nicholas II's assassinated family."

"You're working on that?"

"There is someone in Oyster River that feels a relative of theirs may have been a missing Romanov heir."

"Who?" he asked, sounding very curious.

She gave him a warning frown. "You know that's confidential."

He stopped and then said carefully, "I thought they had found those bones, located in a bog, where one of their murderer's dairies had said? Very conveniently, so they had something to honorably bury before Queen Elizabeth consented to visit the country of her cousins' slaughtering."

Grace had been reading up on the subject in Wikipedia. "By the Bolsheviks' report, the seven members of the Tsar's immediate family and four of their servants were executed in The House of Special Purpose in Yekaterinburg. But when the discoverers put the bones that they found together, only nine individuals were there. It was believed that Alexi and one of the younger sisters, either Anastasia or Marie was missing."

David was selecting his own pink salmon sushi piece, saying, "Who were later found not too far from the first burial, I believe. Weren't those two originally an experiment in cremating the remains? It failed because the murderers didn't have enough gasoline. In 2007, the bones of the last two children were recovered, but they haven't been reburied with their parents as of yet because of politics between the Russian state and the Orthodox church."

Grace wondered how--with all of David's endless business concerns–how did he manage to keep up with an amazing amount of trivia? But having played polo with Prince Charles, he always was a bit of a British Royalty aficionado, so Grace just added, "There were two remains found. From the bones supposedly the two individuals were determined to be Alexi, and Marie or Anastasia, but as for a DNA determination of the bones that had been shot, smashed by gun butts, dumped in a cave, pulled out, wiped with acid, then drenched in gasoline at a failed attempt of cremation, and then finally buried with lime in bog for over ninety years, I'm certainly glad I wasn't doing those DNA profiles."

Chapter 11

Thursday Inger had to remind her at one o'clock that she had the 'power tea' at two. Grace felt she should be wearing a fancy hat and white gloves, but instead, she donned a navy blue pants suit with a pale periwinkle blouse, that had a touch of darker blue lace at the collar. For Christmas Kurt at given her a GPS screen that plugged into the cigarette lighter of her station wagon, so now Grace typed in the Kincaid address. Their compound was over in the direction of Greenwich, so Grace went down to Sound Beach Avenue, crossed over on Summit to get to Riverside, which ran along a finger of Long Island Sound called Cos Cob Harbor. With annoyance, Grace noted she was running about ten minutes late.

The Kincaid estate had a nineteen-hundreds mock Tutor gatehouse, and Grace drove onto the estate overlooking the shining water. To the right, she passed half-timbered, stucco-style garages and a staff house that she'd considered looked like a mansion on its own. Where was the boathouse? Gravel- covered asphalt roads peeled off to the right or left into manicured green lawns and thick old-growth forest. Coming around a curve, Grace saw the road she drove looped in front of a super modern, glass-walled mansion with white cement supports that resembled an alien flying saucer with spreading wings.

When she parked in front, a man came out to open her car door. "Valet parking, mam."

Grace surrendered her keys in exchange for a plastic numbered disk as the guy coldly eyed her beat-up station wagon--probably envisioned his tip shrinking to a dollar. Then she started climbing the building's wide stairs, feeling like she ascended some early Mesoamerican pyramid for a sacrificial ritual.

A gray-uniformed maid answered the door, took her jacket, and led Grace to the right, out of the marble-floored, two-story entry hall, through gold rimmed, antique white double doors to a huge solarium that was a story and half high. Three slate-stone steps led down to an octagonal shaped sunroom, containing three indoor pond gardens at the edges of its walls of glass. A number of women sat at tables clustered in the center like a desert island in some remote blue slate sea. Grace thought she recognized a member of the ORR Board of Directors. The silver-haired woman smiled warmly to Grace and Grace smiled back, desperately trying to remember her name. She had better luck with the woman dressed in a flowing, light wool, emerald-green dress and feverishly blue eyes. This was Maura, she guessed...

"Grace, I'm so glad you could make it." Maura turned to the taller frosted-golden haired woman beside her. "Dr. Farrington is always so, so busy. Grace, this is my mother-in-law, Charlotte Kincaid."

Charlotte held out her hand, Grace took it, shaking the smooth, slightly cool hand as she looked about the startling room saying, "This is amazing. From the gatehouse, I expected something nineteen hundred Tutor."

"It once was," said Charlotte in a velvet voice. "But about five years ago there was an unfortunate fire. We had a terrible time with the Historic Preservation Committee and the Zoning Board. At first, they demanded we rebuilt with the same footprint and exterior."

Grace nodded appreciatively. The fact that the estate went from classical mock Tudor mansion to modern art monument or mausoleum--depending on your esthetics–was a testimony to the power of the Kincaids. Looking at the beveled-glass tables and green-cushioned wrought iron chairs, and not thinking of anything else to say, Grace murmured, "It's beautiful, and it feels warm in here. I would think anything with glass windows and such high ceilings would be too cold for New England?"

Smiling indulgently Charlotte explained, "The

windows are triple-glazed, and the flooring is radiant heat, and you can see the ceiling fans that recirculate. We built with the most advanced green technology. It's actually very energy efficient, and for large meetings, we can get two hundred and fifty people in here."

Grace nodded again and there was dead silence. Finally, Charlotte turned to her daughter-in-law commanding, "Why don't you show Dr. Farrington the buffet and let her get started. Seat her with science people."

The buffet held tropical-flowered china plates and typical British tea table foods: cucumber and salmon-salad sandwiches; potato and macaroni salad; raspberry gelatin molds; and tiered trays of small bakery sweets. Next to it stood a table with bottles of white wine--the choice was only dry and dry. Feeling hungry, Grace-filled up with the salmon salad and shrimp. Maura looked about to see if anyone was listening, and then asked in a soft voice, "Have you found out anything?"

Grace looked at her--did Maura mean found out anything about the caretaker's murder? No, she must mean Dagmar's parentage. "Not yet." Looking out a side window, Grace saw the harbor shore, a narrow sandy rock beach, and yes--nearly screened by the fir trees--a two story rustic building, not in the water, but up on shore. "Is that the boathouse? It's not in the water?"

"We're on the Sound with the tide coming in and out twice a day. There is a railing track that the boats can be pulled inside on, and then they can be raised up along the walls."

"I see an outside staircase?"

"There's the caretaker's apartment above."

How could Grace get into that apartment? "I heard you have a beautiful wood motorboat?"

"It's a twenty-six foot Chris Craft Continental," Maura supplied proudly. "They call it a 'utility,' but the varnished woodwork is beautiful."

Looking at the docking in front of the boathouse Grace asked, "Is that it over here? I'd so love to see it."

Maura seemed eager to please. "If you'd like to, after the tea we can walk over and see it up close."

"I'd enjoy that." Grace said, and that thought kept her sitting through the whole power tea at the 'science table.' Maura introduced her to the other three women as "the renowned Dr. Grace Farrington." Of her fellow 'science people,' one sold educational software to schools, another had no science background at all, but wanted to organize a worldwide movement 'Scientists for Aldon Kincaid,' and the third woman said nothing, just stared at Grace the entire time she ate. She even watched as a mortified Grace dripped scarlet cocktail sauce down the front of her blouse and tried to blot it up with a paper napkin, leaving a big, dark stain on the pale blue.

After they ate a bit, Charlotte rose to the clear plexiglass podium and introduced a woman psychologist, who gave a lecture on 'Turning a Negative Bias on its Head.'

Grace found the woman's talk lively, but her ideas for manipulating people were totally without any sense of morality. Trying to be inconspicuous, Grace looked around to see if there was a clock. Would it look too gauche to take out her phone and glance at the time? As the speaker finished, Grace joined in a polite sprinkling of applause, then hearing faint murmurings, she looked to the entrance as Charlotte sounded surprised and delightedly announced, "It looks like my son, Aldon, can join us."

Wearing a tailored gray suit with a crisp white shirt and red shot silk tie, a tall, fairly handsome man with ruffled sandy hair stepped down to the slate floor. He had a warm smile that he managed to spread to every woman there, as he started going around to each table shaking hands and saying something to almost everyone.

He was followed at an appropriate distance by a stocky, balding man, who Grace was surprised she could recognize as the campaign manager, Harry. The manager stood to the side, looking like he constantly evaluated his politician's effect. Grace looked further about and saw Maura sitting at the head table--with her lips parted in adoration--as her loving eyes followed her husband's every move. No, she didn't get up and join her Aldon–she just contentedly stayed seated as he shook hands and laughed with other women. Fascinated, Grace watched Maura just following her husband around with her eyes, but those Romanov blue eyes showed no jealousy; they only held a love that rose almost to the level of worship.

But it was the impassive, cold green eyes of Aldon's mother that struck Grace forcibly. Retaking her seat at the table, Charlotte followed her son's every move around the room, seeming to be coolly judging his performance and the impressions he made on the power tea women. As Grace watched, Charlotte took short notes on a small pad next to her plate, and Grace had the distinct feeling that tonight Aldon would be up for a tactical assessment of his display during this little 'unexpected, informal appearance.'

As the royal progress drew near them, Grace noted a distinguished brush of gray at   Aldon's temples that belied his easy-going, youthful charm. When he reached her table, Aldon actually held a hand out to her saying, "Dr. Farrington, it's so good to see you again."

She hadn't the slightest idea of where she had ever seen him before, but Grace held out her hand and shook his. "Congressman." His hand was dry and warm with a firm grasp, and with his brilliant smile, he appeared genuinely interested in her as an individual, not an easy thing to project to a table–actually a room--full of people.

Yes, Grace did feel the electricity of his charismatic personality, but as Aldon walked away, she also noticed he moved rapidly, well practiced, and was out of the room with a speed that amazed her.

Charlotte moved to stand in front of the dessert table and suggested to others, "Get some cake, some wine, and we'll network a bit'. Unfortunately, Grace found herself locked in to stay until everybody else left. Fortunately, the woman Grace half recognized as a Board member from ORR came over and started talking about their Spring fundraiser.

Although Charlotte did the grand organizing, Grace noted Maura quietly moved from woman to woman with her gentle smile, soft words. It appeared that as the candidate's considerate wife, Maura gained more kudos for her husband, then the cool, controlling Charlotte.

Finally, others began to leave, and Maura came over to her. "Did you want to see that motorboat before you leave?"

"Yes, I would." And get into that caretaker's apartment! The maid brought their jackets, and Grace followed Maura out the glass door that led to the patio at the back of this house that overlooked the chilled gray harbor. Blue slates matching the inside room floored the softly undulating edges of the patio that ran the length of the back of the house. If you could call that expanse of wide, high glass arches as the 'backdoors' of anything.

"Maura." A voice called out from behind them. They looked back to the door. Still carrying her wine glass, Charlotte had followed them out to the patio without a jacket. "Where are you going?"

"Grace is interested in boats. She wanted to see the Chris Craft."

Charlotte looked at Grace speculatively, then said, "Perhaps Aldon can take you out in it sometime?"

"That'd be nice, but not today," Grace answered pleasantly. "I've only got a few minutes..." She needed to say something here, so she made up quickly, "I'm going out to dinner..."

It was Maura who helpfully embellished her white lie, "She's probably dining with David Gardiner."

That raised Charlotte's eyebrows, and she gave a hopeful little smile. "David? I've heard he's back in town?"

"He's visiting from Greece," explained Grace--might as well drop a big name.

The mother-in-law looked genuinely pleased. "Sometimes we must all get together for dinner. David should hear Aldon's proposals. They're not limited to just 'Democratic' ideas."

Grace forced a smile back. "If we can."

"And," Charlotte extended the offer graciously, "You must come to my next power tea." She made a tight little mouth of displeasure. "We didn't have too great a turn-out today, but we will do better next time."

As a member of the 'disappointing turn-out,' Grace could only smile back.

The jacketless Charlotte evidently took that for a 'yes,' and she withdrew back into the house.

They walked past elegantly green-striped patio furniture, a large gas-fed firepit and a built-in stone barbecue, with a sink and refrigerator arrangement that Wolfgang Puck could have cheffed on. At the end of the patio, they stepped down more wide stairs and walked on the grass, toward the forest lining the narrow, rough, rock and sand shore. Walking outside, Grace could breathe in salty-smelling air, and it felt so good to be out of that huge, hothouse. When they were out of hearing distance, suddenly Maura happily confided, "I'm two months past my last period. Maybe more."

"You're pregnant?"

"I don't know officially yet. I have a tendency to false pregnancies. I want it so much--my period's stop, and then when I get confident that I'm surely pregnant this time...I start to bleed." She looked so bereft, Grace almost wanted to reach out to hug her, but Maura's face quickly shifted to radiant joy. "I haven't taken the blood test yet, but this time I'm sure. My breasts are swelling a bit–it must be hormones. It's just so wonderful–I haven't told Aldon, or Charlotte, or Harry...you're the first to know!"

That seemed strange to Grace, a woman Maura hadn't known a month ago is now her closest friend? "What about your doctor? If you've had problems in the past, your hormone development should be closely monitored."

Worry clouded her face. "You're right, of course, I should go see Dr. Vaster. I'll have to think up an excuse to go into town and check with him."

The fact that a grown woman needed an 'excuse' to go into town made Grace inwardly cringe, but she only said, "That would be a good idea."

Maura stood looking out to the steel gray water. "It's been so terrible. Charlotte says not to worry, I'm only thirty-two, but we've lost three babies..." Maura turned to Grace in almost an appeal. "My mother-in-law is trying to be comforting, but she's talking about getting donor eggs or even using Aldon's sperm to inseminate a surrogate mother." Those intense blue eyes of Maura's seemed almost to glow. "That's wrong! I should be the vessel that carries down the sacred inheritance of the Kincaids."

"Aldon is older than you? As I told you before his sperm should be tested at a fertility clinic. And your child should be tested for Down's syndrome."

"Why?" Maura appeared offended. "That only happens if the mother is in her late forties!"

"No, the risk rises sharply with the maternal age of thirty-five, but women in their early twenties have given birth to Down's syndrome children."

Maura bit her lip. "We couldn't have an abortion–the Kincaids are Catholic."

"It's called a 'reduction,' and it is up to the mother to

make the decision." From the frown on her face, Grace figured Maura actually seemed to be thinking about that, so Grace continued, "The research is difficult, and little has been done, but it seems that with an older father the chance of Downs increases by 50%."

They were getting closer to the boathouse as Maura said, "Oh, I thought older men often produced very intelligent children?"

"Studies have shown that too, but it's unclear at this time if that's a genetic link or a natural selection of a male sensible enough to hold off fathering children until he is established in life and could spend more time with them. I'd love to research it, but there are so many things to be studied."

"Aldon will be a wonderful father," murmured a happy Maura.

They'd reached the two-story boathouse built just above a steep strip of sandy beach. From the grass strip, a white-painted dock led down to floating platoons on the water. Although Grace told Maura she wanted to see the boat, actually what she wanted was to get into that caretaker's apartment, but would have to work up to it carefully. "You keep your boat out here?"

"Unless it's stored in the boathouse for winter, yes."

Following Maura, Grace clopped out onto the bopping platoons. Getting closer she could see a fancy, varnished wooden boat, with sleek, speed lines, and a beautiful, elaborate wooden inlay in the bow. Held only by two rope coils, it floated in the clear water, occasionally rubbing up against blue bumpers hung over the dock.

Silence, so Grace started, "It looks expensive."

"Aldon got it at a reduced price, but even then it was seventy-eight thousand dollars."

Wow, well Grace had to admit the polished wood hull, and two sets of green leatherette covered seats certainly looked pretty–but in no way could that cost be justified with the Kincaid as 'guardians of poor'? She wanted to change the drift of the conversation, looking back to shore at the boathouse Grace said, "There is an apartment over the boathouse? Those upstairs windows must have a fantastic view?"

Maura looked back at the large, multi-paned windows that overlooked the harbor. "Yes, it does. It's a beautiful place. It's small, but rather than live in the main house with Charlotte, I'd love to live up there with Aldon. We'd finally have privacy..." Her voice sounded wistful.

"When you and Aldon have a child, maybe you should insist on your own house?"

She gave a twisted smile at that. "Perhaps."

Keep the focus on the murder scene. "Is the boathouse still sealed by the police?"

"No. They came back out and took their stupid crime scene tape off." Looking cold as she wrapped her arms across her chest, Maura looked back to the path around the trees to the main house. She probably wanted to get back inside.

Grace desperately tried, "Is that woman who lived with the caretaker still in the boathouse?"

"No, Aldon let Sierra move into one of the two chauffeurs' apartments over the garages."

"Then, I could see the boathouse apartment?"

Maura looked surprised. "If you want to, sure. There's a key hidden by the door. We can get in."

Their shoes resounded hollowly as they started walking off the docking floats. Grace saw steel railings that led from under the water to up inside the double doors of the boathouse, but Maura led her to the side and then to the outdoor wooden staircase. But to their surprise, their way was blocked by someone coming down carrying an armful of clothing.

Chapter 12

A tall young woman, nearly six foot, very thin, wearing jeans, a western blouse, and high, suede boots was coming down the stairs, not seeming to be disconcerted to see one of the owners.

"Sierra," said Maura, "I thought you cleaned everything out?"

"No, there's not much closet space in that dump over the garage. Not that it was that great living over a clammy boathouse."

"But it's free, isn't it?" returned Maura sweetly. "Being around here must bring back sad memories for you."

The girl frowned, "Sad memories?"

"Of your great love for Brian. Maybe you should move on so you can forget?"

Ignoring that, the girl asked, "Did you want something?"

"I'm showing a friend the apartment."

Sierra tossed her head and looked down at Grace. "I'd rather you didn't. There are still things of mine and Brian's in it."

That didn't phase Maura at all. "Well, unless you can show a marriage license, anything in that apartment goes to his next of kin."

Now Sierra turned on Maura with indignation. "Somebody's been searching through everything–you don't have a right to do that even if it is your place!"

"The police searched it."

"No," Sierra insisted with resentment. "I saw it after the police finished, someone else has been in there rummaging through our stuff?"

Maura only shrugged. "More reason for you to pack up and find another place to live."

The girl stood there blocking the last step, but Maura

just put her hand on railing saying, "Please move. This is Dr. Grace Farrington, and she doesn't have all day."

"Grace Farrington?" Sierra asked. "Friend to that woman who killed my man?"

"Freya didn't kill anyone," said Grace in a flat voice.

Sierra smiled contemptuously at that, then turned on Maura. "I'll be telling Aldon about this."

Maura looked up at her. "You do that. And keep looking for a new apartment. Charlotte's talking of hiring a second chauffeur."

Not looking too happy, but under Maura's hard gaze Sierra finally stepped out of the way, saying, "Nothing of our stuff better be missing!"

Grace wanted to talk with Sierra, but not in front of Maura, so she just followed up the steep outdoor stairs. From the top balcony, the boathouse below looked to be a story and half high. A wood shingled three-sided enclosure sheltered the door, and from the far side, under a flowerpot with a dead plant, Maura picked up a brass key. The door was painted a dark park-green, and inside the first thing Grace focused on was the three wall-banks of small-paned windows, also trimmed with green paint, contrasting with the mellow, varnished wood walls. They walked down a short hall, which opened to a large room. In the back, there were two doors, probably to a bathroom and a closet. Also along that back wall was an open compact kitchen with stove, microwave, small refrigerator behind a breakfast table with four chairs. But now the cupboards above the sink were ajar, and piles of stuff littered the counter and kitchen floor. The main room, with its brown suede convertible couch--that must serve as the bed--and bark-branched legged tables, looked like it too had been ransacked.

"What happened?" exclaimed Maura clearly, horrified.

"Did the police leave it this way?"

"No. They left it neat."

"Sierra?"

"I don't think so."

"If you been robbed, maybe you should call the police?"

"No! No more publicity!" Maura looked around. "There is nothing here worth stealing. I was up here to take back the keys after the police released the murder site. I had enough trouble making them take down that horrible yellow crime scene tape–you could see it from the patio!"

"But if Sierra and the police didn't do this, who did?" Grace asked.

Maura shook her head and picked up a pillow that had its seam cut with its stuffing falling out. "They left it neat. Looks like someone has been searching? I bet it's Sierra, searching for something...probably for Brian's nonexistent fortune."

Or probably the same thing Grace wanted to search for–something, anything, that would prove Freya hadn't killed Brian. But Grace didn't know where to begin? Desperately she looked about a set of golf clubs in the corner, and a camera bag on the shelf under the windows. Brian had a desk, with an older CPU computer, a LED screen, and flatbed scanner, under a shelf of oversized books. "Oh," Grace started. "You have books on boats." Or should she say ships? "Can I just look through these a bit?" Picking one up, Grace ruffled through it, just a regular book with pictures of sailboats.

Bending down for some magazines on the floor, Maura was automatically straightening up. "Do you want to take them with you?"

"No, I just thought if I could sit down...and read a bit a here."

Maura looked torn. "I'm running late today." She looked around the room. "Let me get the staff over here to clean this place up first...then you know where the key is, you can come at any time." Maura finished brightly.

That sounds like the best Grace could do today, so saying, "Thank you," she left Maura at the mansion. But as Grace walked to her car, she wondered how Sierra knew of her friendship with Freya? During the murder, Grace had been out of the country, so there hadn't been any reason for there to be any media coverage of their relationship?

* * *

After the abortive Tuesday night dinner, on Friday Grace closed up her lab on time, then drove over to Oyster River. She parked in the Town lot and crossed over to the row of eighteen thirties houses, walking past stores selling women's apparel, gourmet foods, and real estate. She reached a brown painted building that sold antiques on the first floor and custom made hats on the second. But to her left, cement stairs led down to a basement, with display windows filled with stained-glass sun catchers, many of them soldered by Freya herself. Inside The Haunts of Wôden were new age books, handmade jewelry, tarot card decks, and glass display cases with Wiccan athames and Santeria saint candles. Alongside that were displayed Freya's rare and beautiful minerals for sale–minerals that an expert like Freya could find on the Internet for a low price, and then resell for quite a bit more.

Grace felt when you walked in the aromas of exotic incense it gave a spiritual feel to the place like you should be genuflecting before one of the Buddha, Kuan Yin, or Horned Hunter statues that lined the windows that overlooked the back parking lot. Freya usually looked up with a smile, but today when her friend saw her, Freya promptly looked away toward two customers browsing among the tie-dyed scarves. Still, Grace walked to stand across the counter from her. "How's it going?"

"Well, I'm not under arrest, so I didn't need that lawyer." Her friend still wouldn't meet her eyes.

Grace just tightened her lips at that. She wasn't leaving until she learned more, but Freya continued to look away from her, picking up the stained glass sun-catcher that she now encased in bubble wrap for a mailing package. "Grace, we'll talk later, okay?" Finally, Freya looked at her. "If on the way home I buy a roast chicken, you want to come over for dinner?"

Actually, as Grace remembered Freya's dictum that they weren't talking, but if her friend forgot, so could she. "Since it's my turn, how about I treat you to a dinner at Captain's?"

As her face relaxed into a smile, that looked to be what Freya wanted. She nodded happily. "Yes. After I close up, that would be nice."

Hearing sounds outside on the steps down, Grace looked up as the brass bell over the door jangled, and two men in business suits entered. She looked to Freya who had paled.

Walking up to the counter the first man spoke, "Mrs. Dell?"

"Ms. Dell, yes," Freya answered.

He took out a leather folder and flashed a silver badge fast, then put it back in his coat. "We'd like you to come with us. We have some more questions."

Obviously frightened, Freya still stood up to her full height, a good half a foot higher than either of the men."I can't right now–I'm running a business...I can come, after six..."

The second man took out an envelope. "Ms. Freya Dell, we have a warrant for your arrest."

Desperately, Grace looked at her. "I'm calling Mark Silverstein. Don't talk without your lawyer! I'll lock up for you."

Picking up her handbag from under the counter, Freya nervously fished out her shop keys, "You know where to hide the money from the register?"

Grace nodded. The first guy led off with Freya following him. The other guy waited to tag after her. Grace saw the two shocked customers watching the perp parade, so she just pasted on a silly smile, and pulled out her phone. Mark Silverstein's number should be in her phone–sweating, Grace thumbed through the contacts. Would he still be there? Yes, she rang, and a cultured female voice answered, "Jones, Durham, and Silverstein."

The Silverstein at the end was Alan Silverstein, a corporate lawyer of David's, who was now also on the ORR Board and Mark's uncle. "This Grace Farrington, I'd like to speak to Mark Silverstein?"

"One moment please."

The phone line switched to soft classical music, then a young male voice came on. "Grace, good to hear from you. Haven't found another body, have you?"

Relief flooded her. Mark's voice always gave one the feeling that everything would soon be under control. "No, I haven't, but a friend of mine..."

"Not Kurt again?"

"No, he's in São Tomé--well probably now he's at sea--headed for the Antarctic ocean..."

Mark put her back on track, "So who are we talking about?"

"You know Freya Dell? She's a businesswoman who runs the Haunts of Wôden." One of the customers carried three tie-dyed scarves up to the counter. That meant Grace had to ring them up. How did she put a tax on that sale? Did Freya have some sort of chart here? Balancing the phone under her chin she took the scarves, looking for the price tags... "They'll be twelve dollars each."

"What?" said the voice on the phone.

While at the same time the customer argued, "No, the sign says they're on sale three for twenty dollars."

Grace looked over. Of course, the sign faced away from her. "I'm sorry, then it's three for twenty."

The woman handed Grace a twenty dollar bill, and Grace rang her purchase up, but the price displayed on the register was twenty-one dollars and twenty-seven cents. Apparently, the register automatically added in the sales tax. The customer looked doubtfully at the register figure. "Make it an even twenty," Grace said firmly putting her phone down on the counter and grabbing for a paper bag to put the scarves in.

Noting the other woman still shopped, Grace picked up the phone again and desperately asked, "Mark, are you still there?"

His voice floated back, "You're running Freya's store I presume?"

"The police came and arrested Freya..."

"Arrested?" he asked sharply.

"They wanted to ask questions, and Freya told them she couldn't leave her store until she closed up, so they pulled out a warrant. That's arresting her, isn't it?"

"Sounds a bit like it."

"They didn't say where they were taking her..."

"You could check the Oyster River police station first," he suggested.

He wasn't offering to work for free to defend Freya. Maybe he wouldn't take her on at all! Grace found herself pleading, "You have to help her! She's innocent."

"Grace–she's innocent of what?"

"Murder."

"Great." He sounded disgusted. "Don't you have any friends getting arrested for something simple like maybe...jaywalking or sheep molestation?"

"What?"

"I'm sorry. Calm down. Let's get this straight, Freya is accused of killing this person..."

"A man."

"Why?"

"She visited him."

"Did she know him?"

"Freya said she only wanted to interview him for one of her books." Grace found herself finishing lamely.

There was silence on the line, then he said quietly, "But you don't believe that do you?"

"It doesn't help that the victim was killed with her tenth-century trimming axe."

He agreed. "That will certainly complicate things. Where did this take place?"

"The Kincaid estate."

"Ah," now Mark's voice held understanding. "The caretaker bludgeoned in the boathouse. I should have wondered if you didn't have something to do with that–or at least one of your friends."

"Will you defend her? I told her not talk until her lawyer got there."

"You're getting this routine down. Now, if it's in reference to the Kincaid murder, she might be being questioned in Greenwich. I'll make some calls. Okay, then she knows I'm coming?"

"She knows I was going to call you...about your fee. Remember what you charged me, can you charge the same thing for her case, only cut it in half when you tell her, and I'll make up the other half, and we won't tell Freya...?"

Silence on his end of the line, then, "Grace, that's not the way legal billing works..." The line became silent again, finally he said, "Let's see if I can get her released and home, and then we'll talk about fees."

"Oh, Mark, thank you so much!"

Before she could say anything else, the phone went dead. Grace looked up at the clock. She would have to keep the shop open until Freya's regular closing. And that other woman now stood at the wall shelves reading one of Freya's books on Tarots; this was going to take a long time.

After Grace could finally lockup the Haunts of Wôdan, she climbed up to the sidewalk and looked around. She could get her car and dinner, but with Freya under arrest, everything felt so wrong. Looking down Main Street, Grace made a decision, she had to do something to help! She crossed to the parking lot, but instead of getting her car, she walked further, past The Blue Peacock dress shop to a white-washed basement of an old seaman's house. Here Abe had his home and in the cellar, his bookstore. To the jangle of a bell over the door, Grace entered, expecting Abe to be on the over-stuffed couch in front of the register counter reading as usual. Instead, he came around a freestanding bookcase, and found her asking, "Freya's under arrest?"

"No...n-n-not really," Grace found herself stammering, Abe would know the truth soon, but she couldn't accept that Freya was really under arrest for murder. "The police are questioning everybody."

Abraham Hoyt was a man about 5' 8" with mussed brown hair and a stringy goatee. He didn't seem to be able to see past his thick-lensed glasses, and rarely left his fortress of books, yet he knew everything going on. "She got a lawyer?"

"Yes. Mark Silverstein." If you want information, you gotta kick in. Saying that Grace walked over to the free coffee urn. Today he didn't have one for hot water, so Grace poured herself a cup, wishing it was tea. To kill the coffee's bitter taste, she stirred in several tablespoons of white powdered creamer. On the small table, there was a package of ginger cookies on a plate and a bowl of M&Ms for the kids. Not for the first time, Grace wondered how, with his lackadaisical sales approach and his thin-margined products, that Abe ever managed to make a living. She sat down on the non-matching armchair across the coffee table from Abe. "Hopefully her lawyer will clear up the misunderstanding."

"Hear the caretaker got bludgeoned with Freya's trimming axe?"

Now, Grace had his complete attention, as she carefully said, "Maybe...maybe it was another axe? Maybe he had one?"

"Aaup. You know why Freya would've had that axe with her?"

Grace shook her head. "What do you know about this victim?"

Abe perked up when he could give information. "His name was Brian Amundsen, he worked for that campaign manager, Harry Corman."

Taking out her small notebook, Grace wrote down the name. "I thought he took care of the boats or the Kincaids' estate property?"

"Didn't hear of him raking leaves or cleaning gutters. Brian tooled around in that fancy wood motor-boat and the Kincaids' Mercedes. Aldon Kincaid even set up an account in Brian's name at Neptune Grotto's marina to gas and repair the boat. Hear Brian also had an American Express card that got paid with Kincaid checks. Guess that's on top of his salary, which was rumored to be very generous for a yard man."

"Do you know who was signing those checks? Aldon or his campaign manager?"

Abe shrugged. "Don't know. Might be able to find out."

"Do it please." *So they paid Brian because he took loving care of their boat? Or because he did things for the Kincaids that people will pay to keep quiet?* "What else do you know about this guy?"

"Freya came here asking about that Brian when he moved into the boathouse." He stopped staring out into the book stacks. "Didn't have his right name though, called him Lars." Abe looked down at the book in his lap. "Got the idea she was a bit afraid of him..." He looked directly at Grace. "Never known any of the Dells to be afraid of anyone...but maybe Freya had a reason. That Brian was a big guy."

"Tall or fat?"

"Tall with more muscle than most middle-aged guys. About the height and build of Freya's son, Mac. 'Course Freya's a pretty good sized woman too. Helped me move that bookcase over there..."

Grace wanted him to stay on topic. "What do you know about the Kincaids?"

He snorted at that. "You can gossip all day about them. Summer people, come out from the City to use that big house only a few weeks a year but still feel entitled to mix in our politics. Now with Aldon in Congress, they claim Connecticut as his home address, but he lives more in the penthouse in New York City overlooking Central Park."

"Know anything more about them?"

"The late Senator, Aldon's uncle, screwed around with the ladies, and he had his special donors club. Had his fatal accident with his target pistol just before he had to testify about that one. Aldon's father, Julius, died of a heart attack in his mistress' apartment 'cause she waited too long to call 911, not wanting to embarrass him..."

"That must have upset Charlotte."

"The wife? No." Abe looked over his thick glasses at her. "She agreed to a marriage union of two great families, but the total focus of her life has always been the son."

"The Congressman?"

Abe gave a little smile at that. "To Charlotte, Aldon's always been the 'President Elect,' just a few years away."

"What do you know of Maura, his wife?"

He shrugged and thought about it. "Nice lady. Usually, a bit preoccupied. Buys any book I have on Russia or Romanov history. Also gets the latest books on making babies–she's had two, no three miscarriages I hear, a shame..."

"Maura seems a very sweet, intense person."

"Why you so interested in them?" Abe studied her, then said, "Ah, I forgot. Heard you were the star at Charlotte's power tea?"

God, he did hear everything. "A very dim star, I'm afraid. But that mansion is something to see. I expected old school stone pile, and it's all cement arches with spreading glass walls..."

"Architect's a fairly young guy, Lewiston, I got one of his books here..." Abe blinked, looking about at the stacks of new and classic volumes that lined the crowded basement.

Grace shook her head. "I'm not interested. I was just surprised to see it."

"Well, the family manse burnt down a few years ago." Abe frowned in concentration. "There were some stories about that too. Of course, when somebody dies young, that always happens."

"Stories like what?"

He gave some thought to it. "Other things going on then, I didn't pay much attention." Abe frowned. "I can ask around for ya to get the full story. The Kincaid housekeeper is coming in for a book she ordered, but you know who will have the real dirt? Stan Lubchek."

"Who is he?"

"Former chauffeur of the Kincaids. Charlotte felt at fifty-eight he was getting too old and she 'retired' him–without a pension. Claimed they only needed one chauffeur. Kept the younger guy. Stan was out of an apartment, and the only job he's found so far is part-time cleaning out businesses at night–at half the pay. Yeah, he comes in here for his hunting magazines, I can ask him." Abe frowned again. "Ought to ask him about that campaign gal too."

"Who?"

"A Miz Brittany Hellas worked on Aldon's Congressional campaign. Hear tell they spend a lot of time working together. Then one day Brittany Xed herself out with a rum and sleeping pill cocktail."

Freya and Samantha had been arguing about a dead campaign worker, maybe this was her? "You don't think her death was an accident?"

"Well, there were rumors about her and Aldon, heard they were doing most of their 'work' at night. 'Course the Hellas family comes from around Cos Cob, and always have been an unstable lot."

"Could Aldon have killed this Barbara?"

"Brittany? Hell, no. Heard he didn't even have the balls to break up with her–had his campaign manager do it for him."

"Have you heard anything about the manager?"

"Harry? He's a piece of work. One day Maura came in looking at my books, and this guy just comes in a few minutes later. Greets her, then walks over to the other corner with books on pruning bonsai trees. Don't see him as a gardener. Didn't buy nothing, in fact, seemed to be covertly looking at her the whole time. When she left, he came over to me real friendly like, then started asking questions about what she bought, how often she comes in. If'n I didn't know better, I'd have said he was a jealous husband shadowing his wife, so she couldn't get anything on the side."

"He followed Maura to my lab too. Asked a bunch of questions about her."

Abe raised an eyebrow at that. "Grace, you messing in a murder again? When's Kurt getting back?"

She flushed at that. "I don't need Kurt MacKay to take care of myself!"

"Aaup." Abe's mouth narrowed to a tight line.

Trying to change the topic Grace said, "You know, I bought a book in here last week. A mystery by June Brown..."

"Juliet Blackwell. Ya got the third mystery in her San Francisco witch series. I'll order the fourth book for ya, but ya might want to try her haunted home renovation mysteries. I got all of them in stock. Think ya'd like it, good to see Dr. Farrington reading just for fun."

Grace had her own hauntings to deal with, but she dug for money to buy that book.

Chapter 13

That night Grace climbed into bed and picked up her new Blackwell book, planning to do a little fun reading before she turned off the lights. Throughout her life, Grace never really read anything but non-fiction--nothing just for mere pleasure-- she hadn't even read Freya's books, but that beach on São Tomé taught her that allowing a little recreational time could make her mind even more productive. She started on the mystery just as the phone rang. Reaching for it, Grace wondered who would be calling at this hour? "Hello?" "Grace? It's Mac."

Immediately Grace felt a shot of fear. "Is Freya okay?"

"She isn't with you?"

Why was he asking? "No. I haven't seen her since the police came to her store. I left messages for her to call me...so she's not at home?"

He sighed into the phone. "No, I found a note taped to my door *'Got to clear out my head. Will be gone for awhile, don't worry, Mom.'* That's typical Freya! Ma gets herself sinking up to her chin in quicksand, then tells you not to worry! And, of course, my girlfriend's not talking to me either."

"Sam? Why?"

"I'll never understand women...we were to go out last Monday, then she texted a phone message saying, 'I can't see you tonight,' and she hasn't returned my calls since."

"Maybe Sam's just busy? But we need to know where Freya is. Maybe your mother is still with the detectives?"

"The police let her go hours ago when she got a lawyer–I guess he's your lawyer."

"Mark Silverstein, a very good criminal lawyer."

"Yeah, well he'd better be, they brought Ma up before a judge–they're charging her with Brian Amundsen's murder. I didn't know about it then, but the lawyer got Ma out..."

"Are you sure she's not hiding out at the boat building barn?"

"Nope."

"Did you call that looney bird lady?"

"Astrid? Yes. Look, I'm sorry I disturbed you," apologized Mac awkwardly.

"No! No, don't worry about that! If you find her, call me. Any hour of the night, please."

After that call, sleep wouldn't come. Restless, Grace got up and made herself a cup of lemon tea, wishing she had some chocolate chip cookies. Not feeling like baking some, Grace rummaged in the cupboards and came up with some chocolate-covered marzipans wrapped in foil Santas and Christmas trees she had bought for Bobby's kids, and forgotten to give to them. Eating one luxuriously rich treat after the other, Grace drifted back into her office. Her laptop sat in its case. She unpacked it and booted up her 'Murder of the Caretaker' spreadsheet. Checking her notebook, Grace changed it to the 'Murder of Brian Amundsen.'

Grace scanned the sheet; she would have to leave Mac, Freya, and Unknown killer's percentages the same, but more possibilities were evolving with the Kincaid family, especially Aldon Kincaid. For generations, the Kincaids were all ambitious, politically minded, and Aldon had the 'Alpha A's' proclivity to fool around. Grace added lines for him, Charlotte Kincaid, even Maura.

As for motive: Aldon fooled around constantly, and Brian knew it, but it probably was Brian's job to cover that up. Does the Golden Boy have a temper? She had assumed the murder weapon was Freya's, but her friend never said so. Could there have been another tenth-century trimming axe floating around that belongs to Aldon? His score came in at a pathetic 40 % based on a bunch of weak assumptions Grace just guessed at. 'To Do': Talk to Maura. Learn more about her husband. Particularly, was he on the property that day?

Next row: Maura. For 'Motive,' well, Harry was following her, but that's not a reason to kill Brian, so 0 %. Still, the wife inhabited the property and could be almost as physically strong as Freya, 25 %, and for a 'Pro,' Maura would do anything to protect the royal family, 50 %. But on 'Con' side, Grace couldn't see a motive whatsoever, - 50 %, leaving Maura with a weak 25 %. And Grace realized that the only reason Maura was being considered at all was that Grace knew her better than the rest.

Charlotte. Here the 'Motive' would be to protect her son's political chances, 50 %; for 'Means', Charlotte looked late fifties and very athletic, obviously strong enough to swing that axe in passion, with added 10 % for proximity; 'Con' Charlotte appeared to be a proactive person, 25 %; but here is where the case fell apart, alive Brian was a henchman, dead he was a liability, so - 50 %, giving Charlotte a total of 35 %.

Finally, Harry, the campaign manager got his line. 'Motive' unknown, but may have been to protect Aldon's reputation, 10 %; 'Means' On the property, 25 %, 'Pro' Harry manipulated the Kincaids for his own reasons, 50 %; 'Con' How did he get Freya's axe? And why kill the guy working for him? Giving Harry a -50 % for 'Con," with a grand total 35 %, but Grace felt it should be higher. Again the 'To Do:' learn more about what the campaign manager was into. Speak with Abe again.

She looked over the unsatisfactory screen: Did the suicidal house campaign worker fit in anywhere? Should Grace add more columns for the campaign worker's suicide or possible murder? Would Harry or Brian have killed the girl to protect Aldon's reputation? She added some columns for–Grace looked at her notebook—Abe had said 'Brittany Hellas.'

What else? Was Maura jealous of her husband's affairs? That would be a reason to kill Aldon, not Brian. Working on the spreadsheet had given Grace a headache and a profound desire to go back to bed. Taking two Tylenol she did just that.

* * *

After a short morning run, Grace balanced her doughnut and newspaper as she unlocked her laboratory door. Her assistants wouldn't be in for hours yet, which would give her a nice quiet time to catch up on e-mails and project details. She'd have to speak with someone at Affiliated Technologies about the joint study on the lobster mold based skin softener she and Kurt were doing. She liked giving positive reports and wanted to hear how Affiliated had been doing with their preclinical toxicology tests. The study was started to give Bobby a job, but it was turning out to be profitable for them all.

"Grace?"

What now? Grace turned around to see the security screen. In black and white she saw a safety-helmeted Adam Greenfield in leather jacket and jeans, not his President of ORR suit. With him dressed for his construction business, maybe this wouldn't take so long.

This hope died quickly when the door opened, and he walked into the lab, over to the coffee maker's pot of hot water. Grace followed him, as Adam himself poured a cup of water then stirred in coffee crystals from a jar that Inger had left out. "You know, being President of Oyster River Research is a voluntary position. I don't get paid for it–and I have my construction company to run."

Having heard this many times before, Grace nodded her head. "It's wonderful that community leaders like yourself will take on the responsibility and give up their valuable time..."

He cut her off, "Grace, you have promised to attend our Spring Fund Raiser?"

"Yes."

"Are you aware that David Gardiner has bought tickets for two tables?"

"Two? That is what...sixteen chairs? Nice donation to ORR, congratulations."

"One is for his lawyer, Alan Silverstein, who is on our Board of Directors, but the table on the front costs more. David plans to have his family there as I understand?"

Why was he asking her? "If you have a question about who is going to be at his table call David's office or ask Alan?"

"I understand he wants you sitting at his table–but ORR needs you at the head table on the dais."

That's the problem–but suddenly Grace realized she might have some leverage here. "Have you given any more thought to my request?"

"Your request?" He looked confused as he drank from the styrofoam cup.

"Yes. When ORR's long-term secretary left, you replaced her with a full-time secretary, who couldn't handle the work."

He only shrugged, drinking the coffee black. "ORR had grown over the years."

She nodded in agreement. "So you added another part-time secretary."

"But that didn't work out," he muttered. "The first one wanted the second one full-time, and they still weren't keeping up with the catalog, the budget, and the student applications, grades, and paperwork."

"So you added a temporary secretary, Gail Travinski."

"Yes, and then the first two quit..."

"But Gail managed to do the work of all three!" pointed out Grace.

"And with what her temporary agency charges, it cost me almost as much as the two full-timers who left," Adam returned.

"So, as I've asked before, why can't Gail be put on the payroll as a full-time employee?"

"Perhaps someday, but not now."

"Why? The agency is charging you her salary and a third more for their profit."

"Actually, I think they charge us her salary and two-thirds profit."

"Then it will be cheaper to hire her..."

"No, it won't. Grace you don't understand. If I hire Gail, ORR will have to pay social security, medical insurance, holidays..."

"You don't pay her for holidays when ORR is closed?" Grace hadn't realized that.

"Of course not. She's a temporary employee, hired by the hour. But if we make her an ORR employee, we'll also have to give her vacation time, and we'll have to put her on the retirement plan, and the temporary agency would charge us a severance fee for hiring away one of their employees--it's in their contract..."

"Adam, Gail has no medical insurance. She doesn't go to a doctor for even an annual physical..."

That made an impression as a worried Adam asked, "Is Gail sick? ORR's medical is self-funded, I mean if an employee on insurance needed something expensive like kidney dialysis, our rates would go way up."

"She's not sick--but she should get check-ups." The whole unfairness of Gail's situation angered Grace, who said, "For the buffet--actually David has invited me to join him at his table, but I haven't decided where I'm going sit. Or whether I'm moving to Greece to work in David's laboratory. I'm going to think about it, and while I'm doing that, I want you to think about hiring Gail full time. Now both of us have work to do." Saying that Grace turned away and headed back to her desk.

Not looking too happy, Adam walked out.

*   *   *

Grace didn't choose to lock her laboratory door when she

worked in the main room, and now, deep in thought as she emerged from her computer screen, she was shaken to see a short, young, dark-haired man in an impeccable charcoal gray suit standing there asking, "Grace. Grace, do you know where Freya is?"

Making the connection with 'Freya', she recognized Mark Silverstein, Grace's lawyer, now Freya's. "She's in jail?"

"No. I've gotten her out on personal recognizance, but her shop is closed, and she's not at her house. Her son says doesn't know where she is?"

"I don't know either–is it important?"

"Yes. It seems Freya didn't exactly tell us the truth about Brian Amundsen, or the same man under a bunch of other names. The police have been notified that Brian and Freya formerly were lovers..."

"That's impossible." Grace sat up with immediate denial. "I've known Freya ever since I came to Oyster River. I mean, she's had relationships...but not with this man who I've never heard of before."

"This apparently was some time ago, probably before her son was born."

This didn't make any sense at all. "How did the police find that out?"

"The murdered man had a woman living with him..."

The 'slut' Freya had mentioned, and Grace had met? " I saw her–what was her name?"

"Sierra Sonheim. Might be a phony name. She looks twenty, thirty years younger than Brian, and didn't seem to grief-stricken at the loss of her man-friend."

"Could she have killed him?" Grace asked hopefully.

Mark shook his head regretfully saying,"Sounds like the detectives feel she had an alibi and no motive."

"Freya didn't do it," Grace stated firmly.

Mark seemed to be mentally getting his case in

order. "There are multiple security cameras on the Kincaid estate. They photographed Freya entering the property, parking, and carrying the axe. Although most of the axe had been wiped, they found a matchable fingerprint of Freya's."

"Well, it is her axe," protested Grace.

"She's also recorded on camera as leaving without the axe."

"The cameras showed her going into the boathouse?"

"Apparently the only two cameras that would've recorded the boathouse stairs had been out of order for months. Looks like someone smashed them deliberately."

"Did Freya admit it was her axe?"

Mark sighed. "Yes, at an earlier interview, without me present. And she wouldn't tell the police or me why she had it." He looked at Grace with a question in his eyes.

A question Grace couldn't answer, so instead, she asked, "Is that all they have?"

"No, Freya refuses to explain why she was on the property. Or how she knew the caretaker."

"She told me she went to interview him for a new book."

"That sound right to you?"

Again, he looked to Grace for an answer, and all she could do was shake her head. "I don't know, but if the police don't know why she was there, they can't have a motive, can they?"

"The detectives got a search warrant for her house and found a blouse in her dirty laundry basket with a brown stain. They've matched it to Brian's blood type. Can they match it to his DNA?"

More comfortable with a question in her field Grace sat back and answered, "Yes, with a relatively recent stain it would be a fairly simple extraction."

Shaking his head, Mark said, "She is out on personal recognizance, and the judge could change that to bail or jail.

The police have to know where she is. Have her call me if you find her."

He left her upset, thinking where could Freya be? Mac obviously had a better chance of finding his mother and would be working on it. She just should get back to her DNA.

But the damned phone was ringing again. She should just let it go to messaging for Inger to pick up, but it might be Freya. "Laboratory 5."

"Grace? Is that you?"

The voice sounded a little upset. "Yes, who is this?"

"Maura Kincaid."

Grace had to set some boundaries. "This is my lab phone, and I'm working right now–what did you want?"

The woman's voice had a hesitate quality as if she knew she was asking too much. "Could you come over for dinner tonight? Charlotte's got a small buffet, and she asked me to ask you?"

"Uhh...no" Grace did not want to do this and decided to lie her way out. "I...have a dinner date tonight."

"Oh, with who?" Maura slipped into best friends mode.

"A male friend."

"You can bring him! That would make an even number at the table."

No way did she want that. "No...it's David Gardiner–he's only here from Greece for a few days..."

"David Gardiner? He'd be fantastic! Charlotte would be so impressed if I got him to come."

Oh, shit, 'when you deceive, what a tangled web you weave.' "He's already got special reservations..."

"Where?" she asked breathlessly.

Where? This was getting ridiculously complicated. "He wouldn't tell me, he said it was a surprise. Dinner at six thirty."

"But you could come earlier, maybe for hors-d'oeuvres, Charlotte would be so impressed with me, just a few minutes, I promise!"

How did Grace get herself into this? "I'll have to call him, then I'll call you."

"Don't bother. I'll tell Charlotte you both are coming at five thirty, she'll be so excited. David is a real plus for Aldon's campaign, and I got him! Thank you so much, Grace!"

The phone line was dead before Grace could come up with enough backbone to say no.

Off the phone, she turned to her computer, but Grace couldn't get back to work unless she did something. Picking up the phone again, she dialed and was relieved to hear it answered. "Gardiner here."

"This is Grace. David, can we go out to dinner tonight?"

"Actually I'm in the City..." he sounded a little confused.

"I just needed an escort–you–tonight at five thirty."

A short pause, making Grace wonder. She'd turned him down so many times, perhaps he had moved on without her? But that reassuring masculine voice came back. "Yes, I can adjust my schedule. That will work out and be quite pleasant. Can I pick up at your condo?"

She needed time in the clean room to catch up, about three hours would do it. "Pick me up in my lab a five o'clock?"

"Fine."

"David, I'm not getting dressed up, so we can't go any place fancy."

"Grace, I've told you before, we do not dress for anyone else, and we'll dress how we wish, and then go where we choose. I'll pick you up, visit your friends, and afterward we can go to the City and pick up a Broadway show and late supper. Now, where is this place that you need an escort too?"

That might be a sticking point. "Do you know who the Kincaids are?"

Again that hesitation. "Yes, I know the Kincaids, and I also know they own the mansion where the caretaker Freya is accused of killing died. I thought you were staying out of this murder investigation?"

"I'm not in it–but I know Maura Kincaid, and they're giving a fundraising buffet tonight. She pleaded with me to bring you, but I don't want to stay more than a half hour."

Silence, then he said, "That sounds right. And for dinner- what do you feel like fish? Chinese? Barbecue?"

She didn't need another decision today. "Surprise me."

Chapter 14

He arrived at her lab at four thirty, so she had him run her over to the condo where she could change into a blue print blouse and black linen pants. Maybe a little too informal, but David smiled to see her come out of the bedroom. Driving to the Kincaid mansion, again Grace appreciated the leather comfort of David's black Cadillac Escalade, and enjoyed the entrance they made.

This time Charlotte opened the door and seemed mildly gratified to see both of them. "Dr. Farrington and David Gardiner, I'm so glad you could make it. Please join me in the living room."

The lady of the manor led them to double doors left of that great, theatrical two-story foyer with its gold veined marble flooring and decorative niches. Grace was relieved not to be in that big solarium sunroom expanse. Instead, Charlotte led them into a gracious living room, with a broad expanse of pale beige carpet, white couches, and bronze-tinted glass tables.

Smoothing her dress, Maura walked over to them holding out her hand, "Mr. Gardiner."

"David, please." He shook her hand.

"Grace has spoken so much about you," gushed Maura.

Grace found herself raising her eyebrow at that, and Charlotte too looked a little surprised as she commented to David, "My daughter-in-law apparently has a formed quite a relationship with Dr. Farrington."

"Grace, please," she said as David steered her to a couch and the maid entered carrying a silver tray of canapes.

Charlotte looked to Maura, smiling sweetly, "Where is Aldon? He knew what time they were expected."

"I'll go find him," her daughter-in-law said, immediately hurrying out of the room.

As the maid waited, Charlotte asked them, "Can I offer you anything to drink?"

Grace looked to David who said, "A scotch and soda would be nice, but we can't stay too long."

They looked to Grace. "I'd like ginger ale."

Charlotte looked to her maid, "I'll have white wine. Maura's should be watching her weight, so she'll have a diet Pepsi, and Aldon would like a Coke."

"With rum," the man himself told the maid as he entered, ignoring his mother's hard-lined mouth. Instead, he continued in a jovial manner, making it sound like he'd already had a few rum and Cokes. "Gardiner, you're here. Have you seen the light? You're coming over to our side? Realizing that a planned society can function so much better than everyman for himself?"

"Not really," returned David amiably.

Quietly Maura had followed Aldon in, sitting on the other end of the second long couch as her husband ignored her and his mother, saying, "My campaign is action happening! My opponent's an old man, with older ideas."

"Ancient at only fifty-two?" David pointed out.

"Old with tired ideas, worn out solutions, an inability to carry things forward..."

"That's strange, your opponent's a man with a great deal of expertise from the military, his family business, and his political career." David pointed out in a moderately friendly manner as he reached for a small plate and tongs to capture a miniature spring roll. Filling his plate with a selection of Charlotte's hors d'oeuvres David observed, "I still tend to believe citizens are best served by a government that can't and shouldn't provide everything. Nor should it control everything from cradle to grave, especially by managing the means of production and distribution."

"Because you have money to buy whatever you want, you don't care about the disadvantaged, the marginalized in our society?" challenged Aldon, who now sat at the edge of a leather couch seat as the maid returned with the drinks. Under Charlotte's disapproving eyes the maid--obviously well trained--served Aldon first. And following that maid, with his own drink already in his hand, was Harry. He moved over to stand behind Charlotte's chair, and Grace wondered if the campaign manager had been listening outside?

David ignored him, speaking directly to Aldon. "No, because however appealing socialism sounds it's always a bad idea in the long run."

"Socialism?" Aldon asked in a mocking tone. "Me? Scion of the wealthy Kincaids?"

Tilting his head to the side, David quietly commented, "As a Congressman, you've voted consistently to increase regulation, expand taxation, and enlarge the role of government control over every facet of American life."

"For the good of the herd," Aldon pronounced, and Grace saw Charlotte shoot a fast look at Harry, who tightly studied David's reaction.

The man sitting beside Grace only finished chewing his spring roll and then said, "Encouraging the breakup of families, subsidizing the production of multiple babies by teenagers, and showing children you don't have to work to receive a check--in the long run you're damaging the very population you're claiming to help. A controlling government, by allowing little mandarin kingdoms to over-regulate business, produce lost jobs, closed companies..."

As Grace reached out for her ginger ale, Aldon argued back, "But look at Grace, spending endless time applying for grants from a myriad of government agencies, profit-oriented corporate entities, and amateur-headed charities like Oyster River. A benevolent government would fund her entire research needs, without her having to waste time begging for sponsorship."

Grace found herself faintly resenting the 'begging'

part, but she only commented, "If the government is the only entity allowed to fund my lab from taxpayer funding, I assume they will also be deciding just what I can and cannot research? And, if those benevolent managers are unhappy with my results, are these all-powerful bureaucrats going to demand I change my findings to agree with whatever the current political script is?"

Aldon actually looked perplexed that anyone would question his statements of 'facts.' "It's just a matter of the right guy on the top picking the best possible person to run the National Science Foundation or the National Institute of Health. In a Kincaid Administration, I'd be picking someone like Dr. Grace Farrington to run either of them."

Just supervising her own lab--with only three assistants--sometimes felt like a Herculean task to Grace, so she pointed out, "By choice, I'm a researcher, not an administrator."

Giving an ironic smile, David quietly questioned, "Aldon, I believe you're running for junior senator from Connecticut? Exactly what authority will a Senator Kincaid Administration's have over the staffing of the National Science Institutes?"

Aldon shot a glance to his mother; it was Charlotte who answered, "As a senator, very little. However, Aldon is visualizing the future. This senate run is merely the preliminary of Aldon's presidential campaign."

David raised a questioning eyebrow, but before he could counter, Maura instantly chimed in to change the topic, "Grace, Charlotte is giving another 'power tea' next week. Its theme is STEM for young girls. It would be such a show of support for the young women if a significant scientist like yourself put in an appearance?"

"Perhaps you can give us a keynote speech?" suggested Charlotte.

Without a doubt, Grace supported any efforts to get

young students--female or male--to study science and mathematics, but she hated all public appearances, and the time they squandered, still, Charlotte's power teas would get her on the Kincaid estate, where Grace might learn more about Brian's killer. "No. No speech at least. I'll arrive late, be introduced, and leave early. And that's it."

Charlotte nodded. "That would be sufficient." A distant doorbell chimed. "Some of the other guests are arriving early." She looked at David. "Can't you stay for dinner? We're expecting the Lieutenant Governor tonight."

Grace did not want to do that, and she shifted to catch David's eye, saying, "That's very nice, but as I explained to Maura, David has limited time in this country so we would prefer to dine privately."

Taking that as his cue, David rose, and Grace followed him. Charlotte and Maura also politely stood, while Aldon just sat there cradling his drink.

"I'm so glad Maura could get you to come, both of you," said Charlotte as Maura followed them out to the foyer. "David, we have some evening policy groups you might find interesting..."

"Perhaps some other time," David returned, as Grace felt his guiding hand on her elbow again. The maid was taking coats from four well-dressed people, who seemed to know David and he went over to shake hands. While the maid went to fetch their coats, Grace looked about in that cathedral of a foyer. Her eyes settled on two tall, recessed niches on either side of the front doors. Not wishing to start talking with the newcomers, Grace moved closer to inspect the nearest niche in the elegant, but sparsely decorated room. She stopped to study an exquisite statue of a woman, about three foot high, masterfully sculpted from a single block of green jade, set with a face of aged ivory carved in an expression of sublime beauty, selflessness, and compassion.

"Notice the richly detailed robe, but bare feet?" Maura

murmured next to Grace. "That's Kuan Yin, the Chinese goddess of mercy. I pray to her sometimes..." she finished in an even softer voice, "I think she forgives all."

"A beautiful piece," admitted Grace.

"Ming dynasty," said Charlotte proudly, coming up behind Maura. "We had to get special dispensation to get a historical object out of China. Some minor museum people created all sorts of obstacles, and then we had more problems getting the statue into this country because of the ivory face–which was ridiculous. It's obviously a masterwork, an artistic treasure that shouldn't be bound by some petty Customs' regulations."

Yes, the Kincaids weren't restrained by the petty laws the rest of us lived under, yet studying that object of absolute beauty, Grace too, lusted a bit in her heart wishing to possess it. And seeing that serene goddess reminded Grace of the similar, but the much less expensive statues in the Haunts of Wôden... and of another tall bronze Kuan Yin standing in a tranquil garden. Suddenly, Grace had a very good idea of where Freya might be found.

Chapter 15

Back settled in that luxurious car of David's she asked, "I expected the Kincaids to be after you more to donate to Aldon's campaign?"

"Not likely to happen, and they know it." David gave that superior look of his. "Aldon is a Democrat, and I'm a registered Conservative Republican." He stopped for a light, looking at her again. "Grace, I've never asked, what party do you support?"

"No party." Not paying too much attention, Grace now worried about Freya. She thought she knew where Freya would be, but she didn't know how to get there.

Again David asked, "You must be something, did you register as an Independent?"

"Registered?" she answered absentmindedly.

"To vote."

Grace thought about that. "Actually I've never voted."

"Why not?" He actually sounded shocked.

She had to think about that. "Well, at first I was too young. Then, in college in California, I was out of my residency. When I came here, my hours were so long, I tried to vote once, but I hadn't registered beforehand, so I couldn't–and, I don't follow politics, so I don't particularly care."

"Well, you should!" He sounded personally offended, as he made a turn on to the Post Road.

"Why?"

"Politicians create the rules of the world you live in. Politicians decide how taxpayers' research and infrastructure money will be allocated. Corrupt politicians use tax money to buy votes and bleed the system like leeches--too many parasites and an organism dies. A populous that doesn't vote will most certainly get lives they'll be unhappy with."

Grace really didn't see the importance of this to him,

but she said, "Will it help if I go to Town Hall and get registered as a Republican?"

That made David frown more. "No! You should get registered, but if you have no preference, sign up as an Independent. Of course, you won't be allowed to vote in the primaries, but you can change parties later. But before the next election, do some reading. Find out what the issues are, and chose your position and candidate."

"Usually I don't want to vote for any of them."

He slammed his hand down on the steering wheel. "That doesn't matter! It is your civic duty to vote! If there is no one you like, then vote for the least objectionable candidate, or use the civil rights strategy-- keep voting the incumbent out until you get someone who at least tries to carry out your wishes."

Grace leaned forward. Something else filled her mind. "I'll think about that, but, now I'd like to go somewhere."

"We are going into the City for a show and dinner," he said.

"Later, but there is someplace else I must go first."

He looked at her with those pale blue eyes. "Where?"

"I don't know, but we've got to go there." Grace looked around at the road, they were pulling away toward I-95 and New York City, not where she wanted to go. "This sounds crazy to you, right?"

That brought a crooked smile to his face as he pulled off the road in front of a pizza parlor so they could talk. "No, dear, I've been married twice. The first year with Lauren was a lesson in the insanity of picking one's mate in a rage of teenage hormones. And, of course, the next twenty-one years were with an intelligent, organized woman, but even Sylvia had her difficult times."

Wryly Grace pointed out, "Wouldn't she have said that you could be a bit unreasonable sometimes?"

He smiled appreciatively. "Yes, she did just that more

than a few times, quite correctly. Very much like you, Sylvia was a brilliant, curious woman for the subjects she was interested in, but like you, she was totally oblivious to most of the world we live in. Now, is this place you want to go to-- is it in the United States?"

"It's around here. A woman's house. Freya's led seances there. It's off the main roads, a beautiful place." Grace struggled to remember; why hadn't she paid any attention to where Freya was driving? "It's not far from your house. You can't see it from the road, it's behind a small pine and birch forest. Then you reach a bamboo plot around the house, with small, beautiful, white-stone gardens, and koi fish ponds. It's a single story house, u shaped around a glassed-in atria. The house is contemporary, exquisitely decorated, with mainly oriental furnishings and traditional early American portraits. The portraits are probably of her family, I guess."

"The lady is very wealthy?"

"She's a friend of Freya's, so I don't think she'd have much...I mean, Freya's friends usually don't care about money. But I don't know... wouldn't a house in your area be expensive?"

He choked a little bit at that. "Yes, dear, a house in my area, with a five-acre zoning minimum, would be a little expensive. What you are describing might be the Perkins estate. Does Evelyn Perkins-Campbell ring a bell? She's noted for her Japanese gardens and for being President of the Garden Club."

Grace thought a bit, "Evelyn? That might be it...but I don't really remember...you know I'm terrible on names and people. You know her?"

"I know of her family, the Perkins have been here almost as long as mine..."

Somehow Grace felt she should defend her friend. "And Freya's the Dells were farmers and fisherman when the Connecticut colony was settled."

Again he smiled gently. "Yes. The Dells are certainly a fine, old, local family. Now we'll have to locate the Perkins house..."

"So we'll need an address," said Grace reaching into her handbag for her phone. "I could call Gail, the secretary at Oyster River, but she probably has gone home by now. Or I could call Abe Hoyt in his bookstore. Abe knows everybody around here, or maybe they might have a telephone directory in the town library..."

David reached out, putting a gentle hand on her arm. "Grace, this is a Cadillac Escalade. We can sit comfortably here, activate that screen, and have the nice lady living in the car dashboard find Evelyn for us and map a route to her house."

Freya had always driven when they went to one of Evelyn's séance circles, and Grace hadn't paid much attention to the route, but she was sure David took the wrong turn off the main road, and she didn't recognize any of the houses along the way. Finally, she was sure he turned off into the wrong piney driveway, but shortly, they were parking on the white gravel lane curving in front of a long, one-story contemporary house surrounded by Japanese gardens. Lovely, peaceful gardens with a five-foot tall green bronze statue of Kuan Yin. "Yes, this it, I'm sure."

Nervous now, Grace headed up to the red-lacquered door and pressed the bell. What would she say?

The door was opened by a petite woman dressed in a blousey, violet silk print Kimono. "Grace?" Alma looked past her to David in his tan suit. "David Gardiner? I thought you had moved to Europe?

"I commute," David said.

Grace had expected the usually courteous Alma to invite them in as she always did. Instead, her would be hostess stood blocking the doorway saying, "I'm sorry. I'm not having a spiritual circle meeting today. Is that why you've come?"

"Actually I'm looking for Freya," Grace said hesitantly.

Alma still didn't move to allow them in. "Oh, I heard she was under arrest... that's such a shame..."

"Freya's out, but she disappeared. I thought she might be here?" Grace tried again.

"Oh, no. No, no, she's not here..." assured Alma.

Grace pulled her jacket closer. "It's chilly today with the clouds, couldn't we just come in for a minute?"

Alma looked torn. "I'm very sorry...I'm not dressed for company...and I'm coming down with a cold, and I'm really not up to guests right now." Alma started to close the door in their faces.

"Grace, maybe we should just go?" asked David.

But if Alma was not letting them into her house, maybe Freya was in there? Sounding a bit desperate Grace begged, "It's going to rain...before we leave, could I just use your bathroom?"

After a moment's hesitation, the ever courteous Alma reluctantly pulled back. "Well, you can come in for just a moment. There's a half bath there behind that door." She pointed across the living room. "But then you'll both have to go," she finished firmly.

Grace needed some private time in the house. "We're also here because David is planning a koi pond garden–he wanted to know how yours had been built..."

That raised an eyebrow with Alma who looked to David and asked in a concerned voice, "You're going to dig up all your mother's lovely English gardens?"

"No," David corrected, then lied like a trooper, "but I have a new area I was thinking of making into a sort of tea house setting, with a Japanese theme."

Their reluctant hostess glanced back through her open living room, that fronted on one side of the glassed-in atria, also with its koi ponds and small footbridge. The second passion in Alma's life was her stone lantern, arched bridged gardens. "They are so restful to look at."

"Yes," David elaborated, "I'm not at all happy with the plans my designers have given me. Outside, could you just show me how they constructed the drainage by the footbridge? Then we will go, I promise."

Their hostess looked unhappy, but she opened a concealed panel of white paper and varnished black framing to reveal a coat closet and pulled out her black wool cape. Ever the gentleman, David moved to help her slip it on, as Alma continued,"Yes, I'll just show you the garden, while Grace uses the facilities, but then you'll both have to go..."

As soon as David ushered Alma out into the yard, Grace rushed about the house looking in neat room after neat room; no clothes lying out in the guest rooms; even the English ivy themed master bedroom looked like a perfectly swept layout in a high end decorating magazine. Grace pulled open the door to a large walk-in closet, nothing out of order. No Freya with her notebooks, half drunk cups of tea, and drawing pencils all spread about. No, her friend wasn't living here.

Defeated, Grace walked back and stood in the quiet dining room where Freya had held so many séances. The furniture had elegant, spare Japanese lines, with the mirror polished, long dark table seating twelve. The matching walnut chairs and furniture included an impressive breakfront, with some of the pieces delicately inlaid with mother of pearl accents. Grace sat down on the yellow silk upholstered chair and stared at the textured, pale yellow walls. Hung on them were lacquered black board artworks formed by the skillful arranging of semiprecious stones into scenes of koi fish and water lily ponds. Very restful, very peaceful, but the room's serenity was lost on Grace.

Where was Freya? Grace was out of ideas. With a

terrific headache, feeling suddenly tired, she just folded her hands together over her eyes. When Alma came back, Grace'd do what she should have done: explain that Freya's shouldn't have run, and Freya's lawyer wanted her back before she got in real trouble, so if Alma knew anything that could help...

"Summoning me by telepathy, Grace?"

At the familiar voice, Grace looked up to see her tall friend in the doorway. Freya's blonde hair dropped in a long braid, and she was dressed in a rainbow Mumu that only came down a little below her knees. "You didn't check the closet in the guest room, but after you left, I stepped out and smelled your aroma."

"What do I smell like?" Grace asked.

"Clean. Laboratories. Citrus disinfectants." Freya moved toward her. "You used your psychic side to track me down at Alma's."

"No," said Grace, smiling again. "I just knew where you could get Panda dung tea and pecan cookies." Freya smiled at that, so Grace continued a little more seriously, "Freya, you shouldn't have disappeared, your lawyer says it's not helping your case."

"Do I have a case?" The taller woman sat down alongside Grace and shook her head. "I needed to get somewhere quiet and safe where I could think, but I don't want to make any trouble for anyone."

"Mark needs you back. So does your son, but first I need to know the truth. The police told Mark that at one time you lived with the murdered man?"

"They found that out?" Freya looked at her with wide-eyed surprise, saying, "that was decades ago..."

"The caretaker has a girlfriend he apparently confided in."

"Oh, the slut," said Freya with contempt. "I've seen her, Sierra something or other, twenty-two at the most,' Freya stopped, then continued with a touch of distaste, "women have always had a fascination for a mean guy who comes across as a sharpy."

"Were you married? You said Mac's father was a soldier, killed overseas before Mac was born?"

"I lied," said Freya lowering her head in shame. "And what's worse, I told the same lie to Mac. Now he's furious with me."

"But this murdered man, is he–was he--Mac's father?"   "I don't know," she said staring off at the pressed woven dried grass wallpaper.

"You don't know?"

"I lived with him...actually it was two men, a mènage à trois. I was young, in art school. Lars Anderson and Wolfgang Eriksson were tall, Nordic guys--a bit scary, but that made it all the hotter. We chose our Viking names: From Alice Dell I became Freya, Wolfgang wanted to be Thor, and Lars called himself Loki. We had a fantastic year, the three of us, in a king-sized waterbed in the apartment I was paying for by dipping and carving art candles. That summer Thor won a Volkswagen Bus in a poker game, and we rode back and forth across the country. But summers must end, and Thor got a signing bonus for the Marines, and he took off overseas... While Lars found a rich widow."

"Lars?" a confused Grace asked.

"Call him Brian, that's the last name he used. He wanted to keep me on the side, but at that point, the glamour of *'being with an outlaw'* had finally worn off. I didn't want to be a back street girlfriend and knowing how he was making his money, I'd grown to distrust him."

"Who fathered Mac? You named him 'Thor' at birth."

"I had been on the pill--but I had the flu--probably threw it up, but they were leaving so we had to have goodbye sex. I was miles away from both of them before I realized I was pregnant. Neither of them was husband or father material, and I knew that. So, when we wrote a bit at first, I didn't tell either of them about the pregnancy. I dropped out of college, came back home, and gave birth to Mac without ever telling them."

"Then this Lars, Brian or Loki found out?"

"That I had a child? Yes, just recently, apparently."

"You told him?"

"No. But he must have been doing some investigating, he was always good at that-- ferreting out people's secrets so he had leverage over them. He must have found out about Mac, and he can count. He also studied enough of me to know I owned the Haunts of Wôden and in my spare time I work building a faering in the boatwright barn. The barn is isolated, and a predator like Brian looks for that.

"He tracked me down to the boat building barn. Inside, I heard a motorboat drawing close, thought it was one of the volunteers and ignored it. But, after awhile, when nobody came in, I got curious and took a walk through the trees where my boat was tied up. Now, there was a fancy woody motor launch tied up to a birch, and on my boat, a tall, sandy-haired man bent over, looking through something. Probably looking for anything he could steal."

"Sounds like a 'Mr. Nice guy'."

"Wishing I hadn't put that trimming axe down, I walked over to find out who was this big guy with his hand in my toolbox, and then Brian straightened up and gave me a big-toothed grin. At first, I just stared, then I confronted him demanding to know what he was doing? He said he was looking for me. I asked him if he thought I'd fit in that toolbox? He just wide-grinned me and wanted to start up all over again, as if the years hadn't washed '*us*' away."

Freya stopped talking, and Grace could see however she might protest it, at that moment her friend had been pulled back into that summer of love. "What did you say?"

"I asked what he was doing in Oyster River?"

"He said his name now was Brian Amundsen, and that

he was making mucho bucks working for a wealthy politician..." She stopped, the memory was obviously not one Freya wanted to continue.

So Grace prodded, saying, "He was working as a caretaker on the Kincaid estate."

Freya's blue eyes darkened. "I doubt that." Grace looked sharply at her friend as Freya explained further, "'*Caretaker*' is what I'm sure he was paid for on the books, but Brian always preferred other jobs, where he had an opportunity to bully, to hurt someone... even in our days he was searching out secrets and pulling in bucks for doing dirty tricks in political campaigns."

"Do you think he was doing that for the Kincaids?"

"Probably." Again Freya got uncharacteristically misty-eyed. "Brian was older, beefier, but still the Loki that I once loved."

"Loki? Isn't that the name for the evil one?"

" Loki, the bad boy of the pantheon of Norse Gods, that fitted Lars–or your Brian--to a T."

"Oh, Freya, do you think this Brian was Mac's father?"

An agitated Alma was coming into the room, followed closely by David trying to distract her, but Alma was saying, "Grace, you both do have to go..." She stopped seeing Freya and Grace sitting at the table. "Oh, dear."

In her calming voice, Freya said, "It's all right, Alma. Grace is a friend. Could you get David some tea and let me and Grace talk a bit more?"

Alma nodded and withdrew, and after glancing to Grace, David left following her. Grace could hear Alma's worried voice saying something and David's polite murmurings in return. When they were out of hearing, it was Grace who said, "Your lawyer has been told they have your fingerprints on the trimming axe and in the boathouse."

"It's my axe, and I was there."

" And that you had Brian's blood on your blouse that the police found in your laundry basket?"

Her friend just kept looking away.

"Freya, this is important. You were there, you brought the axe...why?"

The big woman shrugged her shoulders. "Maybe to kill him."

"**No!**" Grace said. "I don't believe that. You went there. Did you take the axe to protect yourself?"

Freya didn't answer.

"By not talking, you're making yourself look guilty of his murder." Grace studied her. "You want to do that don't you? You're afraid. Not of being arrested, no, you're afraid...that Mac killed his father?"

Her friend's pale skin darkened with a deep flush, and her hands shook as she pressed them against the table. "No! Mac wouldn't!"

With a polite jingling of China, Alma carried in a tray of Japanese tea cups, a black iron pot, and a plate of small round cookies. As she set them down, Alma looked at Grace disapprovingly for having upset Freya so.

Freya looked at the black lacquered tray. "Thank you, Alma. Grace is trying to help, but she really doesn't understand the situation."

Their hostess nodded and left them alone again. Neither of them spoke for some time. Grace sipped some of the smokey tea; Freya's was just left untouched. Finally, Freya spoke, "When I saw Brian again, he already knew I had a son, knew Mac was christened 'Thor,' and guessed I'd never told Mac the truth about his parentage. Brian naturally assumed he was the father, so seeing an opportunity, he tried blackmailing me..." she stopped.

"What did you do?" Grace urged.

"Laughed at him, that he thought I had money. That stopped him a bit. Then he wanted me to sign over my store to him. That was a stupid idea–the space is rented, and what was he going to do: sell incense sticks and Buddhist singing bells? I told Brian to go away but knew if he didn't get what he wanted, he'd tell Mac the truth just to be lousy.

"I realized my son should hear the truth from me first. So I told him. Mac was furious! He stormed out of the house, drove away..." Freya still looked at the wall as she remembered. "Like an idiot, I had told him where Brian was, Mac was so angry, I was afraid he would go to the estate, and that they might fight! I decided I needed to be there. But I knew Brian and was afraid of him, so--stupidly--I took the axe with me for protection."

Oh, God. "Was Mac there?"

"I didn't see him, but Brian was there. I told him that Mac was his son. I begged Brian to be kind...He only laughed and moved toward me. I raised the axe..."

Grace didn't want to hear this but stayed silent as Freya continued, "Grabbing my arms, Brian ripped the axe away from me. I'm strong, but he was always a lot stronger. He tried to force me to kiss him. I bit his lip, the blood spurred out..."

Suddenly it was clear to Grace. "That's where they got his blood on your blouse! What did you do?"

She shrugged. "I turned and ran..."

"Then Brian was alive when you left... Do you think Mac came after you? That Mac and he fought?"

Freya pursed her lips tightly, and then spoke slowly, "If Mac is accused I'm going to admit I killed Brian."

"But you didn't."

Freya only looked at her.

"I don't think Mac killed him either," Grace explained. "He's a policeman, he's an ex-MP, he's been trained to control himself in an emotional confrontation..." Grace tried again. "Can you tell Mark the truth–what you just told me? And then wait to see if Mac is accused before you confess to a murder that neither of you committed?"

Chapter 16

Later, driving away from Alma's, something was bothering her, so Grace asked, "David, what do I smell like to you?" He frowned at the question, keeping his eyes on the road, but inhaling steadily before he finally said, "Something I find very sexy."

"Freya says I smell like laboratory disinfectants..."

He laughed at that. "That's part of you, and there is a very sweet, womanish smell too. Grace, you're never too excited about Broadway shows. Instead of driving all that way into the City, could we just have a quiet dinner at my house?"

Sleeping over at his house was not asked but implied, and after such a long time of not seeing him, Grace really liked the idea. She needed a bit of relaxation for herself. "Yes."

The front entrance to David's estate was just a small brass plate with 936 set in a hillside of mowed lawn, edged by banks of azalea bushes that kept their dark green leaves in the winter. They took a gravel road that led into the trees. The house itself was a long rambling affair of gray wood shingles. David drove past the front and swung around to the back, parking in a cobble-stoned courtyard, bordered by a five car garage, across the way from the horse barn and the hunting hound kennel.

They walked into the kitchen, a large, commercial-looking space with stainless steel everything. This encompassed the domain of Caine, David's butler/housekeeper. David just kept walking through to the low-ceiling hallway, part of the original pre-Revolutionary war farmhouse. He opened a door to one of the newer sections, the foyer dominated by a floor-length portrait of a commanding woman in a white dress, one of David's ancestors painted by John Singer Sargent.

She followed him into that comfortable, but oh so

masculine living room. Leather chairs and sofas with brass studs. Drum tables, Impressionist paintings, stone fireplace, and shelves and shelves of books. David reached for her jacket, as Caine in jeans and slippers walked in. "Sir, I thought you were going to the City?"

"No, we'll be eating in–I'll be sending out for a pizza."

The butler looked horrified. "I am certain we can do better than that! Dr. Farrington, would you like a stir-fry? Or a steak?"

"The quickest and easiest for you," she said.

With a slight bow, Caine left, and David loosened his tie. "I'll be right back, I've just got to make a phone call."

Too restless to sit down, Grace walked to the squared stone fireplace. Above it stretched a huge world map, yellowed with varnish and age. Multiple lines of airplane flights left from the British Isles, with the legend, "Travels of The Prince of Wales 1931". Grace followed dashed lines, dotted, and straight lines of royal progresses taken by the heir to the British Throne. Grace had read once that such a map hung in the Duke of Windsor's home, and that after the Duchess' death their personal effects were auctioned off in Paris. Was this a copy or had David's wealth obtained the original?

When David walked back alongside her, Grace asked, "He never became king, did he?"

"Actually, he reigned as Edward VIII from late January to early December 1936 before abdicating the throne to his brother."

"All for the love of a twice-divorced woman?"

"I've never really thought that the real reason." He studied the map above them saying, "They christened him Edward Albert Christian George Andrew Patrick David."

"Must have been hard to call him for dinner," commented Grace tartly.

"They called him David, too. He was born to rule over the British Empire that they said the sun never set on. He apparently had some fuzzy ideas of modernizing the monarchy and was frustrated in his attempts by the entrenched establishment, but World War I seemed to have really broken him."

"He served at the front?" asked Grace surprised.

"No, he and his brothers were not allowed to–if the enemy captured the heirs to the British throne...no, but he saw the results of trench warfare, all the dead, then the crippled men coming back from what he felt was a useless fight. That may have been his motivation to choose unacceptable women after unsuitable women as lady friends. Culminating with the twice married and divorced American, Mrs. Simpson. Rather than have her for queen, the government forced his abdication. A sad waste of what could have been--with a decent consort-- a valiant king." He walked toward the kitchen. "Would you like something to drink?"

"Wine."

"Sweet red?"

"Yes."

He nodded, left, and came back with two glasses that he put on the drum table as he sat opposite her. Caine followed, carrying a silver tray set with wheat crackers and cut cubes of cheddar cheese.

"Thank you," Grace said. As the butler left and she reached for her glass asking, "David, what do you know of the Kincaids?"

He lifted a contemptuous eyebrow. "Other than they've made politics the family cash cow for generations?"

"One of them was a senator, and now Aldon's a congressman." She sipped some of her wine. "That's a business?"

"That doesn't include the Kincaid lawyers, who find their business enhanced by their relationships with their cousins in office, or the directorships offered to close family members."

"Charlotte is on a number of boards because..."

"Well, she's a shrewd businesswoman, but her rise definitely started with her husband in state politics, and was immensely helped by his uncle the senator's circle of friends."

"They were all corrupt?" Grace couldn't believe it.

David shifted uneasily. "Corruption? Not the best of terms, Grace. Politics is the art of finding allies, forming coalitions, and negotiating consensuses. There is a fine line between baldly asking for a bribe or simply introducing an exceptionally talented businesswoman to the CEO of a company who could use her expertise."

"Then you'll vote for Aldon?"

"No." He seemed surprised at that. "Aldon Kincaid hasn't any non-political experience in the real world, he doesn't seem to have inherited his mother's business instincts, and he has made no effort to reach out to people that know more than himself. He is apparently running on the family name and his boyish good looks–that only carries you so far." David stopped to take a drink and reconsider his statements before adding, "He's not running for my party, and I think his 'answers' to problems--if enacted into law--will actually make things worse for the people he claims to be helping."

"You support Republicans then?"

"Conservative Republicans, yes."

"Your late wife voted Republican too?"

"Sylvia? Oh no, she was a lifelong, rabid Democrat..." Smiling in remembrance, he observed, "We used to have raging arguments over party stances. And the bets we had on election outcomes..." His eyes softened with obviously a pleasant memory.

That Grace couldn't understand. "With both of you sharing the same pool of money what fun was it to bet?"

"We didn't bet cash." She realized he was flushing

with a bit of excitement at the memory. "We'd pick a close race, and the loser would have to...pleasure the winner for at least a week at a time. Sylvia foolishly figured the 2008 election for the Democrats was such a lock-in she gave me very long odds, and after the surprise midterm turn around, she was into me for months of selfless pleasuring."

"You let her serve you for months without a return?"

"Oh, I'm sure a lot of what we did she got hers in."

Oh, lord, seeing him there, looking at the strong arms and fit legs Grace found herself murmuring out loud, "I'm sure she did."

"Maybe we should bet on something?" he asked with that impish grin.

Getting or being a love slave? Getting a bit warm from the talk and wine Grace wanted to steer the conversation to neutral grounds. "Were you always a Republican?"

"No, in college Sylvia and I used to demonstrate together. I think a great man once said 'If you're not a liberal when you're twenty-five, you have no heart. If you're not a conservative by the time you're thirty-five, you have no brains.'

"So you suggest I become a Conservative?"

He cocked his head to the side and studied her. "No, you are definitely not interested in monetary policy or so-called social engineering. I'd say you'd best line up with the Libertarians. "

She smiled back, and to herself, Grace made a mental note to look up the beliefs of the Libertarians.

But as he continued she found out, "The Libertarians believe the less the government interferes with the populous, the better."

"Sir," Caine was in the doorway. "Dinner is set out in the sunroom."

"Thank you," said David rising, holding out his arm to escort Grace.

She rather liked that old-fashioned gesture that let her feel the warmth of his arm.

The glass windowed sunroom had been added probably within the last decade. White wicker chairs with green cushions and matching glass-topped tables, flanked by tall green plants, and white wainscoting. Now the table held two place settings on sap green placemats, and a wok with a shrimp stir fry on a bamboo mat. Grace should have brought her drink with her, she was about to get up and get it when David said to the butler, "Sylvia left her drink in the other room. Could you get it for her?"

Caine's eyes shot from him to Grace, then quietly fetched the drink. Sylvia was the name of David's late wife, and this wasn't the first time David had made that mistake. Well, if you're married to a woman for twenty-one years and raise three children, it becomes second nature to call out to her–still, maybe it wasn't just her holding off...maybe David himself wasn't ready to marry again?

Her host waited for her to take a plate first. Noting the excellent stir fry had huge shrimp, noodles, fresh asparagus, water chestnuts, and sweet peppers, Grace sat eating quietly, as she considered marrying David, with a ready-made family of a daughter and twin sons. Would that wash away the regret of not having her own children?

After eating, Caine cleared the table as they sat back in David's comfortable living room, with him taking business calls, while Grace commandeered his laptop, taking the thumb drive off her keychain to bring up her data. One of the things Grace most liked about David was how comfortable she felt working around him.

Finally, they turned a movie on and just watched and talked. Grace always wondered what she should say on a date–the few awkward times she went out, she tried to plan topics. But with David, the talk just flowed: horses, antiques, the British Empire, the latest DNA discoveries, Oyster River.

What they didn't discuss was the murder charge hanging over Freya. Grace had already decided she would be spending the night before David asked, "Do you want me to drive you back to your condo? Or won't you think about staying the night, because as the song goes *'Baby, it's cold outside'*?"

Actually, in late March, it wasn't all that cold, but Grace only said, "Do you mind if I bring your laptop upstairs to your bedroom?"

"Not if you take me along with it," he said.

While much of the house remained with its colonial roots of low ceilings, slate floors and heavy chestnut beams, David's bedroom suite upstairs resided in a 1940's wing that must have been extensively remodeled in the last ten years. His door opened to a short hallway. To the right she could see his small home office; there was a closed door area opposite it. The wife's dressing room? Grace's office-to-be? Again another closed door to the left and an open one to the right displaying a man's huge walk-in closet, with its cherry trimmed shelves, drawers, bins, racks and shoe slides.

Now she followed him into a large, softly lighted room of beige carpets and tan comforter—obviously 'done' by an expert decorator, but a man's room, from the king-sized, dual sleep number bed to the wall of the video screen, and the chestnut brown circular couch seating near the bay window. From being here before, Grace knew Caine would have that little bag of toiletries David had told her to leave left out on the bathroom counter, rather like the service in some high-class hotel. As usual Grace set his laptop on the end table by her side of the bed as David hit the remote to put his news program on t-v.

"Do you mind if I shower first?" Grace asked.

"Unless you want to do it with me?"

In the past they'd had some fun with lathering each other up under that rainstorm shower-head, but not tonight. Grace just wanted to clean up and crawl into bed and rest a bit, and then see what might happen. "Some other time, I'm really tired tonight."

As he moved near her, David nodded as he stared back to something on his television screen news program, grumbling, "Will those idiots never learn?"

On the couch before the bathroom door, Grace saw two terrycloth bathrobes laid over the chair–his brown and a new sea green, fluffy one which Grace picked up and decided to tease a little, "You keep a robe handy for all your lady friends?"

Raising an eyebrow, Davie reached out to embrace her saying, "Look at the pocket."

As he kissed the back of her neck, she did, and saw script in yellow satin embroidery spelling out 'Grace.' *Oh, God, this was getting too serious!*

David kissed the back of her neck again. "My daughter Madison is driving down from college and is expected here tomorrow. The boys will be down this weekend. I'd like you to meet them."

That seemed a little too much for Grace, who stepped away from him. "Uh...David. We don't have a commitment, and with your children, I don't want to pretend that we do."

"No commitment, but I'd like them to at least meet you. Well, they know I have friends, and both boys are studying science, so I believe they'd like to meet the eminent Dr. Farrington."

What were his intentions? "If you're showing me off like a champion beagle, that's fine, but I rather you didn't push our romantic relationship on your kids..."

He studied her with his head tilted to the side. "You are very right, dear, going slowly is sometimes a good strategy."

And Grace realized he'd turned her denial into a relationship that they were keeping quiet between them. That's not what she told him–why couldn't things just stay the way they were?

In the bathroom, the walls, floor, ceiling, and even the glass-booth shower glinted with metallic, ceramic and crystal tiles. This bathroom always reminded her of Aladdin's jeweled cave. Twin green-glass sinks were set on top of the granite counter; two closed-door toilet stalls with a bidet, and that two-or-more-person walk-in shower, with its choice of side jets, rain storm from above or the hot tub alongside. Caine had been busy, a set of plush sea green towels and her own toiletries bag with a toothbrush rested on the counter. After showering, Grace felt like a mermaid as she wrapped herself in that luxurious bathrobe. She came out and glancing at the t-v, she was pleasantly surprised to call out as she recognized, "*Charlie Chan in the...*"

"*Castle in the Dessert,*" he answered.

"I used to watch all the Charlie Chan's with my grandmother," Grace said, easily slipping into the bed beside him.

"When Sylvia's obstetrician announced she was carrying twins, I floated the idea of naming them Number One and Number Two son."

Grace laughed. "That must have gone over big."

His phone rang, and David looked at the narrow display, "Damn, I have to take this."

He lowered the t-v a bit but left it so she could still listen as he argued animatedly with someone in what Grace thought was British-accented Italian.

As Charlie investigated the Princess Borgia, Grace set up pillows so she could sit up on the bed, as she unhooked the thumb drive from her keychain. Plugged it into his laptop with the data that she always carried, Grace booted up. She'd need a new spreadsheet...there must be some litmus test she could construct to determine a pure Denisovan--if they ever get one--as opposed to a Neanderthal hybrid or a modern human mix. She wanted to devise a data filter that would winnow out the known sequences to reveal an ancient branch or branches of the human tree.

Grace mentally struggled with various methodologies as she stared at Charlie finding poisons and ducking armored assailants. After an hour or so, Charlie's murderer was found, and David's phone conversation finished, but Grace still juggled choices in her mind, searching for a 'Farrington Fusion.' Finally, a frustrated Grace closed the top of his laptop, saying, "I just can't get it," as she leaned back into the pillows.

He slid a warming body on the cool sheets next to her teasing, "Well if you want to get it, stop playing with that damned laptop..."

She teased back. "Are you saying if I have sex with you, I will get the answer to my Denisovan comparison study structure?"

"This Denisovan man, who may be what? Sixty-five million years old?" He ran a hand down her hip, as she shivered deliciously he whispered, "Give me a chance, and I think I can make you not care about him."

Laughing, Grace found herself moving into his lips.

* * *

She woke up with the answer. The alarm clock showed 3:20 in green lights. It took her a moment to realize where she was—David's bed. He slept warmly beside her. In her mind, she had the complete protocol for a new angle of study of the Denisovan remains, but she just needed to get it all down before her Farrington Fusion faded. If she got out of bed, David would wake up, but if she just typed quietly... Grace opened the laptop lid, slipped over on her stomach and brought up the screen she wished, trying to angle the light away.

David rolled over and said in a sleepy voice, "Oh, Grace, not again..."

"I'll take the laptop into the next room." She started to

slip out of bed.

His strong arm slipped over her hip. "No, just type away, I'm getting used to it."

Rolling back he turned his head away from the laptop's screen light and soon he breathed the steady, softness of sleep as Grace rechecked her theory on screen after screen. Finally finished, she noted the clock now showed 4:45, as she saved all her work to her thumb drive, then a tired Grace dismounted the drive, put it on the end the table, and closed his laptop. Snuggled back into the blankets against his warm, muscular back Grace smiled to herself; marriage was out of the question, but being here, smelling David, feeling his warmth, it all felt so right.

Chapter 17

The next morning on his way to New York David dropped her off at ORR. Grace showered and changed in her condo, then hurried down to her lab. Inger already sat at her desk as Grace walked in asking, "What is Nick working on?"

"He's doing further analysis of the Brazilian coffee leaf blight samples..."

"Today, I want you both to switch your focus to the suspected Denisovan sample. We're going to do a study, inclusive of any current material I have that might be Denisovan, then I want to cross reference with benchmark samples taken around the world. You'll set that up. I've laid out the parameters on this...." Inger looked up as Grace dipped into her jacket pocket and then realized her thumb drive wasn't there. Shit. No, she didn't put it in her handbag. Did she leave it on her condo's bed table?

No, last night she was in David's bedroom. He'd already left for New York, but the butler would probably still be there. "I'll be back." Grace headed out. What a waste of time, driving to his estate. Why had she forgotten? Because of her worry over Freya and Mac? Or because of David, his strong arms, his offer of a dream lab and luxurious loving life in Greece?

There were two cars already parked in the cobble-stoned courtyard, a neat blue convertible, and a bronze Land Rover. From the Land Rover Grace saw Caine carrying in two bags of groceries.

"Can I help you?" Grace asked.

He looked surprised at that. "No, I'll get it all. Mr. Gardiner isn't expected to be back until this evening."

"I left my thumb drive...probably in the bedroom."

Frowning a bit, he looked to the blue convertible with its white top up, parked in front of the stables. "It looks like Miss Madison is in the house..."

"David's daughter? I don't really want an introduction right now, I just need to run in and pick up my drive."

"Of course." At the door, Caine hit a security code, and it unlocked. They walked into the kitchen with its blue slate flooring, heavy timbers and Colonial brick fireplace tall enough for you to walk in. A wide room, probably once all of the original farmhouse footprint, now set up as a commercial-like kitchen with double, seven-foot-tall refrigerator and freezer set alongside each other, near the double oversized ovens, microwave, Cuisinart pro, and just about every cooking appliance imaginable. Even the central work island had plumbed water and a small sink. This was a kitchen that an expert like Freya should be cooking in. As they walked through, she heard the dishwasher humming and smelled freshly baked bread.

The butler led her through to a narrow, steep back staircase and then upstairs. This place had been added onto over decades, and it was a bit confusing. Caine left her alone when she came out in what looked like a central hall. Getting her bearings, Grace hurried into David's room. His male aroma enveloped her. At that moment she seriously considered marrying him and working in that lab on his Greek Island. Just for a second, she had a happy dream of having her work, a husband, and a family. Then reality returned, in this life, she only had time for one irrepressible obsession! The bed looked to have been professionally made, and the laptop was gone, but she could see the thumb drive still sitting on the end table. Grace picked it up and was slipping it into her jacket pocket as she heard, "What are you doing?"

Grace looked around, and in the doorway a young, blonde woman stared at her as she repeated, "What are *you* doing in my father's bedroom?"

"Ah...." Grace looked around. "You're Madison, aren't you?"

"Who are you?" came the unfriendly demand.

Grace hesitated, then answered truthfully, "Grace Farrington."

That obviously meant nothing to the young blonde with her arms crossed in front of her, but from behind her the butler, Caine, had joined them, now saying firmly, "Grace, if you're finished with the bedroom, you can leave now."

Taking that as her exit line, Grace started to walk past the girl.

"No!" Madison protested. "She picked up something from the end table and put it into her pocket."

"Yes," Caine explained for her. "Grace left some keys here for the next place she's working on. She had to come back for them." Feeling like a sneak thief, Grace just kept walking out as Caine soothed the girl, "Grace is very trustworthy."

* * *

The 'trustworthy' Grace had barely settled back at her laboratory desk and was inserting that drive in the laptop when a slender, red-headed woman walked in. She did recognize Samantha, the reporter, and Mac's girlfriend, but today Sam walked in more hesitatingly than usual, with her shoulders hunched, her eyes cast down, and even her copper red hair looked dull and stringy.

When she walked up to Grace's desk, Sam said, "My editor insisted I interview you."

The woman looked absolutely like a zombie, as if her spirit had left her body. In the past, they'd had a difficult relationship when Grace strongly objected to an article Sam had written about her–but even knowing Grace probably wouldn't do another interview, the reporter didn't come across like the beaten loser Grace now saw before her. When Sam didn't say any more, Grace prompted "Interview me on what?"

"You were at Charlotte Kincaid's 'power tea.' My editor wants your take on Aldon's science expertise for a series I'm supposed to be writing on him." The way she spoke, Sam sounded like that was the last thing in the world she wanted to do.

God, Grace only wanted to work on that Denisovan methodology, but instead this woman was before her looking so pounded down by life. "Why don't we both go over and get some tea." Grace stood up and walked across the room to the coffee machine that was only used to make endless pots of hot water. She pulled out a small carton of half and half from the office mini-fridge and sniffed to see if it was okay. Like a whipped puppy, Sam trailed after her, saying nothing as Grace poured water, and then handed her a hot cup. "Take your choice from our tea box. It's heavy on healthy camomile, because nobody wants to drink it."

At that Sam smiled, showing a glimpse of her usual outgoing disposition, but Grace had to hand her a tea bag before she filled her own cup. "Sit over here," Grace ordered. When they both sat down, Grace stirred the heat off her mint tea with a mixing stick and said, "I don't have time to waste, what's the matter?"

The reporter only looked down at her paper cup.

Grace tried again. "Mac mentioned you, and he were having problems?"

"It's not Mac!" she immediately defended, then looked broken again. "I just can't face him. I'm going to make some changes, maybe reporting isn't what I should be doing..."

With Sam's dedication to being a journalist, that statement was the equivalent of Grace giving up on DNA research. "What happened?"

There was silence for a long time, then Sam squared her shoulders and started, "My assignment was to write a series of profiles on Congressman Aldon Kincaid. His campaign manager arranged it. It's supposed to be an in-depth study: his values, his career, his shining plans for the country..." Her lower lip quivered. "I've been meeting with Aldon at his house, then for informal lunches..."

Grace waited as Sam took a drink of her tea, then she asked, "His politics mirror your own?"

That Sam could be positive on. "He's a progressive. He wants to improve the country–the world."

Grace drank some of her own mint tea and waited.

Finally, Sam started again. "The first article was published. Aldon said he was impressed with my writing, with my organizational abilities. He talked about my becoming his senatorial campaign spokesperson...the salary's fantastic! Mac and I,...well, we've talked about what kind of house we'd like to buy if we stayed together..."

Sam started to tear up, and Grace knew from her own experiences what was coming, but Grace only said, "I think you should talk to Mac about this..."

"No! Mac would kill him! No–I don't want anyone to know!" Almost pleading, Sam looked into Grace's eyes. "Aldon wanted us to talk privately. He keeps a motel suite, for business meetings. I went there, he said wanted to get my ideas on the campaign strategy with women voters..." Sam stopped talking.

Grace finished for her, "You went there for business purposes, and he wanted something else?"

"How could I be such a fool?" Tears glistened in Sam's eyes. "How could I explain to Mac how stupid I was..."

"You weren't stupid!" Grace found herself almost shouting in anger. "You left yourself wide open because you trusted Aldon--it happens! Often men in a position of power think they can have anything they want, and they're very adept at gaining your trust. Making you feel like it was all your fault for coming on to them."

Sad-eyed Sam looked into the distance. "Aldon asked me if I'd been having fantasies about him, the way he'd been having fantasies about me?"

Grace hated to ask, "Did he rape you?"

"He tried to force me into the bedroom," Unconsciously, she rubbed her sleeve, which covered an arm Grace figured was probably badly bruised. "I kicked him--hard--we struggled...and he looked so hurt. Then when I was escaping, he warned me that if I said anything, he'd see I never worked as a reporter again."

With the Kincaid empire that wasn't an idle threat. "Maybe you should drop this project?"

"No–no, I can't. I've just got to be professional, stay away from Aldon, and get the job done."

"And what about the next woman he gets up there to '*talk about a job*'?"

Now Samantha was openly crying, "I don't want my editor to know. I don't want Mac to know! Maybe I gave Aldon the wrong impression..."

"No, you didn't! I know things you can't put in print about Aldon Kincaid that confirms he hunts any woman he can."

Sam stopped to get control and then said quietly, "Grace, I need my job. I like my work. I don't know what else I would do."

Grace stopped to think about it before she said, "Finish your profile, and then refuse any more assignments that have anything to do with him."

Miserably, Sam stared back at Grace saying, "You think I'm a coward."

The current conventional wisdom dictated you must 'out' the guy to protect any future victims, no matter what it does to your reputation. Grace remembered back to a similar situation early in her career, and the disciplinary board that believed 'his' story over the truth. That man lied, and because Dr. Charles Marshall was in a position of authority, he nearly ended Grace's career. The only thing that saved her was Eric Larsen demanding that Oyster River give her a position...a second chance. "No. I think you are doing the best you can for yourself in a bad situation. You don't have to tell Mac, but don't cut him out. Just go and tell him that life is being lousy to you, you don't want to talk about it, but you need a hug."

"He won't understand..."

"He's Freya's son, he'll understand! And if you are clear that you really don't want to talk about it, he won't ask questions."

Wiping her cheek with the back of her hand, Sam stood up. "You're right. I'm going to call him now. And as for that 'power tea,' I'm going to write about fanatical sycophants, and Aldon condescending to shake hands with his worshiping, clueless followers."

"That should get you off the liberal political beat..." agreed Grace.

Sam smiled, and threw the paper cup into the trash can, and left Grace to her possible Denisovan bones. For Grace, people who died eighty thousand years ago were a lot easier to deal with.

* * *

When David had returned from the City, a luncheon had already been laid out on the sunroom table. He was delighted to see his twin sons had joined Madison. Again, David wished Grace was here, but she was probably right, they should be more stable in their plans before he tried to meld them into a family.

Caine carried a platter of cold cuts to the table. As usual, the boys were always hungry. In college and taller than their father now, but with the same sandy hair, and sun freckled skin, David found himself smiling with pride at both of them. He was proud of all his children. The older Madison had grown into a fine looking woman, but a little scatterbrained for David's taste, as she flitted from major to major, deciding on a degree in business one day, and a degree in education the next. Hopefully, she'd marry a man who could manage her share of the family businesses successfully.

Now his daughter looked up at him with a frown on her face. "I saw that woman pick up something of yours and put it in her pocket."

Reaching for a sesame seed roll, her father wasn't paying any attention.

"Dad," Madison continued, "Don't you care?"

Raising a quizzical eyebrow David asked, "About what?"

"The woman who stole something from you," Madison finished. "One of the cleaning crew in your bedroom."

Now frowning, her father focused totally on the conversation. "The cleaning crew is here on Mondays and Caine supervises them." As the butler returned with a pitcher of iced tea, David looked up. "Was there someone working here today?"

"Grace dropped by, sir, she may have left something-- her keys I believe," answered the discreet butler.

"Oh," said David, knowing he was flushing a bit.

With devilish eyes Jessie exchanged a sly look with his brother, and sounding oh so innocent he said, "Yes, Grace. Madison saw her in your bedroom picking up something she might have dropped on the bed's end table?"

David realized it was the damned thumb drive. He'd seen it on the end table, then forgot to remind Grace about it.

With laughter on his lips, Joshua kept at it. "What are you always telling us, Dad? Keep a helmet on that soldier, or you'll be paying for twenty-one years?"

As their father flushed deeper, his other son chimed in, "Yeah, we don't want our inheritance quartered..."

David glared at the both of his sons, but a confused Madison finally got it. "She wasn't cleaning your bedroom?

She was in it? With you?" Agitated, his daughter started to rise. "What about Mother?"

There was dead silence. Then her brother Josh answered in a sad voice, "Mom's dead, and has been for some time." He looked from his sister to his father. "But, Dad, have you fully considered the financial ramifications if you remarry?"

Raising an eyebrow in contempt his father stared at him. "We're referring to the disposition of *my* money, I believe? Yes, it is always prudent to consider financial ramifications of any major change, but only if you first assess the value to you of your non-negotiable assets. In your life, Joshua, you will often find non-negotiable people have a greater value to you in the long run."

Jessie also answered, "Madison, Mom wouldn't have wanted Dad to be alone the rest of his life. We should all be happy for them."

A stricken Madison looked from one brother to the other, starting to cry. "You can't let him do this!"

"Grace..." her father started awkwardly, "is a friend. A very important person in my life right now..."

"You're marrying her?" Madison looked horrified.

"We've talked about it–but nothing has been decided."

"You can't marry her! You can't forget about Mother! You can't do that to us!" Madison threw down her napkin, turned, and ran out of the room.

Pained, David started to rise, but Caine, who was beginning to clear the table spoke first, "Sir, give her some time to get used to the idea."

"Yeah," said Josh in a disgusted voice, "Madison always thinks the world revolves around her. Leave her alone."

His brother Jessie then spoke softly, "But when she really thinks about you marrying again, she'll understand that's what Mom would have wanted. Your happiness is what we all want."

His father wasn't quite as sure.

Chapter 18

Getting work done, but Grace's mind kept digging at Freya's problems. She pulled up her murder spreadsheet. Should she keep it titled the 'Murder of Brian Amundsen' or make it the 'Murder of Lars Anderson, or Loki', or any of Freya's ex-lover's other probable names? Grace left it the murder of Brian Amundsen. Yes, truly Brian/Lars was a definite Loki.

Alright, Grace scanned the sheet. She would have to increase Mac's scores. Yes, she already had him in the area and strong enough, but before she had 0 % for the motive. A man in his twenties finding out his father was not dead, but very much alive and had abandoned himself and his mother, that could be a strong motivation for a fight, 35 %, but hitting Brian from behind with a fatal weapon? No, and as an MP and policeman Mac had been trained to control his emotions and strength. No, she'd give him a - 20 for probability.

But more possibilities were evolving–the Kincaid family, especially Aldon Kincaid. They were all ambitious, politically minded and Aldon had the Alpha A proclivity to fool around.

Although Aldon claimed he hadn't returned home until late that night, did he really have an alibi? That might be checked. And Brian attempted to blackmail Freya, guessing she had never told her son about his father. According to Freya, Brian had a long history of ferreting out secrets and turning them into personal financial rewards. Although the press carefully kept it out of the papers, Aldon's screwing around could have attracted Brian's attention.

Grace tried to construct a scenario in her mind: Freya went to the boathouse, and confronted Brian, who took her axe away; attacked her; Freya escaped. The killer arrived, maybe even Unknown Blackmail Victim, who was sick of being ripped off? Or Aldon returned early to make a hush money payment, went to the boathouse, and seeing the axe, the politician waited until Brian turned his back, and then struck from behind. Aldon wouldn't have to worry about wiping fingerprints--with the exception of the axe--because it was his boathouse. All Aldon had to do was take care to arrive back at the main house a lot later to give him some sort of alibi. Were there alternate accesses to the boathouse not covered by the cameras? From the water, of course. But there might be hidden lanes or pathways from the back or side that an owner would have known about–Grace would have to check. Grace Googled a satellite map of the Kincaid Estate, but the boathouse area was covered by treetops; she would have to check on the ground.

Returning to her spreadsheet, she put in a line for Unknown Blackmail Victim and then one for Aldon Kincaid. Aldon's line showed Motive: 50 %, Means: 20 %, Pro: it could have been unplanned, a sudden overwhelming of fury. Aldon couldn't have known the weapon would be there, but maybe he paid off, and Brian demanded more money? Brian turned his back, Aldon saw Freya's axe lying there, used it?

Motivation seemed to hinge on any blackmail material that Brian had. He must have had hard copies: photographs; birth certificates; pay off receipts? Did Sierra have that now? Or was it still in the boathouse? Grace needed to revisit that boathouse apartment. She needed an excuse to get on Kincaid property, but not when there were a lot of people about. At lunch, she'd speak to Gail and get her to type up some sort of paperwork for Aldon to sign regarding his upcoming speech at the ORR fundraiser. Yes, then she'd call Maura, ask to come over with the papers, then get Maura outside so they could *'talk.'* Grace would tell Gail what papers she needed at lunch, but not now-now Grace had her real work to finish. She pulled up the Brazil results. What could she tell Señor Cardozo that might save his coffee crop?

* * *

Finally, Grace and Inger could unsuit from the clean room in the airlock, and then head into the front lab room. Grace settled before her computer while Inger picked up the phone messages. One obviously puzzled her as she looked up and said, "A 'Maura' wants to treat you to lunch at two thirty in Neptune's Cave. She says it's very important, and she doesn't want to talk in your lab...she didn't leave a return number?"

"I know who she is." Mildly resented the fact that the Kincaids expected everyone to drop everything to come at their beck and call Grace glanced up at the clock...one forty. She could lie and say she never got the message, or better yet, say she did get the message, but couldn't take the time off from her work. But somehow that sad woman, desperately trying to prove she was descended from a Romanov Grand Duchess to be equal to her husband's 'elevated' family got to her. Poor Maura, valiantly trying to carry on the legacy of two noble families, both of doubtful morals, all the while, her bum husband chased every woman he could get his slimy hands on.

But it was about time Grace ate lunch anyway. "I'll be back in an hour or so," she told Inger. Then she walked back to her condo to pick up her car and drive around the harbor end, to head for Oyster River. Neptune's Cave was on the way into town. The restaurant and parking lot abutted on the water, with rows of docks going down to Neptune's marina. In the summer there would be a little clam shack window open on the side selling hot dogs, fried clams, lobster rolls, and hamburgers that you could eat on the picnic tables outside. Now the water looked gray, and the wind chilled as she walked past the giant statue of a seaweed-bearded Neptune, with his storm stirring trident, that guarded the main bar and restaurant portion.

Inside, the ceiling had been sculpted into uneven stalactites and painted as an undersea grotto. The table tops were poured clear resin with sand, starfishes, doubloons, and other 'seascapes' underneath and there were good views from the windows--nice–, but Grace was not going to be sitting here waiting the whole day. Not seeing Maura in the dining room or the bar, Grace just picked a table by the windows overlooking the harbor and ordered the fried scallop platter. The waitress brought over a basket of cheddar biscuits, just as a harried Maura rushed over, carrying a bunch of fancy shopping bags from the Blue Peacock dress shop.

"Grace...it was so kind of you to come." She looked at the waitress. "Whatever Grace is having, bring one for me too." Maura looked about to see no one was at the tables near them, then she waited until the waitress walked away before she breathlessly said, "I brought the bags so I can show you my shopping–like we're just sitting here being friends."

Grace couldn't believe this. "In case your husband's campaign manager sees us?"

Maura ignored the disapproval in Grace's voice. "You tested my DNA?"

"Yours, yes, Dagmar's not done," said Grace."So I can't complete the comparisons yet."

"Did you see anything wrong?" she asked anxiously.

"Wrong?"

"Aldon and I have no children. We've been trying, but I've had three miscarriages..."

"I'm sorry. Did the doctors tell you what the problem was?"

"They didn't know. ..only that I'm over thirty and I started late."

"A few women have been known to have perfectly normal pregnancies in their forties and fifties. I'll do a superficial look at your DNA again, but I didn't see a Trisomy 18 or anything that stands out as a possible problem, but a real forensic comparison of yours and your husband's DNA might be a good idea. I can refer you to an excellent fertility clinic that specializes in just that?"

"There is nothing wrong with Aldon," Maura quickly reassured her.

"Creating a child is a fifty-fifty proposition," pointed out Grace.

"The doctors just told me to be patient, there seems to be nothing wrong."

"If you have another loss, I think you should be more proactive. Insist that an autopsy plus DNA profile is done on the fetus to determine a possible reason for the miscarriage. And if you wish, we could take a swab of your husband's DNA, and I can look at it to see if there is any incompatibility or outstanding problem. Is he over forty yet?"

"There can't be anything wrong with Aldon. It must be me, and the fertility specialist seems to think everything will be okay. He just tells me to relax...I am trying to produce the Kincaid heir, and they say 'just relax.'"

The waitress carried back with another unsweetened ice tea with lemon and then finally two platters of scallops with fries and coleslaw. Maura didn't look thrilled at Grace's choice. "I would've chosen broiled—fewer calories."

Grace just smiled and ate hers as Maura kept moving things around her plate, obviously trying to get up the nerve to say something. Finally, she started, "Being a Kincaid is very lonely. I mean, my mother-in-law says we must hold ourselves above the herd. We must be something to look up to."

Grace raised an eyebrow wondering if the 'herd' appreciated the sacrifice, but she only said, "That must be difficult at times."

The woman looked so forlorn like she didn't have a friend in the world and could never find one, but Maura was saying, "It impressed my mother-in-law that I'd been to see you."

"You told her?"

"No, Harry did." She shrugged, explaining, "We were

all having dinner, and he said he'd seen me go into your lab and wondered why."

Grace stopped eating. "It doesn't bother you that your husband's campaign manager is keeping tabs on your whereabouts, and reporting them to your mother-in-law?"

Maura looked surprised that Grace should question it. "Harry's always after all of us, he wants the Kincaid image to be pristine."

"So how did you explain to your mother-in-law about seeing me?"

She brightened with pride at that. "Charlotte knows I'm a chairperson for the Horseback Rides for Handicapped Children. I said that I'd thought you might be a draw at one of our fundraising dinners. My mother-in-law actually said that I showed initiative!"

Maura sounded so pathetically proud that she'd done something right, Grace figured that didn't happen too often in the Kincaid household. "Try the cole slaw, they make it here with their own recipe," was all Grace could think to say.

"Yes." She got the point and looked at her plate, and then went on, very business-like. "By the way, the awards dinner is April fifth at seven thirty, at the Captain's Mansion, and you'll need to give a twenty-minute acceptance speech. Don't go over that, please. We'll give you dinner and an award, of course."

Since Grace did nothing with horses or handicapped children, she could only ask, "For what?"

That seemed to stop Maura, but only for a second. "For your consistent interest in the betterment of humanity."

As Kurt would say, 'Aaup.'

Maura continued, "I came up with the idea of taking a discarded horseshoe and painting it gold and nailing it on a stained board–saves a mint on buying awards... which means more money for the kids." This time she at least stabbed a fried scallop. "But my mother-in-law also approved of me being friends with you."

"That's kind of her." Maura seemed to have missed the sarcasm. Grace had finished mostly everything on her plate and wanted to get this meeting over with so she asked, "Was there anything else?"

Again Maura hesitated like it hurt to get this out, but finally forced herself to say, "Yes, I'm being blackmailed."

"What?'

"That bitch, Sierra, the one that was living in the boathouse with Brian. She's still on our property."

"Why is she still on the property?"

"I want her out of the compound. She and Brian were trouble from day one, but for a time the police had closed the boathouse and the apartment over it as a crime scene. They've opened it again, but Sierra says she won't go back, so Aldon felt sorry for her, and is letting her stay in the second chauffeur's apartment over the garage."

Of course, with Sierra being such a hot-looking babe, Aldon would keep her in an apartment nearby. "What is she blackmailing you for? Your husband killing..." Grace started to say 'Lars' then corrected it to, "Brian?"

"No! He wasn't here." Again Maura hesitated--Grace had only been her best friend for a week, but finally everything poured out, "A campaign worker of Aldon's, Brittany Hellas, my husband flirts with everybody--really harmlessly--but this twenty-year-old girl apparently misunderstood, got depressed, and mixed some sleeping pills in her rum, and killed herself. Such a waste." Here Maura did look pained at the loss of a young life, but then those blue eyes hardened, and her voice took on a rough tone, "That bitch Sierra is threatening to go to the press with some story about being Brittany's best friend, and being able to give details about a juicy affair with Aldon that caused her suicide."

"Did the dead girl leave a suicide note mentioning

your husband?"

"I don't think she left one."

This must have been the campaign worker Freya and Samantha argued over. "So what if your husband just denies Sierra's story?"

Again the hesitation, then, "Brittany may have been pregnant. The police asked questions. They asked if Aldon and Brittany had an affair?"

"Did they?"

Maura looked down at her plate, maybe feeling ashamed that she still loved her husband, no matter what he did. "The Kincaids are Alpha males, known to go after money, fame, power... and women. That's what he was born to, it's in his DNA, you understand that?"

Well, everybody made their own heavens and hells in this life Grace thought, but she only said, "I wouldn't pay a blackmailer unless you intend to do that the rest of your life..."

"The police...could they test a fetus and determine who the father was?"

"Yes, if they had a sample of the father's DNA to compare with. Have the police asked your husband to give them a swab?"

"No, but could they take it from something he held or dropped?"

Grace once picked up murder solving DNA from a snot covered Kleenex discarded in a wastepaper basket, but she only said, "Yes, they can do that, and they sometimes do in the preliminary stages of building a case, but when it comes to a serious accusation they are going to have to respect the chain of evidence and make an official request for a swab. If your husband refuses, they will go to a judge to try and force him."

"Will the judge allow that?"

"Depends on the judge and the strength of their other

evidence."

"Then I should..."

Grace cut her off. "How long ago was this suicide?"

"Five months ago."

That changed things a bit, so Grace asked, "And the police questioned you and Aldon how many times?"

"Once."

"So you've heard nothing since then?" Grace forked her last fried scallop.

"From the police, yes."

"Just because a pregnant women suicides, the police don't normally try to identify the male who fathered her child. Generally, the police will only try to get DNA of a man if it was, say, a rape-murder. Did the police tell you how they knew of the affair?"

Maura shrugged her shoulders as she chose the next scallop on her plate. "Brittany worked on the campaign and Aldon's known to be with other women." She looked up saying defensively, "All the Kincaid men are known for that."

Grace wanted to ask Maura if the Kincaid name was really worth enough to put up with that, and then she reflected her own relationships were not what she was raised to view as natural and proper. "Well, presumably Aldon hasn't killed any of those other women?"

"Of, course. And Brittany suicided..." Maura supplied.

"With sleeping pills in rum. That might have been an easier way to do it for a woman distraught, or somebody might have known she'd drink alone, and dissolves the pills in her bottle?"

Maura looked horrified. "Are you talking about murder? Aldon wouldn't have–he couldn't! And that weekend we went away for another 'honeymoon'–the stick test said I was fertile, but it didn't take."

That hypothetical doctored rum bottle might have been sitting there for awhile, but Grace only asked, "How about his good friend, the nosey, protective campaign manager?"

"No, Harry doesn't do violent things--that's what he had people like Brian for. There was this guy following us all around with a sign saying '*Aldon Kincaid Sold Us Out!*' He was passing out brochures making my husband's business dealings look like corrupt payoffs..."

"What happened to him?" asked Grace.

"I heard Harry bragging about it to Aldon. He had Brian dress up in a 'save the ecology' hoody and dark sunglasses, then Brian showed up at a demonstration, got the guy in the parking lot, and beat the hell of him."

That did shock Grace, but she tried not to show it. "Police question you about this?"

"No. And I never saw that crazy guy again. But now Brian's gone..."

And Freya stands accused of murdering him. "So who will Harry get to do his dirty work now?"

That stopped Maura for a moment, then she said, "I can't see Harry murdering a disturbed girl in love–that would be more like Charlotte."

"Charlotte?"

"My mother-in-law." Maura made a dismissive gesture with her hand. "I'm just joking, but since his birth, Charlotte has been so focused on seeing Aldon as president. She had his first baby bib embroidered with 'Hail to the Chief.'"

"Why is Sierra trying to blackmail you about Brittany–why not go directly to your husband?"

"I don't know."

"Did you ask Aldon if Sierra's trying to blackmail him too?"

Maura looked down again. "I couldn't. I'm not supposed to know about the other women."

"Fine. My I guess is Sierra is just trying to see who

she can scare enough to get money out of. But once you pay her, Sierra will know she's hit the motherlode and will be back forever." Maura nodded as Grace continued, "I would suggest you find a criminal attorney and speak confidentially with him, and if 'the family' asks why you are visiting a lawyer's office, just say you're asking some questions on alimony for 'a friend.'"

"If I have to prove that, you'll be my friend I'm asking for?" Maura asked.

Grace had a distinct feeling that Maura less wanted an alibier, than she wanted to feel someone had her back. "Yes, I'll be happy to say I sent you to speak to a lawyer for me."

All radiant smiles, Maura stood up. "Thank you so much! Let me know the minute you have matched Dagmar's DNA. And don't forget the April awards dinner!" With a airy wave, Maura grabbed up her shopping bags and left, forgetting her bill, and that she had said she wanted to treat Grace, which meant Grace got to pay for both lunches.

Since the town was just half a mile down the road from the Neptune, Grace decided to do a fast drop into Abe's bookstore. Inside that basement store, Abe had the heat up cozy and although he had about five people browsing and one standing at his counter waiting to buy, he paid no notice, as he sat on his couch reading a picture book on Houdini and contemporary magicians.

Grace moved and stood in front of him. No sign of life. "Abe?" She started softly, then raised her voice a bit, "Abe,..." Finally, he surfaced with blank eyes blinking behind thick-lensed glasses. "Abe, you have a customer."

He turned his head to the counter. "Ya ready?" Looking hopeful that the guy might decide to look around a bit more...

But customer only nodded his head, so Abe had to

reluctantly put down his book, and slowly get up, looking very put upon to ring up a customer and sell a book. Knowing she couldn't do anything else, Grace walked to the two urns percolating on another table and poured herself hot water over a Greenleaf teabag in a paper cup. Then she headed to sit on the non-matching, over-stuffed couch at right angles to Abe's spot, quickly looking through the stack of picture books on the cigarette-scarred coffee table to find a 1950's paean to camping.

She starting browsing through happy families in the wilderness: with the lake behind them, Dad and boy carried fishing rods and a string of rainbow trout to Mom and the girl, who were playing with the family puppy, in front of a friendly fire and perfectly level tent. Neat, exceptional world in the photos, but Grace had camped out not too long ago on a specimen collection expedition in the Peruvian Andes, confirming Grace's firm belief that human civilization's highest achievement was the invention of the flush toilet, followed closely by central heating, and air conditioning.

Still, the pictures of happy families gamboling in fold-top campers and RV's looked appealing. Yeah, sometimes she did wonder what it would be like to have a little daughter or son of her own. Freya raised Mac without a husband, and still followed her dreams, but Freya fountained endless love and made Mac pretty much the focus of her life. No, Grace couldn't do that--motherhood was out. Grace's research would always come first. Marriage might be possible–if her husband agreed to her priorities. Could David do that? Even Kurt?

Abe settled back near her with a fresh mug of coffee, which he set beside his original mug of coffee as he opened up his book again. She had to act fast, the window of his attention span was rapidly closing. "Abe?"

He looked up from his book, a little irritated. "How's Freya?"

"Out of jail, doing good, but you were looking into the Kincaids for me?"

"Kincaids?" He asked, sounding confused. She could almost feel that book pulling his mind from her.

Grace prompted again, "Political family with a home near here. The girlfriend who suicided."

"Aaup. That suspicious house fire."

"Fire?" Grace asked. "No. The campaign worker suicided with rum and pills."

Now she had his attention as he stared out over the bookcases that marched to the door and windows overlooking the sidewalk. "The pills were Brittany Hellas. The maid killed in the fire was Marylou, no, Marylinn Gleffner."

Grace sat there shocked. Another Aldon Kincaid girlfriend dead? "When the Kincaid house burned, somebody died?"

"Aaup. The Kincaid house burned down on some sort of holiday, Fourth of July I think, with Aldon captaining his boat in a sailing regatta in the harbor. It was a command performance with all the family and servants down cheering him on at the yacht club beach. Charlotte paid to have a clambake catered for the entire lot of 'em. Course the winds came up strong..."

"Abe, what happened to Marylinn?"

"Nobody supposed to be on the estate--all of them was ordered down to the beach. But the wife–Maura-- was pregnant, got feeling sick, and drove home, saw smoke and called the fire department. Course it was too late at that point, and the house burned down to the ground. Got said it might have been an electrical fire that started by itself, that place had some terrible old wiring from the early 1900s..."

"Then it was an accident?" Grace noted he didn't look too certain.

He halted there and looked back out to the display windows. "With the Kincaids so prominent, nobody much got questioned hard. The fire department put it down to bad wiring, but then when they were cleaning out the wreckage, they found a body in the basement. Woman's body. A young housemaid, who everyone figured just left without giving notice."

"That reopened the fire investigation?"

"Never was much of an investigation to start with, and nobody wanted to offend the Kincaids–certainly not our Fire Chief or Police Chief. And with the body burnt past recognition, don't think they even got a decent cause of death."

"An accident? Or something else?"

"Don't know meself." Abe settled back on his couch. "Hear things. Well, when people don't have hard answers, they make up all sorts of stuff. Stories about Marylinn thinking Aldon would divorce his wife to marry her, then when he moved on, a broken-hearted Marylinn set fire to his house in revenge, and got caught inside."

He stopped talking, Grace waited a bit, then tried to prod him. "What do you believe?"

Those thick lenses magnified his dark eyes. "Don't rightly know. Let me ask around some more."

Chapter 19

The first thing Grace did when she got back to her lab was pull up that murder spreadsheet. She had a lot of stuff to modify. If Sierra attempted to blackmail Maura, was she just carrying on a program first started by Brian? That indicated a possible solid motive for a blackmail victim of Brian's to have killed him, say Aldon? Or could Sierra have been blackmailed into being Brian's love slave? Could she have killed Brian to get free? If so, the "Con' would be: what could she have been blackmailed for? And why was Sierra still hanging around town?

This story of the suicidal campaign worker girlfriend of Aldon's--how did that fit in? Could one of the Kincaids have killed Brittany? What of Harry, the manipulative campaign manager? Could he have killed Brittany, and have been blackmailed by Brian, so Harry killed him? She added another row, for Harry's involvement in Brittany's death.

And the formidable Charlotte--Grace could picture her quite righteously killing anybody, especially a mistress pregnant with her son's out of wedlock child. Grace needed to know more about these people. Maybe she could get herself another invitation to the Kincaid Compound, after all, she was soon to be the recipient of the used horseshoe award *'for consistent interest in the betterment of humanity.'*"

* * *

The next week after work Grace headed to Oyster River and the Haunts of Wôden. Freya had a number of customers inside, and Grace found herself manning the sales counter while Freya and her assistant Lilith moved about finding tarot decks and explaining the benefits of burning sage for purification over cedar. When the last buyer left, the store was forty-five minutes over closing time, and Freya had already sent Lilith home.

As Freya turned around the 'closed' sign on her door,

she smiled saying, "Business is booming! The Beltane fertility rights are in May, and everybody is trying to get ready." She looked over to Grace, "and being accused of..."

Grace cut in, "Associated with..."

"A murder," Freya finished, "seems to help business."

"Have you heard anything from the police?" Grace reached to pick up her jacket again.

"They wanted to question me, but I said my lawyer had to be there. I haven't heard anything from them since. Well, I heard from the Kincaid crowd."

"Aldon and Charlotte?"

"No, that smarmy guy who works for them."

"Harry, the campaign manager?" asked Grace.

"Yeah. Claimed that if I admitted to killing Brian..."

"What?"

"In self-defense. Brian attacked me and '*apparently*' Harry heard him attacking me, but I killed Brian and ran before he could help me. Harry thinks he can get the chauffeur to say he also heard the attack."

"Harry expects you to testify to being a murderess under oath?"

"Well, if I give up Mark as my lawyer, and go with the '*high power*' Kincaid law firm, Harry says they can get me a rest cure at some cushy sanitarium."

Grace looked at her, appalled. "You're talking about spending the rest of your life under medical supervision–a four-star jail!"

"Aaup," confirmed Freya. "But Harry sort of indicated that after three years, the law firm might be getting me out, and there would be some unspecified financial consideration, enough so I could make my dream trips to distant islands."

"You're not seriously thinking about doing this, are you?"

Freya finished taking the money out of the register tray. "Harry's got an alternate suggestion. Seems he says I took something from the boathouse--stole something that belonged to him."

"What?"

"He didn't come out and say it, but Lars--well Brian-- used to keep elaborate files on people."

"Blackmail material?"

"Oh, yeah, as a researcher Brian excelled in ferreting out people's secret shames. Harry tells me if I don't turn '*the gold stuff*' over to him, or admit I killed Brian in self-defense, then the Kincaid fortune will be used to help convict me of Brian's murder."

"Document this all with your lawyer. Call Mark now!"

Freya did. Mark said to just wait and see what developed. When she was done, Grace said, "Want to walk down and get sandwiches from the Firehouse deli?"

"Sounds good."

Outside there was still some light, the days were getting longer and warmer. As they walked, Freya said, "Your friend hasn't been around."

"My friend?" Grace asked.

"The girl reporter," answered Freya like she had a bad taste in her mouth.

Aldon's attack on Samantha was told to her in confidence so Grace couldn't say anything other than, "She might be busy..."

"Mac thinks he's been dumped," said Freya with a touch of bitterness.

Grace turned and stepped into her way. "Hold it. You've been itching for them to break up from the beginning, and now you're unhappy because they're not dating?"

"I wanted him to dump her!"

Oh, Lord. "Freya, Mac's got his own life to live. You've been preparing him to be on his own ever since I've known you. You did a good job--let him take it from here."

Her friend just stood there looking down that old road

of clapboard shops and houses. "I want him to be happy..."

"Well, that's something he's got to work for. Maybe he'll find it with Sam, maybe not."

"Now that his mother's about to be arrested for murder, and the girl reporter thinks her insider scoops will be ending you know Sam's been hanging around Mac because he's a cop and can get her leads..."

"Sam told me they never discuss his police work."

"You believe that?" challenged Freya.

"Yes," said Grace firmly. "Yes, I do."

Freya looked away. "Grace, you're supposed to be so smart, but sometimes you are plain stupid!"

Actually, at times, Grace could agree with that.

* * *

The phone rang, interrupting her concentration. Damn, Grace looked about. Nobody here. She could let it go to phone mail, but again it might be important. She answered, "Laboratory 5."

"Grace?"

"Who is this, please?"

"Maura. Maura Kincaid. Is this Grace?"

"Yes."

"The other day, when we had lunch, Harry saw us," she was speaking in an urgent whisper.

Who is Harry and why is that important? With her mind still concentrating on Brazilian coffee blight Grace asked, "Harry is?"

"You know, Aldon's campaign manager."

Yes, that annoying man. "Did you see him come into Neptune's?"

"No, Harry didn't come in. He was passing by outside, and he saw my car and your car parked in the lot. He recognized your license."

"He knows what my car looks like?" Grace found her voice raising. This was ridiculous!

"Yes," Maura confirmed. "Harry knows things like that. He knows anything having to do with Aldon's candidacy, me, you..."

"Why does he care about me? I'm not even going to vote for your husband–or anybody else for that matter!"

"I told him and Charlotte you'd called and wanted to treat me to lunch so you could talk woman-to-woman about your relationship with David Gardiner. Charlotte was impressed that I'm your confidant," She stopped, and thinking about it said, "Of course, they'll see on my credit card that I paid for the lunches..."

"No, they won't. You forgot to pay," Grace reminded her.

"That's wonderful! It's all working out. If they question you, just stick to that story," Maura sounded absolutely joyful. "Thanks so much, Grace."

Grace heard a click as her new best friend got off the phone. She had just settled back to her work when the phone rang again. Steeling herself to tell Maura this nonsense had to stop, Grace picked up the phone and in a frosty voice said, "Laboratory 5."

"Grace?" The familiar strong voice sounded uncharacteristically timid.

"Freya? Are you okay?"

"Yes, I'm fine–no, no, I'm not...I know it's your working hours, but I can't keep closing my store and stay in business..." she sounded near to tears.

But Grace could keep closing her lab she thought testily. Yet, Freya had always been there for her. "I'll be over. Just hold on. Did you have dinner yet?"

"No–I've got the diet cottage cheese in the fridge in the stock room."

"You don't do bad news on cottage cheese." And if Freya was calling sounding so depressed, it could be really bad news. What would cheer her up? "I'll pick up sandwiches for us from the Gourmet Cheese shop. What do you want?"

"Roast beef with mayo and ketchup and a dill pickle?" Freya's voice perked up. "And potato salad and coleslaw and maybe some of their homemade baklava?"

We're really dumping the diet. This must be really bad news Grace thought, but only said, "Give me a few minutes..."

The voice on the phone returned to pleading, "Grace, please don't go back to working again..."

Yes, if she did that they both knew it would be a few hours before Grace would resurface. "Already closed the program. I'll be there as soon as I can."

Inger hadn't been feeling well and had gone home early, and Nick wouldn't be coming in until later, so Grace had to lock the lab up, and that damned 'security lock' wasn't working properly. After a few minutes of struggling with her key card, Grace managed to get it locked, then she walked back to her car parked in front of the condo building.

She arrived early at Oyster River. Parking was impossible. Grace cruised through the small lot twice and then had to park on a side street down by Lord and Toms. With it getting closer to Easter, more people were shopping. As she hiked up the pavement a tall, blonde woman headed her way. Grace didn't recognize her, but that buckskin jacket with the fringe and Indian beading looked familiar.

"Grace," The woman called out in a cool tone.

What was her name? Brian's girlfriend? Sara? No, Sierra?

The woman narrowed her eyes and spoke harshly, "I know what you did."

Say what to that? Grace had seen Sierra last at the boathouse, and maybe if she could keep her talking, Grace could figure out what they were talking about. "You do? That's interesting."

"You searched the boathouse and found something

that belongs to me."

"What does 'it' look like?" Grace asked innocently.

The woman's face hardened and looked older than her years. "You're admitting you searched..."

"There was a murder committed. Your boyfriend was killed. I should think you would like help solving that murder. Anyone's help."

"The police know Brian's murderess--your friend Freya."

"No. No, Freya did not kill Brian."

"He was blackmailing her. Brian knew she'd stolen money..."

Grace found herself frowning, Freya didn't steal any money, this woman was phishing, trying to sound like she knew what was going on, so you'd explain it all to her. Grace only commented, "If you know that, you should call the police. They really don't think Freya had a motive."

"That old woman can't help you–I can. If you have what you took from the boathouse, together we can make it pay!"

Grace didn't think Sierra was talking about 'paying it forward,' so she only said, "I'll think about it. Where can I get in touch with you?"

Sierra stared at her hard as if briefly wondering if Grace was the murderess, but she only said, "The Kincaid estate. I'm staying in one of the chauffeur's apartments over the garage, but it only has an internal phone." She looked annoyed, then said, "Contact Aldon Kincaid and tell him to reach me." Saying that the woman in the suede, beaded jacket walked away.

Chapter 20

With Brian dead, and Maura wanting Sierra gone, Grace didn't think Charlotte would be too happy with her rent-free tenant, so it was logical that only Aldon must be keeping the hot suede jacket babe there. After buying their dinner at the Gourmet Cheese shop, Grace headed to Haunts of Wôden. Grace could hear the peaceful high ringing of the brass wind chimes that Freya hung outside, as she headed down the steps.

Inside an angry, red-faced Freya slashed at cardboard boxes, gutting them for the trash. "Grace. You've got food. Good." Freya looked relieved. "Spread it out on the counter. I'm starved. I'll get the soda cans from the back. Do you want ginger ale?"

Eating her sandwich, Freya's face turned back to normal color, but as they finished, Grace decided she had to get down to business. "I just ran into Sierra."

"Aaup. She was just here," said Freya, relishing every morsel of a sticky piece of honey pastry. "She try to blackmail you?"

Grace thought back on it. "Indirectly, yes. She seemed to think I'd stolen that interesting something of Brian's from the boathouse. His blackmail material?"

"Yeah," said Freya, her face flushing again. "First the little slut tried to bluff me. Demanded I sign over my shop to her, or *'she'd tell all.'*"

"What'd you say?"

Freya laughed. "The shops rented. Most of the stock is on consignment."

"That must have stopped her."

"Nope. She did better research than her boyfriend. She knew my house was paid for, on property overlooking the Long Island Sound."

"So she smells big bucks."

"But still doesn't know how to get them. Maybe we

could get some money out of her. Yeah, I'd bet she'd pay quite a bit for Brian's stack of blackmail scrapbooks and files."

Grace thought about that a bit. "It's strange she lived with him, but didn't know where he kept his business stuff."

"No. Brian was smart enough to see Sierra's chief interest in him was his money, or the ability to make same."

"Where do you think his stuff is?" Grace said as Freya cleaned the lunch wrappings off her counter and then sprayed it with glass cleaner. "Maybe his murderer got it?"

Freya shook her head. "No, Brian wasn't a fool, and the stuff he accumulated over the years would take more room than that small boathouse apartment."

"You think he's got a house somewhere else?"

"Nope. As soon as Brian got any real cash he always gambled it away or paid for the high life..." Freya's eyes softened with the memory. "The three of us once had the high rollers' suite in Atlantic City. Came with a hot tub in the living room and complimentary his and hers massages."

"But you said he had scrapbooks and files of photographs, newspaper clippings, and other paperwork–it has to be somewhere? Do you think he was renting a storage cubical?"

"I asked Mac." Freya looked to the doors. "My son says the police can't find a record of one. At a commercial place, Brian couldn't have paid cash without identification, but in the past, he rented someone's garage."

What is the 'To Do' on this one? "Maybe ask your lawyer to push the police to look harder?"

"And if they succeed in finding Brian's blackmail stash, they'll find out what he had on me..."

"He had material on you, other than Mac's parentage?"

"Oh, yes." Freya nodded grimly. "He was very thorough, and his blackmail stash could supply the police with several motives for me to kill him."

As Grace left Freya, her friend looked beaten, and Grace would have bet she didn't look too good either herself as she climbed up the steps from the Haunts of Wôden to street level. Time to get back to her lab, but as she walked down the pavement, Grace looked across the street to the hillside, with the white-washed basement that was Abe's bookstore. She had asked him to look into the Kincaids, and Abe had a track record of finding something.

When she entered his shop, Abe looked up. As he handed a customer a paper bag wrapped book, he said, "Grace, meaning to call ya."

Since he wasn't referring to her as 'Dr. Farrington' Abe wasn't trying to impress anyone. He came around from his counter to refill his mug of coffee. Although he sat down, Grace didn't. She did not want a social visit and didn't get herself the usual tea. "I'm running late, Abe."

"Aaup." He settled down beside her. "Ya asked me to look into that house fire, the Kincaid mansion."

That got her attention and, she sat down opposite to him. "You heard something?"

He took a sip of his coffee mug, then started again, "Aaup. Stan Lubchek came in. Wants to bone up on the Civil Service exam for a Truck driver."

Who the hell was Lubchek? "Abe, again I don't have much time."

Shaking his head, he started to explain in that clipped manner of a New Englander. "Ya asked me to talk to Stan, he was Charlotte Kincaid's chauffeur when the Kincaid mansion burned down."

That made Grace sit up straight. "What'd he say?"

"Confirmed what we thought. Aldon Kincaid has a reputation for being a ladies man, and Marylinn--what looker that gal was! When that girl walked downtown in those red shorts, some of us found a reason to go outside and check the pavement on the sidewalks."

With the sweet memory he was drifting, so she asked, "Do you think Aldon was having an affair with her?"

"If he wasn't, it wasn't for lack of trying. Aldon commuted from Washington on weekends. Stan would pick him up at JFK, then drop him off at a private house that was broken up into apartments. One day he saw Marylinn running out to meet Aldon. That was jes before Aldon's wife lost their first baby, too."

"Do you think the police knew that?"

"That Aldon's sleeps around, aaup. Might not know Stan knew Aldon was breaking up with Marylinn."

"That would be motivation for her to set fire to his house."

"If'n she did."

A chill spread through Grace, "You don't think..."

"Whal, I also spoke to Beck Judson."

"And he is?"

"Fire Marshall. The construction people called him when they found the body in the basement ruins."

"What were the findings of the autopsy?"

"Autopsy? Grace, that pile of timber had been drying out since the nineteen hundreds. It burned hot and long. By the time the fire department got there, they pretty much concentrated on keeping the outbuildings from going up too. Luckily the wind blew toward the water, so when the fire cooled, the Fire Chief and marshalls came and just took a fast look at a lot of blackened timbers down in the cellar."

"And they found Marylinn?"

"They didn't. Insurance inspectors came, they had to make a decision on accident or arson. The first fireman's report mentioned smelling accelerant."

"So it was deliberately set?"

He shrugged. "Insurance don't pay off under some circumstances. Kincaids started screaming in important ears, so next report said '*old wiring caused the fire.*'"

"When they found Marylinn dead, wasn't a more thorough investigation done?"

"Story pretty much old news by then. Took three, four months to get the second report out. Then the insurance company finally let them start cleaning out the burnt timbers. That's when they found the body. Still, took another month or so until they figured out who she was. Then only 'cause her family from Vermont came down asking why they hadn't heard from Marylinn lately?"

"But a body in the basement, that was news!"

"Whal, you know the Kincaids and his party are real close with the media. Folks felt sorry for them. They lost their house, then construction was held up again. The newspapers and some other folks figured the Kincaids were the victims here. It was in the paper, once, page eight most likely."

"Did they do an autopsy?"

Again he shrugged. "With what they had."

"Did they check to see if Marylinn was pregnant?"

"Grace, until her family showed up, they couldn't even tell she was a woman."

As he spoke, Grace started remembering, "A few years ago, the Medical Examiner's office was having a problem identifying a badly burnt cadaver that had been out in the elements for months. I remembered being asked to extract DNA from a mess of carbonized tissue and bones, then try to match it with three samples from living people."

"You did the work on Marylinn?"

"No names were given my lab. I did the work at the Medical Examiner's office in Farmington. Just a mound on the tray-- the flesh was hopelessly carbonized. It took hundreds of tries on what bones were left before I got a verifiable extraction, then I found a family relationship with samples of the saliva from three other individuals."

"That sounds like it."

"The police were investigating; the fire department must have reopened the case when a body was found?"

Abe looked at the windows as he saw the past, "Whal, police and fire guys looked into, not wanting to find anything much."

"Did they say Marylinn deliberately caused the fire to suicide?"

"Final reports said 'old wires' were the most likely cause of the fire." He stopped and thought about that for a minute and said sadly, "Waste of a really beautiful woman if she did kill herself."

"If she didn't?"

Abe's face fell in tight lines. "Grace, you ain't learned that asking questions about murder can get you hurt?"

Grace's mind flashed over the evidence. "Aldon's alibi for Marylinn's death is no good, no way could the police have known when that body died, or if there was a bomb left to set fire to the house while Aldon was out yachting. Do you think Aldon could have killed Marylinn?"

Abe shook his head. "Aldon's hasn't got the backbone for doing much of anything on his own. That campaign manager and his mother just put their hands up the back of his shirt, move Aldon's arms and make him dance around appearing almost life-like." Customers were walking in, and Abe got up to signal the end of their talk, but he finished by saying, " If'n Charlotte and Harry keep pushing, Aldon might be our president someday."

Like Grace could ferret out the secrets of DNA, Abe had an ability to penetrate the mental layers of all who came within his orbit, so she said, "Keep asking around for me, please, Freya's counting on us."

Chapter 21

The next morning started badly. A call from Inger, saying she threw up all last night and was feeling sicker, and had to go to the doctor, "But I'll be in afterward," Inger sniffled.

"No, you've probably got that nasty bug that's going around. You need to rest and drink fluids. Just go to your classes if you can then go home, I'll be fine. And you can make up your time at the end of the month. "

"But you gave Nick time off for his exams?"

Shit. Grace had forgotten that, and Bobby was chaperoning his daughter's class trip. Still, Inger never complained. She must be really sick. "It's okay, you get some rest. Do you have food in your apartment, or do you want me to pick up some orange juice or something for you?"

"No, thank you. After the doctor, I'm skipping classes and just going back to bed."

"That's good. Call if you need anything, and I'll be just fine here." Grace forced herself to sound positive, but when she hung up, she looked around the lab feeling discouraged. Today, on top of Grace's work, she'd have Inger's, Nick's, and Bobby's--just great. But first she needed an answer for Freya, so she'd have to prioritize: reading journal papers were unpaid work, they'd have to be put aside for the time being; Grace would have to check the extraction logs, to see if everything was being processed that needed work, but Nick usually kept on top of that; the mail, e-mail, text requests, letters, and phone calls were always handled by Inger, and just scanning them for brush fires would leave Grace working in the lab all night.

She would start by reviewing the latest extraction results, but as Grace looked up, the East wall lobster tanks were looking murky gray-green, which meant the filters must be changed, and the water salinity checked and adjusted, usually Nick's job. And since the lobsters are living creatures in her care, they took precedence. That meant finding the step ladder, filters, rubber gloves, cottony-filter material, and a bucket. On her ladder, Grace stared at the top row of tanks, pulling out green slime filter material, and dumping the gunk into the bucket on the floor. Lobsters with that bright turquoise mold on their shells scuttled away from her, as she smelled the rank fish tank. Grace leaned over to dip out more stuff as she heard her front door open. With that security lock acting up, Grace left the doors open when somebody was in the lab. Surprised, Grace looked over--who would be coming in now?

A trim blonde girl, dressed in a cream-colored, light-wool pants suit, carelessly accessorized with diamond earrings and bracelet stood at the entrance of her lab. The girl looked about and then focused on Grace scooping more green slime covered filter material. "Grace Farrington?" she asked coldly.

"Yes." Frowning, Grace wiped her slimy gloved hands on the new filter material. She recognized this girl from somewhere, but Grace couldn't remember where–a student? A reporter?

With an expression of distaste, Grace's guest scanned about the white painted wood lab that had originally been built in the 1920s. Without Inger straightening things up, paper printouts were scattered on lab tables, Grace's lunch burger wrapper and soda cup were still there on her desk, and everything looked messy and old. As Grace straightened up, this girl demanded, "You've been with my father?"

That settled who she was. This must be Madison Gardiner, who Grace had met the other day in David's bedroom. And by '*being with my father*' did she mean being with him as a friend, or being in bed with him? Grace put down the fishnet, and started to climb down the ladder. Should she try to shake hands with the girl? Better take off the rubber gloves first, which Grace did. "You're Madison?"

The girl didn't answer her, so Grace tried again, "How did you find me here?"

"The Gourmet Cheese Shop–they know everybody around here. I asked where Grace Farrington worked and they said you'd be here."

That was true enough. "Why didn't you just ask your father?"

Ignoring that, the girl spoke with deep emotion, "My mother was Sylvia Lasher Gardiner, a social leader, and expert horsewoman, who came from a distinguished family that traces its lineage back to the Mayflower..."

"I thought Sylvia was your stepmother?"

The girl's face fell. "She was my mother since I was a baby..."

Grace cursed herself for the thoughtless question. "And I'm sure Sylvia loved you very much..."

The girl's face hardened again. "My father is still mourning her. You're taking advantage of a wounded man, preying on him! Luring him in..."

Grace smiled at the absurd thought of her as the sultry siren enmeshing someone as coolly cerebral as David Gardiner. "I think your father can take care of himself."

"Do you intend to keep chasing him?" Madison demanded.

This was getting a bit insulting."Our relationship is between your father and me."

Madison reached into her handbag and pulled out a thick envelope which she held out to Grace. "Leave him alone! We have lawyers. You won't be allowed to take advantage of a man..." her voice started to crack, "who is clearly unable to take care of himself."

The girl held out the envelope, which Grace didn't take. Not knowing what to do or say, Grace, started, "Maybe we should sit down and talk a bit..."

"No." Madison threw her envelope down on the

nearest desk. "You will stop seeing my father. You will not try to contact him again...or I will go to the police! You only want money from him, there it is! Now leave us alone!" With a half-sob, Madison turned and walked rapidly to the door.

"Please..." Grace started forward, but the door had already slammed after the girl. Feeling her response was totally inadequate, Grace moved over to the envelope and opened it up. Inside she found a thick wad, which Grace at first thought were tens, but she realized they were all hundred dollar bills. And it looked like several thousand dollars in used, worn bills, the traditional ransom payment. Oh, shit. Grace carried it over and put it in her desk drawer and had to find the key to lock it up.

Her time was running out. She'd have to talk with David, but first Freya needed her. Finishing the lobster tanks, Grace returned home, showered, then dressed in her best black pants suit. She hated asking for favors, but the Medical Examiner's office kind of owed her for all those unpaid special consultations. She picked up her handbag and a small, briefcase-sized sample holder and headed out to the morgue up in Farmington. No problem getting past the front desk, and she certainly knew the way to the autopsy rooms. Through the glass-windowed door, she recognized a friend, even if she couldn't remember his name.

Wiping down a steel table, a stout, middle-aged man looked up, and then walked to her smiling as he asked, "Grace, did we call you in?"

"No, actually I was wondering if I could get a swab off of one of your guests?" she asked, trying to remember the friendly guy's name...was Sam, she wasn't sure, or maybe Joe?

"You working on a case for the police again?" he asked.

"No. This is just personal curiosity." *That did sound lame.*

He looked surprised, but game. "Well, we don't usually let people come in off the street...but we'll probably be needing your expertise shortly, and you've certainly helped us before, so which one do you want?"

"His name is..." She pulled a small to notebook from her pocket. " Lars Andersen."

Moving to a desk, staying standing up he typed in the name and waited for results; getting a blank screen he frowned. "Spelling it L-a-r-s A-n-d-e-r-s-e-n?"

"Yes."

He retyped, searched the screen, then he shook his head regretfully. "Don't have him."

Of course not, what was his name now. She looked deeper into her notebook. "I should have said, Brian Amundsen. A-m-u-n-d-s-e-n. His current a.k.a."

Typing again, he still got no hits on his screen. Looking over his shoulder Grace tried again, "Try cross-reference. Blunt trauma, from the Kincaid estate?"

He sat down and typed in more. "Okay. We've got something, but the name he has here is 'Lou Anders,' and let's see, some other a.k.a.'s, Tim Marshall, Len Butterfield, and Bill Amundsen and Len Anderson. Your guy gets around. I took his fluid samples for the drug scans, we haven't gotten them back yet. We've got several sets of his fingerprints under the different names sent from police files to confirm. Check with the cops, this guy must have some record."

Behind him, Grace looked at the screen as he pulled up a mortuary picture of a big-boned man with blond, military styled hair greying a bit. Brian had a neatly trimmed mustache and blue eyes that were open in surprise. "How tall?" she asked.

"195.58 centimeters roughly that's six foot five. Sound like the right guy?"

"Yes."

"Then we've got a problem. It's a murder case. If you

go in there, I'll have to put your name on the chain of evidence." He looked at her questioningly.

With her being friends with Freya--the current murder suspect--that could be complicating. She could call Mark and ask him if that was legal–but she figured he'd say no. Grace took a deep breath, then asked,"If I stayed out here, and you just went in and did some swabbing for me?"

He nodded. "We've taken a full set of our samples already, and swabbing a little wouldn't be contaminating evidence since I'm already listed on the evidence chain. I can do that for you-- inside of the mouth?"

"Yes." From her briefcase, she started to hand him two collection vials, then decide to make it three. She had to get this extraction right!

Blessing the fact that he wasn't asking any questions, Grace waited. When she finally got back to her laboratory, she suited up and immediately started the process of extracting Brian's DNA. For comparison, she had Freya's and Mac's samples in her computer files. They were some of the first she had taken when Grace moved to Oyster River and ran into the Dells.

As she worked, Grace vividly remembered that time. Having moved across country after being fired and disgraced professionally, Grace spent the days stuttering through teaching undergraduate classes; sure she'd be fired by the end of the month; sleeping in her car because the previous tenant wouldn't move out of the basement apartment she'd rented; and then being very hungry, but not having much money left to buy food until her first paycheck.

Finally, near sunset Grace remembered going out in the woods at the point to gather seaweed samples for her own studies, then slipping on slimy rocks, falling down, pain shooting up her leg. Spilling everything she collected, Grace just sat there sobbing as waves of pain shot from her foot.

"Lady?"

Grace looked up to see a thin, sandy-haired boy, all legs, coming over. He righted her bucket and started putting the seaweed samples back in. Not knowing anyone was about, an embarrassed Grace wiped her eyes and nose. "I'm sorry,..."

"What happened?" the kid asked.

She had thought from his height he was eight or so, but looking at his face, she realized he was probably five? Grace tried to pull herself together. "I slipped. My leg's hurt."

"Is it broken?"

Her attempt at a brave front started to crumble as she bit her lip. "I don't know."

The kid bent down and examined it. "It's swelling bad. I'll get Ma and the boat."

Yes, her ankle was near twice its size. She couldn't walk, the sun would be setting, and she'd be sitting here in the cold, wet and darkness looking like a looney. If she had broken her ankle, she couldn't teach and assist in Eric's lab, and she would lose her last chance for a job.

Hearing oarlocks creak, Grace looked up to see a blonde giantess rowing her boat over with its buckets of clams and black mussels in the prow. A braided Viking maiden listened to a stranger's tale of woe; half carried her over into the boat; rowed Grace and Mac across the harbor to the rickety dock in back of an old house. Freya dragged Grace in, and then taped up her sprained ankle. They all ate baked beans and franks, and being so hungry, Grace made a pig of herself eating plate after plate. Then--not knowing Grace at all--Freya let her sleep on the couch for two weeks until her apartment was ready.

And it had been like that all the years as Mac grew to manhood. Freya helping Grace, Grace helping Freya. She owed Freya a lot–they both owed each other, but that was what friendship was about. So by working on this DNA, Grace knew she'd find out if Loki/Lars/Brian/Lou--or whatever the hell he called himself–had fathered Mac Thor

Dell! She'd have an answer, but whether she would tell Freya and Mac or not, was a whole other question.

And it wouldn't be long until she had her answer. Over the years Grace had taken thousands of DNA samples. Her first work had started with the tracing of the Y chromosome that defined male inheritance, then they discovered that with mitochondria in the cell you could trace the female ancestry. When she entered the field, they were spending months on extracting and analyzing just tiny genetic segments. Then came the breakthroughs in computerized sequencers; where initially profiling a simple bacterial genome had taken her ten years, now a full human profile could be done in less than a week.

* * *

Just about a week later, Inger sat at her desk sorting Grace's e-mails, Nick finalized this quarter's lobster mold studies, while Bobby gathered material for her Denisovan project, giving Grace a little time to work on her side projects. The DNA from Brian/Lars still incubated, so not ready yet, but she had gotten positive results from Dagmar's possible Anastasia DNA. "Inger, you have the number for Prince Philip's genetic profile?"

Her assistant read off the log number, and Grace looked up the serial numbers for the Dagmar's hair extractions, and Maura Kincaid's sample number in her private log book. Grace studied the successful extractions taken from a hair follicle found on the lock of hair from Dagmar, and some skin cells. Three of the skin cells were human, but probably contamination from handling. Yes, one was male. But one skin cell perfectly matched an incomplete profile from the hair follicle extraction. Grace would use that one to benchmark for Dagmar. She set it up on a split screen with Maura's DNA to compare them side by side.

Definite mitochondria transmission mother-to-daughter relationship between Dagmar and Maura, other expected nuclear DNA matches, yes, a definite maternal family relationship. Blanking Maura's profile, Grace decided to compare the strongest extraction of Dagmar's DNA to Prince Philip's, especially his maternal line transmission coming down from Queen Victoria.

And the results floored her. Grace just sat there staring at the product she couldn't believe on the split screen. No mitochondria match, but one after another alleles were the same. Not a large number, but an obviously significant showing. What the hell happened? A mistake in the hair extraction? Contamination of the sample? Grace methodically pulled up the incomplete sample from Dagmar's hair and found herself dumfounded with identical results, no mitochondria match but definitely a relationship. What was happening? She had only a previously extracted sample of Prince Philip's DNA to work with, so no back-checking any of his chromosomes.

She needed more. Hitting the Internet, Grace turned to Wikipedia. She started with studies of the Romanovs-- Nicholas and Alexandra, their murder, burial, discovery, and verification of the DNA trail of their presumed bones. Finally, she leaned back in her chair. "Inger, we need to contact that Russian geneticist. He heads the State laboratory in Moscow...and he had a problem with extracting DNA from frozen mammoth bones, so he contacted me months ago..."

Inger thought about it for a minute and then said, "Dr. Dmitri Yuriev?"

"Yes, that sounds like it. I need to contact him."

"I'll check your database for his record." Inger immediately started typing.

"We should have it–but the problem as I remember was that he doesn't speak English, someone at his end translated for him... We'll have to hire a translator..." and that's going to take time and money. Years of schooling had forced Grace to work patiently, methodically, but she always wanted her answers instantly! She hated delay, red-tape, language barriers...

As she typed, Inger nodded and suggested, "Right now Bobby is teaching one of your graduate classes. I believe you have two Russian exchange students. Perhaps one of them could translate?"

"Great!" That might be an answer, and maybe they could do it today! "It'll save on the budget if we can get one of them. Maybe we could do it now? It shouldn't be difficult, just a simple question. Dmitri's either going to say yes or no." Grace looked at the clock on the wall. "Go over now and ask before the class dismisses."

Inger came back with Sonya, who had long, dark brown hair, and bright hazel eyes. She was both excited and nervous to be signaled out by Dr. Farrington, and Grace quickly explained what she wanted. But then they had a significant time differential to work out. They needed a weekday in Russia, probably from nine a.m. to twelve or two to five Russian time. Sonya suggested ten a.m., so that meant their call from Oyster River would have to be tried at two a.m. Connecticut time. Grace didn't have a problem with that, but she often forgot normal people didn't work her hours.

Inger apologized profusely to Sonya, "Dr. Farrington is so sorry to ask you, but do you think you could do it tonight?"

"Of course," bubbled Sonya. "Should I go back to the dorm? Or should I stay here?"

Again Inger took the point. "Security will come pick you up in the dorm at about one thirty, which would give you time to get some sleep first. Would that be okay?"

"Da," said a happy Sonya. As she started to get up to leave, the student looked all about the big open room with its tables, computer screens, microscopes, and that strange maple, multi- drawered cabinet that once held doctors' pulled teeth. Hesitantly Sonya asked, "May I take a picture?"

Grace looked up at that. Of course, she was asking the poor girl to give up sleep just to satisfy her endless curiosity. "Yes, yes of course. And, Inger, take a picture of Sonya and me with her camera." The young woman's face lighted up as Grace walked over to her, so she continued to Sonya, "Do you have some time now?" The young woman nodded. Grace hit a button on her desk, speaking into the air saying, "Nick, are you doing an extraction?"

A moment for him to get to the speaker, then his voice floated back. "I'm going to start culturing the new twisted lobster shell scrapings."

"Hold for a second, Inger will be bringing in a scientist to observe."

Inger's eyes widen a bit in surprise, but Grace turned to Sonya. "Would you like to suit up and see my clean room?"

"Da–yes!"

She happily nodded as Inger got up saying, "Suiting up will take some time. Let's see what size are you for the jumpsuit..."

* * *

That evening, Grace brought a box of donuts back to her lab and started to make more hot water for the tea. When she spoke at genetics conferences in China, she usually picked up some specialty teas to bring home; now she dropped tiny black leaf orbs into a steel mesh tea ball, giving her a steaming cup of Yunnan black tea just as Sonya arrived escorted by security. Before the call Grace explained what she wanted to be asked: Dr. Farrington understood Grand Duke George Alexandrovich died of tuberculosis, and that his remains had been exhumed, and his alleles analyzed and mapped. Could she get a copy of that?

What Grace planned as a five-minute conversation extended to over an hour and a half, with Dr. Dmitri eagerly asking questions on Grace's research on the Denisovan genome, and Grace wanted to know how the mammoth family tree was coming, and some recent early human bone finds from Siberia now in his laboratory. All of this had to be passed through Sonya's nervous, but seemingly perfect translation.

Dmitri had not done the work on the Grand Duke, but he was familiar with the scientist who did and would see if he could send the eminent Dr. Farrington the readouts. Through Sonya, Grace confirmed her e-mail address, and then she discussed a new method of DNA methylation mapping. And Grace promised to update him on her work with the Denisovan find. Finally, she closed up the lab and escorted Sonya back to her dorm room on the peninsula. Walking back to her condo, admiring the bright pointed stars over the harbor, Grace felt deep satisfaction at what had been a truly successful day.

Chapter 22

For one full day of working without anyone being murdered or arrested, or asking her to marry him, Grace thanked the gods of the laboratory. That evening, in the dark, she started back to her condo, tired, but very pleased with her progress this week. There were lights on in the Admin building, of course, the library stayed open all night. Still, Grace recognized the cherry red 1500 truck with the logo of Greenfield's Construction Company parked in front. That meant Gail would probably be putting in overtime, and Grace needed to talk to her about this baby thing. She headed inside, but Gail was not at her 'fishbowl' desk in the center of the foyer, and, as she walked toward Adam's office, Grace heard soft cursing and plastic scraping noises coming from the side door leading to the supply room, so she looked in.

Ripping open the copy machine back, a flushed-faced Adam now tore out more mangled sheets of red paper, throwing several on top of the over flowing wastebasket beside him. All the machine's paper trays were pulled out. "Grace, do you know how to get this thing working?"

"Gail's the only one who manages to keep it going past ten copies–where is she?" Grace said as she walked to help him.

"She left early. Some doctor's appointment" said a harassed Adam. "I've got to get two hundred more of these fundraiser brochures to be added to the newspaper delivery for tomorrow morning!"

Grace put down her handbag and took off her jacket. "Gail says that on dry days the static makes things worse, so..." She picked up the red paper from the machine's tray and ruffled the stack before putting it back. "Try running only ten copies at a time..."

"Shit! I'll be here all night. "

"Well, that's what Gail would be doing...and she's

only a temporary." She expected to get another rendition from Adam of '*being President of Oyster River Research is a voluntary position, and I don't get paid for this...*'

But in a tired voice, Adam only said, "I spoke to several members of ORR's Board about hiring Gail on full time. They said she certainly deserves to be hired..."

"That's wonderful!" started Grace as she keyed in ten and pushed the copy button.

Adam didn't look so happy. "You didn't let me finish. They plan to hire her, but her salary is not in this year's budget." He put the next stack of finished ten at right angles to the first couple to keep count.

"She's in there as a temporary. Without her agency's fees, it might even cost less to hire her?"

"The Board doesn't see it that way."

"You're president here, you need her..."

"I agree. But my authority does not extent to offering a permanent employment contract to an unbudgeted employee, and you know that."

Grace did and keying up the next ten, she knew she'd have to start working on the Board members, starting with David's lawyer, Alan. "All right. I will work on it from my end."

He sounded not too hopeful, "Have you thought more about your seating at the Spring fundraiser?"

Adam had at least tried to do his part, so Grace conceded, "I will sit on your dais during the speeches, and after the photographs are taken I'll join David at his table." She punched in another ten copies for him.

"I'd appreciate that." Adam pulled off finished copies as she pressed the button for the next set, but still sounding nervous he asked, "Are you planning to leave here to work in Greece?"

She punted. "I have a three-year contract with ORR."

Closing his eyes, he said, "You know, if you want to

leave, Oyster River won't hold you to that. If you decide to go, tell me, and I'll sign your release before we tell the Board."

That gave her an out, but did she really want one? "Don't say anything yet. Let me think more about things first."

As she keyed in another ten, he picked up the next stack of printouts, and said, "Thank you, Grace. If you decide to stay, I would really appreciate it."

She wasn't letting him off the hook. "But if the Board can't get its act together, Gail may find herself another job elsewhere with benefits, and then you'll be paying for three more unbudgeted secretaries to replace her!"

"Oh," someone spoke from the doorway behind them, and they both turned to see Nicole.

As she eyed Grace, Nicole said, "Adam, I wanted to talk with you, but if you're busy..."

"He's all yours," answered Grace, walking to the door. "He needs to run off about one hundred and fifty more copies. You can help him." Grace grabbed her jacket, handbag and was out the door before either of them could say anything more.

As she reached Gail's desk, she heard the copy machine starting again, and Grace could hear Nicole murmuring, "I understand you're arranging the seating for the dais..."

* * *

At the end of a long, frustrating day, Inger told her that Grand Duke George Alexandrovich's DNA profile had arrived. Yes! Delighted, Grace sat at her computer and pulled up the data. Someone had done a thorough job on what must have been a difficult task. Grand Duke George Alexandrovich was the third son of Tsar Alexander III and the brother of Nicholas II. Described as smart and athletic, George unfortunately, developed lung problems early in life and was sent deep within Russia to live in a drier climate. He died in 1899 at the age of only twenty-eight.   She put up a split screen with Prince Philip's DNA. Yes, some differences, which was to be expected, including the male Y from Philip's Danish royal heritage, but many of the other gene repetitions matched, confirming Prince Philip's and Prince George's shared Romanov heritage. She blanked out Philip's profile and this time pulled up Dagmar's patterns to compare to the Grand Duke's.

Of course, since Dagmar was a woman, there were no XY chromosomes to confirm, just the two Xs for female. Grace focused on the nuclear chromosomes, particularly the gene locus on chromosome sixteen. All genes presumably started out as one copy, but after hundreds of thousands of years of procreation and mutations, that one gene often stacked up with multiple copies. Some profiles showed a particular gene with three, four or maybe two hundred copies, or even two thousand copies of the same gene. Genetic relationships were proven by comparing the number of matching gene repetitions that they all had in common. Here the two profiles she studied deviated strongly, but still, a few of the chromosomes carried genes that repeated in exactly the same numbered repetitions, proving both of these individuals did have some sort of a family tie. And Dagmar and the Grand Duke had two in common that Prince Philip didn't have.

Looking at the three profiles--and without more confirming evidence--she'd hazard a guess that a many times great-grandparent of Dagmar's was a member of the Romanov family. Perhaps a distant royal cousin of the Tsar, or a by-blow by some predatory Romanov male, maybe even an earlier Tsar. Yes, Dagmar had Romanov blood, but not a close relationship with Nicholas II, and she certainly could not be his surviving daughter. That would not be what Maura Kincaid wanted to hear.

Grace sighed deeply. Telling the woman she was not descended from the Grand Duchess Anastasia would be very painful for the both of them. Better to get it over with. She looked up Maura's number in her small notebook and dialed.

"Grace?" came the eager voice on the line.

Was the campaign manager also bugging the Kincaid phones? "Ah...can I drop by your house..."

Before Grace could say 'this weekend' Maura chimed in with "Right now? That would work. Aldon and I are leaving for Washington this afternoon. I'll look forward to seeing you." And that bright voice clicked off the phone.

Shit! Now she had to drive out there, wasting more of her time. Grace disgustedly started to roll her chair back from her desk, but something else bothered her. Grace's genius and what lay behind her 'Farrington Fusions' was her recognition and remembrance of patterns and their relationships-- now she pulled up Prince Philip's read out again. Something familiar about that configuration nagged at her. Something she'd seen before, but where? Not recently...Grace stared at the screen. Nothing. Well, she'd think of it in time. She blanked the screen, Grace had to get this stupid Dagmar business over with before she could even start working on projects she was paid to do!

Driving past that imposing gate and the two-story Tutor gatehouse, Grace noted banks of yellow daffodils were blooming along the Kincaid driveway. Admiring them, Grace parked to the left, beyond the house. As she got out of her car, the white gravel crunched under her feet, and Grace looked to the strand of thick woods that marched to the beach. Could she just run over and search the boathouse for blackmail material? Maybe she could talk with Maura and ask if she could go over and look in the boathouse again, because why...? Yeah, right, ask a favor after she shattered the woman's illusions of being a Romanov Grand Duchess. No, it would have to be some other time.

A nervous-looking maid answered the door, as she said, "I'm Grace Farrington. Maura is expecting me."

Frowning, the maid glanced across that enormous foyer toward the closed gold outlined doors to the living room. "She said she wanted to see you..."

From the behind doors, Grace heard a woman shouting. "**My fault? I'm setting a bad example...**"

A man's angry voice--Grace couldn't get the words.

The maid walked to the door, then knocked briefly. There was no answer, but the shouting stopped, so the maid opened the door announcing, "Mrs. Farrington."

Grace walked into a painful tableau: a white-faced Aldon stood stiffly to the side of Maura. She was standing a bit hunched over, with her arms wrapped protectively around her chest, and as Maura forced her usual stunning smile, Grace could see a fresh red mark on her cheek.

With obvious practiced charm, Aldon turned to her. "Tiffany, it's **Dr.** Farrington. Grace really." He held out a hand to shake.

Grace took it and wondered if that's the one he used to hit his wife.

"How do you do?" He asked rotely and then briefly looked in askance to Maura, "You are really a friend of my wife's?"

"Yes," replied Grace firmly.

As the maid left, Aldon gave a boyish shrug. "It's just that you two would seem to have nothing in common?"

Ignoring that Grace said, "I understand you'll be ORR's speaker at our Spring fundraiser?"

"Yes." He straightened into the young candidate. "Scientific progress is at the forefront of my agenda for the future."

Aaup, and wife beating second on the list thought Grace.

Aldon pulled out a thin cigar, and Maura glared at

him. "Don't do that. Charlotte will smell the smoke."

Ignoring his wife, Aldon lit it, and exhaling a long white puff he sardonically asked, "You think my dear mother will reprimand the next Senator from Connecticut?"

"She won't say anything to you–she'll go after me!" shot back Maura.

"I'm sure Dr. Farrington doesn't want to hear this," her husband pointed out taking a deep puff.

Seeing his charm wasn't exactly flooring Grace, Aldon only said, "Actually, I have some calls that have to be made before we leave. Dr. Farrington, if you'll excuse me." Not waiting for an answer, Aldon turned and walked to the doorway, only stopping to snuff out his still smoking cigar in the dirt of a potted palm. Over his shoulder, he growled, "Have the maid get rid of that."

Looking a bit embarrassed, Maura turned to Grace and said, "Charlotte hates smoke. Hates cigarettes and cigars–but he still keeps smoking in her house!"

"Well, it's your house too..." Grace tried.

Maura turned her feverish blue eyes on Grace. "I'm so sorry you drove all this way–because of the traffic, the limo is coming for us earlier than expected–we have to be in Washington for a dinner tonight, at the White House! That's not a recognition a junior Congressman usually gets, but they all know Aldon's on the way up."

"He just hit you, didn't he?"

She cast her eyes down. "In self-defense. I kicked him first--I've been so emotional lately–but we've lost our venue for the Horses for Handicapped children fundraiser, and that bitch Sierra was flirting with him. Grace,..." she started then Maura abruptly stopped when the maid entered. "Yes, Tiffany?"

The woman spoke apologetically, "The phone in your office was ringing, ..."

"What was it?"

"The Country Club--about your awards dinner?"

Maura sighed, "Grace, so sorry, but I must take this. I'll be right back." She hurried out, and the maid followed.

Leaving Grace alone, just standing there...wasting more time.

Still, she looked over at that potted plant by the door, with its cigar soaked with Aldon's salvia. The campaign worker--Brittany--had died, probably after an affair with Aldon. It could have been suicide. It could have been murder. Brian getting rid of a problem for Aldon and Harry? Aldon cleaning up his own mess? Could Brittany have been pregnant? Grace had connections with the State Police and the Medical Examiner's office. If samples had been taken, she might be able to get access. What she needed was the DNA from a possible father to compare with it.

Moving swiftly, Grace dug into her purse for a ziplock collection bag and a latex glove. As she moved to the potted plant, Grace wondered if the Kincaids had security cameras inside their house? With a gloved hand, Grace fished that cigar butt out of the plant pot, slipped it into the ziplock collection bag, and then stuffed it and the used glove into her handbag. She was standing back in place when Maura returned saying, "I'm so sorry, Aldon says we must leave now, but would you like the servants to get you something to drink or eat?"

Maura's bruise had been covered by makeup–she must have practice at that Grace thought cynically. "No, I've got to get back to work, but I did want to look at the boathouse again..."

"Not today. Grace, I promise we'll go look at it again, but now I've got to get going."

As Maura ushered her to the door, she glanced down at the plant pot with its disturbed dirt, then quickly looked up to Grace. Still, Maura said nothing.

Heading outside without a jacket Maura said, "I'll

walk you to your car."

After they walked a bit away from the house, Grace asked, "How can you put up with that?"

"With what?" With the red mark on her cheek fading under her makeup Maura forced a smile. "Oh, you mean his yelling? Aldon's under such pressure. Since he's been born, there have been high expectations of what he's going to do for us all. That's a difficult burden for anyone to live with. It's my job to support him, keep the dream afloat."

"While he's trying to sink the whole thing with his womanizing?"

Maura only gave a lopsided smile as she rubbed her chilled arms. When they reached Grace's old car, Maura leaned against it, speaking in a soft voice she asked, "Dagmar's DNA. Have you proved she's Anastasia?"

Oh, God, this was not the time to tell her. "I'm working on it. Can you come to my laboratory when you get back?"

Maura nodded, her face lighted with a little expectant smile of a soon to be Grand Duchess.

Chapter 23

The next week brought very good news. Grace had an answer for the Brazilian coffee growers. "Your current fungus infestation is genetically related to an Indonesian blight that affects vanilla bean plants."

"That is important how?" asked Señor Cardozo.

"The Indonesians have come up with a very effective bio spray that seems to interrupt the fungus' reproduction cycle. Probiotics for the plants called Effective Micro-Organisms are a safer alternative to protect from roya. The probiotic inoculates against the rust while improving soil quality and strengthening the plants. I think it might help you control in the early stages of infestation, but only in the early stages. Inger is sending you the information on it and where you can purchase some of the spray to test."

"Si!" He sounded relieved.

"But, Señor, that's playing catch up–you have to get ahead of your problem."

He sounded weary. "By breeding whole new crops of low-producing coffee plants? That will cost much too much!"

"Not if you are thinking long term. Your copper sprays will eventually poison your ground soil. And evolving effective probiotics will increase the cost of your coffee. Some of the wild Coffea strains from Ethiopia are rust resistant and look very good, especially the C 14. I think by cross breeding they will be your best option to produce a coffee leaf-rust resistant crop, with the necessary taste and yield. You're extremely lucky C14 still exists."

"These wild strains have lower yields and may have a weaker taste."

"That is true, but further breeding will correct this."

"I will speak with my brothers," he did not sound happy.

"Do that. Your industry must invest funds in maintaining the genetic bio-diversity in Africa and in Brazil, by finding and planting fields of ancestral coffee plants. I know the expense involved, but these strains have genetic value to you..."

"As you requested, we have placed our coffee plant seeds in the genetic repositories."

"That's not enough! You should be breeding alternate strains in your own fields," repeated Grace patiently.

"This takes years."

"I can possibly speed some of that up for you In Vitro, but it will be time-consuming and very expensive. One of my associates, Robert Jamison, is planning to go for his doctorate studying Gene Manipulation in Plants of Nutritional Importance." *If he didn't change his doctoral topic again, this coffee business could be a chance for Bobby's first project as a co-study with herself.*

Silence on the line as he seemed to think about that. "It would be cheaper to breed our own plants..."

"Yes, much cheaper," Grace admitted, "but you are going to have to produce multiple generations, grow them to maturity, test them before you can breed them again."

"How long does this take before we get lucky enough to have a single plant we can use to propagate our new stock?"

"Unknown, but gene transfer in the laboratory works a lot faster than waiting for your plants to appropriately reproduce themselves, even with artificial pollination."

"Is this really necessary?" He did not sound happy.

"Señor, for hundreds of years Brazil was protected from African coffee rust by the Atlantic ocean, then in the 1970's it first appeared in your fields. I ran DNA profiles on your coffee plants, virtually all the coffee plants in the Americas--nearly all the coffee producing plants worldwide-- trace their lineage back to a single tree planted in the conservatory of King Louis XIV in 1713. Interbreeding from one plant for centuries results in a dangerous genetic uniformity that is at enormous risk for devastating epidemics. You will overcome this rust, but there will be other problems in the future. The only thing that might save you is maintaining multiple genetic lines, or at least keeping some greenhouses of specimens that have disease-resistant ancestor genes that might be bred back into your stock."

"The Ethiopian government has forbidden all export of coffee plants and coffee seed from their country."

That would be a problem. "I'm sure they'll let you invest your funds in their country to protect and maintain areas where wild coffee is still found." There was silence, and although it was illegal, Grace felt a moral imperative as she suggested, "If the price is high enough, people will find product to sell to you."

"Maybe they will sell me my own coffee plants?" he complained, sounding bitter.

"Send me leaf samples, and I can tell you if you have plants with ancestral genes."

He picked up on that. "Since we are trying to preserve valuable genes, you test what I buy without cost?"

We had been through this before. "No, Señor, we are both in business. You are preserving the wild coffee plants for your long-term earnings; my lab tests of your DNA are my immediate income."

Again that hesitation on the line. "We will look into it..." he said. "What you suggest is a great expense..."

"As you know there are several very good genetic laboratories in South America that would be a lot cheaper than mine."

"Can you guarantee they will give us disease-proof plants?"

"No. I can't even guarantee that with my laboratory. We can discover, select, splice, manipulate, and combine genes, but we are not God, we can not create them."

"My business is coffee. If my coffee beans cost too much, no one buys them."

"I understand. Now, my assistant Inger, will also send you contact information of some excellent laboratories closer to you that will perhaps be more reasonably-priced choices."

There was silence on the line, and Grace waited until he said, "I must talk with my brothers, then some of the other growers. If we do try this plant manipulation, we would wish the best person--yourself--to do it."

* * *

Grace looked up nervously at the clock. Maybe instead of her lab, she should have done this bound-to-be emotional meeting in the cafeteria or a restaurant somewhere? As Inger headed to the clean room with more samplings from the lobsters, Grace said, "I'm having a confidential talk with someone. Don't come out of the clean room until I call you, okay?"

Inger nodded and closed the door behind her. When Maura came in, she was dressed in tan jodhpurs and a black riding coat. Breezily she explained, "This afternoon I work with handicapped children, giving them rides on horses. That's my excuse for going out today."

Needing an excuse to leave your own house seemed a bit ridiculous, but Grace had to get this over with. "I've completed my work on Dagmar's DNA."

"Have you finished?" Excitement lighted up Maura's face. "You have proved my great-great grandmother Dagmar was the Grand Duchess Anastasia?"

"Why don't you sit down. Would you like some tea, coffee?" tried Grace, reluctant to get started on this.

"Is there something the matter...?" Maura looked confused.

She had to get it over with. "Your ancestress, Dagmar, was a beautiful, wonderful, obviously resourceful woman, but she was not a daughter of Tsar Nicholas."

For a second Maura just stared at her, then the woman said in a brittle voice, "You're saying you can't prove she was Anastasia–is that what you're saying? You don't have enough DNA?"

"No, I'm saying she isn't the Grand Duchess Anastasia because I do have the DNA."

"But she has to be..." said Maura in a broken voice.

"No, she doesn't. In fact, she wasn't."

Maura stood up and started to pace in a tight circle before Grace, "When they were testing for Tsar Nicholas's remains, they exhumed his brother, George, didn't they? Perhaps if you had his DNA..."

"I do. I sent to Russia for Grand Duke George's samples. It confirmed what I had discovered with Prince Philip's." Grace took out several sheets of paper to explain, but Maura didn't look at them. "Mitochondrial DNA is passed from mother to daughter and son. In the female line, it continues on down. Queen Victoria passed her mitochondrial DNA to her children, and all her direct female descendants, such as her granddaughter Tsarina Alexandra and Prince Philip's mother and himself. Dagmar did not have mitochondria inherited from Alexandra so she couldn't have been her daughter."

That fact seemed beyond Maura Kincaid's comprehension. "Maybe you're mistaken?"

"You are a descendant of Dagmar. That is all through daughter to granddaughter transmission, with no male transmission, I can read that in your DNA."

"Yes," confirmed Maura.

"From your sample, I see you have Dagmar's mitochondria, but you do not have Queen Victoria's or the mitochondria she would have given to Tsarina Alexandra."

"But maybe I lost those genes. They say only half your genes come down to your child?"

"That's nuclear DNA. Barring damage or mutation,

mitochondria are passed intact from a mother to her children. In the females, the mitochondria continues to the girl child's children. The male children do not pass theirs on; instead, their wives will pass the mitochondria they received from their mothers to the couples' offspring. Queen Elizabeth the II passed her mother's mitochondria to Prince Philip's children. If you were a female descended directly from Alexandra you would have inherited the mitochondria she received from her grandmother, Queen Victoria.

Maura moved back to the chair, weakly sitting down across from Grace. "You saying Dagmar had no Romanov blood?"

"I didn't say that. Actually, she had quite a few markers in common with both Prince Philip and Grand Duke George."

"What does that mean?" demanded a confused Maura.

"It means that earlier than both of them, an ancestor of yours split off from the Romanov family tree."

"Was that legally by marriage, or just some royal louse fooling around with a peasant girl in the hayloft? Perhaps raping her?" finished Maura bitterly.

Shaking her head Grace said, "Martial status is impossible to tell with DNA."

Grace looked at Maura's pained face. The woman's head was actually hanging in shame, and it made Grace angry. "So your great-great-grandmother wasn't Her Royal Highness Anastasia Romanov, daughter to Tsar Nicholas II! But your grandmother lived under that Tsar. She lived with Russia under siege as the Germans under the Kaiser attacked relentlessly in World War I. Hundreds of millions died of starvation and the cold, but Dagmar survived. Then came the brutal Bolshevik revolution. For three hundred years the Romanovs had ruled Russia, and suddenly that world disappeared. Can you imagine what that was like for the Russian people? For Dagmar? The new leaders assassinated

Nicholas and his family, outlawed the comfort of the Orthodox Church, and executed anyone who looked cross-eyed at them.

"Yet Dagmar found a White Russian soldier who managed to get them both out of Russia during a world war; they made their way to England; then finally they immigrated to the United States. Do you have any idea of what an accomplishment that was? When her husband got run over by a runaway horse, the widowed Dagmar found herself a job sewing. Later, she captivated and married her boss, a well-to-do manufacturer." Grace looked into Maura's eyes but could see she was making no impression. "Even if she wasn't born a Grand Duchess, Dagmar was one hell of a brave, intelligent, resourceful woman. Someone to be proud of."

Only silence as that sank in, then a broken Maura said, "She lied about being Anastasia."

"Yes, she did. Did she do that to get two husbands to marry her? Or did she just get them with her own brains and attractiveness? The Tsar was gone, and a living Romanov could have been hunted down by the Reds and killed, so possibly, Dagmar didn't tell that story to either man.

"But you said Dagmar didn't tell the Anastasia story to your grandmother and family until late in her life? An elderly woman's mind could easily float from anchoring reality. We know by Dagmar's genes she was descended from some branch of the Romanov line. Maybe she was told that as a child, and at the end of her life, she confused her own story with ones she'd heard about Anastasia? Perhaps it was an honest mistake made by an aging mind beginning to slip?"

Maura looked down at her hands, "Thank you for researching this." She looked up quickly. "You won't tell anyone else?"

"Not if you don't want me to."

"But your assistants..."

"They know I've researched Prince Philip and Grand

Duke George's DNA, but I've processed your samples with only code numbers. My assistants will never know of the connection."

"That's reassuring...." she started.

Grace had enough! "This not Tsarist's Russia, or even Royal Britain! This is the United States of America, we have no royalty here, not the Romanovs, not the Windsors, certainly not the Kincaids! Now you say your husband might be President someday; I've heard that is possible. Then you will be the First Lady of the land, isn't that enough for you?"

The woman's face seemed to have collapsed, making her look far older than her years. "I don't know if I'll still be married to Aldon. You know he fools around with any woman he can. I caught him yesterday coming out of Sierra's apartment, that merry non-widow of Brian's."

So Aldon Kincaid was fooling around with the murder victim's mistress—when did that start? Did Aldon kill Brian for Sierra? Grace did not know what to say, but fortunately, Maura was still talking, "Jackie Kennedy knew all about Marilyn Monroe and the other women Jack fooled around with. Marilyn even called her, wanting Jackie to divorce the president. How could she stand that?"

"Jackie obliviously decided staying married to the president was worth it to her."

"I think Brian may have been blackmailing my husband about his affairs. The police don't know that. The detectives did question Aldon about that Brittany woman working for his campaign who committed suicide..." Suddenly Maura realized Grace still listened, so she spoke quite defiantly, "They questioned my husband, but I could say he was with me. He had an alibi."

What could Grace say here? "That's good..."

Still, Maura continued, "Because the journalists covered for him, Jack Kennedy got away with his affairs, but the press wouldn't hide that today. Aldon needs to be President. The country needs to have him as its leader! And he needs me to work alongside him. I just wish Dagmar had told the truth, that I was a descendant of Tsar Nicholas...."

"You are related to the Romanovs, so you are descended from the Imperial bloodline."

"That's right, I do have royal Romanov blood..." Maura said, with a proud voice but dead eyes. "But I need time to get used to this. All my life I've been told one thing told to keep it a secret and now...but you're right. I am a Kincaid, and I will help my husband succeed. Thank you, Dr. Farrington." Saying that she turned and left, leaving Grace wishing that she'd never gotten involved in this mess.

And what had Maura said? The caretaker Brian might have been trying to blackmail Aldon Kincaid over the suicide of a campaign worker? Maura claimed she was her husband's alibi but was she telling the truth? Grace had the definite impression that Maura would say anything to protect her philandering husband.

* * *

David was taking her to lunch, so when he picked her up in his car, Grace handed him the thick envelope, and he asked, "What is this?"

"Your daughter is not too happy about us seeing each other. She tried to pay me to leave you alone."

He raised a quizzical eyebrow as he looked inside the envelope and started to thumb through it, apparently doing a fast count. "Where did she get cash? Her allowance is paid through her credit cards." Grimly, he studied the envelope's wad. "Looks like you've got a few thousand here not to have sex with me." He looked back to Grace, the teasing back in his pale blue eyes, "Well, tonight I'll see that, and raise you another two envelopes for you to have carnal relations with me."

"David!" Grace settled back into his car. "Your

daughter's very upset...and it might help if you explained to her that I'm not a cleaning lady."

"What?"

"Caine gave the impression that I was in your bedroom to clean up, and when she came to my lab, I was mucking out the lobster tanks."

"Why were you cleaning tanks?" he grumbled. "You have assistants for that."

"They were sick or busy..."

"Then you call a temporary agency."

"You can on your budget, not on mine."

He frowned at that. "I'll have a talk with Madison, but she has to understand that even if you are the cleaning lady, this is my choice. Grace, my daughter is not going to run my life. And by the way, my sons are in your corner one hundred percent. Jessie wants a fall wedding for us."

"Oh, God."

"Now, will you be sitting with us at the Oyster River Research fundraiser buffet? My children will be there. I'd be honored if you could join us?"

Such a formal request, but that was David's way. "I'd love to, and maybe at the end, but I'm representing ORR, so I'm expected to sit on the dais with Adam and the rest during the speeches."

He nodded in agreement with that. "Yes, you are Oyster River's shining star."

"They've got others. Huang and his new assistant, Dr. Noreen Dobbs, whatever."

"Dr. Nicole Duval. She's already presented my New York Office with a preliminary funding request for an Epigenetics related study she would like to do."

"Epigenetics?" asked Grace a little forlornly. "That's what she's researching?"

David found that vastly amusing. "I'm being pursued by a sexy young scientist, she's pushing Dr. Huang out of her way, and all you're concerned with is her choice of study area?"

* * *

Back in her lab Grace heard the phone ring. She looked around. It's was after seven p.m., so nobody else was there. Grace answered, "Lab 5."

"Grace? It's Abe. Kurt back yet?"

"No, he'll be gone for awhile, still chasing humpback whales and mermaids."

"Aaup." Abe didn't sound happy. "You ever get that carry permit?"

No, she hadn't. "Why? Do I need a gun?"

There was silence on the phone for a bit, then came Abe's quiet voice. "Ya wanted me to ask questions about that fire that killed Marylinn."

She waited, then when he didn't say anything more Grace urged, "I'm going to keep digging myself. Freya's up for murder..."

"Aaup." He gave in. "Asked about. Spoke to a couple of the fire department guys who worked on that case."

"Was it a murder?"

"They couldn't say yes, couldn't say no."

"Is the case still open?"

"Nobody's working on it if that's what you're asking."

"Why not?"

"Whal, Marylinn might've set the fire and committed suicide–that's what the Fire Chief felt, and he can't try a dead woman."

"But if she was forced into it by a married, lying lover...or even locked in that basement by the arsonist, wouldn't he think that might be a prosecutable crime?"

"If it were you or me, maybe. But when we're dealing with important folk like the Kincaids, nobody much wants to call them on anything without concrete proof to back it up."

"So no matter what they do or who they kill, the Fire

Chief won't take action?"

"That's not true. Ed's a good guy. He's a made a guess as to what happened, so have his guys. They had smelled accelerant during the fire, and after they found the body, they climbed into that burnt timber-filled cellar and really poked about. But figuring out what might've happened four months ago, and having proof to pass on to the town prosecutor are two different animals."

"What do they know?"

"That old mansion was built before zoning pretty much. There were only three entrances to that cellar. The stairway down from the kitchen, a bilco door, and a boarded-up coal slot."

"No windows?"

"Nothing, a grown woman, could have climbed through. The bilco door lock melted, but after they found the body, those fire chief's guys crawled all over those blackened timbers, making sure they were all lifted out of the cellar one by one."

"The Kincaids must have loved that," Grace said with sarcasm.

"The Fire Chief and Police Chief were having senators and governors complain about them, so that made things harder. Course the final report missed a few facts. Weren't in the report, but a guy--who won't go on the record--found the remains of that basement door. It must have burnt out and fell into the basement before the real fireball."

"The kitchen door that led to the cellar?"

"Aaup–he said that when they found it, that door was locked."

"From inside the kitchen or the cellar side?"

"He couldn't tell. Now, Marylinn could of set that fire, then locked herself in the cellar to get back at Aldon." There was silence on the line as Grace absorbed that. Then Abe started again, "Some in the Fire department even whispered–that one of the Kincaids forced Marylinn downstairs, and then locked that basement door, either Aldon or his mother, Charlotte."

Coldness ran down Grace. "Do you think he could have?"

"Aldon's a weak-willy, but if his career was threatened, maybe he could grow some backbone. Maybe, but my money would be on the mother. Charlotte's always had ice water in her veins." Abe stopped, then started again, softly, "But, Grace, be careful, if one of the Kincaids killed once, they can kill again."

Chapter 24

Grace donned a black silk blouse with gold and silver dragons embroideries that she had picked up at a Beijing Genome Conference. She wore it with a long black skirt, then thought about changing it. Should she wear that beautiful dress Freya had gotten for her by trading her huge pink rock-salt lamp? That dress swirled and made her feel young and foolish–but not tonight, tonight was business. She represented Oyster River Research.

Coming downstairs she met Bobby at the bottom.

He looked her up and down. "You look great." Then he glanced back to his apartment. "The babysitter is late...Sara might not come."

"Well, you have to show, but you can be late. Wait to escort your wife, but I've got to go now and fly the flag."

Her assistant nodded, but said, "Make it an early night, Grace, we're supposed to have a bad storm coming in tonight."

Outside a chill wind blew from the harbor, and Grace smelled a fishy low tide. Cars were parking in front of her condo and all the way down to the peninsula point. A big event tonight. Grace had invited Freya, but her friend refused, *'Everyone's looking at me as if they were waiting for me to kill someone else.'* Back on the force, Mac would probably be on duty here, and of course, Samantha would be here, having her pen and pad out to take down the news for her paper.

Grace walked past the Admin building. Some lights were still on, Gail must be fixing up last minute problems. Then past Eric's lab–now Huang's. She never walked past here without some small feeling of gratitude for what Eric had done to bring Grace to safe harbor in Oyster River. Her own lab building looked so dark and empty. With a room full of people ahead, Grace just wanted to run inside her lab and hide. She'd love to spend the evening catching up on work in her apartment, instead of being some Big-Eyed-Monster to be paraded before possible sponsors.

Ahead, the back of the mustard yellow Roost mansion loomed, with its Italianate tower front facing the main road. Outside it was two, no three television trucks with satellite dishes on top–these last weeks Adam had Gail working hard for publicity. Thick clouds now covered the sky and harbor as Grace headed up the slight hill, noting more cars driving in. She looked over and saw private security directing traffic across the street, into the parking lot of the fish hatchery. The traffic might overflow above the berm around the dam, where the tall, white Congregational church overlooked the lake. Water from that lake ran down to the marshlands at the head of the harbor. Grace wanted to keep walking and sit by that lake, blessedly alone.

She can't. She could sneak in the back door through the kitchen addition, but she shouldn't. Instead, Grace straightened her shoulders and walked right into the spill of light from the front doors of the Roost. No badge table had been set up in the tower base foyer, with its elaborately inlaid wood flooring in an eight-foot compass rose design. Today when she walked through the short entrance hall beyond the foyer, there was actually a hat check girl in the cloakroom. Grace handed in her coat and received a blue plastic, numbered token. The first floor had been gutted, and now a meeting hall occupied pretty much the whole building's footprint. It was a story and a half high, and tonight the lighting darkened the ceiling to give a more intimate atmosphere. She looked about and didn't see David. She also certainly missed Kurt; his totally irreverent take on these affairs made them go a lot easier.

Grace scanned the crowd more and did see David standing next to a shapely woman in a red sparkled dress, that plunged way, way below her neckline. She was speaking to him in an animated fashion, and David smiled politely back.

The woman looked like someone Grace should know. Dr. Huang's new assistant, Nicole? Moving in on a man who had money, well, that's how some people got research grants. Grace could go over there and establish that she had some sort of relationship with David, but being in a contrary mood, she decided to walk to the bar in the back. No corporate sponsorship today, so it was pay as you go, Grace ordered a sweet red wine, and dug out money from her fanny pack, realizing she should have brought her smaller evening bag.

For the fundraiser, the room had been set up with gold tablecloths, on round tables scattered about in front of the low dais with its fold-up podium. Now, the wall behind the podium was decorated with American flags. Two long tables had also been set up on each side of the podium, and there Grace would be sitting on display, like a prize turkey. She walked over to put her handbag and wine on a place setting and discovered each plate had a name written on a stiff card in gold ink with Gail's elegant calligraphy. Adam and his wife were seated girl-boy-girl with Maura and Aldon Kincaid. Dr. Huang Wong sat next to the red-dressed Dr. Nicole Duval. Since Kurt wasn't here, Grace should have asked Gail if Bobby and Sara could have been seated up here. Who else? Dr. Apeloko was next to her, and two Board of Directors. Grace didn't see Charlotte Kincaid, but she did see the campaign manager Harry sitting at a table front and center underneath the podium so he could monitor everything. Now, Harry talked earnestly with an elderly couple that Grace knew to be well-heeled.

Under the tall windows that overlooked the harbor, people already lined up at the rectangular buffet tables, spooning veal cutlets, penne pasta, scalloped potatoes, chicken in wine, baked haddock, bean casserole, salads, and rolls. Grace picked up a heavy china plate, selected a few pieces of cheese and green grapes, then spooned some veal cutlet with tomato sauce. She skipped the penne pasta, grabbed a roll, and scooped up some salad and added a fried chicken leg.

"Hi, ma."

Grace looked up. This young man standing in her way was addressing her? A carbon copy of himself came over, "Don't let Jessie frighten you off," the second guy warned.

The boys–well men– were both about six foot, with sandy hair, outdoor freckles, and laughing pale-blue eyes. The eyes clinched it for Grace. "Joshua and Jessie–David's sons?"

"Hey, she remembers us--we must be important," said Jessie to Joshua. Then he turned from his twin back to Grace. "Some of Madison's friends recognized Dr. Grace Farrington, so you've risen a bit in my sister's estimation."

"Not that she wants any woman to marry Dad," added a discouraging Joshua.

Murmuring from the crowd made Grace look to the entrance. With Maura close by his side, Aldon Kincaid marched in, greeting guests and shaking hands as if ORR was his living room. Grace knew she had to get up on the dais, eat a bit before they started the speeches, or she'd be introduced with a mouth stuffed with food.

Jessie looked at her saying encouragingly, "Dad has an extra chair at the table beside him. He's hoping that when you're done working you can join us?"

The boy's request sounded so sincere that Grace nodded and said, "I'll try."

Hurrying a little, she finished filling her plate and carried it up to the dais. Grace started to rapidly eat, noting David's table was to the left, also up front. Following Aldon, Maura carried her plate up to the dais, and stopped as she passed Grace, murmuring, "I asked that I be seated next to you so we could talk, but..." She frowned, looking at the seating cards.

"Don't worry about it, we can talk later," Grace reassured her. Between Maura and David's kids, she'd probably have to stay for the whole event, shit. Soon the crowd filled their plates and settled down.

Getting up to the podium, Adam did a brief update on Oyster River Research's current projects, and introduced Grace, Huang, Apeloko, and Fritz, but not Nicole. Apparently Adam classed her in the 'bring along' category. Then he presented Aldon Kincaid as a "young man who will be revitalizing this country's research."

She heard David below her give a brief snort to that, and was glad Kurt MacKay's sharp tongue now sailed oceans far away, as a vigorous Aldon Kincaid claimed he would single-handedly erase unemployment, eliminate the national debt, and lower the rate of out-of-wedlock pregnancies. Aldon waxed long on foreign relations and getting the U.S. respected again, and Grace wondered how exactly a junior senator from Connecticut could be expected to fulfill all that. But like the others, she clapped politely and wished he would finish up. Pretty much everybody else stifled yawns, but sitting on that dais, Maura Kincaid looked at her husband with worshipful eyes.

Listening to Aldon promise on, Grace got the distinct impression that it was not so much a race for the Senate that he started, but this was the opening volley to Aldon Kincaid's march to the Presidency of the United States. Grace promised herself she would get registered, just so she could vote for his opponent, whoever that might be.

Shifting uncomfortably in her seat, Grace shot a look at the clock and noticed Aldon was droning on over his allotted time. Eventually came the final applause, with a lot more enthusiasm, as the crowd was released to take their pick from the truly delicious looking dessert table with its chocolate dipped strawberries, meringue tarts, and tall, lavishly frosted layer cakes. Naturally, someone on the Board blocked her access, as she gushed about Grace's 'Farrington Fusions.' From experience with these events, Grace knew the first people up online would get all the good stuff--the expensive cheesecakes and slices of a Bavarian layer cake-- and the last online would have broken pecan cookies and peppermint puffs. Finally, after the third science fan blocked her way to gush over *"your marvelous work,"* Grace could line up and was just reaching for the caramel coconut cheesecake when she found someone pulling at her sleeve. Grace looked around to see Maura's radiant face.

"Can we talk?"

Not even meaning to, Grace glanced across the room to see Charlotte smiling with a group of donors, while behind her stood the faithful Harry monitoring. Beyond that, across the room by the bar, Aldon leaned over the red-dressed Nicole, checking out how deep that dress dropped. Glancing back to the dessert table, Grace watched as the last caramel coconut cheesecake slice landed on someone else's plate. "Certainly," she said to Maura in a resigned fashion.

Maura looked about conspiratorially, and whispered, "Not here. Meet me in the foyer."

Grace murmured back, "I'll get some dessert to make it look good." As a happily smiling Maura moved away, Grace realized she was getting as crazy as Maura, but she did get one of the last slices of the Bavarian chocolate layer cake with its topping of cherries. Then she moved over to David's table, setting her plate on the open place beside him. David had a phone to his ear, obviously doing some business, but he looked up at her, smiling warmly.

"I'll be right back," she said returning his smile. His sons were eating huge amounts of deserts and ignored her, while Madison glared from her father to Grace.

Grace moved past the crowd around Charlotte, who now was in an animated discussion trying to get more recruits for her power teas. She also noted that by the bar Aldon seemed to be still in an intimate conversation with the blushing Nicole, but with Harry now standing behind him.

The campaign manager looked about as if trying to find someone. Grace turned to one of the Board members and said hello. Then, seeing Harry looking in the other direction, she quickly moved to the entrance hall. Grace waited a moment to see that Harry was still occupied with Aldon and Nicole before she slipped out the hallway and the double doors.

In the foyer, Maura stood by the windows alongside the entrance door. In that drafty area, her arms were wrapped around her chest, but the face that turned to Grace was flooded with an almost rapturous animation. "Grace, I am pregnant. The doctor confirmed it! I'm taking hormone pills, and getting my blood checked weekly...this pregnancy will work, I know it."

Remembering her husband's mantling stance over the busty Nicole in the next room, Grace found herself asking, "How does Aldon feel about it?"

"I haven't told him, or Charlotte or Harry," she said bubbling with her joyful secret. "You're the first to know."

Freya would probably know what to advise this woman, but Grace only could only think of, "You'll make a wonderful mother."

"Can you imagine--if Aldon makes President, and then his son ... our boy will have to have a presidential name. Or maybe it'll be a girl. She may even be the first woman president?"

"Shouldn't you just start by picking out the colors for your nursery?"

She dipped her head. "Yes. Yes, I shouldn't get ahead of things. That's what my therapist always says. But I'm so happy..."

Grace found Maura's giddiness almost worrisome. "I thought you couldn't stand your husband's infidelities?"

For a brief moment doubt crossed Maura's face, but determination surpassed everything. "It's all different now. I will carry down the Kincaid destiny–and there will be a new Romanov in town." She glanced toward the door. "But you can't tell anyone! You're the first to know, but I need time to tell the others..."

Grace nodded as the door behind them opened, and good old Harry stepped in with his big smile. "Ladies, the party is in the other room."

As if practiced, Maura had an answer. "Oh, Grace was just wondering if I could speak to Aldon about funding her research. We can do that can't we, Harry?"

Harry still stood there saying to Maura, "Sure, but Aldon needs you for some pictures."

Maura immediately moved away from Grace and headed over to Harry, but as she did, the woman looked back at Grace tossing off, "I'll talk to Aldon about your project."

"Thanks," said Grace.

As Maura slipped back into the main room, Harry watched her with calculating eyes. Then he turned those eyes on Grace, who figured she probably should make herself available to any reporters for comments and photographs, but as she started to walk forward, Harry stepped into her path. "Grace, I heard you wanted to go see the boathouse?"

"Did Maura say that?"

"You know you've gotten to be really good friends with Maura, very fast."

"Yes."

"But going forward Maura's gonna be really busy working on her husband's campaign."

"Too busy to talk to me?"

"Much too busy. And you're a very busy lady too. Maybe you should stick to your laboratory."

"I like to get out sometimes." Brushing past him, Grace smelled his too strong aftershave and whiskey--a bad mix when he was too close. And he was following her closely into the main room.

Where Harry started warning again, "Grace, your research depends on the grants you can rustle up, doesn't it? So if important people--like the Kincaids–say stop funding Farrington, then maybe you'll be out of business, won't you?"

"You're threatening my funding?" Grace realized her voice was louder than usual, but who the hell did this guy think he was? Before Harry could even formulate a further reply, David joined them. He had apparently been listening and turned on his best imperial manner as he commented, "You know my late wife, Sylvia, headed many of the Oyster River charities, and even some of the U.N. appeals. She commented once that although the Kincaids like to give the impression they're generous donors, in actual money, not much ever seems to show up."

Harry immediately defended, glaring at him. "The Kincaids are very charitable."

"Only if they think they can get publicity out of it." David levelly stared back. "And then, sometimes what they pledged and what they actually pay are a bit different."

The campaign manager turned on Grace. "You think you can stop speaking to Maura?"

"No," replied Grace firmly. "No, I can't–and she'll hear about this conversation too!"

Harry went almost white and looked like he wanted to punch out someone out, but with David standing there, the campaign manager didn't say anything. He just finished his drink and walked away.

With a worried frown, David's eyes followed Harry. In a low tone he said, "Grace, you should let me know if he gives you any trouble. Contact my lawyer, Alan, Mark Silverstein's uncle. Harry Corman has a reputation for being a nasty SOB, and the Kincaids like to throw their weight around."

And Grace had turned Harry loose on David. "Can the Kincaids hurt your business?"

He seemed amused by that. "No. Actually, there are people who would say I can be a lot nastier to mess with. And, as for Harry, I don't deal with the help." But still, David didn't look happy. "My daughter isn't feeling too well, and boys are bored here, so I was thinking of leaving early..." With a frown, he looked over at Harry and the Kincaids. "But I hate to leave you now..."

"I'll be fine. I'm going to go over, answer any press questions, get photographed, and then leave myself. It's been a long day." Privately Grace felt David's daughter's '*sick feeling*' was more based in a dislike of herself, but she only said, "Tell Madison I hope she feels better."

* * *

Walking home, Grace had to lean against the wind. A Northeaster was blowing in, the cold clung longer this year, now into April. Back at her condo, Grace worked on her computer as she listened to that growing wind howling outside on her balcony. Finally, she felt hungry again, so she poured a can of chili into a pot on the stove. It was just starting to bubble when Grace heard sounds of scraping. It came from nearby...where?...outside. On her balcony. Grabbing a cleaver from the knife drawer, Grace headed to the curtain wall at the end of her apartment. The floor-to-ceiling curtains were pulled closed now for the night, but would open onto to sliding glass doors and the balcony overlooking the short lawn and the harbor. More shuffling sounds slamming against the glass. Could an idiot have climbed up one story on the side of the building?

Grace couldn't stand it. She pulled open the floor-length curtains. It took a moment for her eyes to adjust to the darkness. Outside something white moved near her feet. Even with the glass sliding door between them, she jumped back. But then Grace began to breathe again. On her deck was a huge seagull--maybe an albatross? The bird, fluttering his long wings, obviously didn't like the light and took off from the balcony, having trouble flying against the wild wind. Grace pulled the curtains shut again.

What had Kurt said? Those sliding glass doors could be jimmied by a five-year-old. She should have gotten the locking pole–actually she had bought one, but gave it to Sara in the apartment below. Well, she and Bobby were on the ground level, more likely to be burglarized. But from Aldon's cigar, Grace now cultured what she thought was the DNA of a murderer. A murderer who might be coming after her and all she had was the rifle in her closet, with no ammo. She hadn't bought more bullets since Grace went out shooting at Blue Trails with Kurt. Oh, hell.

Taking her canned chili from the stove Grace dumped it on a plate. Well, she could have just eaten it out of the pot since it was just her alone...and would be just her alone the rest of her life. As Grace ate, she reviewed her actions. Okay, when she heard someone trying to break in she should have run the other way, out into the hallway, then run down to Bobby's apartment and called the cops. Yeah, why do these great ideas always come after the event? The last time when she was robbed, and she came home to find her apartment door smashed open, Grace had rushed in banishing her plastic briefcase as a weapon. Fortunately, the robbers were long gone with her t-v set and microwave.

But now, the idea of going to bed alone here tonight seemed too much. She could leave and spend another night with David, but she didn't relish a confrontation his daughter. Grace looked at the time, it was two thirty, way too early to wake up Bobby and Sara downstairs. With the wind pounding outside and rattling the glass, it left her too uneasy to sleep here. Should she take her sleeping bag and go to the lab? Should she call security to escort her? No, she'd feel like a fool, and her name would be on the guard's report, and with the way that laboratory door lock had been acting up, she wouldn't feel safe there either.

Finally, Grace got her grandfather's pocket knife from the bedroom, opened the main blade, and put her jacket on. Then taking a deep breath to slow her heart a bit, Grace left her apartment and headed downstairs. Yes, the outside door in the lobby still had a broken locking system. Seeing her car outside Grace realized could drive to Freya's, and sleep there, knowing her son-the-cop slept downstairs among his gun safes. No, Grace wasn't going to bother them because of her craziness.

Outside, wind from the water blew damp and cold, and Grace found herself shivering. If some killer did lurk out here, she was stupidly exposing herself. Yet being able to move--to run if she had to-- made Grace feel better. The street lamps on ORR property cast a weak violet-white light that now bounced with shadows from the whipping tree branches. Carrying the knife hidden in her pocket, she walked quickly, along the sidewalk, past Administration, past her laboratory, and headed for the entrance to the facility. Walking under ORR's streetlights made Grace feel exposed and vulnerable, so she tried to stay hidden by the dancing darkness as much as she could.

She crossed the road again, now walking on the grassy hill that led down to the harbor. Grace could hear waves loudly slapping against the pilings of the docks. Even with the waves, the tide was pretty low, which meant the ramp to the docks now ran down steeply. Her shoe slipped a bit on the wet, steel netting and caught on a wooden cross tie. Grace stopped, took a breath, and then continued down much slower. The long floating dock lay ahead, pale gray in the overflow of the single security light at the little key hut. Only one of the small motor boats ORR kept for student use bobbed tied to the dock. The rest were upside down on the grassy hillside. Grace passed Kurt's diesel lobster yawl, the 'Big Un,' and finally walked out to the damaged thirty-six foot Cabo Rico sailboat--'The Lovely Lady'--the boat he lived on.

Seeing it there gave her a protected feeling–like Kurt was still there, sleeping in that soft bed in the prow. But he wasn't. Her white knight now sailed in Southern waters, headed for Antarctica. God, she wished he was here. Or David. Or Mac. Or anybody. Grace climbed up the gangplank and headed up.

Sounds from shore. An animal? A killer hunting her? Security making rounds? Grace jumped down to the deck. She didn't have a key, but she knew where Kurt's was–up by the prow, in a box, under a coiled rope. Grace dug her hand in and pulled it out, then moved sternward to the slanted hatch doors. Opening them up, she quickly slipped inside and down the 'ladder' steps. She bolted the hatch doors behind her, felt for the light switch and pulled the curtains closed across the main cabin portholes. Opposite the compact gallery, she checked for Kurt's automatic under the built-in bench of the dining table. It was gone, probably illegally with him on the ship. Moving forward, she passed the bathroom and storage, to the captain's cabin in the prow with its queen-sized bed. Kurt hadn't made his bed before he left, now she slipped a hand under the mattress near the carved headboard Kurt had built. Feeling for the sliding wood panel. Finding the indent, she pulled it back and was soon dragging out a loaded thirty-eight revolver. Kurt had schooled her in loading and shooting, but she had never gotten around to getting her own carry permit and handgun. Reaching down again she pulled out a cardboard box of ammo.

Looking around, Grace grabbed up a pillow and pulled off the case to wrap the gun in. She could take it back to her condo–but that was a long, cold walk in the dark, where a killer could be lurking behind every tree or shrub. Since she was here anyhow, why not spend the night? With the gun now on the table beside her, Grace felt comfortably safe. Turning up the electric heaters, she stripped off her clothing, climbed into Kurt's bed, and snuggled in the worn sheets, that needed washing, and still held his reassuring scent.

She awoke to sunlight shafting in through a porthole window and felt disoriented as her bed bobbed under her until she remembered coming down to Kurt's boat last night. Getting up she felt better. Leaving Kurt's gun on board, Grace jogged to her condo to shower and change, then headed down to the lab. Several large branches were on the ground from the storm last night, but the world looked scrubbed and clean from the wind storm. Grace picked up a cranberry scone and earl grey tea at the café in the Admin building. Stopping at Gail's desk Grace said, "Good turn out last night. Nice selection of food, the menus, and the tables looked lovely. You did a good job of pulling it together."

Gail beamed. "I saw you guys on Channel Eight last night."

"You arrange that?"

"Yes. But they were only going to cover the buffet if it was a slow night."

"I thought you were going to attend this one?"

The secretary looked down. "I really wanted too, but the tickets are pricey."

"You should have told me. Remember ORR owes me an escort ticket, you can have it next time–you should enjoy your efforts."

"Adam did offer me a ticket..." Gail admitted, "but we completely sold out for the room's capacity, and then Nicole got Adam to add her. She got herself added to the dais next to Dr. Huang. He wasn't too happy about that."

"He complain to Adam, or did Huang pick on you?"

"Me–like I had anything to do with it."

Grace smiled slyly. "When he introduced the dais line, Adam didn't mention her."

Coloring a little bit, Gail said, "I guess I forgot to type her name in his notes. But it did go well?"

To Gail's delight, Grace described the talks, the food, and a group that really seemed to enjoy themselves, even sitting through Aldon's self-serving speech. Later, as Grace walked back to her lab, she kept thinking that with all the extra work Gail did on that event, she should have been there. The secretary should be paid better. Grace would have to speak to Adam again! Gail needed to be a full-time employee, but that talk was not for today. Today that extraction from Brian's cadaver should be completed, and she'd find out who fathered Mac Dell!

Chapter 25

Checking the extraction log Grace noted Nick had completed the culturing and profile on the DNA from Brian/Lars/Loki/Lou, whoever. Now she'd learn if the blackmailing trickster fathered Mac Dell. Grace called up the first sample. The extraction had worked well from the first swab taken at the Medical Examiner's office, but she back checked with a sample taken from each of the other two vials. All matched nicely. Now--taking a deep breath first--she pulled up one of the genetic profiles she had done over the years on 'Mac' Thor Dell.

Grace immediately went to the twenty-third chromosome to compare the tell tale Y, the male heritage from father to son. Relief flooded through her body. The murdered, shifty blackmailer Brain had not fathered Mac! Yes, they had similar ethnicity, height, and coloration, but the tell tale Y chromosome--passed from father to son--was totally different! Lars Anderson or Brian Amundsen or Loki or whatever else called himself did not father Freya's tall son. Now, back to her paying work.

Still, Grace left the lab early, at four-thirty, so she could catch Freya in her shop. She had to circle the Town parking lot twice to get a space; she should have parked behind Freya's store. Hurrying downstairs, Grace found Freya wrapping up herbal concoctions for her mail order customers.

Freya looked up saying, "I've got to finish this before the Federal Express guy comes."

"I'll help you." Grace slid behind the counter. "What can I do?"

Freya handed her a sheet. "Read off what I need for the next box, then hand me the printed label, and cross that order off the list."

Reading from the sheet, Grace followed Freya around the store as she gathered, "Three packages Jasmine incense, one brass-winged dragon incense burner, one book *Tarot For Beginners*, one Gypsy Witch deck, and an amethyst necklace eighteen inches..."

Freya hurried about, packing until finally the last box was sealed and labeled, creating a huge white boxed, blue and orange lettered pyramid just before the Fed Ex driver arrived.

"Thanks," Freya said to Grace as the delivery man came in. "I got behind. Those detectives were here, questioning me again."

That didn't sound good. "You're supposed to have your lawyer with you before you answer..."

The tall woman shrugged. "It was only stuff I've already told them."

"Freya," Grace was bursting to tell all, but she waited until the Fed Ex guy carried his last box out in his canvas bag before she said, "Can you close up a few minutes early? I've got something important to say."

Freya moved to the door and turned around her 'closed' sign and then came back.

"I got a sample of Loki or Lars or Brian's DNA..." She started.

But Freya only interrupted saying, "I figured you would."

"He's not or was not Mac's father!"

The blonde Viking mother closed her eyes in relief, saying, "You're sure?"

"I'm positive!"

Now peace flooded Freya face. "I've already told Mac the tale of two men. He'll be relieved to know it wasn't Lars-- or as he last called himself--Brian." She walked over to start counting the register money tray.

Grace followed asking, "How could you have loved a man like that?"

Freya stood there as she methodically turned George Washington's portraits, so the dollars all faced the same way.

"They were both predatory males, tall and hunting–in those days it all seemed so wildly Nordic. I overlooked Brian's preying on those weaker than himself. While Thor–Wolfgang Ericsson-- he could strip you of everything in poker and chess, but there was a fairness to him. If Thor targeted you, you did something to deserve it. He was more of a Robin Hood to Brian's Sheriff of Nottingham."

As usual, Grace only focused on the question she wanted to solve. "Was Brian blackmailing people in those days?"

"Well, I didn't think about it formally as 'blackmailing,' but he was always collecting dirt on everybody he knew, so sometime in the future, he'd have control over them. That's one of the reasons I left him--that constant need to control you, play with you, like a cat letting a mouse run from him, then clawing him back."

"He sounds like a bum."

"Thank the Goddess he's not Mac's father," sighed Freya.

But Grace's mind still nagged at the problem before it. "Describe the blackmail information he had. What did it look like?"

Freya shrugged. "Newspaper clippings of your drunken driving arrest. He'd hide in the bushes for candid pictures of your wife screwing the mailman, or of your kid selling drugs at the schoolyard. His collection of telephoto lenses cost a small fortune. Did you see them in the boathouse?"

Grace hadn't seen them, but she figured that might be because Sierra had been emptying the boathouse of anything saleable. "That stash sounds like more than you could keep in a safe deposit box?"

"Oh, yes. He had stacks of scrapbooks and plastic boxes of files... It took up half the extra bedroom of the apartment I was renting."

Grace pictured that ."And over the years, it must have grown? Unless he changed his ways..."

Again Freya shook her head. "I can't see him giving up his dark holds over people or his exploitive practices."

"Perhaps his murderer found his hoard and destroyed it?"

"I don't think she did," said Freya carefully.

"She? You think our killer is a woman?"

"That junior miss, his live in–Sierra. She was just here, going after me."

Fear shot through Grace. "How is she going after you?"

Freya sighed. "Brian told her he was Mac's father and that Mac didn't know it."

"Well, that hold's gone now."

"Yes, but there more things that Brian also knew about me..."

"Such as?"

She shook her head. "When you are young--with two wild guys--you do some stupid things."

"All right. Did Sierra bring these things up?"

"No. She thought I had Brian's '*records*.' And Sierra had more smarts than he did. Brian tried to get me to sign over the store, which is rented–Sierra did some research at the town hall and figured out my house, and more importantly, its land on the harbor could be resold for big bucks. She wanted me to sign the deed over to her."

That gave Grace something to think about. "So knowing Sierra's shark-like tendencies, Brian probably hid his stockpile of secrets."

"I would think so."

"Have the police spoken to you about that being a motive?"

"No, and Mac hasn't heard anything in the department about Brian being a blackmailer."

"Which means the police haven't found his records."

"They could be in any storage cubical in the whole of Connecticut or any other state..." said Freya looking hopeless.

"No. Unless he used cash, they would have been able to trace anything on his credit card, so that pretty much lets out commercial storage."

"You know, Grace, I'm frankly hoping his blackmail hoard isn't found for the sake of all of us, and his would-be victims."

Back in her lab, Grace pulled out her murder spreadsheet again and studied it. No blinding 'Farrington Fusion' yet, but she saw an emerging thread: blackmail. Brian trying to get money out of Freya to keep the secret of his parentage from Mac. What was the hold Brian had over the younger Sierra? Sex, love, or some secret only he knew? Brian did the dirty work for the Kincaids, especially Harry. Could Brian have been trying to blackmail him or Charlotte? And Aldon certainly was a candidate for extortion, with his political reputation to protect balanced against his rampant womanizing–Grace's money was on him for the murderer. So had Brian asked too much from someone? She needed to find the blackmail material. Where the hell could it be?

Twenty years ago Freya said he had half a room full of scrapbooks and file boxes. Either he threw the old stuff away when he moved, or he added to it. She remembered when this laboratory used to be half taken over by two runs of seven-foot high steel framed file cabinets. How many of the forty-two inch wide cabinets had marched in two rows that she had inherited with the lab? In those days the computers could not hold the amount of data from one of her DNA profiles, then, bless them, laptops got stronger, and the computers started functioning in megabytes of data. Now, one of her inch and a half drives the size of a thumb-- with one hundred and twenty-eight gigabits-- could hold every profile she'd ever processed, so the file cabinets and paper folders went to recycle. Grace sat stiffly upright in her chair, recalling an image of the boathouse apartment, with its desk, computer, and flatbed scanner. If a geneticist can transfer thousands of her files to a computer, why couldn't a savvy blackmailer? Which meant, to find Brian's complete stash, maybe they should be looking for something smaller than a domino.

She needed another look about that Kincaid boathouse. Maybe she could get Freya to go with her? How late was it? Only eight p.m.--early enough to make a call for people who lived with normal hours. Grace dialed Maura.

"Grace," the woman sounded so happy to hear from her, Grace felt guilty. "Aldon has a fundraiser at the house on Saturday. We're expecting the Governor and Bridgeport's mayor, and some of ORR's Board–can David Gardiner make it?"

"Uhh,...I don't think so...he may be returning to Greece shortly..."

"But you'll ask him?" Maura pushed.

"Uhh....yes, I'll ask.

Maura immediately changed her tact. "But you must come! We need you to head up Aldon's Science team. Just one meeting..."

It wouldn't be *'just one meeting.'* "I don't really have much time..." said Grace reluctantly, "but I was going to ask you something..."

Maura suddenly broke in laughing. "I sound just like Charlotte. Well, with this new Kincaid in my tummy, I've got to start thinking about being the matriarch for the next 'Kincaid for President' generation." Her voice lowered to sound confidential, "Aldon and Charlotte are so excited about my pregnancy. Charlotte wants to call the baby Aldon Julius Kincaid, junior, but Aldon says no way." Maura hesitated for a moment, obviously relishing her new power. "We are going to name him or her something dignified, proper for a Commander in Chief, especially if it's a woman president.

And if it's a girl we're not going to name her Maura or Charlotte, but we may name her Dagmar Anastasia Kincaid."

"That sounds wonderful." This was going to be awkward. "Uhh...Maura, could I come over and take another look at the boathouse? Tomorrow afternoon?"

"Tomorrow, no, Charlotte's taking me into New York City in the morning. We'll be staying there overnight. She's so happy about the baby, we're going to start picking out furniture for the nurseries. There will be one in the Central Park Penthouse and one in this house. And I did what you said--I spoke up to Charlotte and said if Aldon and I are starting a family, we need our own house. So if Aldon wins the state senate seat in November, she'll give this house to us, and we won't be living in his mother's small apartment in Washington. Charlotte will buy us our own house in Georgetown. Although I'd prefer something in Virginia, maybe a horse farm---rural surroundings would be better for our son. Sort of George Washington's childhood..."

Maura sounded so happy, Grace felt like a shit trying to prove her husband guilty of murder, but maybe if she found Brian's blackmail trove she would prove Aldon's innocence? "But you said I could look in the boathouse apartment?"

"Yes, I know, but we're leaving at eight. Uhh...you know where the key is. Couldn't you just go in yourself?"

Perfect! "Yes, I could do that. That would be fine."

"I'll tell security to expect your car. And you'll come to Aldon's fundraiser?"

If you take, you got to give. "Of course." She'd go unless Grace could get enough proof to put Aldon in jail first!

Next step, a call to Freya, who, with her psychic powers, or just her sharp eyes and inbred intuition, had been known to find lost objects. "Tomorrow we're hunting Brian's blackmail material on either a thumb drive or CD's in the boathouse."

Freya thought about it and said, "Of course—he'd

have modernized. Yes, I should have thought of that! I'll try to get someone to watch the store after twelve."

The next day, they both had to wait until one when Lilith–Freya's Goth assistant with black and purple hair–showed up to mind the store. Then they took off for the Kincaid estate. As Grace drove past the Tutor Gatehouse, Freya nervously commented, "The police said there were security cameras at the entrance and the parking lot?"

"No problem. I called Maura. She and Charlotte were going into New York City today, but security has been informed to look for my car."

"Do they know I'm coming?" asked Freya.

As Grace turned off the main driveway, she hemmed a bit about that. "I don't think I mentioned it–but I know where the key is. Hopefully, we wouldn't run into Aldon, Sierra, or any of the Kincaid security people."

Freya nodded and looked out to the acres of grassy lawn bordered by a forest of tall trees. Her friend looked calm, but glancing down, Grace noted Freya's hands were tightly clenched in her lap.

Grace softly asked, "Are you thinking of Brian?"

"He was a bum–but your first loves, they always stay with you. That summer with him as Loki and Wolfgang as Thor, I truly felt like a goddess. That time will never come again--our youth will never come again..."

She sounded so down, Grace needed to say something. "But we're still living and loving...You had a son, that must have been a golden time too?"

"It was–and still is...even if he is following that girl reporter around like a starving puppy looking for a bone."

"She's smart, pretty, and hard working. He could do a lot worse than Samantha Carson."

Freya looked critically at her, saying sardonically, "Well, she must be something, if Grace Farrington can remember her name."

Grace wanted to change the topic as she parked. "Now that you know Wolfgang Eriksson is the father of your son, are you and Mac going to try to find him?"

"No. Mac's curious, but he'll respect my wishes." Freya stopped, looking at the water. "I loved Brian and Wolfgang, but they were born hell raisers. Mac and I have a good life here, I don't want to rock the boat with another berserker."

They got out, and Grace had an overwhelming desire to wave for the cameras. Instead, they just calmly walked to the grass, past the edge of that concrete-and-glass monsterpiece of a mansion. By the smell, Grace knew it was low tide, with the harbor and river mouth shining in the warming sunlight. A beautiful place to live, and the Kincaids only used it for a few weeks in the summer–well now that Aldon was in Congress and would be running for the Senate seat from Connecticut, Maura said this was their 'place of residence' no matter where they really lived. And Maura had prattled on endlessly what a great place it would be for their son or daughter to grow up.

As they walked through the trees to the steep wooden steps of the boathouse, Grace saw a white paper balled up in the grass, strangely out of place in this manicured mandarin's park.

Climbing the stairs, Grace found the key under the flower pot, but when she opened the door, everything was all wrong. Someone had cleaned the apartment, put all the thrown down cans and papers and books back in their places...but the cleaner hadn't displaced the body now center on the floor.

"Oh, my goddess," Freya whispered, coming up behind her and painfully grabbing Grace's arm. Freya looked about as if she'd find the murderer still there.

Pulling free Grace moved closer, getting a disturbing smell. A woman lay spread out on the carpet, wearing high leather boots, green jeans and a fringed, sorrel-colored suede jacket with Indian beading. She could be sleeping, if her bloody blonde head hadn't been bashed in from the back-- probably with the metal headed golf club laying beside her.

The blood on the carpet had soaked in. The blood in her hair had a dry look. This didn't look like a fresh kill. Getting closer, Grace knelt down, feeling for a pulse in her wrist. There was none, and the wrist felt cooler and stiffer than it should be. More sculptured clay than human, the woman lay, with only a little of her face showing toward Grace, who looked up and asked, "Doesn't that jacket look familiar?"

"Oh, you are so clueless!" Freya had just checked out the bathroom and closets for the killer. Now she returned to stand there with pain flooding her face. "It's Sierra, Brian's live-in girlfriend. She was a bitch, but no one deserves this."

"I understood she'd moved to the garage apartment. Why do you think she kept coming back here?"

"Sierra accused me of having Brian's stash of blackmail material. Probably she was still looking for it herself. Or maybe she found it, and tried to get money out of the killer–not the brightest of ideas--but that kid never struck me as working for her master's degree."

Grace stood up. Sierra seemed to have fallen face first. Not far from the body lay a bloody golf club. The shiny shaft and leather grip had no blood splatter. Grace would bet the murderer wiped it clean of fingerprints to leave the police with no suspects other than them. "Freya, do you have Mark's number..."

With no answer from Freya, Grace looked up and noticed her friend's eyes were fixed, as, in a trance-like state, she walked in front of the victim's head. Freya's--eyes unseeing but seeing all--looked to the body. Her hand--flat palmed out-- hovered over Sierra's head, then moved above Sierra's shoulders as in a far away voice Freya pronounced,

"She was leaning over, reaching for something valuable..."

"Brian's blackmail files?" Grace said softly, afraid to break Freya's connection.

"No... no. Something base, sordid, unworthy... in a bag, probably cash...Sierra knew who she was dealing with. She should've been on guard, but greed overcame her fear. She wanted that bag. Sierra leaned over and then the golf club was raised behind her..."

As Freya spoke, Grace pulled two collection vials out of her fanny pack. Dipping both of their cotton-tipped sticks into Sierra's blood. "Is the bag still in here?"

"No..." came that floating voice of Freya, "They took it." Suddenly Freya snapped out of her trance, rising to her full height. "We've got to get out of here before anyone sees us!" whispered Freya, hurrying around to grab at Grace's arm.

"Wait," said Grace rising, "Who killed her?"

"How should I know?" asked Freya.

"You were just in a trance communing with the murder victim or the killer..." That even sounded weird to Grace.

Her friend shook her head. "It doesn't work that way, Grace. I didn't see the killer, I became the killer, and felt the killer's hatred, fear, anger, fury... does that help?"

"Not enough to get an APB out."

Again Freya said, "We've got to get out of here before someone sees us."

"We can't." Grace looked at the phone on the desk, but thinking of fingerprints, she decided she'd better go with the cell phone in her bag. Hopefully, it will be charged and get a signal. "We've got to call the police."

"Why?" demanded a horrified Freya. "They'll arrest us!"

"We have to call because we're on camera as entering the property, and this morning I asked Maura for permission to look at the boathouse. Somebody is going to find this body some time, and when they check the cameras, you and I are 'it,' so we'd better admit to things from the start."

"Oh, God. I can't tell him..." Freya moaned.

"You can't tell Mark?"

"No, not my lawyer, I can't tell my son-the-cop!"

Double shit! 911 answered and Grace started, "I need to report a..." What was it? Not an accident from the skull that was bashed in with what looked like multiple hits... "a death. In the boathouse on the Kincaid estate." Reluctantly Grace gave her name and was told to wait there, not touching anything until the officers arrived.

Freya looked helplessly. "I should've reported it. They're going to think you killed him with me... I'll tell them I went in alone, and you stayed down at the bottom of the stairs..."

Grace was already dialing Mark, which she should have done first. Looking to Freya, she said, "Stop it! We will say what your lawyer tells us to."

When she heard him answer Grace started, "Mark, the police are coming..."

He cut in, "Oh, I hate conversations that start like this! This is Grace, right? Who's dead now?"

Mark gave his instructions and told them to wait outside the boathouse, but before they did Grace studied the golf club. Under the head, the shaft shined like a mirror. Blood should have splattered or dripped on it. Had it been wiped? Just on chance, Grace pulled out another collection vial and did long streaks of swabbing, leaving more than enough for someone else.

Looking at her, a dazed Freya said, "Are you allowed to do that?"

"No."

"But you are," said Freya in a dull voice as she looked around at Brian's former home. "Oh, Goddess, what are we going to do?"

"Follow Mark's instruction. Go down the stairs and wait for the cops."

They headed down. Way in the distance Grace could hear a dulled police siren. Feeling like a trapped fox with the hounds closing in, Grace looked about. And again she saw that white paper ball and started walking to it.

"What are you doing?" Freya asked. "Grace, you'll be on camera!"

"No, the boathouse cameras were deactivated–probably by your friend Brian," said Grace.

"Yeah," Freya responded. "With the things he was into, Brian treasured his privacy."

Having reached the scrap of white, Grace kneeled down on one knee studying it. Crumbled in the grass was a balled up paper towel with smears of brown--dried blood? It was obviously evidence, but would the police be able to check it out like she could? Pulling latex gloves from her fanny pack and a small collection bag, Grace started to rip off half of the paper towel.

"What are you doing?" Freya loomed over her as they could hear the police car pulling into the estate.

"Nothing."

"Yes, you are–you're destroying evidence!"

"Not really destroying, but police labs have limitations that my lab doesn't," Grace said, stuffing her prize into the plastic bag, then stripping off the latex gloves, stuffing it all into her fanny pack. Looking down, she brushed the grass blades off her knee, and as they walked away she wondered if the police would see the damp stain on her knee and figure out what it was?

A young officer responded from the Old Greenwich police. Freya didn't recognize him, but he appeared very polite. He took their names and addresses, then asked them to wait as he climbed upstairs. Coming down he seemed a bit less friendly as he told them they had to wait for his superiors.

Soon the police swarmed all over, with blue and red flashing lights staining the Kincaids' fortress of pristine concrete and glass. Everyone had asked questions before Mark Silverstein showed up. Having a lawyer arrive gave them a lot of suspicious looks, but some cop had already pulled up the fact that Freya was connected to the previous murder in the boathouse. "Why are you here–this was the scene of a murder your friend is out on bail for?" he demanded of Grace.

"Well since no one else has cleared Freya, we were here to prove her innocence."

The cop looked at her incredulously. "By finding another body?"

"That was an unexpected deviation from the plan," admitted Grace.

"But Sierra was dead when we got here!" insisted Freya.

"You'll both have to come down to the station with us." The cop announced, only to be contradicted.

"Actually, no." Mark Silverstein walked to them and said to Grace, "Have you both told them why you were here and how you came to find the body?"

Freya nodded, and Grace said, "Yes."

Mark continued, "Have you made it clear to the officer that you did not kill the victim and you do not know who did?"

Again they answered in the affirmative and Mark turned back to the cop. "I'm Ms. Dell's attorney. And you can ask any further questions in front of me now, or they will have to go about their business."

The cop signaled a big man in plain clothes coming down from the boathouse apartment. "Detective Kimball, he says we can't hold them?"

"Why not?" asked a gruff voice.

Mark answered him first, "Unless you have enough evidence to charge them with some crime?"

The detective looked very unhappy. "They were on private property..."

Grace quickly answered that "I–we–had permission from Maura Kincaid."

Not looking at her, the detective looked to the lawyer. "Since they were up in the apartment, we'll need their fingerprints."

Mark answered. "You already have Ms. Dell's, and Dr. Farrington will appear at your precinct and give you hers. However she will not answer any questions without her lawyer present."

Grace wondered if they still had her fingerprints from the octagon houseboat murder, but she decided not to bring that subject up.

Again the detective started sounding official, "We'll be getting the cameras' footage, which will have the time you drove on to the property and crossed the lawn in front of the main house..."

"Which should clear us," added Grace quickly. "The woman's body up there, the blood had already dried on her hair when we arrived. If your medical examiner can give you a time of death, I'm sure it will prove our innocence."

Grim-faced, the detective angrily looked to Mark. "Tell your client it is the job of the police to solve murders! In the future, she and her friend should just stay out of it!"

Grace and Freya walked out to the cars with Mark, as he said, "Don't speak to the police again without your lawyer."

"You'll be my lawyer again?" asked Grace.

He shook his head. "With me representing Freya, that could be construed as a conflict of interest. No, I think you should be represented by my Uncle Alan. He's not a criminal attorney, but he can certainly guard your interests."

How much will that cost, Grace wondered, and seeing the look on her face, Mark added, "It should be reasonable. Remember, Uncle Alan, is David Gardiner's lawyer, and wants to keep one of his 'A' clients happy."

"I'll pay standard rates," said Grace, fervently hoping the police didn't question her again.

The front lawn now was now bathed with flashing lights from police cars, the Kincaid's security car, and an ambulance was arriving as Grace drove her station wagon out past the gatehouse. "You want me to take you back to your store?"

"No. I've had it for today. Lilith can close up, take me home."

For a long time they didn't speak, then Freya said, "Now we're both suspects in another murder."

"One time wise we couldn't have committed."

"Unless we killed her and came back to create an alibi," finished Freya forlornly. "Mac is going to be so mad at me. He's a cop, and his mother is accused of murdering two people now. My son might lose his job because of me."

"When the murderer is exposed you'll be totally exonerated," said Grace, trying to sound confident.

"And how is that going to happen?" asked Freya angrily. "The cops won't be looking for anybody but us, and we've lost our number one suspect!"

Grace did feel a little down right then too, but she only said, "There are other suspects. So Sierra's dead. That leaves Harry, the Kincaids, and anyone else Brian and Sierra were trying to extract money out of. I'd assume the motive was blackmail, with Sierra following in Brian's large boot steps."

"Probably," agreed a glum Freya.

Following the shoreline, Grace turned for the back roads to Oyster River. "So, I want you to tell me every detail you remember about your meetings with Brian?"

"I already did."

"Do it again!"

The big woman beside her sighed. "He came to the store. Loki --I mean Brian-- knew I'd had a son out of wedlock. He just assumed it was his..."

"Maybe not. He probably took a positive stance, trying to force you to confirm or deny his fatherhood."

"He also assumed I hadn't told Mac."

"You told him that?" Grace glanced from the road to her.

"No, but I didn't deny it." She looked ashamed.

"Okay, then what?"

"He gave me that wolfish smile of his and said we were going to be partners. To seal the deal, he wanted me to sign over the deed to store building to him."

"What did you say?"

"I laughed at him. Told him I only rent the basement of this building. And asked him how he'd like selling incense from door to door--I'd take him on as a part-time stock boy."

"And?"

"I also told him he'd gone to fat and wrinkled, so I suggested he didn't confront Mac if he valued his front teeth. It was mostly bluff, but he walked out." Her voice went from defiance to pain. "But that night I told Mac the story of the two men and year of love."

"The next time you saw Brian?"

"We had lunch."

"What?"

Freya shrugged. "He called, wanting to come over for some of my '*home cooking*,' and knowing Brian that meant more time in the bedroom than the kitchen, so I said I'd meet him at The Captain's Mansion and he'd better have a credit card to give them up front."

"Brian agreed to that?"

As Grace was stopped for a traffic light, she could glance over at her friend again. Freya had a dreamy expression on her face. "Yes, he did. And I expected him to stick me with the check. He didn't. Ordered a delicious local microbrew beer, jumbo shrimp cocktails, and Porterhouse steaks for the both of us. He always did go first class, but usually on your dime."

"How did this lunch go?"

"It was more of an interrogation. He wanted to know everything about the Kincaids' past, present, and future. He also asked if there were any golden sheep in Oyster River we could shear as a team?"

"But he was living with Sierra?"

Freya smiled softly at that. "He mentioned what fun we had with me, him and Wolfgang, so maybe a threesome might not be too bad."

"You, him, and Sierra?" asked a shocked Grace.

"Aaup."

"Okay. Next meeting with Brian?"

"He called. Told me to bring five hundred as 'loan' to the boathouse, or he'd introduce himself to Mac."

"What did you say?"

"I said I had already told Mac."

"He asked if a cop really wanted a father with a police record? I didn't bite, so he got nastier and said that he had other things on me."

"Did he?"

"Oh, yes."

"So he was playing hardball."

"Aaup. He apparently was in a tight bind, for only five hundred bucks."

"You felt sorry for him? Is that why you picked up your trusty trimming axe, and went out to him?"

There was silence from the seat beside her, and then Freya sighed again, saying, "Oh, Grace, it's so hard to explain." She was silent for a time again, then said, "There was a time that I truly loved that man, but I was always afraid of him. We'd wrestled some in the past, and I knew I wasn't any match for Brian physically, and the axe was more to give me strength..."

"Wouldn't a gun have been better?"

She nodded her head. "I should've gone downstairs and got one of Mac's," she finished regretfully.

"So you went to visit Brian with an axe. Did you bring money to pay him off?"

"No. I didn't have any--the store's been slow, I just paid the taxes..."

"What happened?"

"He was mainly focused on getting the money–he apparently needed it badly. He'd 'borrowed' some from the Kincaid house funds and needed to pay it back before anyone noticed it was missing. He wanted me to pawn something."

"You said?"

"I suggested he pimp Sierra out."

"Freya!"

"A man his age with a kid like that? And I don't think it would be the first or fortieth time for her."

"What else happened?"

"Brian tried to kiss me–I bit his lip."

"Did you tell the police that?"

"No...it never came up. Why is that important?"

"They've still got his body. Your lawyer should get a picture of the damage to Brian's mouth to explain his blood on your blouse. What did he do?"

"He laughed and reached for my handbag. I raised the axe, and he ripped it out of my hands, nearly lifting me off the floor-- and I'm no lightweight! I let go, grabbed my bag, and I ran out the door to his roaring laughter."

There was silence, and then Grace said, "And shortly after that he was found dead bludgeoned to death by your axe." Grace turned on to Main Street and headed into the town of Oyster River. "That's it?"

"Aaup," said Freya.

"How did the killer get behind him?"

"Probably the same way as they did killing Sierra. Someone Brian felt he had buffaloed focused Brian's attention on money."

Grace turned down that narrow old road toward the harbor, and another left on to Freya's dead-end lane. Freya's van and Mac's truck filled the driveway, and another car that was probably Freya's renter was parked on a gravel spot on the small lawn. Grace parked in the street, cutting off a lane to traffic, but she'd be leaving soon. "No, those are not the only times you saw him. You said he'd come to the boatwright's barn? When was that?"

Freya started to say 'no,' then remembered, saying, "Yes. Yes, he did. That first time I saw him in Oyster River."

"How did he know you rented the barn from the historical society?"

"Supreme talent and skills of a blackmailer--research, research, research! I don't know how he found out, but I am fully convinced he could have."

"All right, tell me about that meeting." Grace stared at her hard, as they both just sat in the parked car.

Remembering Freya started, "I was working there. I opened up the two big doors because it was warmer outside then it was in the barn without heat. The fearing's almost done, we'll be christening her soon..." She was getting excited at the thought.

"Stick with Brian," Grace admonished.

Her friend got back on track. "I heard a motorboat, but a real quiet one, and thought one of the volunteers might have decided to show up. I walked outside, and in the woods, I saw something red flashing in the trees. Curious, I walked over into the trees and down the path to the little beach. There was this shining Chris Craft with its bow pulled up on the sand next to my old trawler, and there was this huge guy climbing about my boat, rummaging through the toolbox in the prow."

"Looking for what?"

She shrugged. "Brian and Wolfgang were always checking things out, hunting for prey or booty..."

"Would he have stolen from you?"

Freya smiled ironically. "When I was young I believed friends don't steal from friends, but I learned --when you know a thief --it's not if they are going to steal from you, but when."

"Oh, Freya..."

"I started to walk over, and he must have heard something. He looked up and gave me that old, lopsided grin..." She stopped, her eyes staring back years. "He was older, heavier, but still that man I'd loved once. I got the biggest lump in my throat; I think he did too."

She stopped talking, and Grace waited, then finally she said, "What did he say?"

"Long time, no see. Well, Loki or Brian never was very original or eloquent. That wasn't his specialty. Brian said he was living nearby, and that we should get reacquainted again." Freya stopped, looking torn. "Part of me wanted to take him home to my bed that minute, the other part realized that if he were around Mac my son would be ashamed of his mother." Freya face hardened. "My son came first. I told Brian that it was over, and he'd better remember that, and to get the hell out there."

Breathing heavily, Freya stopped and then she continued. "Brian ignored me. Said he'd heard I was building a faering and he wanted to see it. He walked right past me, up that path through the woods."

"He liked boats?" asked Grace.

Again Freya's face softened with the memory. "Always. He and Wolfgang had found a small sailboat--they said they'd 'won' it. That summer we went out every evening on the lake." Then her eyes hardened. "Brian liked the faering, but, of course, he had to tell me how he would have built it better."

"How long was he in the barn?" asked Grace, getting an idea.

She shrugged. "I don't know how long. He just walked about probably looking for something to steal. Then not seeing anything worth the effort, he kind of hunched over, looking sickish, and asked if I had a drink–he had to take a pill."

"A drink?"

"Well, he said he'd like mead, but he'd settle for water, so I had to walk back to my boat and get a water bottle from my tool sack."

Which would have given Brian a chance to hide something -- probably his plan all along. "We're going to have to search the boatwright's barn."

"All of it?" demanded Freya. "For what?"

"I'm not sure, but I'm guessing a thumb drive."

"Search all of that huge barn for something two inches long? Oh, my Goddess."

"I'll drive." Grace turned to head to her car.

"No, park your car behind mine. The lock to that darn gate to the bird preserve is rusted closed again. Mac and I haven't had time to saw it off, and having the road blocked keeps the boatwright's barn safe from 'pickers.' We'll take my diesel."

Still thinking they could park outside and just walk into the preserve, Grace reparked her car then followed her friend around the pre-Revolutionary War house. The first time Freya motored her here the dock had been half rotted out. But it lasted until Mac was ten when they had a hurricane force storm on a full moon that washed the old dock away. Freya cobbled together some boards, a float of beer barrels and two repurposed ladders that lasted another few years, but when Mac was taking woodshop in middle school, he had come to

Grace for money to buy supplies. While his classmates were making wobbly, three-legged tables, Mac-- with his carpenter Boy Scoutmaster's help--rebuilt a solid upper deck, tide ramp, and a floating dock, with actual iron tie-up cleats for Freya's diesel and whatever else she wanted to tie up.

Now two boats were bobbing up and down at that dock. A beat up aluminum rowboat and that old wooden diesel, the Vengeful Valkyrie, that Mac had named when he was fourteen years old. The boat was ancient when Freya saved enough money to buy it, and now that Mac was an ex-Marine M.P., and a cop, that indestructible Valkyrie keeps chugging along. Freya got in, turned the key to warm up the glow plugs as Grace cast off the stern. Freya had the motor idling when Grace cast off the bow and, pivoting with her hands on the gunwale of the boat, she hopped in. Moving slowly, Grace centered herself on a hard front bench to distribute weight, although the flat-bottomed trawler Valkyrie was a pretty steady boat in low seas. As the Viking gal backed the diesel out to clear the dock, Freya's face glowed in the sunlight with an almost bubbling joy. Always happiest on the water, Freya swung the boat free and plowed a course parallel to the coastline, chopping through low green waves. Even Grace felt the exhilaration of being out on the harbor as she pulled her jacket close, and tried to keep her shoes away from the rainwater slopping under the slatted decking.

Making good time, they chugged passed old houses and docks as the boat motored with the waves. They passed the area where Grace knew the Whaler's Museum was and more houses, finally reaching the thicket of trees that formed the bird preserve. Ahead, the ruins of a long, deep water dock in front of the boatwright's barn that had been a dangerous navigational hazard for over one hundred years; so much so that it had gained historical protection, left there to rot until there were funds to properly 'excavate' it archeologically.

So before that Freya aimed her flat-hulled boat

starboard into the small beached inlet. As Freya cut the engine, Grace handed her a boat hook pole and took one herself to cut the boat's drift in as it ran a foot or two up into the sand. Freya hopped out with a long bow rope to tie up to a tree, saying, "Grace, hand me that canvas bag in the bow please." Grace did and then followed her onto the sand. The little beach was fringed with knee-high grass and thickets of trees. Easily carrying the heavy bag of tools from the boat, Freya headed up on a well-worn path snaking through the saplings.

They came out parallel to the water in a large open area of wild grass and an overgrown gravel parking lot before a three-story, dark-wood barn. At its front--angled to the water--the boatwright's barn had two, twenty-foot-high doors and a third, human-sized entrance. All were padlocked from the outside. Freya unlocked the tall, rolling doors, as Grace asked, "Why don't we just unpadlock the small door?"

"We need the light," returned Freya as she rolled the first door open, Grace pushed back the other.

Inside, the boatwright's barn was totally open for three stories to allow an unobstructed building area. The barn's three other long sides were set with waist high, five-foot tall banks of small-paned windows for lighting the cadaverous opening, with its work benches built into the sides.

To the left, a Y shaped tree limb was being debarked on Freya's makeshift clamp. Probably a keel support for the next project. In the place of pride was a finished looking sixteen foot, four bench Viking style faering that took up the center. With its sleek racing lines of the timbers sledging to the cutting prow, Grace had to admire it as both a working boat and a sculpture of elegant beauty. Yes, it had taken Freya, Mac, and anyone she could shanghai into slave labor for weeks, no, months, but the result certainly looked worth it.

Freya studied her work critically. "As soon as the

water warms we'll be christening her. I'd like you to do the honor. I've already got the mead fermenting for the christening party and breaking bottle."

"Oh, no, not that breaking the bottle over the bow again. Last time it took the two of us twelve hits to break it over the Valkyrie's bow! You shouldn't want to hurt this little beauty."

"This time I'll score the bottle with a diamond tipped cutter." Freya studied the trim ship. "We should have done that last time."

Grace envisioned a disaster in the making, but she only said, "What are you going to name it?"

"Her," corrected Freya. "Well, as usual, I gave that honor to my son. Mac said she's 'slim, reliable and will go where nobody else would think of...so he's decided on the name, and everybody who has worked on the project was polled, and they all agreed."

"I worked on it, and nobody asked me?" protested Grace.

"Yes, you weren't consulted." Freya gave a big self-satisfied smile. "That's because Mac named our faering 'Grace' in your honor."

A sudden warmth spread through Grace. By choice, she was solitary most of her life, but she'd been blessed with a few deep relationships and knowing they were reciprocal really mattered. How could she marry David and leave Oyster River? Time to change the subject. "We've got search this place, and it's got to be done with a standard methodology."

Freya raised a skeptical eyebrow as she looked from wooden box after wooden box of every kind of nails, screws, nineteenth-century planes, and two-handed saws, piles of wood shavings, boxes of pegs, plans pinned to the walls, timber piles, rope coils, pegboards of tools, oil cans, and even a coat scuttle next to a Franklin stove, next a row of glass kerosene lanterns...

"Grace, turn on the lights."

Automatically, Grace turned to the wood wall looking for a switch box, only to hear Freya's chuckling, "A little boatwright's humor." That's right. This building was constructed long before electricity came to Oyster River, and the barn was never updated. Still chuckling, Freya carried a battery lantern for herself and handed Grace a flashlight. "What are we looking for that Brian couldn't just as easily stashed a million other places?"

"A thumb drive or a safe deposit box key--anything else that's out of place," said Grace, walking to the nearest table to get a pad of graph paper. "We're going to have to break it down by zones and check off each one completed."

"Aaup." Freya didn't look at all hopeful, but she started at the first table of planes and hand saws and chisels. "But we're losing the light."

The battery light lasted until they finished a fruitless search, but the temperature had started dropping, and Grace wished she had a pair of gloves and knit cap before they went back out on the water again. "I'm sorry I came up with this snipe hunt."

"It was a good idea," admitted Freya.

Back on the beach, the tide had come in, and the Vengeful Valkyrie floated free on her tether. The sun had sunk below the trees on the peninsula that housed Oyster River Research, but a golden sky reflected in the rippled metallic gray water that looked like glass.

They took off their shoes and threw them on board as Freya used her rope to pull in the boat. It took the two of them to pull the bow up on what was left of the beach. Climbing up on board, they both used the poles to push them into deeper water as Freya said, "Yes, Brian needed somewhere where none of his victims could find his stash of evidence. And I'll bet Sierra was one of them."

"You know, today there aren't many things you can blackmail people for," stated Grace.

"Brian would find something," said Freya, settling back in her seat by the engine.

"Don't turn on the engine," Grace commanded. "You said the first time you saw Brian he was standing on your boat?"

"He always checked out your car, your boat, your apartment–as he once told me he wanted to keep track of '*his*' inventory."

"Let the boat float in. While we still have some light, you check the stern, I'll search the bow." Grace rose, and moved to the same side as Freya, tipping the boat bit.

Freya stood up, carefully shifting her weight to the opposite, portside. "Move more slowly, Grace, it's a floating deck, not a floor. And we're looking for something Brian left? I don't know if he would have had the time."

"The Vengeful Valkyrie is moored on an open dock while you, Mac, and your renter's cars are at work."

Freya sighed.

"Is there a flashlight?" Grace asked.

"Look in that starboard toolbox..." Freya looked over at her confusion. "Grace, that's the right side facing the bow."

Grace found two flashlights. Only one worked, and toolbox was filled with wrenches, oil rags, oil cans, various sized galvanized turnbuckles, and ropes. After trying to move things about, Grace gave up and just started to unload everything. Soon she had a pile on the bench board beside her while the Valkyrie scraped against the beach as small waves pushed her in. Refilling the toolbox, Grace looked around. The portside box held life jackets, flares, water bottles, and a leaking caulking tube. Grace stuck her hand in.

"Be careful," Freya warned, "there might be some loose fish hooks in there."

There were. Rusty fish hooks. Grace nicked her finger

and, as she sucked blood, wondered when she had her last tentaus shot, but at least the barb hadn't stuck in. But no thumb drive or safe deposit box key or mini notebook full of password codes. Standing up stiffly, Grace walked the length of the boat from bow to stern and started running her fingers under the gunwale. Nothing. Freya had opened the cover over the motor. "Grace, I need that flashlight."

Grace handed Freya hers, then they both searched the engine, the lines and pistons, and greasy whatevers. Closing the hatch cover, Freya wiped her oily hands with a gray cotton cloth, Grace took back the flashlight and headed forward again. The bow itself was covered on the top, with a dark hole underneath. Grace had to kneel down on the slatted decking, getting her pants wet from the bilge water. She angled the light into that pointed hole-- not too much under there to see. What if the thing they were looking for was under the decking in the water? As Grace probed with her fingers under the wood covering, she kept thinking they should pull up the slatted decking–should they do it here on the beach–or wait until they got back to Freya's dock? Maybe do it in the full sunlight tomorrow?

Suddenly, Grace's probing fingers hit something disgusting, like dried chewed gum. She angled the flashlight and got down with her shoulder against the wet decking as she tried to see up under the wood bow cover. What was sticky like gum looked light gray and had something small and black stuck deep in it. "Freya!"

With her nails, Grace frantically dug out two inches of a small black plastic piece with a ribbed surface.

"What is it?" Freya leaned over her, sounding frightened.

Grace pulled the two sections apart exposing the silver metal USB connection. "A thumb drive." Before Grace struggled to position herself to get up off the decking, she slid it closed again and then held it out to Freya. As Grace grabbed the gunwale with one hand to rise, she looked to Freya. With her other hand Grace was holding out the drive, but her friend looked like she was holding a scorpion getting ready to strike. Finally up, Grace stood looking at Freya. "I'm assuming you didn't glue that thing with caulking to your bow?"

"No."

Grace couldn't believe it. "He found you living here, found out you owned a boat, and that you worked in the boatwright's barn, so he planned to hide the computer drive on your ship..."

"You're giving him too much credit, Grace. He knew where I lived. He could see my boats, and one day he saw me on the water and followed. Seeing the boat alone, he saw an opportunity and probably even used my own caulking."

"Okay. He stashed his blackmail material on your boat, so he wasn't planning on being killed by you."

Freya just stood there. "What are you going to do with it?"

"I don't think it could be fingerprinted with this ridge design along both sides."

"But you're giving it to the police?"

"Of course–Brian was probably killed by someone he was blackmailing. The murderer might be on this drive."

Freya only looked at her in a tired manner. "Grace, I assume things about me are on that drive and probably a whole bunch of other people who did something stupid, or loved the wrong person, or anything Brian figured he could hold over them. It wouldn't have had to be a crime, just something a person didn't want to come out. Handing it in might destroy many lives." Saying that Freya turned from her, and headed back to the rear for the tiller, leaving Grace to wonder what she would do with their discovery.

As they plowed across the harbor, Freya stayed silent, even when Grace hopped out to tie up. She still said nothing as Grace followed her up the log steps to the house. Inside

Freya took off her jacket and asked, "How about a hot toddy and a grilled cheese sandwich?"

Rubbing her cold stiffened hands Grace asked, "Drink first?"

Freya nodded. "A strong one."

"Can I use your laptop?"

Her friend tightened at that. "Yes, I knew you would have to. It's in the workroom. You don't ever stop digging do you, Grace?"

Inside Freya's workroom, Grace inserted the thumb drive and watched it pop up on the screen, showing rows of folders. She clicked on a folder and hundreds of files scrolled along. Some were titled with six-figure dates, some had names, and some were in some sort of multi-number and letter codes. All of it would be encrypted. How could they break that? Bobby did a lot with computers, and he had friends who knew more. And maybe through her contacts with the Medical Examiner's office, they could get Grace hooked up with the State police who might have someone who could hack this?

Freya stood over her frowning, as she handed Grace a steaming copper mug smelling of lemon, honey, and whiskey. "Click on a file–try that 'sierra kostr 4' there."

"No, he would have password protected it..." said Grace, clicking on the file to prove it. And to Grace's immense surprise something started opening up. "What does 'kostr' mean?"

"In old Norse, 'marriage,'" supplied Freya sipping from her own mug. "It's coming up slowly. Must be a photograph, taking up lots of memory."

"He was a blackmailer and a thief, but he didn't encrypt his own stuff?" Grace stared at that screen with disbelief.

"I knew Brian. I slept him. He was a pretty direct guy, who believed his size, strength, and sneakiness were enough to keep control of whatever he called his. Brian used to repeat that old poem, '*If I want it, it's mine, If it's in my hand, it's mine, and if I can take it away from you, it's mine.*' He wouldn't have bothered with fancy computer nonsense."

That Sierra kostr 4 finished opening up. Fascinated, Grace scrolled down a Baltimore marriage certificate for Sierra Sonheim and Willam F. Dolan. There were five other sierra kostr files, and Grace suspected they would all be marriage certificates. She pulled sierra kostr 3 up. Another certificate for Sierra Sonheim and Anthony Marcello in Arizona. Grace moved to go back and click up the next one, but Freya said, "No. Scroll down this one."

Obediently Grace did and then saw what Freya was looking for. "In this one, Sierra is nineteen and Anthony is eighty-three?"

"Aaup, and if you noticed the previous husband, William Dolan was ninety-two."

"So Brian had proof that Sierra was a bigamist?"

"Maybe. Maybe not. I'll bet Brian had proof that Sierra had married multiple elderly men, some of whom died of exhaustion on their wedding night...or had some help making her a rich widow."

A horrible thought hit Grace. "He wouldn't have killed them, would he?"

Freya face looked older as she sighed, "Brian and Wolfgang would ask me to do outrageous things...me marrying an elderly man and the guys killing him was one. Just for fun, I agreed once. Wolfgang roared with laughter and said it was all a put on, but when I looked at Brian, I saw darkness in those Loki's eyes of his. I think Brian was entirely serious."

"How would it have worked?"

"He and Wolfgang would be my brothers, who would push their lonely, shy sister to a lonelier older man, with hopefully a heart problem or the guys would smother him in his sleep. All the time we were together, Brian would bring it up again and again. While Wolfgang was there, he didn't dare push too hard, and when Wolfgang left, he warned Brian not to touch me. But Brian wasn't afraid of warnings from a man who wasn't there, and when I refused to date this nice old Greek man, Brian beat the hell of me."

"What did you do?"

"I ran."

"Back here, he'd have known where your family has lived for centuries. Could he have followed you?"

"Yes, but I was pregnant, and I had to go somewhere. I had protection: my Dad Mike was alive, my Uncle Mac too, and I bought myself a handgun. And, to be honest, Brian would never have made a good pimp--he's too lazy and crude with his forcing. I'm sure Sierra went along with his schemes willingly."

"Well, she didn't willingly smash the back of her head in. If she killed Brian, then we've got two killers...or just one, if someone thought he had to get rid of both his blackmailers?"

Grace looked down at the list of documents. Aldon, hyphenated with a different woman's name, was on about thirty of them. Maura had ten or twelve by herself, and the mother-in-law Charlotte had a whopping twenty, but Harry had nearly a hundred of the deadly little files. "If we sent a letter to each of them, saying we'd found Brian's stash..."

"Blackmail a killer?" Freya asked tartly. "I think that's the bright move Sierra tried."

Grace opened up another folder, and there were files on Shy Alice. She looked to Freya "That's you?"

"Aaup."

There was one labeled 'My Son.' Grace opened the document. A photo of Mac's birth certificate. "He shouldn't have been able to get that–it's not public information."

"Brian always had his ways," said Freya pulling the

keyboard from her and starting to delete documents.

"Aren't you going to see what he had on you?"

"Nope."

"Freya, if we hand this drive to the police, they might still be able to pull up documents you deleted?" Grace looked at the thumb drive. "If we copy file-by-file to another drive and maybe give that to the police, that might keep you clear?"

A tired Freya looked to Grace saying, "We're both tampering with evidence in a murder case."

"I know you and Mac did not kill Brian or Sierra, but if we hand this drive in, it will give the police motives for the both of you."

Freya looked down at the drive. "If we give this to the police, a lot of people who did some stupid things a long time ago can be badly hurt." Freya pulled the thumb drive out of her computer and held it out to Grace. "But you do what you think is best. I don't want to see it again."

After eating Freya's grilled cheese and not being able to taste anything, Grace returned to her office and slipped that blackmail drive into her desk drawer, locking it. She's got to go through it, but only when she has some of her regular work done. Suiting up for her clean room, Grace told Nick to start extraction on Aldon's cigar tip saliva and the swab of Sierra's blood, while with a high powered microscope, she studied the portion of that balled up paper towel she found on the lawn. Blood streaks. She chose one to begin an extraction, but she figured most likely it would be Sierra's. No, what she was looking for was in the towel itself. Fibers that looked stained, as if they were soaking up sweat or body oil from a desperate killer. And it looked like she had something to extract!

A voice crackled from the speaker in the main office-- Inger. "Grace, I'm sorry to bother you, but there's a Maura Kincaid on the phone. She says she must speak to you now!"

Annoyed at being disturbed, Grace only said, "Patch it in." She listened to the phone line do its dings and clicks as it came over the speaker. "Maura?"

"Grace? Is that you?"

"What did you want?"

"You sound funny like you're underwater?"

"I'm in a face mask and shield."

Silence, then, "Are you going to take it off?"

"No. I'm working right now–you said you had something important to say?"

"Charlotte got a call from the maid," Maura sounded upset. "The police are all over the estate–Tiffany said you found another body in the boathouse?"

She should have called Maura herself. "Yes."

"Who was it?" demanded Maura.

"Sierra."

"Sierra's dead? What happened? Did she have a heart attack? She's so young."

Grace remembered that bashed-in head. "I don't think it was natural."

"Why was she there?"

"You'd have had to ask her."

"Oh, God," moaned Maura. "Why did she have to get herself killed in our boathouse? Why couldn't she have done it elsewhere?"

"I don't think she had a choice in the matter," Grace said tartly. "And it would help if you told the police we had permission to be on the property."

"What?"

"Charlotte or somebody told the police we were trespassing–you remember giving me permission, don't you?" Grace spoke very strongly.

A silence, then, "Oh, yes. I will tell them. But who do you think did it? I mean it must be a passing serial killer... "

"Who passed by twice? The police probably think it was someone on site."

Her voice was starting to sound frightened. "It wasn't

Aldon. He was with Harry discussing the campaign all day..."

She didn't think that was much of an alibi, but Grace only said, "And you and Charlotte went into the City shopping." And those weren't really good alibis for anybody either.

"What will happen now?" Maura's voice sounded terrified.

"The police will ask more questions, the media kept Brian's death to the back pages, I guess they'll do the same for Sierra's..."

"Yes, yes they will!" Maura now sounded relieved. "And it'll be all over, and won't affect my baby or us at all. At least I hope so," said Maura before she hung up.

And thus ended her sorrow over Sierra's untimely death.

* * *

When Grace finally came out of her clean room, she found a note on her desk; whoever wrote it obviously knew she didn't check her e-mail or phone messages too frequently. *'Please call me–Adam's in the office now and wants to talk to you. Gail.'* She could just ignore it, but it was probably something that would have to be faced sometime. Did Adam know she and Freya found another dead body? She wouldn't bring it up unless he said something. Maybe Gail would know. Grace called Admin, expecting her to answer.

"Greenfield Const–no, ORR–Oyster River Research," finished a harried male voice.

"This is Grace. Where is Gail?"

"Picking up the summer catalogs from the printer..." said Adam, obviously annoyed with her absence--although it wasn't Gail's fault.

And Gail was probably not getting paid mileage for using her car and gas, Grace thought, but she only asked, "You wanted to talk with me?"

On the phone, she could hear another phone ringing,

and someone speaking in the background. Again a stressed sounding Adam asked, "Can you come to Admin? I'm supposed to be out of here by now."

"I'll be over." What did he want? Adam didn't mention another dead body. Since Gail was out, would he want Grace to make the coffee? Run copies? No, that wasn't happening! Adam wouldn't dare! Grace just looked about, Nick was still in the clean room, she hit the speaker on her desk. "I'm going over to Admin. Continue with your work, I'll lock the outside doors."

"Will do," floated the disembodied voice back.

Well, she tried to lock the outside doors, then just gave up. Nick would have to handle any visitor or intruder, and he should be out soon. Outside, the harbor looked like smooth steel under a gray satin sky. She could see green buds poking out on the lilacs, and hoped they didn't have a late freeze. Still, it felt good now as Grace headed in the beige brick building, through the foyer, and to Gail's desk where Adam stood, bend over talking into Gail's phone. "You promised delivery. It's here tomorrow, or we'll find another supplier!" Saying that he slammed down the phone and looked at her saying, "Where in the hell do you go to buy horseshoe crab blood?"

"Gail will know when she gets back," reassured Grace. The first line on the desk phone started ringing. Adam looked at his watch as the second line also started ringing, and Grace suggested, "Have you thought any more about hiring Gail as a full-time employee?"

Shrugging off the ringing phones, Adam turned, "Let's talk in my office."

Grace followed him in and noted that more papers spread over the desk in a mess deeper than usual. "How long has Gail been gone?"

He sat down behind his desk, indicating a chair in front of it, "This morning, I told her to stay there until we get our catalogs!"

Grace sat down, wanting to get this over with. "I had to leave my lab open--that fancy door lock isn't working."

"Gail knows about this?"

"Yes."

"Then it'll get fixed." He settled back in that chair and looked directly at her. "David Gardener visited me with his lawyer today."

What was this? Forcing a neutral tone, she said, "Alan's a Board member."

"Yes, to basically represent David's interests. They were inquiring about getting you out of your contract with ORR so you can move to Greece with him." Adam shook his head in defeat. "He showed me plans of the laboratory he has built for you–it's better than anything we can provide, although I could move you into one of the newer labs when Dr. Apeloko returns to Nigeria?"

Newer at Oyster River would be the nineteen eighties, hardly topping what David was offering, but Grace only said, "I'm content where I am for the immediate future. I wish David had not spoken to you, and I thought he knew that." She sighed."What did you tell him?"

"Nothing. I said that your contract was a private matter. The Board will only see the new terms before your renewal date, and before that, I will only speak with you about your future plans."

"You've already told me that you would release me if I wished it."

"Very regretfully. You're our foremost scientist right now. Huang is a bit of a disappointment, and although MacKay's work is interesting, Kurt is a public relations disaster in the making! So ORR will hate to lose you, especially if you'll working somewhere else when you get your Nobel."

"I'm perfectly happy working here...but what David is

offering is not just a place to work, he's offering marriage and a ready-made family..."

Adam studied her. "Grace, as a friend, I don't think you can turn that down."

"It wouldn't be for his money..."

"No, I don't think it would be. I know you're married to your work, but it must be lonely. I can't imagine living without Rachel's companionship, and the kids...my children are my future. And don't push off having money–money matters in this world! If you married David, it wouldn't have to be forever. If it didn't work out, people get divorced. Maybe just give it a try?"

Grace sat back, and said, "I don't really know what I want. I've always known all my life what I wanted, but now..." She shook her head, feeling lost.

"Has he given you a deadline?"

"Not really...but holding David off is not really fair to him."

"And the longer you wait, the more chance he might change his mind."

She had factored that in, and still couldn't come up with an answer. "And if I leave, what about my people?"

He thought about it. "They're all exceptionally trained lab assistants, and putting working for Dr. Grace Farrington's lab on their resume will help. I might be able to absorb Bobby back on my budget as a full-time instructor–but no promises. And anybody taking over your laboratory would need Inger and Nick, at the beginning at least." Adam waited for her to speak, then finally spoke for her. "If you decide to leave, we won't go through the Board. Come directly to me. My construction company lawyer can draw up the papers releasing you. I'll sign them before the Board knows."

Would he be getting himself in trouble for her? "Is that within the scope of your authority?"

He shrugged. "I don't know, but in the event, they

don't like it, my signature as ORR President will be binding for you, and if I get lucky, they'll fire me." She smiled at that, as Adam continued, "I've also been speaking to the Board members individually about hiring Gail from her temporary agency." He ran fingers through his hair. "Working with a bunch of people, trying to come to a consensus with everybody, it's the worse part of this job..."

"But Gail...?"

"Two members are holding out–they admit Gail's a fine worker–they just don't want to commit to another permanent employee at this time."

"But you don't need unanimity, just a simple majority...that would do it, wouldn't it?" Maybe if she spoke to every Board member herself.

"Well, I pushed, and I've got enough votes..."

"Then she's hired?" asked excited Grace.

"I'm going to offer her the job...but it'll be just like any other employee. There'll be a ninety-day probationary period, and the medical insurance won't kick in until that's finished. And her salary will go down..."

"Down?" That Grace didn't understand. "Why? Now you're paying the agency her salary and the agency's fees..."

"ORR's standard compensation rates governs salary. Gail will be starting as a new hire, on Secretarial Level One."

"I thought they didn't have secretaries anymore, that everyone was now an Administrative Assistant?"

"Administrative Assistant is six levels above Secretarial One," he said. "Grace, we could have started her at Receptionist One, that's six levels below."

Grace found herself flushing with anger at the unfairness of it all. "No, you couldn't, because I would have told her to quit and find someplace where they appreciate a good worker! In fact, I'm going to tell her that!"

"Grace, she'll be getting a salary, plus benefits that the temporary agency can't give her."

That really angered Grace. "She's worked here for how many years? She was better than how many senior hires?"

"Do you know what her agency is paying her now?"

Grace told him, and Adam shook his head. "With what we're paying that agency, they could double that and still make a profit."

"Fair's fair, Adam. Gail goes above and beyond her job requirements! She's smart and loyal, and, believe me, if you think your job is hard now, lose her and you will really find how difficult things can be around here!" *What had Kurt told her? No guts, no glory!* "Adam, what you are offering is unacceptable–and I'm going to tell Gail to take the other offer."

"What other offer?" He asked straightening up.

Grace was getting comfortable with lying. "I wasn't supposed to tell you. Gail didn't want to pressure you, but she's had another offer, and it's more than what you're paying."

"How much more?"

"Adam, this discussion is over!" Saying that Grace moved in her seat as if preparing to leave.

He said nothing and Grace just sat there staring back at him, her lips tight. *What if tomorrow Grace had to tell Gail she was jobless? Grace couldn't afford another assistant.* Still, it was so unfair, Grace sat there saying nothing.

"All right." Adam gave in. "If I bring her in as a Level Four Secretarial, she'll have the same salary..."

"But she'll be giving up the flexibility of temporary work, where she can take time off whenever she wishes."

"Gail never takes any days off..." But as she was about to object again, Adam held up his hand. "Okay. Level Five Secretarial. That will be a raise in pay **and** include benefits, but she comes in with a ninety-day probationary period, like everybody else."

Relief flooded through Grace. "I think she might accept that, I'll talk to her," Grace said, rising to leave.

He said softly, "You negotiate better for her than you do for yourself."

"Kurt has been teaching me."

Smiling ruefully at that, Adam also rose. "Can we talk as friends?" She nodded, and Adam continued as he walked her to the door, "In a relatively short career, you've accomplished more than most scientists can even dream of. Your name will go down in the histories of science as a pioneer in the field of DNA. Maybe it's time you should stop pouring all your energies into clean rooms, and you explore some of the other joys of living. Grace, as president here, it's my job to keep you working at ORR, but as your friend, I advise you to think hard on what David is offering, and--for a change--do the best for yourself."

* * *

Getting back to her office, Grace tried to reach Gail on her cell phone, then left a message for her to call as soon as possible–before she spoke to Adam, Grace wanted Gail to know she had '*another job offer.*'

So when the door buzzer rang, Grace looked at the computer screen expecting Gail, only it wasn't. The fuzzy figure on the screen looked like Samantha. Grace just shouted out, "The security buzz-in isn't working. It's open, come on in."

This time the reporter walked in carrying her body proudly like she used to--but still, she spoke a little hesitantly, "Grace, I mean, Dr. Farrington,..."

"It's Grace. You're dating Mac, that makes you part of the family."

Her smile had a touch of dreamy happiness. "Mac's a great guy."

"So it's back going good?"

"I took your advice. I told Mac I was having some

problems that I didn't want to talk about, but it had nothing to do with us." She stopped and thought a moment and finished a bit shaky. "But he asked me if it had anything to do with Aldon Kincaid..."

"Get used to it," Grace said. "Freya and her son seemed plugged into a world of knowledge that the rest of us don't know."

Sam frowned commenting, "Jung's Collective Unconscious?"

"Sometimes it seems more than that..." mused Grace. "They both seem to know things before they happen, or know things that no one could have told them..."

Still smiling softly Sam said, "I reminded Mac that I didn't want to talk about it–so he just said, '*You're the boss,*' and Mac kissed the top of my head and hugged me."

Lovely, but Grace wanted to get back to her work, São Tomé was fun, but it had put her way behind in her rigid self-imposed schedule. "And you're here for?"

"My editor is pushing Aldon's connection with Oyster River Research."

That could be a problem. Grace shifted in her chair. "You'll have to interview that clown again?"

"No. I've made that clear to my editor. He didn't ask for an explanation–I guess he could figure it out. But for the piece, with Aldon's connection to ORR, he's assigned me to interview you about your work here, just a few quotes ..." And she finished lamely, "He'd like a picture."

Right in the middle of everything. "Uhh...Today? I can't do an interview today."

"No, it doesn't have to be today," Sam quickly said. "In fact, I told Mac, and he said Friday night we could both treat you to dinner at the Captain's Mansion or the Pier, and I could get my interview then?" She coaxed.

That would be expensive for them. "How about burgers at Neptune's instead?"

Sam nodded to that and then said reluctantly, "And Mac thought we could talk about Freya...and how I can get her to like me?"

Mission impossible thought Grace, but she only said, "Freya loves her son. You treat Mac well, and she'll come around." *Grace didn't add that with Freya's stubbornness it just might take thirty or forty years...*

"Could I just get a picture for the story right now?"

Grace didn't want this, but she owed it to Sam and ORR and whatever. "Yes, a shot of me here at my desk."

Sam dug into her voluminous handbag and came out with a small camera. "Better lenses than my cell phone." She snapped three or four different angles, and then seemed to be hesitating before passing out the next bad news, "My editor thinks Freya's going to be prosecuted for Brian Amundsen's murder."

"Why? She had no reason to kill him?"

"Mac said she had a history with him..."

"That was before Mac was born!"

"And...that he might be Mac's father..." said Sam unhappily.

"Actually Brian's not, and that can be proven with genetic testing," Grace pronounced.

"The police have Freya's trimming axe and some blood evidence?"

Oh, God. "Mac told you that?"

"No, he never talks about police work, but I've got other sources in the department."

"I know it looks bad–I also know Freya didn't kill him or Sierra."

"Sierra?" Sam asked with shock. "Sierra Sonheim is dead?"

"In the boathouse. Freya and I discovered the body."

"Oh, my God. Why didn't my paper call me?" Dialing her cellphone, Sam looked over her shoulder. "You used the word 'killed'?"

"Off the record?" Sam nodded, so Grace continued, "Her head was smashed in by a golf club."

Talking into the phone, Sam rapidly fired questions and then listened. Finally, she got off. "They didn't tell me because I said I wanted off the Aldon beat. The Kincaids are saying they didn't know why you and Freya were on the property, and that you guys didn't have permission..."

"We did! I asked Maura. She said I could look over the boathouse. She's supposed to tell the police that."

"Was that a text? Or in writing?" Seeing Grace's face, Sam closed her eyes asking, "Grace, have you guys got a lawyer?"

After the reporter left, Grace had forced her mind back on her work when that annoying buzzer from the door rang again. Deep with her computer screen DNA profiles Grace just yelled out irritably, "Come in!"

When she looked up, Gail was standing before her desk with an armful of catalogs, saying apologetically, "I've had the repair guy working on your remote door lock. He needs a part. He's sent for it."

"Uhh...thank you," said Grace reemerging back to the world. "Did you need something from me?"

Gail put the stack on catalogs on Inger's desk. "Adam wants each lab to have a stack of these in case you have a stampede of prospective students visiting. And you left a message for me to come over as soon as I got back?"

Yes. Yes! Grace got up saying, "Let's make ourselves some tea."

Obediently, Gail followed her over to the counter with the hot water machine, with a look on her face that must be the same as Grace's when she was forced to interrupt her work for another time waster.

Grace had to ask, "Adam hear that Freya and I found another body?"

"Yes," said Gail. "He says he's getting used to it."

Pouring their cups, they both sat down. As Grace swirled her black cherry tea bag, she said, "You're still thinking of having a child alone?"

Probably having heard this before Gail stiffened her back. "You disapprove?"

"It's not my choice to approve of or disapprove. Life is hard, and I just think that you are making it harder for yourself and another person," Grace finished, feeling like a dream killer.

Gail tossed her sodden green apple tea bag in the wastepaper basket. "It's not my first choice. I mean, I want to be married, with a husband who loves me, and have a home with a yard. But I'm over thirty, and that's not happening, so it probably never will. If I want any kind of a family, I'll have to make one myself."

"I don't think you realize how hard it will be?"

Those soft blue eyes of Gail's looked back her. "I know that. And I'll dedicate my life to making that child happy."

Grace could well understand pursuing goals that appeared hopeless to others. "Okay. I've spoken to Adam. He told me you are going to be hired as an ORR employee."

Looking relieved, Gail said, "He's had me look up the Secretarial One paperwork. I was worried he was finally hiring somebody else and letting me go..." Then she looked conflicted. "But I became a temporary so I could work a bit and pay the bills, then stay home and do some writing."

"I didn't know you wrote?"

"Nobody does. I only sold one short story to a Science Fiction magazine, and even if I could sell one a week, that's not enough to pay the rent for my apartment, but I thought as a writer I could work at home and raise a baby."

Grace got a flash of Sara slaving with her babies but only said, "You can still keep writing, but you're getting a job here with paid holidays, medical, and a pension some day. Whatever you do in this life, those are important."

"Yes," Gail admitted without enthusiasm.

"Well, Adam's going to offer you Secretarial Five."

"Secretarial Five?" she sounded genuinely surprised.

"And you're going to try and look a little disappointed. Remember, you're turning down another job offer that pays more, but you like the people here."

She looked confused. "I have another offer?"

"Yes, you do. The one I told Adam you already had."

Gail smiled conspiratively. "Okay."

"Now, even though you've worked here for years, you'll be on probation for ninety days. So no sick days taken, no doctor's appointments...well, just work the way you usually do."

"But I am seeing this fertility specialist..."

That could be a problem. "Put it off for the ninety days..."

Gail frowned, "I should tell Adam I'm planning to get pregnant..."

"No! You will not burden him with your personal business! And in those ninety days, you and I are going to research your options and work up a plan..."

"A plan?"

"A life plan. We'll start with a spreadsheet. What a kid needs, how you're going to arrange daycare. Who's going to father your baby–my vote is a sperm bank--no troubles with the boyfriend afterward. And as part of this plan, you and Freya, or maybe you and Sam Carson, are going out to some single places."

"Pick up bars?" asked Gail, coloring.

"Have you ever tried going to any?"

"No." Gail lowered her eyes.

"Well, neither have I, but I had an Aunt who was widowed in her sixties. She joined three different denominations-so every Sunday she attended three different church services, and she saw three different groups of possible husbands. Aunt Marie did remarry within the year. Do you know what the odds were against a widowed woman-- over sixty--getting a man?"

"Grace, are you going to marry David and move to Greece?"

That did stop Grace. "I don't know. Kurt will be coming home soon from the Antarctic, and for years I've been so comfortable with the set up I have here..." Grace stopped to think and then said, "But the pull of getting in bed every night with a man you love, having a ready-made family with children–even grown children-- is very tempting. I don't know what I'm going to do. David's coming today to take me out, and he's leaving on Sunday..."

"Grace, I'll miss you so much...but I think you should marry him."

After Gail left Grace resumed her work, and the next time she looked up David stood there at her desk watching her. "Why didn't say you were here?" she asked.

"The door's still broken?" He didn't look happy.

"The part is ordered."

"I understand you, and Freya found another body?"

"Yes, in the Kincaid boathouse," Grace sighed. "Alan Silverstein is going to be my lawyer if I need it."

"And your security door isn't working while you are undoubtedly hunting down another murderer."

Grace found herself closing down her computer. She really wanted to spend time with this man, but still had to ask, "Your daughter isn't warming to me, is she?"

He chuckled at that. "Madison came into my study and gave me an ultimatum, told me if I married you when she finished college, she would not live with us."

"Oh, God."

"I acted like it was a wonderful idea. I explained I

certainly wouldn't be buying her a house, but I would be extremely proud when she moved out and started supporting herself on her own earnings."

"What is she studying to be?"

"This week?" He raised a quizzical eyebrow. "She's planning to be an archeologist. I did point out she's not likely to find any ancient tombs to excavate in Westport, but reality never seems to bother Madison... However, surprisingly, she did seem to understand what is going to happen when I decide to stop paying her bills."

"Your sons? One of them seemed a bit reserved."

"Joshua?" Those blue eyes of his sharply turned back to her. "Did he say anything?"

"No, but the other one obviously seemed to be more welcoming of the idea."

"Jessie. And both of the boys have a much more realistic picture of what will happen when I stop paying their bills. Now, let's forget all this until Sunday, so you and I can just enjoy our time together."

But first, there was something else that had been bothering Grace. "The other day at your house you called me 'Sylvia.'"

He sighed. "Yes, Caine thought that might have upset you."

"David, it's not the first time, and I certainly understand that living with a woman for twenty-one years, of course, you'd use her name out of habit. And I'm happy that you had such a love in your life...but I'm just concerned that by marrying me you're unconsciously trying to stop mourning Sylvia."

"No!" He said firmly. "I asked you to marry me because I want **you** as my wife."

"Is this an ultimatum? Either I say yes or your offer is withdrawn?"

He evaded her question totally. "I'll be returning to

Greece Sunday night, but I'd like to spend time with you beforehand with no pressure. So I'll a make deal with you, I won't ask for your answer until we have dinner Sunday night. Is that acceptable?"

It was.

Chapter 26

On Friday, her laboratory door buzzed, and Grace clicked on the screen icon. In the darkened lobby she could see an unidentifiable woman standing in the shadows. Grace checked the time. Yes, Samantha and Mac were dropping by now to pick her up for her dinner and interrogation. Between David and Freya and Sam, Grace hadn't had to eat her own cooking for a week. That was a plus, but she had too much work to do to be taking time off. Still, Grace had agreed to dinner with Mac and a short interview for Sam's paper, so she just called out, "The door lock is broken, just turn the handle and come in."

Okay, she had promised Sam and Mac an interview, but if Grace had a few more minutes she might know who killed Sierra! Looking up, expecting to ask Sam to wait for just a few moments, Grace was surprised to see Maura Kincaid, her usually perfectly made-up face ravaged by tears that ran black mascara down her cheeks.

"Maura, what happened?"

"I can't take it anymore! Aldon's cheating, Harry's manipulation, my mother-in-law's bullying..."

God, another time waster, but Grace tried to sound sympathetic as she soothed, "And you're pregnant, which is going to make you more emotional, and even the smallest things will seem overwhelming." Grace looked regretfully at her screen. With the samples she had taken from Sierra's murder scene, Grace might have the answer that would put Maura's husband in jail, but she was going to have to calm down his wife first.

Moving closer to Grace's desk, Maura nodded and sniffed. Grace rolled her desk chair back and pushed a box of Kleenex toward her, and tried again, "Why don't you sit down?"

The woman didn't but was obviously trying to get

control. "That last time you were at our house, you picked up Aldon's cigar butt–you took his DNA, didn't you?"

What did she answer here? Go with the truth. "Yes, I did."

"Why?" Maura sounded hurt like Grace had violated their friendship.

"I also collected DNA off a paper towel used to wipe the golf club that killed Sierra."

Maura looked shocked. "You think you can match that DNA to the murderer?"

"Possibly."

Instantly Maura was all Kincaid again. "It can't be Aldon. He's been bred to lead, he's one of the chosen ones. The day Sierra died, my husband was with me the whole night!" The woman restlessly pacing behind her chair making Grace feel penned in. With Maura wearing an overblouse, Grace thought she could see the beginnings of a baby bump; what was the woman going to do if they convicted her husband of his mistress' murder? Of his henchman's killing? Maura stopped, standing behind Grace, looking over her shoulder at the screen before them.

Yes, Maura could now see the split screen before Grace. The woman could obviously see the two profiles, but could not understand how Grace now compared a possible murderer's DNA with the profile she had just developed from Aldon Kincaid's saliva. The irony of it stung: the poor pregnant wife looking over her shoulder as Grace proved her husband a killer.

An anxious Maura shifted her weight nervously, seeming to both want confirmation and denial. "You don't think Aldon killed her? You can't prove that with those marks? Can you?"   On the split screen, Grace studied Aldon Kincaid's profile, focusing in on the twenty-third chromosome with its short, male telltale Y. Then she turned to the best read out from what she presumed was the killer's

DNA. Grace zeroed in on the twenty-third chromosome, the sexual determinate.

But there was no short Y chromosome in the murderer's DNA, only two long Xs. In shock, Grace stared at her screen. The killer of Sierra--and probably the killer of Brian Amundsen too--was a woman. Freya? Certainly not, Grace knew Freya's profile too well, this was entirely different. Someone at the estate? Charlotte, the mother-in-law? Grace didn't have a sample of her but could get one. Still, the killer's pattern scrolling before her was a pattern Grace recognized from a previous extraction.

With a cold, wet chill Grace realized that the presumed murderer's profile she studied belonged to the woman standing alongside her right now. Had Maura lied about her husband's alibi, not to protect Aldon, but cover up for herself? Yes, Grace should certainly have taken the time to read Brian's blackmail drive that was still locked up in this desk drawer. Read those documents under 'Maura'.

Feeling sick, but desperately trying to look calm, Grace stared up into Maura's feverish blue eyes as the woman asked, "What is it, Grace? Your DNA tells you everything, doesn't it?" Now--too late--Grace saw the small gun in her hand.

The door from the outside opened, and the tall redhead Samantha Carson walked in.

Concealing the gun alongside her leg, Maura just smiled, calling out in a friendly fashion, "The more, the merrier, why don't you join us..."

But Grace yelled out, "**Get out! I'm not being interviewed by a slimy, lying reporter!**" Slipping behind her, Maura shoved the gun painfully against her arm where Sam couldn't see it, but Grace kept yelling, "**You're not going to misquote me again! Go!**"

Looking like she'd been slapped, Sam froze, and then started backing out saying, "I-I-I hoped you'd changed your mind."

The doors closed behind Sam, and a furious Maura stepped back from her, banishing the gun. "You shouldn't have done that, Grace!"

"She misquoted me! I'll not have her in my lab!" Nervously Maura looked to Grace. This obviously wasn't going the way she expected, but Grace just continued, "Why the gun? Look at the screen. There is your husband's DNA," she pointed to his Y chromosome, "And this is the unknown murderer. Look, even you can see they're totally different. Aldon is completely innocent." And in her mind's eye, Grace could see Maura's pattern that she had matched against Dagmar's. That same pattern was before her now as the murderess' DNA.

Maura relaxed her stance a bit, lowering the gun, but not moving closer. Grace wondered if she could jump her? Could she even prevail against the younger, athletic Maura? Especially when the woman appeared to be driven by madness? Maura was talking, she'd better listen.

"I knew Aldon didn't kill Sierra or Brian. Or Brittany. But even if he did, it would have been right. The Kincaids are meant to rule as god-kings. They can save our world, we need them!"

Grace knew they weren't really talking about her husband. "So you're saying even if Aldon killed Sierra, his political ambitions justify that?"

"The country needs Aldon--mankind needs him--the world needs leaders with his heritage...his genetic destiny. It's the predestination of my own baby..."

If Grace could keep Maura talking, there might be a chance to get the gun. "Fortunately, we have your husband, and he will do what's right for the country."

"Aldon will lead successfully, and the child I carry will keep his tradition alive. My son too will be President."

Thinking Maura had been around Charlotte too long,

Grace only said, "Is it a boy?"

Maura smiled fondly, touching her stomach briefly with her other hand. "Oh, yes. They could see that with the ultrasound."

"That's amazing. Congratulations..." babbled Grace. Would Samantha realize Grace needed help, or would she just think Grace was angry again over the latest article she had written? *Maybe if Grace shook Maura up?* "The police are investigating your maid's death. They had me culture Brittany's DNA..."

Frowning at that Maura said, "Brittany wasn't a maid–Brittany was an aide working on Aldon's campaign."

Shit–Grace got the name wrong! "No–the other one...the maid."

"Marylinn?" Maura took a breath and unconsciously put a comforting hand on her belly bump again. "She killed herself too. Aldon got her pregnant, then offered Marylinn money for an abortion, but she didn't want that! She wanted to marry him–he couldn't be president with that scandal following him!" Obviously remembering, Maura's face hardened. "I was at the clambake that day, but I felt sick...so I drove home and found the mansion on fire." Maura studied Grace as if calculating just how much Grace believed. "There was no way I could have known anyone was inside the mansion. She must have set the fire, then hid in the cellar, when the fire cut off her escape..."

Grace didn't believe that. In fact, she figured Maura sent the maid downstairs, locked the door, then set the fire, and that maybe Maura managed to sneak sleeping pills into the campaign worker's rum, but how did she get that doctored rum into her husband's mistresses' apartment? Harry and Charlotte must have also come to that same conclusion; that was why they followed Maura so closely. But knowing she could never rise and jump for the gun faster than Maura could shoot her, left Grace paralyzed. Trying to keep the woman talking Grace only pointed out, "But Marylinn was locked in that cellar–the fire chief's investigation discovered that."

Maura wet her lips. "She did it to herself! Marylinn set fire to the house to get back at Aldon. Then to punish him, she hid in the cellar, locking the door to keep us from saving her."

Getting one of Freya's psychic feelings, Grace knew Maura was lying, but to stay alive, she immediately agreed with her saying, "That's right, it's Marylinn's fault. And since you're my friend, I'll lose that DNA the police gave me."

"You'd do that for me?" Maura sounded pathetically grateful, but then those fierce blue eyes hardened again with the madness of the Romanovs. "Harry told Charlotte that he thought I did it. He had Brian pay off someone to close down the fire investigation...but then Brian wanted money from me to keep it all quiet." Sanity seemed to slip in and out of her eyes, but Grace figured when she was sane again Maura obviously planned to kill her.

"It's so good that we're here to protect Aldon..." Grace tried. "We need him to be our president."

The lab doors swung open with the rumble of the cleaner's cart; Grace looked up followed by Maura as that cart was pushed open by a tall man in a khaki uniform shirt. But instead of the usual cleaning guy, Grace realized she was looking at Mac, who pushed that white canvas cart topped with mops toward them.

"Working late again, Dr. Farrington?" Mac called out in an amiable voice.

Getting further behind her chair, Maura painfully nudged Grace with her gun barrel that he couldn't see, as she said, "Dr. Farrington is doing an important experiment. She doesn't want you to clean tonight."

Ignoring that, Mac reached over, and picked up a wastepaper basket and dumped its contents into the cart, and then he started it rolling again. "Got to clean now. Got a schedule to keep. The administration warned you about that, Dr. Farrington. Even you are not allowed to get in the way of a laboratory cleaning."

While Mac spoke, he didn't look directly at them. He just kept checking trash cans along the way as he rolled his cart closer to Grace's desk. Finally looking at them, Mac smiled as he picked up another wastebasket and dumping it in. "Dr. Farrington, you just go on ignoring me as usual."

A calculating Maura looked from Grace to him, as a terrified Grace's mind flashed images of the growing Mac as a boy; more than her own life, she wanted him out of here to safety, so she said most firmly, "But you've cleaned enough tonight! You **must** leave now...I'll be all right."

Getting closer, Mac grabbed a stack of data sheets from a sorting table and just threw them into his garbage cart. Now he was within ten feet of Grace's desk. Maura had backed up slightly to get a clear shot at him, and to Grace's horror, she realized there was nothing she could do to stop this!

A terrified Maura now showed the gun to him, "Stay there!"

Mac appeared surprised. "Hell, lady, you don't need to have a gun! If you don't want the place cleaned, I'll just leave. No skin off my teeth..." But even as he raised his empty hands in a gesture of harmlessness, Mac kept moving forward, talking as Maura swung her arm to zero in the gun on his chest.

The kid that Grace helped raise was in danger–that frozen feeling melted as Grace used all her strength to shove her wheeled chair back against Maura's hip. The woman staggered back–and not caring what happened to herself-- Grace grabbed for the gun. A flash of light and explosion as Maura pulled the trigger once, and Grace felt heat burn her hands as she struggled with Maura's stiff fingers, before the stronger Mac grabbed both their hands in his bigger ones. He twisted Maura's arm hard as she screamed, but he also locked onto that gun.

At the sound of the shot, a terrified Sam pushed through the doors followed by the shirtless, regular cleaning guy.

Grace found herself just collapsing into her chair.

* * *

Grace gave over her 'paper towel' profile's evidence to a police detective, claiming the killer's ripped paper towel had been left anonymously at her laboratory door with some other papers. Those papers consisted of printouts of the material Brian had to blackmail Maura about the murder of Marylinn. And Grace had been right, Maura had planted the sleeping pills in Brittany's rum, but she had mistakenly trusted Brian to sneak the pills into the campaign worker's apartment. Brian had also documented a lot of the other dirty tricks he had committed for Harry and the Kincaids.

Without the proper chain of evidence, her DNA samples and printouts were technically worthless. But knowing what had happened the police could back check the dirty tricks, and Grace pointed out that their own technicians might be able to replicate her DNA results if they had picked up the rest of the paper towel? The police had. And after warning her of the penalties for tampering with evidence the police left. Having Alan as her lawyer by her side might have helped.

Maura's family lawyers immediately had her placed in a private psychiatric clinic for *'a rest cure related to severe prenatal depression.'* Her doctors cited medical necessity to keep her from being questioned by the police. Finally, a deal was apparently arranged, with no trial as long as Maura remained in a private sanitarium–the Kincaids still had a lot of power. Even they probably couldn't suppress the blackmail evidence Brian had amassed on Maura's killing of Marylinn and Brittany, but agreeing with Freya that turning the thumb drive over to the police would hurt a lot of people Grace didn't do it. If it ever looked like Maura would be free to kill someone else, Grace and Freya could always '*find*' Brian's drive.

However, those print outs Grace did turn over about the Kincaid campaign's dirty tricks could be confirmed from other sources. But only Harry-- the loyal closed-mouthed campaign manager--wound up on trial for the beatings, faked news, and break-ins that Brian had committed for the Kincaids. It was a short trial. An expensive legal team–probably paid for by the Kincaids--defended Harry and he only got five months in jail. Still, Aldon Kincaid canceled his senatorial campaign and resigned his congressional seat, announcing he wanted to spend more time '*with his family.*' Mac said the local cops weren't too happy about the Kincaids walking, but their Connecticut estate went on the market for fifty-three million dollars. Mac didn't think there would be a buyer soon; still, he doubted the family would be summering in Oyster River again.

Over a steak dinner at The Pier, Grace and David talked it all out, but it was a bit bittersweet time, both of them knowing that tomorrow would be their last evening together before David returned his island in the Mediterranean. He took her home and spent some time there until he kissed her good night. She couldn't sleep knowing they'd have one last meeting tomorrow before he left. He'd been fair with her and made an honorable offer of marriage, now she owed him an answer, but the problem was Grace still didn't know what that answer was?

Epilogue

For her last date with David, before he returned to Greece, Grace dressed carefully with her new gold silk blouse and black linen pants. She had told him to pick her up at her lab, for Grace just wanted to check one more thing, something that kept nagging at her. She couldn't even tell herself what it was.

While waiting for David, Grace sat at her desk, aimlessly pulling up screens of chromosome profiles. Looking for one...could it be in the early files when she moved to Oyster River? No, she thought it was within the last few years–and it was. Grace pulled up a screen and discovered it! The mitochondria were different, so was the Y allele that is passed through the male line, yet the other configurations after configurations looked eerily familiar.

She pulled up Prince Philip's DNA. Yes, there were repeated allele matches. Obviously, both were lines descended from German, Danish, and Russian nobility. Starting to type quickly she pulled up Grand Duke George's profile, then more carefully studied the maternal line that came down to Tzarina Alexandra and Philip's mother. Of course, the subject she studied didn't match with what must have been Alexandra's mitochondria, but there were several nuclear chromosomes in Philip's DNA that matched, that might have come down from Queen Victoria herself.

With a shock, Grace stared at her screen. She knew a man descended from the European royal families!

The lab door buzzed. She looked up. Yes, tonight she had locked it with David's entry system that was working now. On the side screen, she could see him standing outside waiting in a dark suit. What would she tell him about his marriage proposal? Still unable to make up her mind, Grace buzzed him in.

David looked about her lab, commenting tartly, "Still

looks like the 1920's in here."

"Not inside the clean room. Thank you for having Alan push the Board to pay for the new positive pressure air control system."

"The lab I've built for you in Greece is leagues above this."

"I thought we were just going to enjoy tonight..." she cautioned, standing up to join him.

"Yes, and I was hoping you would wind up in my bed tonight. But since I'll be leaving early tomorrow, I would like to finish our discussion first."

She finally knew the answer. "On me marrying you and moving to Greece, I've given it some thought. It is a very tempting offer, but it is not going to happen." David studied her, not looking surprised, but not looking defeated either. Still, Grace had something more on her mind. "David, I told you I've been studying Romanov DNA."

"Trying to establish some woman as Anastasia?"

"Yes. Actually, she did have some things in common but was a distant relative on the Romanov side, and she had nothing of Alexandra's line from Queen Victoria so she could not have been any of the Tsarina Alexandra's daughters."

"A shame, I'm sure she was disappointed. I've heard there were many claimants that have tried to claim Romanov wealth that doesn't exist anymore. "

"But, David, I also have a sample of your DNA. I reviewed it tonight, and I think you're related to the European royal houses."

His face showed no reaction. "Is that so?"

"You have a slightly different male Y than Prince Philip's, who is a male descendant of the Danish line that married into the Romanovs, but there are many markers in his nuclear DNA that match yours. And there were also some in common that must have come from Philip's mother, Princess Alice of Battenburg, who was a great-granddaughter of Queen

Victoria. Victoria was a descendant of the German royal houses."

"Yes, I believe she was of Brunswick-Lüneburg-Hanover line, bringing with it a wealth of connections to the ancient German and Austrian royal houses of Welf and Este, and her husband, Prince Albert, was Saxe-Coburg-Gotha, a branch of the eminent House of Wettin."

"You have DNA matching theirs." He still showed no surprise at all, so Grace asked, "You knew all this, didn't you?"

David gave that little half smile of his. "Yes, I did. It's a little family secret. In 1924, the son of King George the fifth, then the Prince of Wales--who later became the Duke of Windsor--was fox hunting on Long Island. My family had an estate on the North Shore, and my great-great-grandmother, Priscilla Gardiner, was widely known as an expert horsewomen on a sidesaddle, and she must have been a bit good in bed too. Remember those were the 'liberated' flapper years. Priscilla and the prince danced the night, then obviously spend some more time together, before His Royal Highness moved on to his next princely visitation. And soon Priscilla found herself very pregnant."

Grace tried to remember her history. "That was before David Windsor became King Edward VIII..."

"And before the Simpson woman came along..." David explained.

"Yes." Grace folded her arms remembering. "Mrs. Simpson, the man hunting double divorcee. The other David reigning as Edward VIII relinquished the British throne for *'the woman he loved'*."

David mused a bit, "Funny how trails seem to predetermine the run. Perhaps your DNA is responsible? Prince Charles appears to be a retread of his great-uncle, trading a marriage of duty for his own personal happiness."

A thought occurred to Grace. "David, are you in line for the British throne?"

He laughed at that. "Unfortunately no. Under English law, a child born on the wrong side of the blanket inherits nothing, even if the original David had not abdicated for himself and all his prodigy."

She stared at his face, thinking how much he did resemble photos she had seen of the late Duke of Windsor. "Did you ever think about..."

"Fantasized about be crowned at Westminister? Of course. But actually, Priscilla's father was very unhappy about *'the honor bestowed on his daughter.'* He wasn't at all thrilled about the British connection since his family had fought in the Revolutionary War to free us from the yoke of King George. He felt that an American asks no one to bow to him, and an American bows to no one. With his daughter in an embarrassing situation, he arranged for a marriage to a distant Gardiner relative in the military, who had the correct bloodlines, but no estate to speak of.

"So your great-great-grandmother married quickly..."

"The excuse was given that her sergeant husband was being posted overseas..."

"And then she had a 'premature' delivery?" Grace finished.

"Yes, and with a bit of whimsy Priscilla named the baby David Edward Albert Gardiner." He sat on the edge of her desk. "Actually, although Priscilla resented the forced marriage at first, I hear she grew to love her husband, and John Gardiner turned out to be an excellent businessman, doing wonders to increase the family holdings, while Priscilla gave him five daughters."

Grace continued to muse, "That first baby and any following in your line--were they male?"

"Yes."

"Then possibly your Y chromosome came down from

Prince Albert and the German royal houses."

"Do I have anything from Queen Victoria?" he asked.

She thought about that. "Obviously, not mitochondria, which the mother passes to her daughter and son, but it's lost immediately in the son's offspring. But your DNA has some alleles that appear in Philip's profile--and his mother was a great-granddaughter of Victoria."

He just smiled. "Of course, the royal families of Europe were heavily interbred."

As always, the DNA fascinated her. "Your great-great-grandmother Priscilla..."

"Was a romantic, headstrong girl in her late teens. I understand she grew to be a very straight-laced matron. A stickler for the proprieties."

But Grace was continuing on her lifelong obsession. "Nuclear DNA is a jumble, with both parents contributing half of the genes, but one never knows what will be passed down. Without Victoria's DNA profile or her both her parents, I couldn't properly determine what came down to you from Victoria. We might get a clearer picture if I can obtain more records of her descendants' DNA?"

"Or we might not," he said dismissively. "It was just a passing whim." David now studied her intently. "Now, Grace, your Greek lab is finished. What will we do with it?"

"Can you sell it?"

He shook his head. "No--it's constructed right in the middle of my private island."

"It sounds fabulous, and it shouldn't go to waste. Perhaps you can lend it out to some scientist..."

"Yes, I can lease it, but by the year only, because, my dear, I still hope to see you working there someday. You know, Grace, there are several guest cottages on the island. You could live there without us being married?"

God, it was so tempting, but, "David, my work is set up here. My staff is here...my friends are here. For the foreseeable future, I will be working at ORR."

"So, I'll lease the lab for the short term." David Gardiner stared at her with deceptively mild, pale-blue eyes. "How about that Dr. Nicole Duval? She seems to be doing some cutting edge work I hear, and Adam tells me she's indicated some interest in having me as her patron?"

Grace found herself tightening up. That would definitely be an answer. If Nicole and David were in close proximity, working together on his island, well, nature might take its course and Nicole would wind up as his wife. That would solve her problem, but perversely Grace didn't want to let that happen. "Ah...you know there is a Greek scientist...I can't remember his name at this minute, but I was thinking it would be so good if he could use that lab...I'll look up the name and text it to you..."

David cut in, "'A 'he,' not a 'she'?"

She felt herself blushing. "Yes, a h-he. Yes,...an...an...important figure in the scientific community."

"So important that you can't remember his name?" That impish Duke of Windsor grin. "So, if we are bypassing Dr. Nicole Duval, then there is still some interest in me, isn't there?"

She smiled in embarrassed acknowledgment as he reached to kiss her. Grace found herself willingly moving in to snuggle against his chest. Complications could be a problem, but she had to admit they could be fun.

The End

For **further books in this series see www.lynnmarron.com**

To comment or talk with the author I'm at lynn@lynnmarron.com

Books by Lynn Marron
All Published in Print and
E-book editions of Kindle or Nook

OTHERS IN THE GRACE FARRINGTON DNA MYSTERIES

ORR: THE NOBEL PRIZE MURDER

Turned down for this year's Nobel Prize, fortyish genetics pioneer Grace Farrington finds out the new Head of Research at Oyster River is the man who stole her research! When Dr. Marshall is murdered on ORR's houseboat, Grace finds herself the chief suspect. Grace is further implicated, when following an1800's witch's *Curse of Three*, two more people die in Oyster River Harbor. While finding herself romantically involved with a wealthy patron and a red-necked colleague, Grace must use her scientific reasoning and her eclectic group of friends (scientists, cops, psychics and some other slightly eccentric New Englanders) to solve the murders before she's arrested or killed herself.

ORR: FATAL DNA

Grace Farrington is considered a genius in her field, so it is not surprising that when doing some special DNA sleuthing she discovers a convoluted motive for murder (as she attempts to desecrate a body). Her life suffers further complications when her new age friend Freya involves her in a seance that triggers a desperate search for a lost Revolutionary War ransom. Of course, no one has found the treasure in over two hundred years, but they didn't have Grace's skill at reading the secrets of Colonial DNA!

Distracting entanglements are the three men on her romantic horizon: roughly edged fellow scientist Kurt MacKay; old moneyed David Gardiner; and a new billionaire, the handsome Jack Stuart, who arrives in the New England town of Oyster River Harbor with an intense interest in both her research and her body. Grace is determined to keep her mind on mitochondria, even as Kurt is attacked by a local fisherman. But when her sometime lover is accused of murder, Grace has to act, only to find out too late that the next targeted victim is herself!

ORR: MURDER GENETICALLY ENGINEERED

In this, the third book in the Grace Farrington DNA mystery series, Grace is returning from winning the prestigious Guru award, when she finds Oyster River Harbor Research is being picketed by Anti-Genetic Engineering protestors. Her rival-- Dr. Huang Wong--has signed a research grant with a conglomerate run by the handsome, wealthy bachelor Axel Jensen. C.E.O. of Humanity's Harvest, Axel has a reputation for marrying brainy women, and is under the impression that his generous contract also includes Grace.

Tension is building up with the demonstrators, as Grace and the other researchers start getting anonymous death threats. These threats are ignored until a body is found floating in the Connecticut harbor. Humanity's Harvest tries to cool things off with a December outdoor-in-the-snow bar-be-que, while Grace is hunting for traces of the elusive '*food for the Incan Lord God*'' in the University Museum. In New Haven, she stumbles on to an intriguing DNA puzzle left over from the Conquistadors conquering of Peru. Can even Grace solve it all before the next murder?

THE MYSTIC TRIPLETS MYSTERIES:

THE PSYCHICS' SEAPORT MURDER

After the 'suicide' of their witch mother, the young triplets, Holly, Frost and Noel Corey were separated for seventeen years. The day of their long-awaited reunion in Mystic, Connecticut, a New England seaport, a murdered man is found on their mansion grounds, making brother Frost the police's chief suspect. Knowing nothing of her Old Craft heritage, Holly starts to learn the skills of her ancestors as she struggles to open Witch House as a viable Bed and Breakfast. To save Frosty, she must also find the murderer haunting her family, while she is being so thoroughly distracted by the tall, muscular police sergeant, Paul Travinski.

MURDER ON THE ALTAR

Brother Noel is accused of poisoning a fellow Beluga trainer at the Aquarium. When Holly Corey starts investigating she visits her Old Craft mentors, Sarah and Abby Hoyt. Unfortunately, against their advice, Holly accepts two new long-term guests at the Corey Bed and Breakfast: Lilith (once a member of her father's coven) and Lilith's younger warlock architect (and sometimes lover) Gregory St. Clair.

Lilith is pressing to buy the Old Mill that the triplets' mother ritually suicided in, while Gregory is trying to seduce Holly up onto the high altar at Grace La Fleur's Church of Nature's Bounty. Afraid of the Wiccan ritual, but needed to know more, Holly drags Sgt. Paul Travinsky up to the beginnings of the naked Yule celebrations that wind up being raided by his fellow cops. While the Sergeant is being told to stay away from Ms. Corey or give up his job, Holly finds herself in danger of losing her life--or her soul--to the combined efforts of the Rasputin like Gregory, and the powerful, mind-controlling Lilith.

A LAWYER WITH PARANORMAL CLIENTS:

ADAM'S UNORTHODOX, UNNATURAL LAW PRACTICE

Inheriting his Great Uncle Quentin's unconventional law firm in Missouri Adam Martin finds himself defending the rights of a succubus, a semi-senile seer, mermaids, zombies, and gorgons. Soon he is writing contracts for werewolves, consulting with ghosts, and protecting unfairly accused fire starters. While this is going on, he is trying to stand up to his six foot tall *'Cherokee'* law secretary, and deal with his staid, disapproving family of conservative lawyers led by the formidable, 'hang them high' Judge Jeremiah Martin. Still, while struggling to save his clients and his law practice, Adam has time to romance some very intriguing and unusual females.

CENTAUR WARRIOR FANTASY SAGAS:

CENTAURESSES OF THE SILVER DRAGON

The Regiment follows the hoof prints of Jace, a ruggedly handsome centaur of Clydesdale proportions. Warriors winning on their last field, but betrayed by treacherous princes, these sword-wielding mercenaries are outlawed. To keep his band together, the legendary fighter finds a patron in the stunningly beautiful Silver Star, a long-legged centauress with sea foam white hair, a luxurious silky tail, and ominous cloven hoofs. The Lady promises a vast treasure, if the Regiment but free her rich mines from a rampaging dragon, but Jace knows dragons do not exist...